Jump attacked the intruder. Sparrows followed like feathered brown darts, gouging the newcomer's face. Kel threw herself out of bed to yank her glaive from the wall.

———◆———

"Trollop, you killed my boy!" shouted the man who fought Jump and the birds. Kel pulled a shutter open, admitting cold air and early morning light—it was shortly after dawn. Jump gripped one of the man's wrists in his jaws, drawing blood. The birds continued to strike his face and eyes as he flailed at them with his free hand.

Kel didn't know this well-dressed, white-haired stranger. Neither did she know the woman and man who ran in to grab him, the woman clinging to his waist, the man with one hand on the stranger's tunic as he tried to knock Jump away. . . .

"My nephew is dead," the other stranger cried. "The Chamber of the Ordeal opened on his corpse."

TORTALL BOOKS
BY TAMORA PIERCE

❧

The Song of the Lioness Quartet

Alanna: The First Adventure

In the Hand of the Goddess

The Woman Who Rides Like a Man

Lioness Rampant

❧

THE IMMORTALS QUARTET

Wild Magic

Wolf-Speaker

Emperor Mage

The Realms of the Gods

❧

Protector of the Small

First Test

Page

Squire

Lady Knight

Protector
of the
Small

Squire

TAMORA PIERCE

Random House 🏠 New York

To Ms. Gloria Barbizan and Ms. Dorothy Olding—

strong businesswomen long before women's liberation

www.randomhouse.com/teens

Library of Congress Cataloging-in-Publication Data
Pierce, Tamora. Squire / by Tamora Pierce.
p.   cm. — (Protector of the small)
SUMMARY: After becoming a squire to Lord Raoul, commander of the King's Own,
Kel of Mindelan must face a terrifying test in the Chamber of the Ordeal before she
can be a knight.
ISBN 0-679-88916-7 (trade) — ISBN 0-679-98916-1 (lib. bdg.)
ISBN 0-679-88919-1 (pbk.)
[1. Knights and knighthood—Fiction. 2. Sex role—Fiction. 3. Fantasy.] I. Title.
PZ7.P61464 Sq 2001
[Fic]—dc21 2001019280

First Random House paperback edition

Printed in the United States of America

10 9 8 7 6

RANDOM HOUSE and colophon are registered
trademarks of Random House, Inc.

CONTENTS

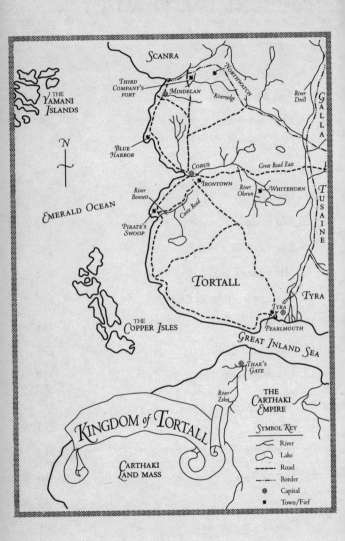

Corus, the capital of Tortall;
Summer,
in the 17th year of the reign
of
Jonathan IV and Thayet, his Queen,
456 H.E. (Human Era)

⊰ one ⊱

KNIGHT-MASTER

$\mathcal{D}$espite the overflow of humanity present for the congress at the royal palace, the hall where Keladry of Mindelan walked was deserted. There were no servants to be seen. No echo of the footsteps, laughter, or talk that filled the sprawling residence sounded here, only Kel's steps and the click of her dog's claws on the stone floor.

They made an interesting pair. The fourteen-year-old girl was big for her age, five feet nine inches tall, and dressed informally in breeches and shirt. Both were a dark green that emphasized the same color in her green-hazel eyes. Her dark boots were comfortable, not fashionable. On her belt hung a pouch and a black-hilted dagger in a plain black sheath. Her brown hair was cut to earlobe length. It framed a tanned face dusted with freckles across a delicate nose. Her mouth was full and decided.

The dog, known as Jump, was barrel-chested, with slightly bowed forelegs. His small, triangular eyes were set deep in a head shaped like a heavy chisel. He was mostly white, but black splotches covered the end of his nose, his lone whole ear, and his rump; his tail plainly had been broken twice. He looked like a battered foot soldier to Kel's young squire, and he had proved his combat skills often.

At the end of the hall stood a pair of wooden doors carved with a sun, the symbol of Mithros, god of law and war. They were ancient, the surfaces around the sun curved deep after centuries of polishing. Their handles were crude iron, as coarse as the fittings on a barn door.

Kel stopped. Of the pages who had just passed the great examinations to become squires, she was the only one who had not come here before. Pages never came to this hall. Legend held that pages who visited the Chapel of the Ordeal never became squires: they were disgraced or killed. But once they were squires, the temptation to see the place where they would be tested on their fitness for knighthood was irresistible.

Kel reached for the handle and opened one door just enough to admit her and Jump. There were benches placed on either side of the room from the door to the altar. Kel slid onto one, glad to give her wobbly knees a rest. Jump sat in the aisle beside her.

After her heart calmed, Kel inspected her surroundings. This chapel, focus of so many longings, was plain. The floor was gray stone flags; the benches were polished wood without ornament. Windows set high in the walls on either side were as stark as the room itself.

Ahead was the altar. Here, at least, was decoration:

gold candlesticks and an altar cloth that looked like gold chain mail. The sun disk on the wall behind it was also gold. Against the gray stone, the dark benches, and the wrought-iron cressets on the walls, the gold looked tawdry.

The iron door to the right of the sun disk drew Kel's eyes. There was the Chamber of the Ordeal. Generations of squires had entered it to experience something. None told what they saw; they were forbidden to speak of it. Whatever it was, it usually let squires return to the chapel to be knighted.

Some who entered the Chamber failed. A year-mate of Kel's brother Anders had died three weeks after his Ordeal without ever speaking. Two years after that a squire from Fief Yanholm left the Chamber, refused his shield, and fled, never to be seen again. At Midwinter in 453, months before the Immortals War broke out, a squire went mad there. Five months later he escaped his family and drowned himself.

"The Chamber is like a cutter of gemstones," Anders had told Kel once. "It looks for your flaws and hammers them, till you crack open. And that's all I—or anyone—will say about it."

The iron door seemed almost separate from the wall, more real than its surroundings. Kel got to her feet, hesitated, then went to it. Standing before the door, she felt a cold draft.

Kel wet suddenly dry lips with her tongue. Jump whined. "I know what I'm doing," she told her dog without conviction, and set her palm on the door.

She sat at a desk, stacks of parchment on either side. Her hands sharpened a goose quill with a penknife. Splotches of ink stained her fingers. Even her sleeves were spotted with ink.

"There you are, squire."

Kel looked up. Before her stood Sir Gareth the Younger, King Jonathan's friend and adviser. Like Kel's, his hands and sleeves were ink-stained. "I need you to find these." He passed a slate to Kel, who took it, her throat tight with misery. "Before you finish up today, please. They should be in section eighty-eight." He pointed to the far end of the room. She saw shelves, all stretching from floor to ceiling, all stuffed with books, scrolls, and documents.

She looked at her tunic. She wore the badge of Fief Naxen, Sir Gareth's home, with the white ring around it that indicated she served the heir to the fief. Her knight-master was a desk knight, not a warrior.

Work is work, she thought, trying not to cry. She still had her duty to Sir Gareth, even if it meant grubbing through papers. She thrust herself away from her desk—

—and tottered on the chapel's flagstones. Her hands were numb with cold, her palms bright red where they had touched the Chamber door.

Kel scowled at the iron door. "I'll do my duty," she told the thing, shivering.

Jump whined again. He peered up at her, his tail awag in consolation.

"I'm all right," Kel reassured him, but she checked her hands for inkspots. The Chamber had made her live the thing she feared most just now, when no field knight had asked for her service.

What if the Chamber knew? What if she was to spend the next four years copying out dry passages from drier records? Would she quit? Would paperwork do what other pages' hostility had not—drive her back to Mindelan?

Squires were supposed to serve and obey, no matter what. Still, the gap between combat with monsters and research in ancient files was unimaginable. Surely someone would realize Keladry of Mindelan was good for more than scribe work!

This was too close to feeling sorry for herself, a useless activity. "Come on," Kel told Jump. "Enough brooding. Let's get some exercise."

Jump pranced as Kel left the Chapel. She was never sure if he understood her exactly—it grew harder each year to tell how much any palace animal did or did not know—but he could tell they were on their way outside.

Kel stopped at her quarters to leave a note for her maid, Lalasa: "Should a knight come to ask me to be his squire, I'm down at the practice courts." Gloom overtook her again. As the first known female page in over a century, she had struggled through four years to prove herself as good as any boy. If the last six weeks were any indication, she could have spared herself the trouble. It seemed no knight cared to take The Girl as his squire. Even her friend Neal, five years older than their other year-mates, known for his sharp tongue and poor attitude, had talked with three potential masters.

Kel and Jump left her room to stop by Neal's. Her lanky friend lay on his bed, reading. Jump bounced up beside him.

"I'm off to the practice courts," she said. "You want to come?"

Neal lowered his book, raising arched brows over green eyes. "I'm about to commence four years obeying the call of a bruiser on a horse," he pointed out in his dry voice. A friend had commented once that Neal had a gift for making someone want to punch him just for saying hello. "I refuse to put down what might be the last book I see for months."

Kel eyed her friend. His long brown hair, swept back from a widow's peak, stood at angles, combed that way by restless fingers. Her fingers itched to settle it. "I thought you wanted to be a squire," she said, locking her hands behind her back. Neal didn't know she had a crush on him. She meant to keep it that way.

Neal sighed. "I want to fulfill Queenscove's duty to the Crown," he reminded her. "A knight from our house—"

"Has served the Crown for ages, is a pillar of the kingdom, I know, I know," Kel finished before he could start.

"Well, that's about being a *knight*. Squire is an intermediate step. It's a pain in the rump, but it's a passing pain. I don't have to like it," Neal said. "I'd as soon read. Besides, Father said to wait. Another knight's supposed to show up today. I hate it when Father gets mysterious."

"Well, I'm going to go hit something," Kel said. "I can't sit around."

Neal sat up. "No one still?" he asked, kindness

in his voice and eyes. For all he was five years older, he was her best friend, and a good one.

Kel shook her head. "I thought if I survived the big examinations, I'd be fine. I thought *somebody* would take me, even if I am The Girl." She didn't mention her bitterest disappointment. For years she had dreamed that Alanna the Lioness, the realm's sole lady knight, would take her as squire. Kel knew it was unlikely. No one would believe she had earned her rank fairly if the controversial King's Champion, who was also a mage, took Kel under her wing. In her heart, though, Kel had hoped. Now the congress that had brought so many other knights to the palace was ending, with no sign of Lady Alanna.

"There are still knights in the field," Neal said gently. "You may be picked later this summer, or even this fall."

For a moment she almost told him about her vision in the chapel. Instead she made herself smile. Complaining to Neal wouldn't help. "I know," she replied, "and until then, I mean to practice. Last chance to collect bruises from me."

Neal shuddered. "Thanks," he said. "I've gotten all the bruises off you this year that I want."

"Coward." She whistled for Jump, who leaped off the bed to follow her.

The practice courts were deserted. Lord Wyldon, the training master, had taken the pages to their summer camp earlier that week, ahead of the traffic that would clog the roads as the congress broke up. The combat teachers had gone with him;

Kel saw only servants near the fenced yards where pages and squires practiced. She'd thought that older squires might come out to keep their skills sharp, but none were visible.

She saddled her big gelding, Peachblossom, murmuring to him as she worked. He was a strawberry roan, his cinnamon coat flecked with bits of white, his face, stockings, mane, and tail all solid red-brown. Except for the palace horse mages, he would tolerate only Kel. Abused when he was younger, Peachblossom was no man's friend, but he suited Kel nicely.

Practice lance in hand, she guided Peachblossom to the tilting yard. There she studied the targets: the standard quintain dummy with its wooden shield, and a second dummy with a tiny black spot painted at the shield's center. They were too solid to fit her mood. Though it was a windy June day, she set up the ring target, a circle of willow twigs hung from a cord attached to a long arm of wood. It was always the hardest to hit due to its lightness. Today it whipped on its cord like a circular kite.

Kel rode Peachblossom to the starting point and composed herself. It was no good riding at the ring target with an unsettled heart. Six years of life in the Yamani Islands had taught her to manage her emotions. She breathed slowly and evenly, emptying her mind. Her green-hazel eyes took on their normal, dreamy cast. Her shoulders settled; her tight muscles loosened.

Kel gathered her reins and resettled her lance. Part of the bargain she and her horse had made to work together was that Peachblossom would answer to verbal commands and Kel would never use the spur. "Trot," she told him now.

The big horse made for the target at an easy pace. The ring flirted in the air. Kel lowered her fourteen-foot lance until it crossed a few inches above her gelding's shoulders. The lead-weighted wood lay steady in her grip. Her eyes tracked the ring as she rose in the stirrups. On trotted Peachblossom, hooves smacking hard-packed dirt. Kel adjusted her lance point and jammed it straight through the ring. The cord that held it to the wooden arm snapped. Peachblossom slowed and turned.

With a hard flick—the movement took strength, and she had practiced until she'd gotten it perfect—Kel sent the ring flying off her lance. Jump watched it, his powerful legs tense. He sprang, catching the ring in his jaws.

A big man who leaned on the fence applauded. The sun was in Kel's eyes: she shaded them to see who it was, and smiled. Her audience was Raoul of Goldenlake and Malorie's Peak, knight and Knight Commander of the King's Own guard. She liked him: for one thing, he treated her just as he did boy pages. It was nice that he'd witnessed one of her successes. The first time she'd seen him, she had been about to fall off a rearing Peachblossom. That her mount was out of control was bad; to have it witnessed by a hero like Lord Raoul, and ten more of the King's Own, was far worse.

"I'd heard how well you two work together," Lord Raoul said as Kel and Peachblossom approached. He was a head taller than Kel, with curly black hair cropped short, black eyes, and a broad, ruddy face. "I'm not sure I could have nailed that target." Jump trotted over to offer the ring to the big knight. Raoul took it, tested its weight, and whistled. "Willow? I don't think I *could* nail it—the ring I use is oak."

Kel ducked her head. "We practice a great deal, that's all, my lord. Jump wants you to throw it for him."

With a flick of the wrist the knight tossed the ring, letting it sail down the road. Jump raced under it until he could leap and catch the prize. Holding his tail and single ear proudly erect, he ran back to Raoul and Kel.

"Practice is the difference between winning and being worm food," Raoul told Kel. "Do you have a moment? I need to discuss something with you."

"I'm at my lord's service." Kel stood at ease, Peachblossom's reins in her hand.

"I owe you an apology," the knight confessed. "I'd meant to see you right after the big exams, but we were called east—ogres sneaked over the border from Tusaine. We just got back. If you haven't accepted an offer from some other knight, would you like to be my squire?"

Kel blinked at him, unable to believe her ears. Over the last four years, when she hadn't dreamed of serving Lady Alanna, she had slipped in a day-dream or two of being Lord Raoul's squire. It wasn't that far-fetched—the man had shown he had a kindness for her in the past—but when he didn't visit after the big examinations, her daydreams had turned to dust. It had never occurred to her that he might have been called away. Palace gossip, usually accurate about who was in residence and who was not, had crumpled under the flood of guests for the congress.

Finally she blurted out, "But you never take a squire!"

Jump barked: Lord Raoul still held the willow ring. He flipped it into the air, straight up. Jump gave him a look, as if to say, *Very funny*, and waited until the ring was six feet from the ground before he leaped to catch it.

"Oh, all right." Raoul sent the circle skimming across the training yard. Jump raced after it gleefully. To Kel Raoul said, "I had a squire once, about twenty years ago. Why don't we sit"—he pointed to a nearby bench—"and I'll explain."

Kel followed him over and sat when he did. He took the ring from a victorious Jump and sent it flying again.

"See, I haven't needed a squire since I joined the King's Own." The big man leaned back, stretching brawny legs out in front of him. He was dressed not in a courtier's shirt, tunic, hose, and soft leather shoes, but in a country noble's brown jerkin and breeches, a crimson shirt, and calf-high riding boots. He shifted so he could watch Kel's face as they talked. "We have servants with the Own, and a standard-bearer, so my having a squire wasn't an issue. But you know the Yamani princess and her ladies arrive next year."

Kel nodded. She felt very odd, as if she occupied another girl's body. Was he asking her out of pity? That would be almost as bad as service to a desk knight—though she'd still take the offer.

"Once they get here, Chaos will swallow us," the man went on. "Their majesties plan to take the court on a Grand Progress—do you know what that is?"

"Yes, sir," Kel replied. "Master Oakbridge, our etiquette teacher, talked about it all last year. It's to show Princess Shinkokami to the realm, so people can see the heir's future wife."

Raoul nodded. "Which means a grand parade throughout the realm. Two mortal *years* of balls, tournaments, banquets, and other nonsense. Oh, some useful things will get done—they mean to survey the roads and hold a census, paper-shuffling, mostly. I have no problem with that, since I don't have to do it. But fuss and feathers make my blood run cold."

Kel's lips quivered in the tiniest of smiles. The Knight Commander was infamous for dodging as many ceremonies as he could.

"Servants and our standard-bearer won't be enough when I have to deal with every jumped-up, self-important toady in the country." He thumped his knee with a fist the size of a small ham. "And I know nothing about the Yamanis. You lived six years at their court and speak the language."

Enlightenment struck Kel like fireworks. He wasn't taking her as a favor, or because he liked her, though that was nice. She would be useful to him as no one else could!

"I liked how you handled yourself when we hunted those spidrens, four years ago," Lord Raoul explained. "You knew when to speak up and when to be quiet. Wyldon and Myles of Olau say you don't lose your temper. After your fight with bandits three years ago, I know you can keep your head in a fix. You'll see plenty of combat with us. I'll warn you, it's more work than most squires get. Plenty of knights come here for the winter months, but the King's Own goes where it's needed, whatever the season. And we'll be in the thick of all the progress antics. If you want out—if someone else you'd prefer has asked . . ."

Kel smiled at him. "I'm not afraid of work, my lord," she replied. "I would be honored to be your squire."

"Good!" he said, grabbing her hand and giving it two firm shakes, beaming at her. "Come down to our stables. You can bring the charmer." He nodded at Peachblossom. "He's going to move there anyway, and I'd like you to have a look at a mare I think would suit you."

As Kel scrambled to her feet, Raoul slung an arm around her shoulders and led her out of the yard. Kel made sure to hold out the hand that held Peachblossom's rein, keeping the gelding on her far side, well out of reach of her new knight-master.

"See, with the Own, everyone has at least one spare horse," Raoul said. They walked down one of the roads that crisscrossed the acres behind the palace. They were in an area of stables: those for couriers, heralds, and officers in the army, those for visitors, and those that served the King's Own. "We live in the saddle. One horse isn't up to all that. Your Peachblossom is heavy—you'll need a horse with good wind and endurance to ride. You can keep Peachblossom for combat." He looked across Kel at the big gelding. "I asked Onua—horsemistress to the Queen's Riders—to help me find a mount who could get on with your charming horsie."

The "charming horsie" snorted, as if he understood. Kel gave his reins a tug, a silent order to behave.

"Here we are," Raoul said, taking his arm from Kel's shoulders. The insignia over the door on this stable was familiar: a silver blade and crown on a blue field, the emblem of the King's Own. Kel, Peachblossom, and Jump followed Raoul inside. The stable was big. There were three hundred men in the King's Own: younger sons of nobles, wealthy merchants' sons, and Bazhir from the Southern Desert. Each was required to supply two horses when he joined, though the company replaced those killed on duty. Kel eyed the ones in the stalls as she walked past. These were some of the kingdom's finest mounts.

Once the Own had been a cozy assignment for wealthy young men who liked to look good and meet ladies with dowries. Under Lord Raoul it became the Crown's weapon, enforcing the law and helping local nobles deal with problems too large to handle alone. Since the arrival of the strange creatures called immortals seven years before, enforcing the law and handling problems required every warrior the Throne could supply. Not all giants, ogres, centaurs, winged horses, and unicorns were peaceful; other, stranger creatures saw humans only as meals. Even those who did coexist with humans had to find homes, make treaties, and swear to obey the realm's laws.

"Here we go," Raoul said, halting. The glossy brown mare in front of them was a solid animal, smaller than Peachblossom. She had broad shoulders and deep hindquarters, feathery white socks, and a white star on her forehead. Kel hitched Peachblossom out of harm's way, then approached the mare and offered a hand. The mare lowered her nose and blew softly on Kel's palm.

"Take a look at her," Raoul said. "Tell me what you think."

Kel stepped into the stall to inspect the mare thoroughly, feeling as if this were a test, at least of her knowledge of horses. That made sense, if she was to spend time with some of the realm's finest horsemen.

The mare's eyes were clear, her teeth sound. She seemed affectionate, butting Kel in fun. Someone had groomed her; there were no burs or tangles in her black mane and tail, and her white socks were clean.

"She's beautiful," Kel said finally. "Looks like she'll go forever. Not up to your weight, my lord." She smiled at the six-foot-four-inch Knight Commander, who grinned. "But she and I should do well." Jump crawled under the gate. He sniffed the mare's hooves, as if conducting his own inspection.

The horse turned her head, keeping the dog under observation, but she seemed to have no objection.

"Very good," Raoul said. "As your knight-master, I give her to you, as is my obligation. What will you name her?"

Kel smiled at the mare, who lipped her new rider's arm. "I'd like to call her Hoshi," she replied. "It's Yamani for 'star.' " She touched the white star between the mare's eyes.

"Hoshi it is. Now, why don't you settle Peachblossom there," Raoul nodded to the empty stall beside Hoshi's, "while we discuss other details?"

Kel led Peachblossom into his new stall and unsaddled him. More than anything she wanted to run back to the iron door of the Chamber of the Ordeal and snap her fingers at it. You see, she wanted to tell it, not a desk knight after all!

Neal was out when Kel returned. She stood before his closed door, disappointed. None of her other friends among the first-year squires—Seaver, Esmond, and Merric—were in their rooms either. Her news must wait: she had to pack. Unlike her friends, she would not be returning to the squires' wing most winters. She was to live in rooms adjoining the Knight Commander's, in a palace wing closest to the barracks that housed the King's Own.

She was explaining things to the sparrows who had adopted her when Jump and the birds raced for the open door. Neal walked in. He was dead white; his green eyes blazed.

"Neal, what's wrong?" Kel asked.

He actually wrung his hands. "Sit down," he told Kel. "Please."

Kel sat.

He paced for a moment. Jump looked at him and snorted; the sparrows found positions on Kel and the furniture to watch. Crown, the female who led the flock, lit on Neal's shoulder. She rode there for a moment, then peeped loudly, as if telling him to speak.

Neal faced Kel. "This wasn't my idea," he said. "Remember that knight I was to see today?" Kel nodded. "Well, the knight wants to take me," Neal continued, "and Father and the king say I should do it. They said that you are getting a very good offer, too. I want you to know I argued. I said it should be you. They say that's a bad idea. That people might question if you were really good."

Kel stared at her friend. What was wrong with him?

Neal took a deep breath. "Lady Alanna has asked me to be her squire. She's a healer, Kel. That's why Father wants me with her. Maybe that's even why the king stuck in his oar. You know I wish I'd had more training. Lady Alanna says she'll teach me. But I swear by Mithros I had no idea she was going to ask."

Kel nodded dumbly. After all her hopes Lady Alanna had taken a squire, though she had done without for her entire career. The problem was, that squire was not Kel. It was Kel's best friend.

"Kel, please . . . ," Neal began. Then he looked

around. "You're packing. You're—why are you packing? You're not leaving?" The worry in his face made her heart ache. Yes, he had the place she wanted, beside the realm's most legendary knight, but this was Neal. They had fought bullies, monstrous spidrens, and hill bandits. They had studied together and joked on their gloomiest days. He'd shown her the palace ropes; she knew about his unrequited passions for unattainable ladies. The only secret between them was Kel's crush on him.

I can't turn on him, she thought. *I can't not be his friend, even if I can't be his love.* "Lord Raoul asked me to be his squire."

Neal collapsed into a chair. "Raoul? I'll be switched," he said, awed. "Lady Alanna told me you were looked after, but this? Gods all bless. Goldenlake the Giant Killer." He whistled. "This is *very* good. I love it. Not even the conservatives will question your right to a shield if he's your master. He may be a progressive, but he's still the most respected knight in Tortall. Even the ones who claim you're magicked to succeed will have to shut up."

"What do you mean?" Kel demanded. Sometimes Neal took forever to get to the point; sometimes, even when he got to it, the thing didn't feel like a point at all. This was starting to feel like one of those times.

"You'll be in public view most of the time," Neal explained. "Not everyone you meet will be your friend, so they won't lie for you, and some will have enough Gift of their own to tell if magic's being worked on you. No one will be able to claim you did anything but what was under everybody's nose after four years in the King's Own."

"If I cared for their opinion, I'd be relieved," Kel informed her friend. "So you think this is good."

He nodded vigorously. "I'm envious," he admitted. "Lord Raoul's got to be the most easygoing man alive. My new knight-mistress is famed for wielding sharp edges—sword, knife, and tongue."

Kel scratched her ear. She hadn't considered the Lioness's temper, though the realm's sole female knight was infamous for it. "You'll just have to get on with her," she said. She knew her words were silly as they left her mouth. Neal couldn't just get on with anyone. He could no more resist poking at other people's conceits or ideas than he could resist breathing.

"I'll manage," Neal said. "She and Father are friends, so she probably won't kill me. Now," he went on, changing the subject, "why are you packing, if you have such a wonderful knight-master?"

"I have to be ready to go with him at any time," she explained, sitting on her bed. "My room's next to his. I don't even know how often I'll be in the palace—he's on the road all year."

"We'll see each other during the Grand Progress," Neal pointed out. "Unless—maybe you won't . . . I know you wanted Lady Alanna."

Kel had to make this better. "Not see you, when you won't eat vegetables like a decent human?" she demanded. "I'll bet Lady Alanna—" Her throat tightened. Dreams died so hard, and this one she had kept for most of her life. "I'll bet she doesn't care what she eats, let alone what her squire does. I should send Crown along to peck you as a reminder."

Neal's answering grin was shaky, but it grew stronger. "As if these feather dusters would be separated from you," he retorted.

"I hope they can," Kel told him. "I doubt even Lord Raoul will welcome fifty-odd sparrows."

Neal slung his legs over the arm of the chair. "I bet he and Lady Alanna planned this. They're friends, and she did say you were looked after. And she has to know what people would say if she took you."

"That maybe I was right to look up to her all these years? That if anyone can teach me how to be a lady knight, it's her?" Kel asked bitterly. She wished she hadn't spoken when she saw the hurt in his face. *Most times I can keep silent,* she thought, folding a tunic with hands that shook. *But the one time I say the first thing in my mind, it's to Neal. I should have said that to anyone but him.*

His eyes were shadowed. "You *are* angry."

Kel sighed and straightened to work a cramp from her back. "Not with you." *Never with you,* she thought, wishing yet again that he liked her as a girl as well as a friend. "To tell you the truth, I don't know what I feel. First I was just about as low as I could be—Neal, I had a vision."

He raised an eyebrow. "My dear Kel, I'd say Jump, your sparrows, even Peachblossom are likelier to have visions than you. I have never known anyone who had both feet nailed to the ground."

She had to smile. He was right. "It didn't come from me," she informed him. "I was in the Chapel of the Ordeal—"

"Finally!" he interrupted. "You took your own sweet time in going—"

It was Kel's turn to interrupt. "Do you want to hear about my vision or not?" She described what had happened when she touched the Chamber's iron door. "And then I went to the tilting yard and Lord Raoul found me," she finished. "But Neal, it felt just as real as anything."

He smiled crookedly. "Then here's a word of advice—don't touch the door again. That Chamber is a law to itself. No one knows how it works. It's killed squires, Kel. Killed them, driven them mad—"

"And left plenty to become knights," Kel pointed out before his imagination galloped away with him. "Like it will us." She refused to admit he'd raised goose bumps on her skin. *I climbed down from Balor's Needle,* she thought, reminding herself of the day she'd finally lost her terror of heights. *I can handle the Chamber of the Ordeal.*

Remembering the realness of her vision, Kel shivered. She checked her hands to make sure there were no ink blotches on them, then picked up a shirt.

When Kel's maid, Lalasa, returned from signing a lease for her dressmaker's shop, she found Kel and Neal trying to fit Kel's weapons-cleaning kit into a trunk that was nearly full. After shedding tears over the news—Lalasa was sentimental—she banished them, saying the palace staff would see to everything. There was nothing to do but go to lunch and share their tidings with their friends. They talked there until the second bell of the afternoon about where they all would go.

When Kel returned to her room, only her night-things remained. Everything else had gone to her new quarters, though she wasn't to report for duty until noon the next day. "I like to sleep late when I can," Raoul had explained. "It's not something I get to do often. Neither will you, so take my advice, and sleep in."

Lalasa sat by the window, sewing basket open beside her, a wad of green cloth in her lap. A stack of neatly folded green clothes lay on a stool beside her.

"I took the liberty of getting your new things from the quartermasters for the King's Own, my lady," she said as Kel closed the door. "These are some of Lord Raoul's spares—he gave word to use them—but grain sacks have a better fit." She clipped a thread and shook out the garment, a tunic in Goldenlake green bordered in yellow. Though Kel would ride with the Own, she served Raoul the knight, not the Knight Commander. "Try these, and the breeches," Lalasa ordered. She held out both. "I measured them against your clothes, but I want to double-check."

Kel stripped off tunic and breeches and donned the new clothes. Something had changed her retiring Lalasa into this brisk young female. Kel suspected that Lalasa's getting her shop and dress orders from Queen Thayet may have caused it. They had both changed since their long, frightening walk down the side of Balor's Needle six weeks ago. Kel thought that Businesswoman Lalasa was a treat; she still wasn't sure about Squire Keladry.

Lalasa gave the clothes a twitch and nodded. "Now these." Kel tried on two more sets of Goldenlake breeches and tunics while her maid pinned and straightened. Kel's shirts, at least, would be the same white ones she'd worn as a page; it was one less piece of clothing to try on.

"You're not to take things to those sack stitchers at the palace tailors'," maid informed mistress. "They come straight to me, and not a penny will I take for the work." Her brown eyes filled with tears. "Oh, my lady," she said, her voice wobbling. "Out with all those men, and just a dog and some little birds and that dreadful horse to look after you."

Kel had to chuckle. "The animals look after me just fine," she said, offering the older girl her handkerchief. "And surely you'll be too busy to work on my clothes."

"Never," Lalasa said firmly, and blew her nose. "Never, ever."

Kel looked at the sparrows perched on her bed. "I need to talk to you, all who can come," she said. "Crown? Freckle? Will you get the others?"

The chief female and male of the flock that used to nest outside Kel's window in the pages' wing sped outside. The sparrows already in the room found perches. The rest of the flock soon arrived.

Kel shook her head. Even after four years she

felt odd talking to them as she would to humans, but they understood far more than normal birds. Ever since Daine, known as the Wildmage, had come to the palace, her magical influence had changed every animal resident. Kel's dog Jump had refused to live with Daine, and deliberately worked his way into Lord Wyldon's good graces so the training master would let him roam with the pages. Peachblossom had negotiated his no-spur agreement with Kel through Daine. The sparrows had moved in with Kel, who'd been feeding them, with the first winter snows. In less than a year they were defending her and acting as scouts for a spidren-hunting party. They had even found Lalasa on Balor's Needle and fetched Kel to help.

"I mentioned this, remember," Kel told the flock. "I have to go with my knight-master. It'll be hard to keep up. I don't know how often we'll be here. Do you want to leave your nesting grounds? Salma told me she'll go on feeding you, so you won't go hungry. You don't have to stay with me. It's not that I don't love you all," she assured the fifty-odd birds. "But this isn't practical." She stopped, seeing all those black button eyes fixed on her. They were dressed as soberly as merchants in brown and tan, the males black-capped and black-collared, but Kel knew they were far from sober. She had seen them in battle, their tiny claws and beaks red with the blood of her enemies, or riding gleefully on Jump's back. Most had come to the flock as newborns, raised in the courtyard and introduced to Kel by their elders.

At last Kel sighed. "I can't think of anything else. Either you understand me or you don't."

Crown, named for the pale spot on her head and her imperious ways, hopped to Kel's shoulder. She chattered at the flock, looking from face to face as a human might. At last she uttered a series of trills. Most of the flock took to the air. They circled Kel like a feathered cyclone, then sped out the window. When Kel walked over to see where they had gone, they were settled in their home courtyard one story below.

Kel turned to see five sparrows—three females, two males—land on Lalasa's chair and sewing. The one-footed female named Peg settled on Lalasa's shoulder with a peep. Lalasa smiled as she stroked Peg's chest.

"Who needs to talk?" she asked, her voice wobbling. "I know what you mean. You are all welcome at my home."

"Peg fetched me the night Vinson grabbed you," Kel said. "I suppose she feels you belong to her now." She took Lalasa's hand. "You are still part of Mindelan, too. If you need a voice at court, or help, or just a friend, I hope you will come to me."

Lalasa wiped her eyes on her sleeve. "I am still your maid, so it only makes sense that you bring me your clothes. I can never repay you for all you have done. I don't even want to." She stood. "If you'll excuse me, my lady, I need more green thread. You will sleep here tonight?" Kel nodded. "Good. I should have the rest of these done by bedtime." She left before Kel could say anything.

"These aren't goodbyes," Kel told herself. "Just the next chapter in our lives." She looked at her bed to see who had stayed with her and Jump. Crown, the white-spotted male named Freckle, and ten other sparrows perched there.

"You'll come with me?" she inquired.

Crown nodded.

"Thank you," Kel told them. "I hope you like our new quarters. Do you want to see them?"

⇥ two ⇤

THE KING'S OWN

*K*el needed only a key to enter her quarters, no magic password. It seemed unlikely that anyone would maul her things and paint on her walls, as they had her first year, when the connecting door now led to Lord Raoul's suite. Once inside, she looked around. This room, bigger than her squire's and page's quarters combined, boasted a desk, a bookcase, armor and weapons racks, and a map of Tortall over the desk. A dressing room with its attached privy was opposite the door that led to Lord Raoul's rooms.

Her belongings were here. Lalasa had set Kel's collection of Yamani waving cat figures on the mantel. Kel's old books were beside those already in the case. Her clothespress, weapons, and all the things she exercised with were neatly arranged; her silk painting of two Yamanis dueling with glaives was hung. The bed had fresh sheets and pillows: Kel or Lalasa would bring her nightclothes and blankets in the morning. Even the birds' and Jump's dishes were there, filled and ready. The twelve sparrows flew to them instantly.

Looking around, Kel suddenly realized the connecting door was ajar. From inside Lord Raoul's rooms she heard voices.

". . . isn't decent. You know court gossips, Raoul. They'll have you in bed with her before today is done!"

"Now I'm confused, Flyn." That was Lord Raoul's voice, slow and good-humored. "I thought they've had me in bed with other men for years, since I'm not married."

"Not around me or the lads, they haven't," was the growled reply. "We've explained it's nobody's business."

"Then explain the same thing about Kel and me, Flyn," Raoul said. "That's easy enough."

Flyn—she knew the name. Of course: Flyndan Whiteford, nominally in command of Third Company in the King's Own, in reality second in command to Lord Raoul, who personally led it whenever possible. Kel had met Flyn three summers ago, during the spidren hunt at the end of her first year as a page.

"Stop joking, Raoul," Flyndan replied. "I've served with you for fifteen years. I've a right to be heard."

Raoul sighed. "You know I listen to you."

"Then be serious. The girl will have no reputation, and neither will you. The conservatives will be furious you picked her."

"So?" Raoul asked. "They dislike me anyway, just for the changes I've made in the Own. How much more can they hate me because Kel's my squire? And she's had four years to think about her reputation."

"She's fourteen—she can't understand all the consequences," Flyndan grumbled. "As a noble she wouldn't be thinking about marriage and babies for another couple of years."

Raoul continued, still patient. "But as a commoner she might be married—and producing babies—right now. Stop fussing. She's intelligent, and she's steady. Some people always believe the worst."

"You only did it because Lady Alanna asked you to," snapped Flyndan.

Kel swallowed a gasp. Now she was *really* glad they didn't know she was listening. She shouldn't be. It wasn't right. Educational, but not right.

There was a sigh in the next room. "Alanna mentioned it, but I've had Kel in mind since the spidren hunt. Everything I've heard just confirms that she'll do well, given a chance. That's what I'd like you to do, Flyn—give her a chance."

Kel knew she had to leave or say she was there. Cat-quiet, she went to her door, then yanked it loudly shut. She walked into the center of the room, saying, "Your food and water dishes are here—"

A man poked his head through the connecting door. He was in his early forties, blunt nosed, with the dark skin, hair, and eyes of a Bazhir. He wore a white cotton shirt and loose dark green breeches, casual dress. "Good afternoon, Squire Keladry. Do you remember me?"

Kel smiled at the Bazhir. "It's Qasim, isn't it?

You fed my birds on the spidren hunt." He'd been paired with her that day and had treated her just as he had the male pages. That, and the fact that he liked her sparrows, made him a friend in Kel's eyes.

"Have you still the little ones?" he asked.

"Some. The flock got too big for me to keep them all." Kel's new flock left their dishes and flew to Qasim, fluttering around him. "They remember you," she said.

He reached into a pocket and withdrew a handful of dried cherries. "I hoped they would," he admitted with a smile. The birds grabbed the treats. "Come." He led Kel into Raoul's quarters.

The Knight Commander occupied a suite of rooms. The one connected to Kel's was a study, complete with a desk, a number of chairs, and full bookcases. Maps of Tortall and its neighbors were mounted on three walls. Beyond the study was a dining room of sorts, though the table was covered with armor and weapons. From her tour that morning Kel knew Raoul's bedroom was on the other side, with its dressing room and privy.

Raoul sat at his desk, stacks of paper and books spread around him. He grinned at Kel. "I see you remember Qasim ibn Zirhud. He's a corporal now, in Volorin's squad. I don't think you were properly introduced to Flyn, though—Captain Flyndan Whiteford."

The man who sat in a chair opposite Raoul nodded curtly. He was stocky and fair skinned, his red-brown hair cropped short on the sides and left tightly curled on top. His brown eyes were set under thin brows, over a small nose and small lips. His voice, a light baritone, carried a hint of a northern burr, all but erased by years with the King's Own.

"This isn't a menagerie," Flyndan objected as Jump and the birds explored the study.

"The sparrows carry their own weight, Flyn," said Raoul. "Or did you forget, *they* led us to the spidren nest?" He reached down to pet Jump. "Her gelding's a piece of work, too." To Kel he said, "I'm glad you stopped by. I forgot to see to your kit. Do you have an hour? I know you'll want to sup with your friends, but we should handle some things while we can."

Kel nodded.

"We'll see to personal armor tomorrow, but as you know, such things take time. Qasim will help you draw pieces to tide you over when we're done talking," Raoul explained. "Until you get your own weapons, use company issue. You need a sword and dagger, a small axe, a shield. That's a company shield, Qasim—I'm having a proper Goldenlake shield made, but that takes a week. Kel, which are you better at, longbow or crossbow?"

"Long, my lord," Kel replied. "And I have a bow, sword, and dagger."

"Let Qasim review them," Raoul said. "He may ask you to use ours for now." He nodded to Qasim. "Standard field kit. Now, long weapons . . ." He gazed at Kel thoughtfully. "Lances are good for tournaments, giants, and ogres, but they're unwieldy in a scramble. Most of us carry spears—"

"A third use halberds," Flyndan added.

"I know you can use a spear," Raoul continued, thinking aloud. "Have you tried a halberd?"

Kel hesitated. Lord Wyldon had never let her use her favorite weapon, which was similar to a halberd. I won't know if I don't ask, she thought. "One moment, my lord?" she asked. At his nod she returned to her room.

"She's polite enough," Kel heard Flyndan say.

"What did you expect?" Raoul was amused. "Wyldon trained her. He's serious about manners."

Kel's wooden practice glaive and a standard glaive hung on a rack behind the connecting door. She took the live weapon down. The five-foot-long staff was teak, the base shod in iron. The blade was eighteen inches long at the tip and broadly curved. The blue ripples under the polished surface marked it as the best steel money could buy. It was a gift from her mother and Kel's prize.

"I can use this, my lord," she said as she returned to the next room. The three men were talking. When they stopped to look at her, Flyndan's jaw dropped. Qasim smiled.

Raoul walked over to her, eyes on the weapon. "May I?" he asked, holding out his hands. Kel gave him the glaive and stood back. He spun it in a circle, as he might a staff. "Nice weight," he commented. "Hey, Flyn, look here." He extended his arm and balanced the glaive on one finger. It remained steadily horizontal. He picked up a quill and set the end on the blade's edge. The steel cut it in half without Lord Raoul pressing the feather down.

Flyndan whistled. "What's this?"

"It's a glaive, sir," Kel replied. "The Yamanis call them *naginata*. Noblewomen fight with these. Since we were at court, we learned, too."

"Can you use it?" Flyndan demanded. "Don't take this the wrong way, but that looks awkward for a—" Flyndan swallowed a word and finished with "youngster."

Raoul handed the glaive to Kel and pushed back some chairs to make room. Kel began the cuts, turns, and swings of a pattern dance. She picked up the pace, until her blade was a silver blur shadowed by the longer dark blur of the staff. She finished with a rapid spin and halt, the blade stopping just short of a chair.

"Captain Whiteford." She offered him the weapon. Flyndan took it in one hand and nearly dropped it; he'd been unprepared for the weight.

"So you've got a long weapon," Raoul said calmly, resting his behind on his desk. "Chain mail?"

"I will find something to fit," Qasim promised as Kel shook her head.

Flyndan, expressionless, returned the glaive to Kel. Qasim dusted his hands—the birds had eaten every cherry—and jerked his head toward the door. Kel bowed to Raoul and followed Qasim, her animals in their wake. She stopped to put her glaive on the rack.

"I chose a tent and bedroll for you already," Qasim remarked. He pointed to a tightly wrapped bundle on Kel's clothespress. "The bedroll is inside the tent. So too are the stakes and rope you will need. May I see your weapons? I need also to look at your travel gear."

Qasim checked everything, eyes sharp as he tested edges and cleanliness. He then inspected her travel packs. "This is all very good," he said. "I am envious."

Kel wasn't sure if she ought to tell this man, however kindly disposed he was, about her anonymous benefactor. That person had sent her gifts during her page years, from exercise balls to help her strengthen her grip, to weapons. She decided to be quiet for now. There was a Yamani saying: "You need never unsay anything that you did not say in the first place."

They went to the stables, then to the armory that served the King's Own. All of the equipment she chose passed Qasim's painstaking inspection. He loaded her with things she did not have—tack for Hoshi, a chain mail shirt, a padded round helm, even a square leather carrier that fastened onto the back of her saddle. The men of the Own often traveled with hawks and dogs in case they had to hunt or track. Like the company's terriers, Jump would ride in style.

Putting her gear away, Kel realized that an important moment in her life had come and gone as she chose a riding saddle and inspected shields. For the first time a warrior had thoroughly tested her knowledge of equipment, and she had passed. Qasim had rejected none of her choices. It was all the more startling to Kel because he'd done it in such a matter-of-fact, commonplace way.

Today she'd dealt with two men who took her on her own terms. Thank you, Mithros, for this gift, she thought to the god of war and law. Then she remembered that she was at her window, grinning foolishly. Shaking her head at her own folly, she got back to work.

It was nearly suppertime when Kel finished putting everything away. She had one more thing to do concerning Peachblossom. She had thought to go to Daine—the Wildmage was home, Kel knew—but she chose to talk to the gelding on her own first. She didn't know if this was because she respected Peachblossom so much that she thought he might listen, or because she resented the idea that he would listen to Daine and not his rider. Whatever the reason, she prayed this would work. Like other palace animals, Peachblossom had grown more intelligent in human terms over the years. By this point, surely, Kel didn't need Daine to translate.

The stable was deserted. No one was there to snicker at her. "Um, Peachblossom? Could I have a word?" she asked the gelding. She hadn't brought any treats. This was too important for bribes.

He walked to the front of the stall and, in a rare gesture of affection, thrust his long brown muzzle against Kel's chest. He snorted at the smell of old iron left by chain mail but didn't move away.

Kel stroked him. "We're going to be with plenty of other horses," she told him. "Hoshi's just the start."

Peachblossom threw up his head to eye Hoshi. The mare, quietly eating hay next door, switched her tail as if to say, Go away, boy.

"Nobody will be able to work if you're forever biting them," Kel said. "We could get in trouble if you start fights. They might make me leave you behind."

Peachblossom fixed her squarely with one eye.

"I don't know if they will," she amended, scrupulously honest. "But it seems likely. We'll always be together when I'm a knight—surely you know that. But consider getting along here? You don't have to be friendly. Just don't make trouble."

The thought of having to leave him made her eyes sting. She loved every scarred, irritable inch of Peachblossom. She knew she would like Hoshi: she was a gift from Lord Raoul. She also seemed like a horse who could view disaster with a calm eye. But Peachblossom was the friend of Kel's heart, her staunch ally. She hugged him fiercely around the neck.

"Think about it," she told him, and left him to it.

Kel, Lalasa, Jump, and the sparrows were asleep in Kel's old rooms when thunder broke through Kel's dreams. Sitting up in bed, she realized what she heard was not thunder, but someone pounding on her door.

She leaped to answer it without pulling on her robe. Qasim almost rapped her nose when she yanked the door open. "We are called away tonight," he said. "When you are dressed, go to the stable and ready your mounts. I will pack the gear you will need."

"But my lord's armor, his gear and horses—that's my job," she protested.

"Another time," Qasim ordered. Kel was about to close the door when he stopped her. "It will be bad," he said. "Haresfield village in the Royal Forest was attacked by robbers. The messengers say it is a bloody mess. Be ready."

Is anyone ever ready for such things? Kel wondered as he left. She took a breath and concentrated on what had to be done. Lalasa was placing a basin full of water and a towel on the desk. As Kel washed her face, cleaned her teeth, and combed her hair, Lalasa put out her clothes, including a fresh breastband and loincloth, and one of the cloth pads Kel wore during her monthly bleeding. It had begun the day before.

"I'll need more pads," Kel said, fastening her breastband and hitching her shoulders until it fit properly. "And three days' worth of clothes—how much do I have here?"

"More than that," Lalasa said. Kel glanced at her. The maid smiled sheepishly. "I just wanted to give everything a last look-over," she explained. She briskly folded and stacked shirts, breeches, tunics, stockings, underclothes, and, in one of the shirts, more cloth pads.

"You'd think I rip my seams every day," Kel grumbled, pulling on her stockings. By the time she straightened her tunic, Lalasa had put her clothes in a wicker basket.

Kel hugged the girl, who was as much friend as maid, then grabbed the basket and gave her key to

Lalasa. "Tell Neal and the others I'm sorry I didn't say goodbye," she said, and raced down the hall with Jump and the sparrows.

In the stable Kel and over a hundred men saddled riding horses and put lead reins on their remounts. Qasim had left a pack with Kel's name on it for her spare clothes; she filled it from her basket and gave the pack to the supply officer when he collected them.

Qasim had put a burnoose, weapons, mail, helmet, and shield with her tack. Kel popped out of her tunic, slid into the mail shirt, then pulled the tunic over it. The men of the Own wore burnooses as cloaks. Kel fastened hers at the neck, hoping Qasim would show her how to shape a hood from it and fix it to her head when there was time.

She fastened her shield and weapons to her saddle, then donned her helmet. She was ready. Looping Hoshi's reins around one hand and Peach-blossom's around the other, Kel walked out of the stable with her mounts and Jump. The sparrows had vanished into Jump's carrier on Hoshi's back.

Kel tethered her horses on the edge of the courtyard where the company assembled. The torches, blown by the wind, gave the scene a dream-like feel as the faces of the men were first brightly lit, then shadowed. The night itself was a cool one, the wind smelling of water and the first hay cutting of the summer.

Kel watched the men unnoticed. Some were thirty or older, but most were young, single men in their twenties—married men were not allowed to join the King's Own. A third were Bazhir. Of all the realm's forces the King's Own had done the best at enlisting the once-scorned Bazhir. That was Lord Raoul's doing: he had taken the Own to live among the Bazhir for two seasons and recruited new men from their sons.

"So who's this youngster?" someone asked. Hoshi's bulk shielded Kel from the men's view. "We've got Lerant here for standard-bearer."

"A squire," sneered a young man's voice.

The one who'd first spoken exclaimed, "He's never wanted a squire—"

Kel stroked Peachblossom's nose. Eavesdropping had become a vice for her. She strained to hear a whispered remark, but didn't catch what was said. Then:

"The *Girl*?" someone demanded.

"I don't care if she's the Wave Walker," someone drawled. "She's green as grass."

"She better not foul us up in the field," another voice proclaimed.

"Don't you saddle rats have better things to do?" a gruff voice demanded. "Let's have an inspection. Mithros witness, if I find one strap undone, heads will roll."

"But, Sergeant Osbern, sir, I like my head," someone muttered.

"Very well, Gildes of Veldine. Let's inspect you first and put you out of your misery," the decisive voice said.

Now that they were no longer talking about her,

Kel emerged from between the horses. Gildes must be the drooping fellow who led his mounts to a blond, barrel-chested man. The others were double-checking their things.

"Did you eat?" someone asked Kel. A young man about four inches taller than she approached her. He gave Kel a warm turnover. "Just rolled out of bed and came charging on down, I bet. You'll learn. Eat."

Kel bit and discovered sausage and cheese inside the turnover. "It's good!" she mumbled, her mouth full.

The stranger grinned cheerfully at her. In his early twenties, he was broad-shouldered, big-handed, and very handsome. He wore his dark hair cut just below his ears. His mouth was long and made for smiling. He wore the uniform of the Own: loose dark trousers, chain mail shirt, blue tunic with silver trim, and a white burnoose. The crimson band around his biceps showed a dark circle with a black dot at its center: a sergeant's badge.

"I see you've still got your overgrown horse," he remarked with a nod toward Peachblossom. "I was new to the King's Own that day we saw you tilting. Everybody but me bet you'd come straight off his back when he reared. I won a meal at The Jugged Hare because I bet you'd stay on." He bowed to Kel as she wiped her fingers on the handkerchief she kept tucked in her boot top. "Domitan of Masbolle at your service, Squire Keladry. Your page-sponsor was a certain mad cousin of mine."

She squinted to get a better look at him. His

eyes—impossible to tell their color at the moment—were framed by wide, arched brows and set over a long nose slightly wide at the tip. It was Neal's nose, on someone else's face. Kel smiled. "You're related to Neal?"

"Sadly, yes. I call him Meathead. Have you ever met anyone so stubborn?" Domitan tucked his big hands into his breeches pockets with a grin.

"He can be difficult, um . . . Sergeant?"

He shook his head. "Technically you're not in the Own. Besides, he's written me so much about you I feel like I know you. Call me Dom." He offered his hand.

"Kel," she said, taking it. He gave her a firm squeeze, reassuring, not trying her strength as so many young men did, and let go. She felt breathless and tingly.

"You sure grew into this bruiser," Dom remarked. When he offered a hand for Peach-blossom to sniff, Kel yanked him back just as the gelding struck. "Oh, I see," Dom remarked, unruffled. "A testy pony."

Kel giggled, then saw that Lord Raoul, Captain Flyndan, and two men, farmers by their clothes, had emerged from the palace. Stablehands brought horses and remounts forward.

"We're ready to do business," Dom remarked. "Welcome to the Own, Kel." He swung himself onto his saddled mount, a dappled gray gelding.

Lord Raoul rode over. "All set to give Hoshi a try?" he asked. Kel nodded. "Mount up. Normally our remounts go in a string at the rear—the servingmen lead them with the supply train. We'll make an exception for Peachblossom. You ride a neck length back on my left, and keep him with you. Behave," he told Peachblossom, speaking directly to the horse. "Or I'll muzzle you like a dog."

Peachblossom shook his head vigorously. Kel hoped that was restlessness, not disagreement. With no time for another word with him, she gave a silent prayer to any listening gods for his good behavior and swung into the saddle. Hoshi stood patiently as she settled in.

Kel twisted to look into the carrier behind her saddle. "You have to move," she told the drowsy sparrows huddled there. "Otherwise Jump will squash you."

The birds hopped out. Once the carrier was empty, Kel nodded to Jump: he sprang neatly into the leather box. Hoshi flicked two ears back, then swung them forward again. Not even Jump could shake the mare's calm.

"Well, *I'm* impressed," drawled Raoul, who had watched. "Come along, Squire Keladry. Time to get your feet wet."

Following him to the front of the mounted force, Kel took note of the dogs. Thin, fine-boned greyhounds sat on the ground beside three riders. Four other men rode with terriers in carriers like Jump's. Six wolfhounds stood beside Captain Flyndan, tails wagging. There was no sign of Third Company's hunting birds—probably they were in carriers, asleep.

Lord Raoul faced his men. "Doubtless you

know as much as I do," he said, his calm, steady voice carrying over the fidgets of horses and the creak of leather. The men fell silent the moment he began to speak. "Haresfield in the Royal Forest was attacked by a band of centaurs and humans. We've got reports of twenty-three dead. Balim's squad is there now. Chances are the raiders cleared the district, but they could be stupid enough to stay around. Keep your eyes open."

He wheeled to face the gates, raised a kid-gloved hand, and brought it down, nudging his big bay mare into a trot. A brunet young man with a snub nose rode on his right, carrying the flag that announced they were Third Company of the King's Own. Captain Flyndan rode on the standard-bearer's right. Obeying her instructions, Kel followed Lord Raoul on his left. Behind her she heard the thunder of hooves as the riders took places in a long double column.

Kel felt a thrill of pride. I could be a general, leading an army to war, she thought, and smiled. She had no particular interest in armies, but it was fun to imagine herself a hero from a ballad at the head of a mighty legion.

Except that ballads never mentioned horses like Peachblossom, or one-eared, ugly dogs like the one who sat behind her. Nor did they mention sparrows perched in a neat row on a horse's mane. Used to these passengers, Peachblossom ignored them. Crown had claimed her place on Kel's shoulder.

Once they rode through the Least Gate and across a bridge into the greater world, Kel looked back. The company made an impressive display; two columns of fifty men, each in the white, blue, and silver of full members of the Own, followed by ten men in blue and white. These were the servingmen, who led the remounts and supply train. In the predawn light she could see that five of the Own rode with hunting birds on their shoulders.

"You mind those hawks," she told Crown. "You're safe while they're hooded or caged, but keep out of their sight when they're hunting. At least we'll eat well enough."

"We do try to eat," Raoul called back to her. "I go all faint if I don't get fed regularly. Only think of the disgrace to the King's Own if I fell from the saddle."

"But there was that time in Fanwood," a voice behind them said.

"That wedding in Tameran," added the blond Sergeant Osbern, riding a horse-length behind Kel.

"Don't forget when what's-his-name, with the army, retired," yelled a third.

"Silence, insubordinate curs!" cried Raoul. "Do not sully my new squire's ears with your profane tales!"

"Even if they're *true*?" That was Dom. It seemed Neal wasn't the only family member versed in irony.

Suddenly Kel's view of the next four years changed. She had expected hard work mixed with dread for the Ordeal of Knighthood at the end of it. Never had she guessed that other Tortallan warriors might not be as stiff and formal as Lord Wyldon. Never had she thought that she might have *fun*.

Thank you, Goddess, she thought. Thank you, Mithros. I'm going to learn, and enjoy myself while I do!

They followed the Conté Road southwest into the forest as the sun rose. About the time Kel used to eat breakfast, Raoul held up his arm. Everyone slowed to a walk, Kel a beat behind the others. She had to learn the hand signals. Maybe Qasim would teach her.

Third Company halted beside a river to rest and water the horses—Haresfield lay farther still inside the forest. Kel dismounted, Hoshi's and Peachblossom's reins in her hands. When Raoul climbed down from the saddle, Kel whisked his mare Amberfire's reins from his grip and led the animals to the river. Caring for a knight-master's horses was a normal part of a squire's duties. She glanced back: Raoul grinned and raised his hands in surrender.

Once all three horses had drunk, Kel turned them. Her path to Raoul was blocked by the snub-nosed standard-bearer. He was an inch taller than Kel, a broad-shouldered eighteen-year-old with level brown eyes and a firm chin. He wore his blond-brown hair cropped short at the sides; his bangs flopped over his forehead.

"My lord only took you because he felt sorry for you," he informed Kel icily. "*I* did his chores before you came. I was good at it."

Kel returned his look with Yamani calm, her emotions hidden. This young man's words stung a little. She knew that Raoul wanted her Yamani experience on the Great Progress. She also knew many would see it as the standard-bearer did. "I'm sorry you feel that way," she replied. "If you'll excuse me?" She took a firmer grip on Peachblossom's reins. The gelding watched the young man with too much interest for her comfort.

The standard-bearer gripped her arm. "Watch your step, *squire*," he informed her. "Just because Wyldon didn't have the brass to get rid of you doesn't mean *we* won't."

Kel flexed her bicep. He stared at her as muscle swelled under his fingers, forcing them open. With a quick jerk Kel freed herself. "Excuse me," she repeated, and walked off with her charges, keeping Peachblossom away from the standard-bearer.

Of course he's resentful, she thought as she joined the column. I've taken his place with my lord—or what he sees as his place. There's nothing I can do about that.

"You spoke to Lerant of Eldorne." Qasim appeared at her side to offer Kel a piece of cheese.

"No, thank you," she said politely, turning down the food. She added, "He talked, actually. I listened."

"He is a good fighter, and devoted to my lord," Qasim explained, eating the cheese. "He took an arrow for Lord Raoul last year, when we fought bandits in the Tusaine hills. He was unhappy to learn my lord took a squire." He offered some cheese to Jump, who gobbled it.

"It's all right," Kel said.

"There is more to it," the Bazhir told her softly.

"He applied for a warrior's post in the army, the navy, even as a man-at-arms, though his birth entitles him to better. No one would take a son of House Eldorne after his aunt's high treason. They feared the king's displeasure. My lord Raoul heard of it, and brought Lerant into the Own."

Kel felt a twinge of sympathy. She knew what it was like to be unwanted. Lerant's jealousy was understandable, even if it wasn't likeable. "Thank you," she told Qasim. "I'll keep it in mind."

"He will come around," Qasim assured her as the Own mounted up. "His is a good heart, though temper makes him sharp. He regrets it later. You will see."

Kel led Amberfire to Lord Raoul, steadying his mare as he swung into the saddle. "Thanks, Kel," he said as he accepted the reins.

Kel remounted Hoshi. Of course she understood Lerant's feelings. There was no treason in her family, but hadn't Lord Raoul rescued her, all the same?

⇥ three ⇤

CENTAURS

Smoke rose over the wooden stockade that surrounded the town of Haresfield. The wind carried scents of burned, wet wood and cooked meat. Kel knew those odors; she had smelled them often in raided Yamani and Tortallan villages.

They picketed their horses with those of the squad sent to the town earlier, in a field within view of the walls. The servingmen remained to guard them. Raoul explained to Kel that he didn't want the Own's tracks to blot out those left by the bandits. Anyone who entered or left the town had to skirt the broad space of trampled mud and grass before the gate, leaving the ground untouched until the raiders' signs could be properly read. Third Company entered Haresfield on either side of the gate. Once inside, the men formed their squads. Assigned areas by Captain Flyndan, they dispersed to survey the damage.

The headman, a priestess of the Goddess, the blacksmith, and Sergeant Balim, whose squad had arrived before dawn, met Raoul in the square. They led Raoul and Flyndan through the town, showing the damage. Kel followed silently.

Inside its untouched, fifteen-foot stockade wall a third of Haresfield had burned to the ground. Other buildings stood, but fire damage made them unsafe. The blazes had weakened support beams: roofs sagged, upper floors drooped into lower ones. Smoke drifted everywhere, burning Kel's eyes and filling her nose with the reek of ash and burned flesh. Her stomach had already tried to reject her breakfast twice.

People labored in the ruins. Bodies were set along the streets, pieces of cloth over their faces. Kel could only glance at those who'd burned; the sight of their swollen black flesh was too much. Worse, in a way, were those who looked as if they only slept: they had suffocated. Some charred animal bodies, mostly dogs and cats, lay with their masters. Every animal of monetary value—horses, cows, goats, poultry—had been stolen.

Raoul crouched beside a dead man who clutched a long-handled war-axe. He hadn't died in a fire: five arrows peppered his corpse. Turning him slightly, Raoul showed that the arrows had gone clean through him.

"That's a longbow," Flyndan judged, fleshy face set. "One of those six-foot-long monsters the king wants archers to train on. Just as bad as crossbows for punching through armor."

Raoul checked the arrows' fletching. "Centaur work," he said. "They like feathers from griffins and other winged immortals. They say the arrow flies truer. Kel, feel this, so you'll know griffin fletching the next time you see it."

As Kel obeyed, touching a feather like ridged silk, Flyndan commented, "Not that they can't do plenty of damage with human-made weapons. I've never seen a centaur miss what he shot at. Or she," he added. "Festering things are born archers."

"*This* isn't centaur," Raoul said, rising to yank a crossbow quarrel from a shutter. He showed it to the locals, Flyndan, and Kel. "A human shot this. Centaurs are snobs—they hate crossbows."

"I don't understand," the headman complained. He was an innkeeper, a short man with a barrel chest and straggly beard. "We're on good terms with Graystreak and his herd—they wouldn't attack us."

"They had help," said the priestess.

"You don't know for certain," the blacksmith snapped.

"I know the evidence of my eyes," retorted the priestess, crossing her arms over her chest. "Your nephew Macorm and his friend Gavan had gate duty last night. There's no trace of them, and the gate wasn't forced. It was wide open."

"Macorm's a good boy," argued the blacksmith. "Wild, a bit—"

The priestess interrupted. "You always defend him!"

"I know he's family," said the headman, "but it looks bad—"

Raoul cleared his throat. The villagers looked at him. "Arguing without facts is pointless," he said, kind but firm. "Flyn, have Volorin's squad bring this Graystreak in. If it wasn't his herd, he may know whose it is. Send a squad to the palace for aid: healers, clothes, food, and so on. And I want someone to go to the Riders."

Flyndan opened his mouth.

"No jealousies, Flyn," Raoul told him. "We can use one—no, two, Rider Groups here. Get the rest of the boys to help these people recover what they can."

"Two squads to start digging?" Flyndan inquired.

Raoul looked down the main village street. Bodies lined it on either side, more than the twenty-three reported earlier. "Two's fine," Raoul said, his face bleak.

As Flyndan, Balim, the smith, and the priestess went about their business, Raoul continued to view the damage with Kel. The headman left to oversee the inn's kitchen so those who worked in the ruins might be fed.

When Raoul and Kel had seen the entire village, they returned to the gate. "Well, squire?" Raoul asked. "What do you make of this?" He indicated the ground at the stockade gate.

Kel looked at the churned mud. "I'd guess twenty-five, maybe thirty centaurs," she replied, not sure if she had read the signs correctly. Lindhall Reed, one of her teachers in immortal studies, had shown the pages centaur hoofmarks in plaster so the pages would recognize their tracks. "Twenty or so humans. The humans left their horses outside the gates—there's marks of horseshoes and picket stakes beside the wall. Centaurs aren't shod."

"Very good," Raoul said. "I wasn't sure you'd seen that. Go on."

"I agree with the priestess. The gate was opened." She motioned to the gate. "It's whole, the hinges are solid, there's no blood or anyone dead. Even if the guards were fooled into opening up, there'd be signs of a fight. And they'd have shouted. We were told everyone was abed when the raiders got into the houses." Something in the mud caught her eye: a doll, half-buried in muck. She picked it up and began to clean it with a handkerchief. "Setting fires after they stole, that's mischief, or settling old scores," she remarked. Her hands trembled with rage. The waste and cowardice—robbing their own people in the middle of the night!—had to be punished. "They took every animal they could sell. People are saying they cleaned out the valuables before they set their fires. And if folk here recognized the humans with the centaurs, they're keeping quiet."

"They'd have to, wouldn't they?" Raoul asked. "Villages like this, cut off from most of the world, everyone's related. A raider could be an uncle, a cousin, a brother."

Kel nodded, cleaning the doll as people reported to Raoul and the squad bound for the palace left. This was the lowest kind of betrayal, for kinsmen to steal what little people had. She could not understand those who liked romantic songs of highwaymen and pirates. Anyone who took poor people's life savings was not worth a song.

The centaurs were just as bad. They'd been given homes after they had sworn to heed the realm's laws. Now they were robbing those who had taken them in.

She waited until Raoul had finished talking with his squad leaders before she asked, "My lord?"

Raoul looked at her and raised his eyebrows.

"They won't stay local, will they?" she asked. The doll was as clean as she could get it. Kel thrust it into her belt. "They took all they could move. They're on the run, looking for a place to hole up or another village to rob."

"Absolutely," her knight-master replied. "We've got serious work ahead. Don't worry, though. With help, we'll bring these muck suckers to bay."

The local centaurs arrived. Kel watched the introductions, happy not to deal with these creatures, particularly the centaur chief, Graystreak. His black-and-gray hair was twined and oiled into ringlets, a style she disliked. Graystreak wore a dirty wrap-around shirt with a tangle of ribbons, beads, and chains around his neck, wrists, and pasterns, and braided in his tail. Only the belt at his waist was unornamented by anything but weapons. His human parts were those of a fair-skinned man in his fifties; his horse parts were blue roan.

Suddenly the chief broke off greeting Lord Raoul to approach Kel. He walked around her as if she were a filly for his inspection, ignoring Jump's low growl. On his second circuit the centaur was smiling. "A female. A strong one, not a pitiful two-legger stick girl," he commented. "You will breed easily, perhaps even bear sons of my kind." His voice slid over Kel like oil.

She swallowed hard. Keeping her face Yamani-blank, she imagined Graystreak put to dray horse work in the northern mines.

The sparrows leaped from their perch in a nearby tree to dart shrieking at the centaur. Gray-streak backed up, trying to shield his face. Jump advanced on him, hackles up, snarling.

"Jump, enough," ordered Raoul, coming over.

The dog shook his head.

"I need to talk to him. You aren't helping," the knight told the dog.

Jump sighed. He walked away, frequently glanc-ing over his shoulder as if to say, "I *have* to let him go?"

"This is unnatural," Graystreak snapped, still warding off sparrows. No matter how quickly he swatted, he never touched them. "Take these things away!"

"It's rude to single out the squire and ignore the knight," Raoul said politely. "I didn't give you per-mission to address her. Kel, call off the birds."

Without a word from Kel the birds flew to her. Crown and Freckle perched on her shoulders. The rest lined up on a branch.

Graystreak looked at Raoul. "I will give three slaves for her," he announced. "Two more if she breeds successfully within a year."

Kel stiffened. Slaves? There were no slaves in Tortall!

Raoul thrust his hands into his pockets, still the picture of goodwill. "You forget our customs, Chief Graystreak. Offer all the horses you like, human females are not for sale. And you can't have heard—I said she is a squire. A knight-in-training. She's busy. Now, explain to me how you are not at fault for this." He jerked his head toward the ruins of the village.

Graystreak spread his hands as his expression slid from greedy to innocent. "These young stallions give me no peace," he whined. "I cast them from the herd. Some females were silly enough to follow them. They are no longer my problem."

"You never thought they'd turn on us?" demanded the headman. "Centaur females leave males who can't give them gifts. If you kicked young bucks out with nothing, how were they to get presents if they didn't steal?"

Graystreak looked shocked. "I assumed their two-legger friends would warn Haresfield, since they live here. Had I known this would happen, of course I would have given warning. I prize the goodwill I have built up." He looked at Kel again and sighed before turning to Raoul. "Since I know nothing more, I take myself off. I'm sure you will catch these brigands." He shook his head woefully. "There will be no trade for us here for some time. I shall have to find another market."

The headman cursed and snapped, "Fair-weather friend, aren't you, Graystreak? When we can do business, you and your people are in and out all the time. When it looks like we'll be months restoring what we've lost, you're on your way!"

The centaur raised his brows. "My friend, I too have females. Without gifts, they attack males." He offered his bare forearms for inspection: they were covered with old scars. "Our females can be"—he hesitated, looking at Kel once more—"overly spirited."

She met his gaze levelly. I'll show you how spirited human females are, you sideslipping sack of ooze, she thought.

Graystreak walked toward the gate, only to halt. Somehow Peachblossom and Raoul's warhorse, Drum, had pulled free of their pickets. They stood between the centaur and the gate. Black Drum pawed idly at the ground, as casual as if he had stopped to graze in this bare spot. Peachblossom's head was slightly lowered, his ears flat to his skull. He kept one eye on Graystreak.

The centaur reared to show the geldings his stallion parts, and hissed at them in his own language. Drum flicked one ear forward and the other back, all equine blandness. Peachblossom waited until Graystreak settled onto his fours, then struck, snakelike, his teeth coming together with an audible click as he missed. Graystreak scrambled to get out of range; he nearly fell.

But they're geldings, Kel thought, flabbergasted. Geldings don't face down stallions!

"Get these slaves out of my way," snarled Graystreak.

"That's the interesting thing about having the Wildmage about." Raoul was relaxed and cheery. "Palace animals are changing. Soon most will work for us only if they want to. Some animals are further along, of course."

More of the King's Own mounts had freed themselves of the picket lines. They walked through the gate to stand behind Peachblossom and Drum, forming a barrier of horseflesh between Graystreak and escape.

"I told my lord the other day that horses in particular are showing a smart streak," Flyndan added. "You'd best be careful, Chief Graystreak. Your own slaves might rebel."

Graystreak glared at the humans, trembling with rage. "Tell them to move," he said, his polite mask in tatters. "You've corrupted them! No gelding defies a stallion, not in the history of horsekind!"

"You don't think history gets rewritten, sometimes?" Flyndan inquired mildly.

"I'll ask them to step aside in a moment," Lord Raoul told the centaur. "There is one thing. I know you weren't trying to avoid the issue—I'm sure it just slipped your mind—but under your treaty, you're required to supply a third of your people to help capture these rogues. I know you'd have remembered in a moment. Our horses just saved you the extra steps."

Graystreak's fists clenched. Then he smiled, his mask back in place. "Forgive me," he said. "I was trying to decide who to send with you, and was preoccupied."

The wagons from the palace arrived shortly before noon. Kel got to work ladling out soup in a mess tent. Raoul stood beside her to issue bread to the diners as they filed by. Only when everyone else had been served did they eat.

"You won't get a traditional squire's education with me," he told her between mouthfuls of soup. "Serving refreshments in meetings, well, you'll do that. It's the best way for you to hear what's said and who says it. I'll want your impressions afterward, so be sharp. But waiting on me hand and foot is plain silly. So's caring for my horses in the field. For one thing, I like to do it. For another, you'll be too busy. Tend to your own mounts first."

Kel nodded. After she swallowed a mouthful, she asked, "Why Rider Groups, my lord? Aren't there enough of us?" He had led all one hundred warriors of Third Company into the forest that morning, not counting the servingmen.

"A different tool for a different job," explained Raoul. Flyndan, seated across from them, made a face and nodded. "We're conspicuous, in our blues with the pretty silver mail and all," Raoul continued. "Our horses are big—good for open ground, slow over broken terrain and forest. Third Company does the main sweep, talking to other villages and making noise. The Rider Groups scout on our left and right flanks—our sides. Their little ponies will cover rocky terrain, marshes, and so on. The enemy will be on the move. Once we know where they are, we'll send half the company around to their rear, to set up a trap. Then we drive 'em into it."

"We've done it before," Dom told Kel. He sat with Flyndan, polishing his empty bowl with a crust of bread. The smile he directed at Kel made her heart turn over, just as Neal's smile did. "We clank around, make a lot of fuss, let the bandits think they'll always be two steps ahead. Then we close the net and haul them off to royal justice."

"They'll have to sing a sweet song to get out of a hanging," Raoul said grimly, picking up his empty dishes.

Kel shuddered: she hated hangings. No matter what the crime was, she saw no malice in those hooded and bound silhouettes dangling against the sky. Worse, to her mind, was the thought that the condemned knew they were to die, that a day and time had been set, that strangers planned each step of their killing.

Flyndan misunderstood her shudder. "That's right. It's not glamour and glory. It's hard, mud-slogging work. If you wanted it easy, you should have taken a desk knight."

"Stop it, Flyn," Raoul said, his voice firm. "See her in action before you judge."

"I know, she rallied those lads while we handled the spidren nest. You'd think she'd be over this warrior thing by now." Flyndan carried his dishes away.

"Kel?" Raoul asked.

Kel was buttering a roll. She knew what he wanted. "I've heard it before, my lord."

Raoul patted her shoulder and took his dishes to the scrubbers.

"He's not the easiest second in command, but he's good at it." Kel looked up to meet Dom's very blue eyes. "You need someone a bit stiff to offset my lord. He's too easygoing, sometimes. Flyn will let up, once he sees this isn't a hobby for you."

Kel shrugged. "I don't need to be liked, Dom. I just need to work."

When she rose with her dishes, he did as well. "And you've a knack for it. I heard what you did with the spidrens, your first year. And then with the hill bandits, your second summer."

Kel glanced up at Dom, startled. "How did you know about that?" She handed her bowl, plate, and cup to the dishwashers. One of them was Qasim. He smiled at Kel and Dom, and meekly bore a scolding from the village woman beside him, who said it took more than a swipe with a cloth to get a bowl clean.

"How did I know?" Dom asked, and chuckled. "My cousin the Meathead, remember? He wrote about both in great detail. I feel sorry for him these days, though."

"But he's got the *Lioness* for knight-master!" protested Kel.

Dom grinned down at her. "You think that's *fun*? Maybe we're not talking about the same Lioness. The one I know rides with us a lot—my lord's one of her best friends. She's the one with the temper. And if Neal's learned to keep his opinions to himself, it'll be more than any of us were ever able to teach him."

Kel started to argue, and changed her mind. Dom was certainly right about Neal.

"Trust me," Dom said, resting a hand on Kel's shoulder, "I bet he wishes right now *you* had his place!" He went to help some men carry a heavy beam down the street.

Kel resisted the temptation to rub the spot where Dom's hand had rested. She needed to find work. Was she some kind of fickle monster, that Dom's smile and touch could make her giddier than Neal's had? Was she one of those females who always had to moon over a man? Did other girls' emotions flop every which way? Lalasa had never mentioned it, if hers did, and she was quite good at explaining such things.

"That's my doll."

Kel looked down. A small girl stared up at her with accusing brown eyes. She was streaked with mud and soot; there were charred places on her skirt, but there was nothing afraid or weary in those eyes.

"I looked and looked and looked. I thought Gavan stole it because he knew I would cry. She's my favorite."

Kel had forgotten the doll she had cleaned and thrust into her belt. Now she gave it to its owner, who informed Kel that "Mama needs help lifting."

"Take me to your mother, then," Kel said.

The girl's home was a shambles. Soot streaked the walls above the windows. Men and boys were on the roof, tearing off burned thatch as they searched for hidden fires. A figure the size of an infant lay in front of the house, covered with a cloth square.

"That's my brother," the girl said, her face stony. "We were running across the street. The house was on fire, and men were shooting arrows, and one hit him. He died."

She led Kel into the house. A woman whose eyes were red and puffy from weeping struggled to right an overturned table. A toddler clutched her skirt. Kel got to work with the table while her guide took charge of the toddler. The young mother was happy for the assistance, and asked nothing of Kel past her name.

They had set the room in order and put the beds out to air when Kel heard someone yell for her. She apologized to the family and ran out, to find Lerant in the street.

"What have you been doing, rolling in muck?" he demanded scornfully, looking down his short nose at her. "Well, never mind. The Rider Groups are here, and the centaurs, the ones who are going to help search. They're in a tent outside the main gate. My lord wants you to wait on them. The wine service is in the bags with the blue rawhide ties, with the packhorses. There's two small kegs of wine in general supplies." He trotted away, not giving Kel time to reply.

She drew a bucket of water from a nearby well and poured it over her head to rinse off most of the dirt. Then she went to find the supplies outside the stockade.

The packs lay on the ground. Raoul's personal ones had his crest pressed into the leather. Those with blue rawhide ties lay beside them. She had gone through one and was opening the second when a man shouted, "Hey! You! What are you after, grubbing in the captain's things? Get out of there!"

A servingman ran over to grab Kel's arm. "You think you can steal whatever you like, is that it? Well—"

"Hold it, Noack," someone interrupted. It was the burly Sergeant Osbern. "What's this noise? They can hear you at the council tent."

"He was in Captain Flyndan's bags, and I'm not to squawk?" the man Noack demanded.

"Squire Keladry?" Osbern inquired. Kel nodded.

"Squire?" cried the testy Noack. "Squire or no—"

Osbern raised his eyebrows. Noack went silent and let go of Kel.

"I was told my lord's wine service was here, and that I should bring it and the wine to the council tent," Kel said evenly. "I didn't know those were Captain Flyndan's bags."

"Who told you?" the sergeant inquired.

Obviously Lerant was having fun at her expense, but she would keep that to herself. "One of the men, Sergeant," she replied. "I don't know the names yet."

Osbern pursed his lips. "Too bad, because I would have a thing or two to say to that man," he told Kel, his voice dry. "It isn't just the captain's bags, Squire Keladry. My lord doesn't drink spirits, and he doesn't serve them. He says he had a problem as a young man, so he doesn't care to have liquor about. Captain Flyndan likes a glass or two. He serves it in his tent, but only when my lord isn't there. A water service will do today."

Kel nodded and found the pitcher, tray, and cups in Raoul's general supplies. The company mages had declared the town's wells to be clean, with no sickness in them. Kel used the well nearest the gate to fill her cups and pitcher, then carefully took the whole into the council tent.

Its sides were raised to accommodate five centaurs, who stood with the humans around a large table on which maps had been placed. These were younger than Graystreak, and looked to be in their twenties and thirties, though with centaurs it was hard to tell. Their youth lasted for two centuries; like other immortals, they never aged past mature adulthood. Unless an immortal was killed by accident or in a fight, she or he might live forever.

There were four human newcomers in plain white shirts, brown tunics and trousers, and riding boots. They wore the emblem of the Queen's Riders, a crimson horse rearing on a bronze-colored field, circled by a ring. One Rider wore a crimson ring around his badge, the sign of a Rider Group commander. Two wore a crimson ring with a thin black stripe in the middle: they were second in command. The Riders had a looser command structure and did not follow traditional military rankings.

The fourth Rider was a woman with golden brown skin and straight black hair. She was five inches shorter than Kel, with a short nose, firm mouth, and level black eyes. She was stocky and muscular. Her hair, braided tightly back from her face, framed high cheekbones and a square chin. The ring around her Rider insignia was gold.

Kel blinked, surprised. As she set cups before the guests, she eyed the Commander of the Queen's

Riders. Buriram Tourakom—Buri, as she was known—was as famed as Lord Raoul or the Lioness. She'd been made full commander during the Immortals War, when Queen Thayet, the previous commander, had seen she was too busy as queen to serve the force she had created. Buri had been Thayet's guard before she was queen; she had been co-commander since the Riders' creation, and had done most of the everyday work in the company. She was a ferocious fighter, armed or unarmed. No one tangled with her, given a choice. When Kel placed a cup before her, Buri murmured her thanks.

Once everyone was served, Kel stood at ease behind Raoul and listened. These centaurs, three females and two males, were very different from Graystreak. They were eager for the hunt and the fight to come.

The meeting ended late. Kel fought yawns as she followed Raoul to the inn where he, Buri, and Flyndan had been given rooms. While the inn was largely intact, the scent of smoke filled it from cellar to garret. Kel didn't care; neither did the others, she suspected. The men and Buri went to their rooms immediately. As Raoul's squire Kel opened her bedroll in front of his door. The sparrows protested this odd way to sleep, but found places around Jump. Kel was pulling off her boots when someone down the hall whispered, "Pst!"

She looked up, squinting. The wall lamp was nearly out of oil; its flame barely cast any light.

"Pst!"

Kel unsheathed her sword and walked toward

the noise, stockinged feet silent on the wooden boards. If she had to go out of sight of Raoul's door, she would wake him. This could be an attempt to draw her off, an attempt on his life.

The attempt was only Lerant, standing at the top of the stairs. "What do you want?" Kel demanded, in no mood to be polite. She wanted to sleep.

He glared at her. Kel turned to go back to her bed. "No, wait!" he whispered.

She turned back as she considered smacking him with the flat of her sword to teach him respect. Such thoughts only told her how bone-tired she was. Normally the idea would never occur to her.

"Why didn't you tell?" Lerant kept his voice low.

"Tell what?" she asked, her own voice barely audible.

"Come on. I heard Osbern set you straight. You didn't tell him who steered you to the packs, or he'd've had me up before Flyn."

"You couldn't ask in the morning?" she demanded, cross.

"I want to know now!"

Kel sighed. "I don't tell on people," she said. "Good night." She walked back down the hall, sheathed her sword, and crawled into bed.

⊰ four ⊱

OWLSHOLLOW

*I*f the Haresfield renegades were new to forest robbery, the centaurs and other humans with the band were not. Lord Wyldon had taught the pages much about tracking, but the next two weeks saw Kel's education expand ferociously. Whenever the robbers could mask their trail by walking in streams and over rocks, they did. It reached the point where the hunters moaned at a glimpse of water or a patch of stone. The robbers often split into five or six groups to confuse their trackers.

The centaurs used magic to hide their passage and their appearance in scrying crystals. They buried or hid loot so it wouldn't slow them down. The Riders found two caches; Dom's squad found a third. Everyone knew more was hidden away, because the bandits attacked every village they could, no matter how slim the pickings. In one village they sold loot from other raids, taking it back with everything else of value when they struck that night.

Clean clothes became a delirium dream. Kel

washed hers cold and wore them wet, thanking the gods she didn't get sick easily. She learned why Raoul had said she would do few of the things that squires normally did for knights. She barely had the strength to care for their mounts and weapons. Waiting on him as he ate and putting out his clothes for the morning would be ridiculous.

On the ninth day they ran out of the lotion that repelled insects. Lord Raoul growled under his breath and sent a party to the palace for supplies, for Riders and centaurs as well as Third Company.

By and large Kel thought the centaurs who hunted with them were decent people. They worked hard and never complained.

"Rogues make us look bad," Iriseyes, their female leader, told Dom, Qasim, and Kel one night as they gnawed stale flatbread. "Enough two-leggers call us animals as is, without this crowd making it worse. We *told* Graystreak he ought to cull Maresgift, Jealousani, Edkedy, and their crowd, but he wouldn't do it. I suppose it's hard to cull your own brother."

"Cull?" Dom asked.

"Kill 'em," Iriseyes said. "Herdmasters like Graystreak can do it. You don't want bad blood in the herd, particularly not in the slaves. It ruins the slaves, so you have to get rid of them, too. That's probably what Graystreak's doing now, culling the slaves that bred with that crowd."

Kel got up abruptly and walked away. Killing horses because they'd been mounted by wicked centaurs was obscene, she thought, hands shaking as she washed her dishes. It was as obscene as babies' being shot as their families ran from danger.

That was the eleventh night. The next morning the party with fresh supplies found them. Clean garments and insect repellant gave everyone, including Kel, a more cheerful outlook. She could even talk to the centaurs, though she had to banish the word "cull" from her mind when she did.

On their fifteenth night they got a piece of luck: Osbern's squad picked up Macorm, a Haresfield renegade. The young man was filthy and afraid. A bite on his arm was infected. He was bound hand and foot, wounded arm or no. Osbern told Raoul it was to protect Macorm as much as hold him: Osbern's men had not liked what they saw in Haresfield. They knew Macorm had been one of the two who had opened the gate.

"It wasn't what I imagined, my lord," the prisoner told Raoul. "There was no feasting or pretty girls or wine. Just take and run, and run. Gavan likes it, but he likes killing, too." A tear ran down his face, drawing a clean track in the dirt. "All I did was ask to go home. I swore I'd never tell, but they didn't believe me. They said they'd cull me at sunset for the Mares with Bloody Teeth—"

"Our goddesses of vengeance," explained Iriseyes. She and two other centaurs were listening to Macorm's tale.

"They said they'd eat my heart. I believed them. They tied me up, but I got away." More tears followed the first.

"We'll just shackle you, then," Raoul said. "To

keep you from repeating the experiment."

"I know where they're bound next," Macorm told him, desperate. "They thought I ran straight off, but I went up a tree. They never thought I'd stay close, let alone right on top of them, and I hid my scent with pine sap. I heard them talking after the searchers went out. For the king's mercy I'll tell you what they said."

"*If* we catch them, we'll speak to the king," Raoul said after a moment's thought. "If you lie—if it's a trap—"

"Gods, no!" Macorm began to weep in earnest.

Raoul and Flyndan traded looks. Flyn raised his brows; Lord Raoul nodded. "Time to call the Riders in," Flyn said with a thin smile. "Buri would never forgive us for leaving her out of the party."

"I'd never forgive myself if she were left out," Raoul told his second. "Kel, get Noack up here with his tools," Raoul told her. "I want shackles on this lad. If you're good, we'll feed you," he told Macorm. To Kel he added, "We'll need Emmet of Fenrigh." He'd named one of the men with a healing Gift. "He's out of—"

"Aiden's squad," Kel said.

Raoul grinned. "You learn fast. Under thankless conditions, I might add. Off you go."

She went to find the men he'd requested.

The Rider Group under Commander Buri came just after sunset; the second Group arrived soon after. Maps were produced, laid flat, and anchored by stones and cups of steaming tea. Kel was kept busy pouring tea and bringing food for the hungry Rider leaders. She even served Macorm, chained to the tent pole for this conversation. Raoul had asked her to do it, though what she wanted to do was take him to Haresfield and rub his nose in the streets filled with the dead, like a bad puppy. Two things stopped her: she was on duty, which meant keeping her feelings to herself, and she knew that Haresfield had surely finished burying the dead by now.

From what she had overheard, a village called Owlshollow was to be the next target. A human bandit had heard the son of that village's biggest fur merchant, apprenticed to a tanner in another town, talking drunkenly. The son complained that the old man wouldn't die and let his son inherit while he was young enough to enjoy it. He was too miserly to buy a horse for his heir to ride. He mistrusted fast-talking Corus goldsmiths and their banks, and hoarded the coin he took from each year's fur harvest. Probably his cronies did the same: they all lived as meanly as they could and whined about the foolish young.

That was enough for Maresgift's bandits. They would descend on Owlshollow and clean it out. If necessary, they would torture the fur merchants into revealing where they'd hidden their gold.

Macorm was taken away under guard after he finished. Once he was out of earshot, the blond, blue-eyed Evin Larse, in command of the second Rider Group, produced a crystal from his sleeve. It glowed a bright, steady gold. "It would have turned black if he'd lied outright, gray if he'd lied even a bit."

"You're sure it works?" Flyn asked. "I don't trust bought magic. I like to see it worked right in front of me."

"It works," said Larse. "It ought to. I paid enough."

"We *did* reimburse you," Buri pointed out.

"Half," retorted Evin. "At the rate I use it for the Riders, they ought to pay me double."

"He only bought it to find out if the ladies he courts have husbands," Buri's second in command put in.

There was a chuckle from the people in the circle around the maps. The air emptied of the tension that had filled it while Macorm was still present.

"Here's their last known position." Buri marked the place on the map with a blunt brown finger. "If they're bound for Owlshollow, traveling at . . ."

The hunters broke into a flurry of talk, figuring the bandits' speed based on what was known. Suddenly the mud-streaked, hollow-eyed, grim bloodhounds had become a lively group of humans and immortals again. The end of their chase was in view.

They calculated the robbers' present location, leaving a margin for error. Raoul sent Kel for a large leather tube packed with his things. When she brought it, he pulled off the cap on one end and slid out a heavy roll of sheets. He looked through them, checking marks on the corners until he found the one he sought, then drew out the sheet and opened it on their worktable. It showed part of the Royal Forest, the district that contained Owlshollow.

Reaching into his shirt, Raoul produced a gold

key on a chain and pulled it over his head. Using the key, he drew a circle around the dot labeled *Owlshollow*. It included the bandits' last known location. When he closed the circle, the map vanished. They were looking down at real terrain, forested hills, streams and rivers, marshes. Owlshollow appeared as a small town at the junction of two roads and a river. It was situated on rocky bluffs, protected on two sides from raiders who came by water.

"Show-off," murmured Buri. "Bought magic *still* isn't as good as what you do yourself."

"As if you did any," retorted Raoul.

Iriseyes ran her fingertip from the bandits' last known camp, where Macorm had left them, to Owlshollow. "Well, well," the centaur said, showing teeth in a predator's grin. "Look at this."

"The river blocks them outside the town," said Flyn.

"Marsh blocks the southern escapes," Buri said, her eyes glittering. "The stone ridge boxes them in on the north."

"I know this town," Volorin said. He wore his dark hair long and braided, with ivory beads carved like skulls at the ends of the braids. "No one can get through the marsh, and that ridge is a hard climb, not easy for centaurs. If we spread out in an arc . . ." He sketched the arc on the map with his finger.

"We'll have them," said Evin Larse.

"We split up," said Raoul. "Our hunter force takes position at Owlshollow, where they'll seal off the river escape routes. The rest of us will form a crescent of hounds, and drive our playmates to the hunters." He looked around at the others; all were nodding.

The Rider Groups, the centaurs, and half of Third Company were given places along the crescent. Raoul would command the fifty men of the Own in the field. Flyndan and the rest of Third Company would make a fast ride at dawn, slipping far around the bandits to reach Owlshollow. The robbers would never realize the trap was set until it closed.

As everyone prepared to go, Raoul said, "Kel, you'll report to Captain Flyndan and his sergeants."

Kel and Flyn stared at him. Flyn protested, "She's your squire, my lord—"

Raoul shook his head. "I want her with you."

One of the first lessons pages learned was never to question a knight-master's command. One pleading look was all Kel allowed herself before she began to clean off the table. By the time she was done, everyone had gone to their beds. She went in search of hers.

Raoul crouched between his tent and Kel's, giving Jump a thorough scratch. "Walk with me," he told her, rising to his feet. They strolled across the large clearing that held their camp.

Raoul finally stopped to lean against a massive oak. "You want to know why I'm sending you with Flyn."

"Sir, I'm to obey without question," Kel pointed out, though she did want to know.

"That's fine if you're to be a lone knight—you have to figure out things yourself," he said quietly.

"But if you get extra duties someday—like command—you should know why you're asked to do some things, particularly those that aren't part of regular training.

"Putting you with Flyn at Owlshollow accomplishes two goals," he explained. "You'll deal with his not liking you. He'll probably give you scut work. You need to show you'll do your part no matter what. Plenty of nobles won't take orders from a commoner, and they balk when there's no potential for glory. You need to show that you'll do what's needed, not just for me, but for others. And I'll see how Flyn manages you, if you change his thinking at all. I know you want to be among the hounds, but trust me, this is important."

Kel nodded. She understood his reasoning, though she hated the assignment. And she still couldn't argue, because proper squires didn't.

Raoul clasped her shoulder lightly and let go. "There will be other chases," he said. "Now get some sleep."

Owlshollow was larger than Haresfield, and better fortified, with a double stockade wall to shield it. Late that first morning within the walls Flyn called a meeting with the men of the Own and the town's officials. The squads would wear farmers' clothes over their mail and work in the fields, so anyone who scouted would think all was normal. Flyn gave each squad a position, then looked at the townsmen. "Did we forget anything?" he asked. "Any side trail, any hole that might let a few escape?"

The chief herdsman was in a whispered argument with the son who had accompanied him. Finally he sighed and looked at Flyn. "My son Bernin reminds me of the old game track, b'tween the bluffs an' the marsh. It's overgrown—I don't know how bandits from outside would know of 't, or see 't to escape."

"If I've learned nothing else in my years of service, master herdsman, it's that the unexpected always happens," replied Flyn. "I would hate for even a single louse to escape." He looked around until his eyes found Kel. "Have your son show this track to Squire Keladry. That will be her post when things warm up."

Kel left with the shepherd lad Bernin, swallowing disappointment again. She'd hoped that Flyndan would relent and let her take part in the main fight. There's a waste of hope, she thought bitterly.

As Bernin led her through the gates, he kept peering at her. Finally, as they trudged around the outermost wall, he asked, "T'n't Keladry a *girl's* name?"

Bernin was right. The trail was clearly still used, by animals if not people. Someone desperate could take it to reach the river. A bridge two hundred yards downstream would provide a clean getaway if a fugitive got that far.

She wasn't sure she could hold it alone, so she asked Captain Flyndan to look. He had done so, then told Kel, "Just be ready to take anyone who actually makes it here. I doubt they will."

They waited for the rest of that day and through the next. Word finally came that Maresgift's band had camped just a few hours' ride from Owlshollow. Raoul's hound forces in the forest would start their push at dawn. Maresgift would have two choices: to stand and fight, or to run for Owlshollow—and Flyndan.

The next morning the raiders came. Lonely at her post on the bluff, Kel heard the battle chorus: horn calls, yells, the clang of metal, the scream of horses. It would be a desperate fight in the fields. The bandits knew that capture meant hanging.

It was maddening to guess how it was going from sounds blown to her through the tangled briars that hid the trailhead above. She stood on a broad ledge halfway between the town and the River Bonnett. It was reachable only by the track down from the heights or up from the river. Here she had flat dirt and room to fight. The river's edge was all tumbled stones, where it would be too easy to break an ankle.

Kel got a coil of thin, strong rope and took it down the trail from the top of the bluff. Using spikes to anchor it, she stretched the rope at knee height across the trail, six feet above her guard post. It would bring any fugitives tumbling onto the ledge, where she would be ready for them.

She kept her fidgets to the occasional walk to the edge of her post, where she could look at the swift, cold Bonnett thirty feet below. When she caught herself at it, she felt sheepish. You act like the edge is going to creep up on you till you fall, she told herself sternly. Now stop it!

The morning she had climbed down the frail, rusted outer stair on Balor's Needle had marked the end of her fear of heights, though she still disliked them. Looking at the Bonnett from her ledge was like wiggling a loose tooth with her tongue—it was silly, but she had to remind herself that she would no longer freeze in panic at the sight of a drop. She also wanted to be sure her body would remember that a cliff lay only ten feet behind her.

The battle sounds grew louder. She smelled smoke: had the bandits set the fields on fire? If she climbed to the top, she might see. Her orders were to keep quiet and mind her post. She ought to be like Jump. He crouched at her feet with the patience of the born hunter, ready for game to be flushed. The sparrows were among the briars above, preening, sunning, and doing whatever birds did when bored.

Suddenly they zipped down the bluffs past Kel, screeching the alarm. Gravel rattled down ahead of whoever was on the trail. Kel settled her hold on her glaive and checked her stance. She heard scrambling feet . . .

Was that a *child* crying?

Someone shrieked. Stones flew as the fugitive hit Kel's rope hard enough to rip it from its anchors. A centaur skidded onto the ledge half on his side, tangled in her rope, brandishing a short, heavy cutlass.

Kel, hidden by a large boulder where the trail met her ledge, lunged into the open, driving her glaive down. She halted her thrust a bare inch from a squalling girl tied to the centaur's back by crossed lengths of rope. A cool part of her mind noted that this was why no one had shot the centaur: they had feared to kill the child.

The centaur hacked at Kel with his cutlass as he wallowed, fighting to get to his feet. Kel's moment of panic—had she cut the girl?—ended. She jerked away from the sweep of the enemy's blade and cut the rope that held the child. "Jump!" she yelled. The dog leaped over the fallen immortal, seized the child's gown in his powerful jaws, and dragged her free.

"Get her out of here!" Kel ordered him. The centaur heaved himself to his feet and backed against the stone, cursing breathlessly. She ignored what he said: she had one eye on Jump, who towed the shrieking child back up the path, and one eye on the centaur's blade.

The immortal sidled, trying to find room for his hindquarters as he fumbled to yank a saddlebag over his head. He tossed it to one side, out of the way. Its contents thrashed and squealed like a large, frightened animal.

The centaur chopped at Kel, trying to draw her away from the opening where the trail continued down to the river. Kel blocked his cutlass, keeping herself between him and escape. There was nowhere for him to go on her right, unless he were mad enough to try that thirty-foot leap to the foaming, rock-studded river. If he ran that way, she half-thought she'd let him go. It would be a quicker end than hanging.

The centaur groped at a heavy leather belt around his waist with his free hand. He yanked out a throwing-axe.

My luck, thought Kel. He comes the way no one's supposed to come, *and* he can use weapons in both hands.

He hurled the axe. Kel dodged left, still between him and escape, and stepped in with a long slash across his middle. He blocked it with his cutlass and hacked down at Kel's head. She caught the blade on her weapon's hard teak staff, angled the glaive, and rammed the iron-shod butt straight into the spot where the creature's human and horse parts joined.

The centaur went dead white, uttering a gasping whine. His eyes rolled back in his head. Kel swung the glaive's blade around, placing it where the centaur's jaw met his neck. She pressed until a drop of blood ran down the razor edge.

"Yield for the Crown's mercy," she ordered.

Even as he snarled a reply the centaur kicked out with his forelegs, ramming Kel back. Her right side was on fire; her left thigh hurt so fiercely she thought she might faint. Instead she clung to her glaive and staggered to her feet.

The immortal charged, cutlass raised, and nearly speared himself on Kel's blade. Kel silently thanked the Yamani armsmistress who had bruised her all over to teach her one simple rule: never drop the weapon.

Pain made her weak—she tried to ignore it. Her main attention, her serious attention, was on the foe.

He spun and kicked, his back hooves showering

her with rock and dust. Kel shut her eyes just in time. She whipped her glaive in a sideways figure-eight cut to keep him back until she could see. Warm blood trickled down her cheek where a stone had cut her. The sparrows shrieked. Kel knew they were at the centaur's face. Terrified he might kill them, she opened her eyes. The creature roared his fury, shielding his face against the birds, forgetting his cutlass as he spun, wildly hunting for an escape route.

Kel lunged, sinking the eighteen-inch blade deep below the centaur's waist and yanking up. His belt dropped, cut in two; his forelegs buckled. Kel pulled her glaive free as her foe went down, clutching his belly. Blood spilled around his hands. From the stink, she knew she'd hit his human intestines.

He would die even if a healer could be found. No healer could save anyone from a belly cut. The foulness in the intestines spread, infecting all it touched. Kel gulped hard and cut the centaur's throat, a mercy stroke. Blood sprayed, spattering her with drops that burned. He was dead when she lowered her glaive. His eyes never left hers. Even after he died, they were still wide, still fixed on this human who had brought him down.

Kel braced her glaive on the ground and hung onto it, swaying, her ribs and leg on fire. Her stomach was in full revolt over the mess she had made of the centaur—Kel swallowed rapidly until she defeated the urge to vomit. She prayed that no more fugitives came her way. She wouldn't be able to stop them.

"Jump?" she called softly, not wanting to attract attention from the battlefield above. "Jump, where are you?"

She heard a scrambling noise on the trail, and a human whimper. The dog walked onto Kel's ledge with the rescued toddler's wrist held gently in his teeth.

"Guard the path," Kel ordered. "Don't let anyone take us by surprise." Jump wagged his tail, freed his charge, and trotted back the way he had come. The little girl ran over and clutched Kel's injured leg. Pressing her face into Kel's leather breeches, she began to cry.

Pain made Kel turn gray; sweat rolled down her cheeks. The girl clung to Kel's bad leg with all of her strength, sending white-hot bolts of agony shooting up Kel's thigh. Using the glaive for support, she gently pried the toddler's arms open and lowered herself onto a stone. Once down, she pulled off her tunic and wrapped it around the girl, listening to the sounds from above. Either the battle was moving away or it had ended: she heard a handful of horn calls, and no clanging metal at all.

"We'll be fine," Kel told her companion. The girl curled up on the ground, sucking her thumb, with Kel's tunic for a blanket. She was asleep almost instantly. For a moment Kel looked at her own thumbs, thinking it might be reassuring to do the same. But centaur blood was on her hands. Also, the thought of the teasing she would get if anyone found her doing it kept her from tucking her thumb into her mouth.

A shrill, quavering shriek reminded her of the centaur's leather pack. Looking at it, she saw the pack thrash. Something was alive in there. Kel carefully got to her feet, moving like an old lady. Using her glaive for a crutch, she hobbled over until she could grab the pack.

"Calm down," she told the occupant, lurching back to her seat. "It's all over." Settling the pack on her lap, she opened the buckles that held it shut and thrust a hand inside. Later she would wonder where she had misplaced her common sense. She had known too many animals in her life to grope blindly for one. All she could think was that pain and exhaustion had betrayed her this once.

The creature in the pack took exception to her hand. It clamped a hard, sharp beak on the tender web between Kel's thumb and index finger. Kel yanked her arm free. The creature hung on, emerging with Kel's hand. It was an orangey-brown bird, its feathers caked with dirt and grease. Blood welled around its beak as it held onto Kel. She didn't want to hurt the thing, but she did want it to let her go!

Kel shook her hand, to no effect. She tried to press the hinges of its beak to open it. Catlike paws armed with sharp talons wrapped around her captive wrist, gouging deep scratches where they found flesh. She pressed harder on the hinges of that murderous beak until it popped open. Kel yanked her hand free.

The creature leaped free of the pack to wrap fore- and hind paws around Kel's mail-covered arm. Kel grabbed its curved, yellow beak with one hand to keep it shut. She yanked her captive arm free of the creature, pressed it onto her lap, and wrapped the leather pack around it to neutralize the thing. Only when she was certain it couldn't free itself did she pick it up to look it in the eyes. They were the hot orange of molten copper. She'd never heard of an animal with copper eyes.

The creature hissed. Its body, paws, and tail were all rather feline, except for the feather covering. The head, beak, and wings looked eagle-like, though she wasn't sure. Unlike most nobles, Kel didn't like falconry and had never tried to learn it.

"Cat paws, cat tail, eagle . . . ," she murmured, then stopped as the hair stood up on the back of her neck. "Oh, no," she whispered. "Oh, no, no, no."

The baby griffin stretched out its head and grabbed a lock of her hair. She yelped as it yanked, and dragged her hair free before stuffing the griffin into its pack. The small immortal protested its renewed captivity at the top of its lungs. Somehow the little girl at Kel's feet slept on.

Kel tried to think as she wound a handkerchief around the still-bleeding wound between her thumb and forefinger. Griffins were protected by law, but that didn't stop poachers. The traffic in both griffin parts and live griffins was deadly, but not because of the law. If a griffin's parents smelled their offspring on a stranger, even years afterward, they would kill the person. Whatever made up the scent, it could not be washed off. Mages weren't even sure the parents detected an actual smell. The fact that it stayed for years seemed to indicate the scent was magical rather than actual. It didn't apply to those who handled claws or feathers, only to those who had held an infant griffin. This one's parents would have to be found, and someone would have to explain to them what happened before they ripped her to pieces.

Kel put her head in her hands. She straightened instantly as pain stabbed her ribs. Not now, she thought, despairing. I don't need this now.

⇥ five ⇤

THE GRIFFIN

*K*el sat bolt upright with a gasp. In her dream the centaur had come alive again, scaring her out of sleep.

She was in the dark, cased with sun-dried cotton that carried a fishy scent. She was not hot, sweating, dirty, or in pain. Now she remembered: they had lifted her up the hill on a loading platform and brought her to a makeshift hospital. She'd warned them about the griffin before someone else could touch it. A healer had told her she'd broken bones, then given her something vile-tasting that put her to sleep. She was in the hospital now. It was night. A few oil lamps supplied the only light.

She was just wondering how the others had done when the healer brought her another dose of medicine. After that she slept well into daylight until she woke, alert and ravenous. Someone had put a metal cage beside her cot. Inside it was the pouch, the griffin, a dish of water, and a dish of what smelled like fish scraps. If the immortal had eaten, she couldn't tell.

They must have just stuck the pouch in the cage and let the griffin crawl out, she thought, yawning. She could see the small gate in the side closest to the dishes: whoever had fed the griffin and given it water could just change the dishes that way. If the griffin didn't mind the cage, perhaps Kel could transport it that way until she found its parents. Her hands throbbed from the mauling they had gotten from those claws. Kel would rather not let it have any more of her blood, if she could help it.

A woman brought Kel a bowl of clear broth.

"The bandits?" Kel asked her, forgetting what she had been told when the others found her.

"Captured, them that aren't dead," the woman replied with grim satisfaction. "They'll face the Crown's justice soon enough."

Kel nodded and finished her broth. Within a few moments of handing the bowl to the woman, she was asleep again.

It was nearly sunset when the baby griffin's squall roused Kel. She peered at him over the edge of the cot. He was flapping half-opened wings, objecting to the cage. When he saw Kel, he peered up at her through the openings in the metal.

Kel flopped onto her back. I wanted that to be a dream, she thought.

Another woman brought Kel water and a bowl of noodles in broth. Kel was so hungry she nearly inhaled the food, looking around as she ate. She counted twenty beds, most filled with sleeping men. The two beside Kel held female Riders.

She was about to put her bowl on the floor when something small and wet struck her cheek. She wiped it off, then inspected it: a ragged bit of fish skin. With a frown Kel wiped it onto a napkin. She put the bowl next to her cot; when she straightened, something wet struck her eye. Kel removed it. More fish skin.

She looked into the metal cage. "Stop it," she told the griffin. She was impressed with the little thing's aim. It must have taken innate skill or lots of practice. . . .

Inspection of her blankets revealed pieces of scaled skin and fish bones in their wrinkles. Kel touched her pillow and the sheets around her head, to find more samples of the griffin's target practice. She leaned over to glare at the creature.

A large, smelly scrap hit her squarely in the mouth. Kel picked it off with a grimace and dropped it into the cage. The griffin bowed its shoulders, lifted its head, opened its beak, then spread and fluttered its wings. Kel had raised young strays; she knew begging when she saw it.

"Ridiculous," she told the griffin. "You've been feeding yourself from your dish. Keep on feeding yourself." She lay down with a thump. A gobbet of fish entrails landed in her ear. She sat bolt upright with a cry of disgust, wrenched off her blanket, and threw it over the griffin's cage.

The griffin began to shriek. Even with the blanket to muffle it, the hall echoed. Seeing other patients sit up, Kel snatched the blanket off the cage.

The griffin opened its beak and fluttered its wings.

Kel lifted the cage onto her lap. "Little monster," she growled. She opened the grate and reached in for the dish. The griffin lunged and clamped its beak on the tip of her index finger. Kel bit her tongue to keep from waking anyone with a scream. She fought the griffin for possession of her finger. The moment she shook it off, the griffin assumed the begging position.

Kel glared at her charge. It was still filthy, shedding feathers, its keelbone stark against the skin of its chest. It was half starved. Keeping a watchful eye on it, she took a fish off the plate. The griffin opened its beak and tilted its head back. Kel let the fish drop. In three bites the prize was gone. Once again the griffin begged. Kel fed it two more fish without problems. When she fumbled getting the next fish out of the cage, the griffin hissed and swiped at her arm, leaving four deep scratches.

"I guess you've had enough," Kel said grimly. She closed the cage and put it on the floor. The griffin began to scream again.

Five fish, a bitten finger, and three more scratches later, the griffin stopped begging. It closed its eyes and went to sleep in its cage. This time, when Kel put it on the floor, it didn't protest.

She was still picking fish remains out of her bed when the nurses came to light the night lamps. With them came the shepherd's boy, Bernin.

"You look better," he told Kel frankly, parking his behind on a stool beside her cot. "You was green when they brung you up."

"I'm not surprised," Kel replied. "I felt green." Her ribs and leg were bruised, but the deep aches were gone. The vile liquid must have been a healing potion.

"The mayor di'n't even want you here, 'cause o' that—" Bernin pointed to the griffin. "My lord roared at 'im an' the mayor changed his mind." He grinned so infectiously that Kel had to grin back.

"I'd do what my lord said if he roared at me," she admitted.

"Well, you *got* to, bein' his squire, an' all," he pointed out. "That little 'un you saved? The girl?"

"Jump saved her," Kel said firmly. "I just distracted the centaur." Jump, asleep on the opposite side of her cot from the griffin, thumped the floor with his tail.

Bernin rolled his eyes at this city girl nitpicking. "Anyways, her folks is charcoal burners, caught in the woods by them bandits. They took a bunch of lone folk, them that on'y come into the walls for winter. Cowardly pukes." He spat on the floor, winning a disapproving glare from a healer. "But the little's fam'ly wants to show you gratitude. They wanna know what they could do."

Kel winced. She'd done nothing to be thanked for. Jump had saved the child. She'd simply killed a centaur and almost gotten killed herself, because she had forgotten he was part horse. Any thanks would only grind it in that it was a miracle any of them had survived.

"If they want to give Jump a bone, or thank Captain Flyndan, who put me there, that's fine," she told the boy, smothering a yawn. "I just did what I was told."

"Don't you *want* to be thanked?" Bernin asked, baffled. "I'n't that what you go heroing for?"

"No," replied Kel. Remembering her manners, she added, "Say I thank them for thinking of me."

Bernin wandered off, shaking his head. He passed Raoul on his way out. Kel watched her knight-master walk along the rows of beds, talking with those who were awake. Hers was the last cot he reached.

For a moment he looked down at her, hands in his breeches pockets, shaking his head. "Young idiot," he said, amusement in his sloe-black eyes. "You forgot the forelegs, didn't you?"

Kel smiled wryly. "Yes, sir."

"You'll remember next time." He spotted Bernin's stool and lowered himself onto it. It was so short that his knees were at the level of his chest. He straightened his legs with a sigh. "A pretty trap, though. The rope was a nice touch."

"I got lucky," Kel said, shamefaced. "If he'd fallen wrong, that child could've died. Or my friend, here." She nodded at the griffin's cage.

"You can 'if' yourself to death, squire," he said, patting her shoulder. "I advise against it. You're better off getting extra sleep. Once you and the others are up and about, we have to take these charmers to the magistrates for trial."

He grinned as Kel made a face. "When people say a knight's job is all glory, I laugh, and laugh, and laugh," he said. "Often I can stop laughing before they edge away and talk about soothing drinks. As for the griffin . . ." He looked down at the cage and sighed. "I'm surprised he's still in there. Griffins usually don't put up with cages for long. We heard testimony from the robbers we captured. They knew about the griffin, of course—the centaur killed the peddler who stole it from the parents. Did they teach you about griffin parents killing anyone who's handled their young?"

Kel nodded.

"Until we find them, I'm sure the Own can protect you long enough that we can explain things. And I've sent for Daine. She can search for this one's family."

Kel sighed with relief. She had thought she might have to leave Lord Raoul's service and work in the palace until the griffin's parents were found. "Then I can go on tending it, I suppose," she said, not looking forward to that beak and those claws.

Raoul grinned. "Think of it as a learning experience, Kel," he advised, eyes dancing with mischief. "I'd suggest you get a pair of heavy gloves like the falconers use." He got to his feet. "Now sleep. I expect you to be walking around in the morning."

In her dream, Kel faced Joren of Stone Mountain, Vinson of Genlith, and Garvey of Runnerspring, the senior pages who were her greatest enemies in the palace. They had made her first two years as a page into a running battle with first Kel, who could not stand by while others were bullied, then with Kel and her friends. Vinson had even attacked Kel's maid, Lalasa. Once they became squires, with knight-masters to answer to, Garvey and Vinson seemed to lose interest. Joren changed, too. He claimed to have seen the error of his ways and wanted to be friends.

Although she rarely saw them, Kel still dreamed of them, and they were still her foes. In this dream Joren—white-blond, blue-eyed, fair-skinned, the loveliest man Kel had ever seen—grabbed Kel's left ear between his thumb and forefinger. Smiling, he pinched Kel's ear hard, fingernails biting through cartilage to meet. Kel sat up with a yell. Her dream vision of the older squires vanished. The red-hot pain in her ear went on. She grabbed for it and caught a mass of feathers and claws that scored her hands. The griffin had gotten out of its cage, climbed onto Kel's bed, and buried its beak in her ear.

She tugged at him, making the pain worse. She stopped, gasping, and fought to clear her mind. It was hard to do: the monster growled in its throat, distracting her, as did the complaints from the other patients.

Breathing slowly, trying to forget the pain and distractions, she found the hinges of its beak and pressed them. Her fingers slipped in her own blood. It took several tries until she could apply enough pressure to make the griffin let go. The moment it did, Kel wrapped both hands around it and stuffed it under her blankets, rolling it up in them briskly. She then grabbed the cage.

It fell apart in her fingers. Only a handful of metal strips, badly rusted, and a pile of rust flakes remained. The dishes that had held the griffin's water and fish were whole—they were hard-fired clay.

"Griffins don't like cages," she muttered. "That's not how *I* would put it."

One of the nurses hurried in with a plate of fish. She thrust it at Kel; the moment Kel took it, the woman fled.

Kel got to her feet. Someone had laid fresh clothes on the stool next to her cot. Using her nightshirt as a protective tent, Kel dressed under it, muttering curses on griffins as she tried to keep blood off her clothes. When she shed her nightshirt, she found a healer standing there. The woman bore a tray that held swabs, a bowl of water, cloths, and a bottle of dark green fluid.

Kel peeled away enough blankets to free the griffin's head while the rest of it stayed under wraps. As she fed it, the healer worked on Kel's ear.

When the griffin lost interest in fish and closed its beak, Kel put the plate aside and glared at her charge. What was she supposed to do without a cage? She certainly couldn't leave it wrapped in sheets.

As if to prove Kel's point, the griffin wavered, blinked, and vomited half-digested fish onto Kel's bedding. Mutely the healer gave Kel a washcloth and left. Kel used it to gather up the worst of the vomit. The griffin wrestled a paw free and swiped four sharp claws over Kel's hand. She was trying to think of a merciful way to kill it when a muffled blatting sound issued from inside the blankets. A billow of appalling stench rose from the cot.

Knowing what she would find, Kel pulled the bedding apart. The griffin clambered out of a puddle of half-liquid dung and threw itself at Kel.

When she raised her hands in self-defense, it seized one arm, clutching it with its forepaws and shredding her sleeve as it clawed the underside of her arm. Kel gritted her teeth, shook her pillow free of its case, and shoved the kicking immortal inside.

The healer had returned. "I'd better leave this with you." She placed a fresh bottle of green liquid on the stool beside Kel's cot. "It will clean your wounds and stop the bleeding."

Kel yanked her captive arm free and closed her hand around the neck of the pillowcase. The thin cloth would hold her monster only a short time. "If I might have swabs and light oil and warm water, I would be in your debt," she said politely, one-handedly folding her bedding around the griffin's spectacular mess. "I need to clean my friend."

"Might I recommend the horse trough outside?" the healer suggested, as polite as Kel. "I will bring everything to you there."

The glove idea failed. Kel tried falconers' gloves, riding gloves, and even linen bandages on her hands. The griffin would not take food from a gloved hand, and now that Kel was better, it took food from no one else, either. With regular practice, Kel's skill at incurring only small wounds improved. She hoped that, with more practice, combining her duties as squire with multiple feedings for her charge would leave her less exhausted at day's end. Most of all, she hoped the griffin's parents came *soon*. There were two of them to care for their offspring. Surely they never felt overwhelmed.

Five days after she left her cot, Third Company and the two Rider Groups took the road with the griffin and thirty-odd bandit prisoners. Their destination was the magistrates' court in Irontown. The journey was tense. Everyone knew that death sentences awaited most of the bandits, who made almost daily escape attempts. Twice the company was attacked by families and friends of the captives, trying to free them.

The Haresfield renegade Macorm was the first to see Irontown's magistrates. In his case the Crown asked for clemency, since Macorm's information had led to the band's capture. His friend Gavan, who faced the noose, testified that Macorm was a reluctant thief who had killed no one. The magistrates gave Macorm a choice, ten years in the army or the granite quarries of the north. He chose the army.

Kel attended the trials as Raoul's squire, watching as the bandits' victims and the soldiers, including her knight-master, gave testimony. She heard the griffin's history for herself. The centaur she killed, Windteeth, had murdered a human peddler who offered griffin feathers for sale when he saw the man had a real griffin in his cart. Windteeth knew the risk he took, keeping a young griffin, but the prospect of future wealth had meant more to him.

"Nobody went near him after that," Windteeth's brother told the court. "Nobody wants to tangle with griffins, and that little monster has sharp claws, to boot."

Not to mention a beak, Kel thought, looking at her hands. Her right little finger was in a splint, awaiting a healer's attention. The griffin had broken it that morning. Why couldn't she have left that cursed pouch alone?

The court reached its verdicts with no surprises, ruling on hanging for the human robbers, beheading for the centaurs. Kel put on her most emotionless Yamani Lump face and attended the executions with Raoul, Captain Flyndan, and Commander Buri. She had seen worse—the Yamani emperor had once ordered the beheading of forty guards—but not much worse.

Looking at the crowds as they gathered for the hangings, she wondered if something was wrong with her. Many people acted as if this were a party. They brought lunches or purchased food and drink from vendors, hoisted children onto their shoulders for a better look, bought printed ballads about the bandits and sang them. Did they not care that lives were ending?

Kel's jaws ached at the end of the day, she had clenched them so hard. For the first time in years she felt like an alien in her homeland. Then she realized that the three human commanders were not at all merry. They ate together both nights after the executions, with Kel to wait on them. Their evenings were spent in review of the hunt and in plans for better ways to do things in future, not in having fun at the expense of the dead.

The second night Buri followed Kel as she took away the dirty plates and stopped her in the hall outside the supper room. "We do what we must," she told Kel, her voice gentle. "We don't enjoy it.

Remember the victims, if it gets too sickening."

"Do you get used to it, Commander?" Kel asked.

"Call me Buri. Get used to it? Never. There'd be something wrong with you if you did," Buri replied. "Death, even for someone just plain bad, solves nothing. The law says it's a lesser wrong than letting them go to kill again, but it sows bitterness in the surviving family and friends. Bitterness *we'll* reap down the road."

"Do the K'mir execute criminals?" Kel wanted to know.

Buri's smile was crooked. "In a way," she replied. "We give them to the families of those they've wronged, and the families kill them. After all these years in the civilized west, I'm still trying to decide if that's good or not."

Kel thought of Maresgift, fighting his bonds wildly and screaming curses as they brought him to the headsman. She couldn't decide, either. The only good thing about that execution was that it had been the last.

The next morning Veralidaine Sarrasri, also known as Daine the Wildmage, came to Irontown in search of Kel and the griffin. She found them with Third Company and the Rider Groups, in the barracks at Fort Irontown.

"Let's have a look outside," Daine said, looking queasily at the walls around them. "I've been spying in falcon shape, and this feels a bit too much like the mews."

Kel retrieved the griffin and carried him outside, where Raoul and Daine sat on a bench in the shade. As Kel approached with the griffin in his battered leather pouch, she heard Daine say, "No, just for a couple of weeks, but it was enough. I'm afraid I freed every hawk there." She smiled up at Kel and held out her hands for the pouch. "And this must be as thankless for you as it gets."

Kel held the pouch, worried. "Its parents . . . ," she began.

Daine smiled, her blue-gray eyes mischievous. "Unlike you, I can talk to them, and they'll understand me," she reminded Kel. "Let's have a look."

She lifted the griffin out of the pouch, gripping its forepaws in one hand and its hind paws in the other. Once it was in the open, she handled it deftly, checking its anus, opening the wings to feel the bones, prying open the snapping beak to look into its throat. Kel and Raoul watched, awed. From time to time the immortal landed a scratch or a bite, but not often.

"We tried keeping him in a cage at first," Kel said. "The metal rusts to nothing overnight. He just rips through straw and cloth."

"No, metal's no good," Daine replied. "They learn how to age it young. Even a baby like this can break down an average cage overnight, once they have the knack of it. You don't really need a cage. He'll stay with you now that you've hand-fed him."

"Oh, splendid," Kel grumbled. "If only I'd known."

Daine continued as if she'd said nothing. "Make him a platform to sit on, or get him a carrier like they have for the dogs. He should exercise his wings." She bounced the griffin up and down in the air. Instinctively he flapped his wings, scattering dander and loose feathers. "Do it like that. He's got to build them up to fly." She inspected the griffin's eyes. "You don't have to feed him only fish—other kinds of meat won't kill him, and I know fresh fish is hard to come by. He can have smoked fish and meat, even jerky." She held the immortal up in front of her face. Kel was fascinated to see Daine's brisk treatment produce a cowed youngster: the griffin didn't even try to scratch her now, but stared at her as if he'd never seen anything like her. "Yes, jerky's good," Daine said with a smile. "He can chew on it instead of you."

"It's a he?" Raoul asked. He was fascinated. Jump sat at his feet, as attentive as Raoul.

Daine nodded and opened the griffin's hind legs, pointing to the bulges at the base of his belly. "Just like cats," she said as the griffin squalled. She tugged fish skin off one of his feet before she let the legs close again.

"Keeping him clean is fun," Kel said. At least he looked better than he had in Owlshollow. It had meant several days' work with diluted soap, oil, and balls of cotton, as well as nearly a pint of her blood lost to scratches and bites, but it had been worth the effort. The grease clumps were gone, and his feathers were now bright orange instead of muddy orange-brown.

Daine looked at Kel's tattered sleeves and hands. "I'll show you how to trim his claws, so he doesn't do so much damage."

"Easier said than done," Raoul pointed out.

Daine laughed. "You've done well by him, and it's a thankless job. I can see he was hungry for a time, but he's gaining weight at last."

Kel shrugged, embarrassed. "He's a vicious little brute," she muttered.

"I'll bet you are, just like the rest of your kind," Daine told the griffin. "Preen his feathers with your fingers—that helps shake out the dander. And I know you're aware of this, but don't get too fond, Kel. He's not like this lad." She stirred Jump with her foot. He pounded dust from the ground with his tail. "He belongs with other griffins."

"You can't take him?" Kel asked. "Really, he's too much for me. I can't even ask for help with him."

"If you could—" Raoul began.

Daine shook her head. "He's fixed on Kel. He won't take food from anyone else until he's with his true parents again. I could try, all the same, but I'll be on the move, looking for the parents besides what the king asks of me. And I can't talk to him to make him understand things. He's much too young." She plucked a two-inch feather that stuck out at a right angle. The griffin snapped at her, but Daine pulled out of reach. "You have to be quicker than that," she told him. To Kel and Raoul she said, "I know caring for a griffin is hard, and I'm sorry. He'll calm down as he gets used to you, and with luck we'll find his family soon." She looked at Kel. "Don't even name him if you can help it," she said firmly.

"I know," Kel replied. "It's easier to let go if I

don't name him. Not that I'll be sorry to let go, but
still."

Daine thrust the feather into her curly hair and
gripped the griffin by his paws again, turning him
onto his back in her lap. As he struggled and
squawked, she took a very small knife from her boot
top and unsheathed it. "Here's how to trim his
claws."

Not long after Daine left, Raoul took Third
Company back into the Royal Forest. In those
weeks Kel met the charcoal burners, freshwater
fishermen, hunters, miners, and hermits who eked
out life in this wild part of the kingdom. She also
met more immortals than she had ever seen as a
page: centaurs, including Graystreak and his herd;
an ogre clan working a mine; winged horses large
and small; a basilisk mother and her son; a herd of
unicorns; even a small tribe of winged apes.

This was no tour, however. They captured nearly
twenty robbers, burned three nests of spidrens, and
killed nine hurroks of a band of thirteen; the others
fled. Dom showed her a griffin's nest—the parents
and the yearling watched them from high in the
trees, but there was no sign of that year's chick.
Daine had gone there the same day she had examined the griffin. She had returned at nightfall to say
that these griffins knew exactly where their current
chick was; neither had they heard of a pair missing
a child.

Strangest of all was a Stormwing eyrie. Kel
watched the immortals circling their home, sunlight

flashing off perfectly feathered steel wings. How did they live when there were no battles? Had they been overhead at Owlshollow? Did they come after the fight to rip at the dead? Kel was ashamed to realize she didn't want to ask. Surely a squire ought to be tough minded enough to deal with the desecration of corpses.

Next year, part of her whispered. We made it through those executions; we *watched*. Next year we'll be tough minded enough to ask about Stormwings.

"We're giving them a chance," Raoul said as they watched the gliding immortals. "They don't bother us, we don't bother them. But I'll never trust them. Not after Port Legann."

Someone called him away. That night, once supper was done, Kel asked her knight-master, "What happened with Stormwings at Port Legann?"

Raoul told his part of the story of the fight for Tortall's third richest city in the Immortals War. When he was done, Flyn, Qasim, and some other veterans told their versions. Kel had seen the battle as movements of armies on a model the king and Daine had used in Lord Wyldon's strategy class. Now she heard what men on the ground had seen. Their maps were sticks, stones, and lines in the earth. On other nights other battles were picked apart, giving Kel and the junior members of Third Company an idea of the many aspects of war.

There were a few amenities on this sweep. They often stayed in villages, hunting for meat and adding their supplies so the inhabitants didn't suffer with extra mouths to feed. They paid women to launder and mend their clothes. Baths were still cold—Kel had gotten hot baths in Irontown, but few villages were big enough for bathhouses. Most people made do with tubs in their homes.

Kel's guardianship of the baby griffin improved when she made leather sleeves to protect her arms from wrists to shoulders. Some accidents resulted when the griffin found he could hook his rear paws through the laced openings between the upper and lower guards to dig at her elbows, but Kel got better at blocking him. Her hands were still vulnerable. With time she acquired scars on every finger.

six

LESSONS

*W*hen the leaves began to turn, the Own returned to the palace. All the way there Kel daydreamed of hot water. As soon as she had tended Raoul's horses and armor, then her own, and had settled the griffin in her rooms, she headed to her usual bath-house. There she soaked until her fingers looked like flesh-colored raisins. In the morning, filled with virtue, wearing a leather jerkin and arm guards, she gave the griffin a warm bath.

Now Raoul gave orders for Kel's formal instruction as a squire who rode with the King's Own. Qasim and Dom showed her through the Own's barracks, mess hall, and storehouses. In the mess they introduced her to the stiffly dignified Captain Glaisdan of Haryse, Commander of First Company. He regarded Kel as if she were a beetle, treatment Dom assured her Glaisdan gave everyone whose degree of nobility came after *The Book of Silver*. Dom, whose family was in *The Book of Gold*, was safe; Kel, whose family had been ennobled only two generations back, was not in any of the noble genealogies. She wanted to meet Captain Ulliver Linden, in charge of Second Company—she'd heard he was nearly as deadly in hand-to-hand combat as any Shang warrior—but couldn't. Captain Linden and his command were on the border shared by Tortall, Scanra, and Galla. He was not expected before winter set in, if then.

On their second day in quarters Raoul told Kel to report after breakfast. When she arrived, he took her to the master smith in charge of armor for knights. There Raoul watched as Kel was fitted properly for her own breastplate, a chain mail shirt, and chain mail leggings.

"A coif, my lord?" the armorer wanted to know.

Raoul shook his head. "She's been wearing a round helm in the field—let's get her that, made to fit. Too many things come at us from overhead," he explained to the smith and to Kel. "Having someone dig links of chain mail out of your scalp is not pleasant."

Kel winced.

"Leave some allowance in the sleeves and legs, an inch or two," Raoul instructed the armorer. "She's been shooting up like a weed—I'm not sure she's done growing yet."

Kel made a face. She had gone from five feet one inch to nearly five feet ten inches in four years, growing so fast that she half-expected to hear her clothes straining. She was thankful that a knightmaster outfitted his squire. Her parents' budget, with dowries, school fees, and other expenses, could never pay for all the armor squires and knights required.

"Now, sword and dagger. Let me see yours," Raoul said when the armorer finished with Kel.

Qasim had inspected them originally; Raoul had not. Kel handed the weapons over.

The big knight whistled as he looked the weapons over and peered at the underside of their cross-guards. "I thought so," he said. "Raven Armory." He showed Kel an enameled raven on the bottom of the cross-guards. "The best in the realm. Lerant has a dagger from them that's a family heirloom, passed down through four generations. Your parents must have sold two children to pay for these."

Kel hitched her shoulders. "It wasn't them, sir. I don't know who gave them to me."

"You didn't find them in the street," he joked. He balanced the sword on his finger, flipped it in the air, and caught it by the hilt as it came down.

Kel told him about the anonymous well-wisher who'd sent her gifts over her years as a page. "I still don't know who it is," she finished. "Was it you?"

"It never occurred to me, I'm sorry to say." He shook his head. "I can't give you better," he said, handing the weapons back to Kel. "Now, how about some practice? Have you ever tilted at another person before?"

An hour later Kel rode Peachblossom to a tilting yard used by squires. Qasim had come to help: he put a coromanel tip, one that spread the force of the strike over a greater area, on Raoul's lance and Kel's. He then secured padding around them to further lessen the shock of impact.

Both Kel and her knight-master wore padded jackets and leggings and round helms. "Just hit my shield like you would hit the quintain target," Raoul ordered. "Hit square enough, maybe I'll go out of my saddle; if I hit you square, you might get to fly like your friends." He nodded to the sparrows, perched on the fence in an attentive row. Jump sat below them. The griffin was in Kel's chambers, sleeping on the three-foot-high platform she'd had built for him. If she was to learn anything new, she didn't want him there to make Peachblossom uncomfortable.

"Chances are we'll stay on our horses," Raoul continued. "Don't tense up, Kel. This is just the next step. Watch the target point on my shield."

Kel nodded, gazing at his black warhorse, Drum. She remembered something she had wanted to ask for weeks. "Sir, why do you ride a gelding? All the Own rides geldings or mares, when most knights prefer stallions."

Raoul smiled. "The Bazhir taught us the flaw in riding stallions into battle, back when we weren't so friendly with them. They rode mares—smaller, nimbler mares. All our wonderful warhorses, the terror of the infantry? They smelled mares and the Bazhir hardly needed to bloody their weapons. The stallions left battle formation to chase them, and their riders got cut to pieces." Kel winced as Raoul mounted his gelding and trotted to the end of the tilting yard.

"Ready?" His call reached Kel easily over the distance between them. She moved Peachblossom into position and pumped her lance up and down in a training yard "yes"—it was hard to tell when someone in armor nodded. She settled her lance on her stirrup and tried to swallow, her mouth paper-dry. *What if I hurt him?* she thought. *Even with padding and a coromanel I bet this hits the other person hard. Mithros, don't let me mess this up.*

Qasim walked to the center of the tilting lane. He raised an arm, checked Raoul and Kel, then dropped his arm and got out of the way.

"Go faster," Kel told Peachblossom softly, her heart thudding. This would bring her at the target at a quick, light run, not a headlong gallop. She didn't want to use his best speed, not when so much depended on accuracy. As the gelding surged forward, she lowered her lance.

She looked at Raoul. His shield, like hers, was white. The target was a hand-sized black circle at its center. Seeing it, Kel instantly noted the difference between her old targets, which stayed in nearly the same place, and this new one. Raoul surged up and down with his horse's movement, shifting in the saddle as he prepared to strike. Kel rose in her stirrups and leaned forward slightly, trying to aim her lance point at the onrushing black circle.

She hit his shield. She knew that much before a battering ram struck her shield arm to slam her into the high back of the tilting saddle. Her entire left side went numb as Peachblossom curved away from Raoul's charge, both horses taking their riders into open air. Kel's ears rang with the impact.

Numbness was quickly replaced by a bone-deep

ache in her left arm. It almost matched the savage pain shooting through her right side, as the force of her contact with Raoul rolled through her lance to her body.

Peachblossom turned, bringing Kel's knight-master into view. Kel saw Raoul was under siege. The sparrows were darting at his face as they screeched insults. Jump had the man by one leg and was hanging on, swinging as Drum sidled and danced, trying to escape this crazed dog.

"Jump, Crown, Freckle—stop!" Kel shouted. "He's *supposed* to do that! I don't always need help, you know!"

Jump looked at Kel over a mouthful of quilted legging and let go, dropping to the ground with a thump. He trotted to Kel, his lone ear flat, rump and shoulders down, the picture of the apologetic dog. The sparrows hovered briefly, looking from Kel to Raoul, then returned to their perch on the fence.

Raoul, to Kel's relief, was laughing. "Next time, explain it to them first," he suggested. "I think they scared poor Drum." He patted his black gelding's neck. He looked at Kel. "A bit different from the quintain, isn't it?"

Kel nodded fervently. "It is, my lord."

"Most squires don't get anywhere near the shield, their first time," he said with approval. "That training Wyldon had you do with the wood circles paid off."

"But what if I hadn't hit the shield?" Kel asked, worried again. "I might've speared you, sir!"

Raoul smiled. "My dear squire, I'd be a poor

knight if I couldn't dodge an off-target lance, don't you think?"

"Oh," Kel said sheepishly. She hadn't thought of that.

"Ready for another go?"

Kel shifted her lance to her shield hand, shook out her right arm, then transferred shield and lance to her right hand and shook out her left. Both ached, but not too badly. "Yessir," she replied, settling shield and lance again.

Raoul trotted Drum back to their place as Kel took hers. Qasim walked out into the center, looking first to Raoul, then Kel, to make sure they were ready. He raised his arm, dropped it, and dashed for the fence.

"Go faster," Kel told Peachblossom, trying to grip her lance properly in her sore hand. She was grateful that she used an ordinary lance, not her practice weapon. That was weighted with lead. She doubted she could hold onto a weighted lance right now.

Grimly she lowered her weapon as Peachblossom raced down the jousting lane, headed for Raoul. There was the black target circle, jiggling with the beat of Drum's hooves and Raoul's movement. She stood in the stirrups and leaned forward, bracing herself for another clash.

Only later did the pain in her lance arm tell her that she must have struck Raoul's shield. She didn't notice it right away because she had taken flight. As she watched the blue sky above, Kel shed her lance and shield. She turned in the air to take her fall on the flats of her arms, as she did in hand-to-hand combat. Breath exploded from her lungs as she hit. She rolled onto her back, wheezing as she tried to breathe. Jump leaped onto her chest to lick her face frantically.

"Standing there does no good, Jump," Qasim said. He moved the dog and helped Kel to sit up. Jump whined. "Your wind is knocked out, my friend," Qasim said, slapping Kel's back. "Was flight as glorious as it looked?"

Kel gasped, then began to cough. Qasim offered his water bottle to her. She took a hasty gulp, coughed some more, and finally got her body under control. "I tell you what," she croaked, "why don't you take the next run and see for yourself? I won't begrudge you." She patted Jump so he would know she was alive.

"Do you remember how I did that?" Raoul had cantered over to see how she did.

Kel squinted up at her big knight-master. "I *felt* it," she said, marveling that she did remember. "You hit—and then you popped me out, like—like somebody levers a clam from the shell."

"Exactly," Raoul said with approval. "There's a trick to it. Often as not the other fellow knows, and nothing happens, but sometimes he's green or over-confident, and you can dump him on his behind. Ready for another go?"

Never again! cried her inner, sensible self. Her traitor mouth replied, "Yes, sir." She forced herself to stand, mount Peachblossom, and take the shield and lance from Qasim. Running away would be far more sensible, she scolded herself as she guided Peachblossom to his place and settled her lance. But *whoever said I'm sensible?*

After two more runs, Raoul's lance shattered. Kel rested while Qasim secured a coromanel and padding to a fresh lance.

On the next run Kel struck the center of Raoul's shield, but at an angle—her lance skidded off. His took her squarely, slamming her into the saddle's quilted back.

Kel thought over and over, *I love my saddle, I love my saddle.* In a plain saddle she would have flown over more ground than her birds. The high front and back of the tilting saddle kept her ahorse, and the quilting on it meant her bruises weren't as bad as they could be.

"You're done in, and I've worked up a sweat," Raoul said. "We've both time to soak before supper. I'll care for Drum, Kel. You can't see straight."

"I ought to argue, but I won't," she croaked. Her throat was caked with dust, and Qasim's water bottle was empty.

She looked up in time to see Raoul's grin. "I knew when I took you on you'd learn quickly."

She grinned back at him, pleased that he was pleased. Qasim tugged on her shield. She gave it to him, then passed her lance down as well. *I can do this,* she thought, gripping the saddle as she readied to dismount. *It's how I got up here in the first place.*

Gritting her teeth, she pulled one trembling leg over the saddle's back. She slid to the ground and gathered Peachblossom's reins in her hand. The sparrows fluttered over, cheeping as anxiously as if she were a fledgling they had misplaced. Tiny beaks ran through the sweat-matted hair that stuck out from under her helm.

When one of them stuck his beak into her ear, Kel sighed. "Stop it. I'm fine," she told them softly. "Just . . . pounded. For hours. Like you pound salt fish before you can eat it." She turned to lead Peachblossom to the gate and got a surprise. They had an audience: servants, men from the Own, and a few Riders, including Commander Buri.

I'm so glad to entertain people, Kel thought. She put on her best, most unreadable, Yamani Lump face and led Peachblossom to the gate.

Dom held it open, shaking his head. "You're alive. Most people who go five rounds with my lord can only babble about funeral plans."

"Their lances were padded, for Mithros's sake," Lerant pointed out crossly. "How much harm could they do?"

"Good," Buri said. "You get one and have a go."

Kel ignored them as she and Peachblossom trudged to the stables. She wasn't at all sure that she *didn't* need to make funeral plans.

How she groomed Peachblossom she had no idea. It felt as if she simply leaned against him while he rubbed his side along the brush. Once he was settled, she fed him and Hoshi, then lurched outside. She knew she'd want to live after a soak.

The women's baths were empty when she sank her throbbing flesh into the hottest pool. She dozed briefly until a group of women, servants by their talk, waded into the far end. With them came bath attendants: one gave Kel a sponge and soap scented with lily of the valley. Kel scrubbed herself and washed sweat-sticky hair as the women talked of work and families.

She caught an attendant's eye and stood; the woman came over with a large towel. As Kel climbed out of the water, the conversation behind her came to a halt. The attendant took a step back. Kel frowned, puzzled, and reached for the towel.

"My dear!" someone called. "My dear, wait!"

Kel looked behind her. Two women swam over and climbed out beside her. Everyone in the pool seemed shocked or frightened; the two who approached her looked worried.

"Your back is covered with bruises," the older woman said as her companion touched Kel's shoulder. "They look painful, and recent. And your arms and hands are scarred."

Kel twisted to look behind her, wincing as her ribs protested. She could see only a large bruise covering one hip. The scars, tokens of the griffin's regard for her, were easy to find. The worst, the deep pockmark between her thumb and forefinger, was swollen after her afternoon's lance work.

"You don't have to bear this," the younger woman said. "The Moon of Truth Temple will take you in. They'll protect you."

"They'll get the man who did it," the older woman said. The younger one and the attendant nodded. "Even if it's a noble. After the rapes last winter, they have a new commander for their troops. She's *very* aggressive."

Kel suddenly realized what was wrong, what

they were trying to say. They thought a man had beaten her. She began to giggle, then to laugh.

It took some time to convince them that her injuries were normal for a squire who was silly enough to joust with Lord Raoul and get stuck with a baby griffin.

Kel dressed, fed the griffin, and went to eat supper with the men of the Own. Raoul nodded to her as she came in, then returned to his conversation with Flyn and Glaisdan of Haryse. Kel knew better than to try to wait on him. When he sat in the mess hall with the Own, he was Knight Commander, and fended for himself. Only at banquets was she expected to wait on Raoul of Goldenlake and Malorie's Peak. Kel usually thought it odd to calculate things for two different Raouls, but tonight she welcomed it. Sitting with Dom, Qasim, and their friends was as much effort as she wanted to make today.

After supper she walked back to her quarters and fed the griffin. All she wanted to do after that was lie down and read.

Looking around to make sure she had nothing else to do that was pressing, she saw that the connecting door to Raoul's study was open. She looked in. He sat at his desk, sorting through papers.

He grinned when he saw her. "Kel, my squire, pull up a chair. Tonight we start lessons in calculating supplies for different numbers of men under your command."

Kel looked at him, seeing unholy amusement in his face. He had to know how her body felt. Finally she said, "Begging my lord's pardon, but you are a bad man."

He laughed. By now she had learned that she could get away with remarks Lord Wyldon would call insubordinate. "I *am* a bad man," Raoul said, falsely contrite. "Chair, squire. If you'd like a cushion, there are some in the window seat."

Kel hobbled over to a chair and carried it to his desk. Putting it down, she eyed the papers, slates, chalk, and abacus he'd laid out, then fetched a cushion.

Some time later she reviewed a problem he'd just set her: to calculate the number of bowstrings a company of archers might need for a six-week campaign in damp country, using a formula he'd given her. Kel put the slate down. "My lord, if I may . . ."

He was writing in an account book, waiting for her to solve the problem. He put his quill down. "What?"

"You say to calculate for people under my command. These problems are for large groups, not the ten-man squad sizes we learned as pages. Um . . ." She hesitated. How could she phrase it so he wouldn't think she felt sorry for herself?

"And?" he nudged.

"Sir, people never wanted me to make it to squire. They won't like it any better if I become a knight. I doubt I'll get to command a force larger than, well, just me."

Raoul shook his head. "You're wrong." As she started to protest, he raised a hand. "Hear me out. I have some idea of what you've had to bear to get this far, and it won't get easier. But there are larger issues than your fitness for knighthood, issues that involve lives and livelihoods. Attend," he said, so much like Yayin, one of her Mithran teachers, that Kel had to smile.

"At our level, there are four kinds of warrior," he told Kel. He raised a fist and held up one large finger. "Heroes, like Alanna the Lioness. Warriors who find dark places and fight in them alone. This is wonderful, but we live in the real world. There aren't many places without any hope or light."

He raised a second finger. "We have knights—plain, everyday knights, like your brothers. They patrol their borders and protect their tenants, or they go into troubled areas at the king's command and sort them out. They fight in battles, usually against other knights. A hero will work like an everyday knight for a time—it's expected. And most knights must be clever enough to manage alone."

Kel nodded.

"We have soldiers," Raoul continued, raising a third finger. "Those are warriors, including knights, who can manage so long as they're told what to do. These are more common, thank Mithros, and you'll find them in charge of companies in the army, under the eye of a general. Without people who can take orders, we'd be in real trouble.

"Commanders." He raised his little finger. "Good ones, people with a knack for it, like, say, the queen, or Buri, or young Dom, they're as rare as heroes. Commanders have an eye not just for what they do, but for what those *around* them do. Commanders size up people's strengths and weaknesses. They know where someone will shine and where they will collapse. Other warriors will obey a true commander because they can tell that the commander knows what he—or she—is doing." Raoul picked up a quill and toyed with it. "You've shown flashes of being a commander. I've seen it. So has Qasim, your friend Neal, even Wyldon, though it would be like pulling teeth to get him to admit it. My job is to see if you will do more than flash, with the right training. The realm needs commanders. Tortall is big. We have too many still-untamed pockets, too cursed many hideyholes for rogues, and plenty of hungry enemies to nibble at our borders and our seafaring trade. If you have what it takes, the Crown will use you. We're too desperate for good commanders to let one slip away, even a female one. Now, finish that"—he pointed to the slate—"and you can stop for tonight."

Kel wrote the answer without working the problem out on the slate. She liked mathematics, and could do far more complicated sums than this one in her head.

Raoul glanced at her answer. "Show-off," he told her. "Begone!"

Kel obeyed, bowing to him before she closed the door behind her. Then she sat beside her window, staring out at the torchlit courtyard. He had given her serious matters to consider.

Her days took on a pattern. In the morning she fed the griffin, bathed him if he needed it, preened him while trying to keep him from savaging her fingers, and got him to exercise his wings. She took care of her latest griffin wounds, then tended Lord Raoul's armor and weapons. After that she looked after her own gear and fed the griffin again. In the early afternoon she practiced weapons with men of the Own and rode Hoshi to get used to the mare and her paces. She gave the griffin yet another feeding and more exercise, picked up the things he knocked over as he prowled the room, then left for the stable. There she saddled Peachblossom and rode him to her flying lessons from Raoul, always with far too many people gathered to watch. A hot bath and gossip with the serving women followed, then supper, a last meal for the griffin, and finally lessons in logistics and supply, the proper military names for planning and paperwork.

It was nice to have a routine, if only for a while. Two emergency calls came in during those days, but they required one squad or two, not Third Company. Kel knew Raoul would have liked to go, but he seemed to feel her tilting and logistics instruction to be more important.

They had been jousting for three weeks when Raoul came to the grounds with two new men. They were dressed for practice and leading mounts with tilting saddles. Kel knew the knight, Sir Jerel of Nenan, only because she had been interested in the man who chose Garvey of Runnerspring as his squire. Garvey had belonged to the clique led by Joren of Stone Mountain. Seeing Kel now, Garvey made a face and murmured something to his knight-master.

Raoul introduced them to Kel—if he knew of the feud between Kel and Joren's old crowd, he hid it. "We need a change of pace," Raoul explained. "You want to tilt against different opponents, to learn their techniques."

"You're going to enter her in the tournaments during the Grand Progress, Raoul?" asked Sir Jerel with a smile.

Raoul nodded. "I'm going to win money on her," he said, with a wink at Kel. "Squire Garvey, why don't you two give it a try?"

Garvey bowed and led his mount to the far end of the tilting lane. Kel watched him go, wondering if he planned anything nasty. Joren claimed that he had changed after he became a squire—perhaps Garvey had, too.

Kel led Peachblossom to her starting point and mounted up, then positioned her lance and shield. What had Garvey been up to during the last two years? Had he matured at all? Sir Jerel had been posted on the southwestern coast, helping to defend that part of Tortall from slave traders and freebooters. Garvey would have seen a fair bit of combat.

Raoul gave the signal. Garvey kicked his horse into a gallop as he brought his shield down and his lance up. Kel followed suit, narrowing her focus to her target.

Garvey hit her shield squarely, thumping her back in the saddle. Kel struck his shield as well; he didn't falter. She rode back to her place, taking inventory of her pains. Apart from the fading ache of impact in both arms, she barely had any. Even those weren't as bad as they would have been had she clashed with Raoul.

There was the signal. Now Garvey galloped down the lane hard: he meant business. He and Kel struck each other's shields squarely. Kel resettled herself and came on for their third pass, knowing just where to strike to slam the shield into its bearer. Instead, her lance shattered on contact. Garvey's skidded off her shield. Instead of turning his mount, he surged forward. In a slide/hook motion, he locked Kel's shield with his, trapping her.

"Getting fancy, aren't you, Lump?" he asked with a crooked smile. "When do you surrender and go home?"

Kel shoved sideways, freeing her shield. "Never," she retorted. "You want to dance, or do you want to take another run?"

"I'd love to knock you on your rump, but I'm late for my appointment at the perfumery," he retorted, turning his mount. "The scent I've been wearing just isn't fussy enough." He shook his head. "I *need* a feminine perfume, the way court is going to the girls." He rode over to speak to his knight-master.

Raoul walked out. "Are you all right?" he asked Kel. "Was he being unchivalrous?"

Kel sighed. "No—he was just being Garvey."

"I see," Raoul commented, his voice dry. "Are you done in, or would you like a go with Jerel?"

"If he wishes to, I'd be honored, my lord," Kel said, forgetting about Garvey.

Jerel mounted and took his place at one end of the lane. Qasim brought Kel a fresh lance with coromanel tip. He hadn't padded it, as he did the lances she and Raoul used. Kel hoped he knew what he was doing. As she took her place, she realized Garvey's lance had not been padded, either.

I guess—I hope—Sir Jerel doesn't hit as hard as my lord, she thought. Raoul gave the signal. Peachblossom surged into his mild gallop without being told: he was used to the routine. Kel thundered toward Jerel, focusing on his shield, and struck him squarely. He did the same to her. There was more force behind his impact than Garvey's, but it was still bearable. Taking her place for the next run, Kel wondered if she would measure every opponent by Raoul.

At least I'm not flying yet, she thought as Raoul gave the signal.

She and Jerel hit one another perfectly. Kel rode to her start point, thoughtful. Jerel wasn't as strong in the saddle as Raoul. And he didn't surge hard behind his lance—because she was a squire, or because she was a girl?

Raoul gave the signal. Kel and Jerel came on, Kel studying the knight. She rose, changed position, and jammed her lance into Jerel's shield, just to one side of the center boss. As she struck she threw her entire weight behind the thrust.

Jerel's shield jerked aside; Kel's lance rammed through. Jerel swerved to avoid being hit. Kel jerked her lance up as Peachblossom turned.

"Whoa," she ordered. The gelding halted.

Sir Jerel turned, shaking his head. "Well done, squire!" he called. "If I'd been in armor you'd've had me on the ground!" He shook out his shield arm as Kel always did after a pass with Raoul.

Kel wondered if she ought to go again and see if she *could* unhorse the man. A look at Peachblossom changed her mind. His withers were sweat-streaked. While he could go longer and might have to one day, she saw no reason to exhaust him to satisfy her pride.

"Thank you, Sir Jerel," she said politely instead. "You're too kind."

Raoul walked over to take her shield and lance; Dom came to do the same service for Jerel. "Well said, Kel," he told her quietly. "I see you know it's bad form to gloat."

"If I'd actually had him out of the saddle I'd have gloated a little," she replied. "Maybe not. He's a decent sort."

Raoul grinned up at her. "And so are you. Go on, take Peachblossom in. I'll see you at supper."

⇥ seven ⇤

OLD FRIENDS

A week of flying lessons later, Raoul took his squire and half of Third Company into the Bazhir desert. They represented the Crown at a headman's wedding and negotiated the end of a blood feud between two tribes. In Haresfield they hunted and fished, and then smoked the meat to add to winter stores for the victims of Maresgift's band.

Kel did it all with the griffin in tow. He rode in Jump's carrybox on Hoshi's saddle, where he had a view of the leather jerkin she wore to protect her back from his assaults. Nothing protected her ears from his rich vocabulary of squawks and screeches. Jump ran or rode with Dom or Qasim, while the sparrows claimed perches on Peachblossom's mane. They had already learned that the griffin would try sparrow meat if they came too close, and Peachblossom couldn't abide the immortal.

Third Company took its time on its ride back to Corus, passing from autumn on the southernmost edges of the Royal Forest to nearly winter on the northern. Once they were on the palace wall approaches, it took some time to reach their quarters: an uncommon amount of traffic clogged every gate. The men grumbled; even Kel felt cross by the time they groomed their mounts and washed up.

That night she went to eat in the pages' and squires' mess for the first time since she'd joined Raoul. It was November, the end of the raiding season in most of the country. Many knights and squires would be returning for the winter.

In the mess she was greeted boisterously by her friends among the pages: Owen of Jesslaw, in his fourth year and still unable to keep his foot from his mouth, and his third-year kinsmen, Iden and Warric. Of the squires, Balduin of Disart and Prosper of Tameran were already seated, along with Garvey and Zahir ibn Alhaz, a Bazhir who had once belonged to Joren's circle. Kel got on with Balduin and Prosper and was setting her tray beside them when the doors flew open. In came a big redheaded squire in the colors and badge of Fief Mindelan, Cleon of Kennan, who was not only her friend but squire to her brother Inness. Neal followed him.

They headed for the servers' line without looking to see who was there. Kel watched them, feeling odd. Neal looked like any other male. There was no special luster about him as she watched him put food on his tray. She was delighted he was there—she had missed him—but she didn't feel her normal quivery blend of happiness and pain at the sight of him.

I don't love him anymore, she thought, relieved, then distressed. Relieved, because it had hurt to know he barely remembered she was female, distressed because she had believed she would want him forever. Immediately she thought of Dom's bright blue eyes and bold, flashing grin, the way his shoulders fit his tunics. The way he made almost anything seem funny.

I'm fickle, Kel thought gloomily. Who falls in and out of love over a summer? Were my feelings even real?

Suddenly she was very grateful that he'd never guessed how she felt. How embarrassing, if they'd cared for each other and she stopped!

Spotting her, Neal shouted: "Mithros defend us, it's the King's Own squire!" He came over to the table, clapped Prosper on the shoulder, nodded to Balduin, then slid into the space across from Kel. "When did you get back?" he demanded. "And where's your fledgling?" He picked a tiny orange bit of down from Kel's shoulder.

"Um, Kel? Is this place taken?"

She looked up, and up, and up. Cleon seemed to stretch toward the ceiling. "Please sit," she begged. "It hurts my neck to look at you. Since when do you ask for permission to sit, anyway?"

Cleon sat next to her. "When did you get back?" he asked. "We weren't sure how long you'd be gone—"

"Or if you'd ever eat here again," added Neal. "We heard you mostly take meals with the King's Own."

"Because my friends were away," Kel pointed out. "When did *you* get back?"

"I've been here a week," Neal said, "hiding from

my lovely knight-mistress. She doesn't need a sword—that temper sharpens her tongue just fine. This redheaded giant's been in three days."

"Scanran border's cooled down," Cleon said, still looking at Kel. "All the weather auguries are for a bad winter. Bursetin Pass is already snowed shut. Sir Inness decided if we were to reach the palace this year, we'd best go now."

"You see much action up there?" asked Balduin. "We've been on the Gallan border—not that it's a picnic, mind."

"The Scanrans are fidgety," Cleon replied. "Used to be, the border clans would raid on their own. Annoying, but you don't need an army to pound them, just whoever's about. Last year, though, one of the southern clans elected a war leader, Maggur Rathhausak. He brought five clans together and they overran Northwatch Fortress in June." Every-one who could hear winced: he'd named the key to the northern border defenses. "We got it back. One of the haMinches, General Vanget, took command and cleaned Northwatch out."

"Who was in command when it was overrun?" Prosper wanted to know. "And where was he?"

Cleon grinned. "Hunting. General haMinch court-martialed all the officers but the junior ones." He looked at Kel. "What about you? Is Lord Raoul kin—" He changed his mind and used another word. "—easy to work with?"

Kel smiled up into Cleon's eyes. "He's the best master I could have hoped for. And working with the Own is interesting."

"Meet anyone worth having a conversation with?" Neal asked wickedly.

"You mean relatives of yours?" Kel asked, all innocence. "You know, Neal, I think your branch was cheated when they handed out brains, because Dom—" She ducked the roll Neal threw at her.

"My cousin Domitan of Masbolle's a squad leader in Third Company," Neal told the others. To Kel he said, "And he says *you* tangled with a centaur—"

"Heads up," Balduin said, getting to his feet.

Everyone stood as Lord Wyldon entered the mess, accompanied by Kel's brother, Inness of Mindelan. Once Lord Wyldon had given the evening prayer, he and Inness sat at his table. The pages and squires jammed themselves onto the benches and began to eat.

"So what's this about a centaur?" Balduin inquired. "You fought one?"

"Oh, that," Kel said, cutting her vegetables. "Yes, on foot, and he almost kicked my belly through my spine. I'd rather hear about Scanra."

"Did you use sword or spear?" demanded Prosper.

"My lord lets me use my glaive," she replied. "All the men carry some kind of pole arm." She turned to Cleon. "So who's this new warlord?"

Cleon was telling what he knew when the door opened. A bright figure walked into the open space between the tables and the dais on which Lord Wyldon and Inness sat.

The newcomer wore two of the floor-length

wrap dresses known as kimonos, one over the other. The outer one was cream-colored silk with orange and yellow maple leaves printed on the fabric; the edges of her inner kimono were orange. The kimonos were secured by a wide, stiff sash called an obi, this one of bronze silk. The lady's feet, in brown silk slippers, made a shushing sound in the suddenly quiet room. Her ebony hair was parted at the center and combed out straight to her waist. Two short locks framed her face exactly.

Placing her palms on her thighs, she bowed to the men on the dais. "Please excuse me," she said in accented Common, her pretty voice audible throughout the room. "I come at the request of my mistress, her imperial highness, Princess Shinkokami."

Lord Wyldon put aside his napkin and stepped off the dais to stand on the Yamani woman's level. He gave her a bow, the kind done in the Eastern Lands, and said, "I am the training master, Lord Wyldon of Cavall. How may I assist you and your imperial mistress?"

Kel, her face Yamani-still, thought, You'd never believe he once called the Yamanis savages. She put aside her napkin, guessing what had brought the woman here.

"My mistress says, she has been told that Squire Keladry of Mindelan is here," the lady said, bowing to Wyldon again. "Might this unworthy servant of the princess be permitted to speak with her?"

Wyldon beckoned; Kel was already excusing herself to Cleon as she slid out of her place. At the front of the hall she bowed to the training master as she always had. She turned to the Yamani, placed her palms on her thighs, and offered the correct bow due a noblewoman in the emperor's service. The Yamani did the same. Kel looked at her searchingly. There was something familiar about the round face under its mask of white rice powder, shadow-dark eyebrow color, and lip paint. Then she saw a familiar glint of mischief in the Yamani's almond-shaped brown eyes.

"Please excuse me," she said in Common. It would have been rude to speak Yamani in front of Lord Wyldon. "But have I the honor of addressing the Lady Yukimi noh Daiomoru?"

Now the corners of the lady's eyes crinkled, the Yamani equivalent of laughing aloud. "You have changed very much too in six years, Keladry of Mindelan." Yukimi, only a year older than Kel, looked up at her. "There is more of you than there was."

"If you will excuse me? I know you have much to discuss with Squire Keladry," Lord Wyldon said politely. "Outside, perhaps?"

Yukimi bowed to him. "My lord, may I ask if Squire Keladry is permitted to visit my mistress when her meal is complete?"

"Keladry must ask her knight-master," Lord Wyldon said. He bowed to Yukimi and returned to his table.

"Let us go outside, if you please, Lady Yukimi," Kel suggested in Yamani. "My friends' supper will go cold because their attention is on you." She bowed to the lady, who bowed in return.

"They stare so," the Yamani remarked. Turning, she bowed to the room. There was a sudden clatter as every page and squire tried to stand and bow.

"Now you've done it," Kel said in Yamani. "They won't be able to talk sense for weeks."

Yukimi drew an orange and gold fan from her obi, flicked it open, and used it to screen the lower part of her face. Someone sighed with longing. Yukimi's eyes danced as she asked, "Easterners normally make sense?"

Kel held the door and bowed her out of the room. It seemed that Yuki, as she used to be called, still had a lively sense of humor. Glancing back at the squires and pages, all still on their feet, Kel shook her head. Her mess-mates were romantic. Probably half of them were in love with Yukimi right now. The other half would fall just as hard for the princess or her other ladies in a week.

Closing the door, Kel explained in Yamani, "I answer to Lord Raoul of Goldenlake and Malorie's Peak, the Knight Commander of the King's Own. I have to ask him if it's all right. We just got back. How many of you came? How long have you been at court?"

"So many questions!" Yukimi said. "We arrived three days ago at Port Caynn." She made an effort to pronounce the city's name properly in Common. "We were met by a procession and escorted here. My mistress was so happy to see your mother I think she would have wept if it were not entirely rude. There is a delegation with us, of course— Prince Eitaro noh Nakuji is its head. He will act as stand-in for his imperial highness the emperor, and he will go after the wedding. Only Haname noh Ajikuro and I will stay. My mistress felt she would be more accepted if she did not surround herself with our people."

Kel whistled, impressed. She and her family had known that the emperor would not spend a first-rank princess on a nation of foreigners. That he had chosen a second-rank princess like Shinkokami, instead of a fourth- or fifth-rank one, and sent the prince to act for him told Kel he wanted the alliance to succeed. "I think my lord will give me some time," Kel said. "Where are you housed?"

"In the royal wing," Yukimi said, tucking her fan into her obi. "But please, finish your meal. Think how shameful it would be if you were to faint before my mistress. There is so much more of you to feed now."

Kel bowed to the Yamani girl, knowing her amusement showed in her eyes. That was all right. For a Yamani, Yukimi was easygoing. "I will visit later, if my knight-master agrees," she told Yukimi. They bowed, then separated. Kel went back to her supper, Yukimi to report to the princess.

As soon as she reentered the mess hall, Kel was besieged with questions. How many pretty Yamani girls had come with the princess? Did they all dress so colorfully? Did they all bow so much? Were they all beautiful?

Kel answered questions between bites until Cleon finally growled, "Let her eat! We'll see plenty of the ladies soon. Master Oakbridge posted the schedule for entertainments today."

"We'll hop so hard at those things we'll be lucky to get a whiff of perfume," Prosper complained, but Cleon had reminded everyone that supper was growing cold.

Kel looked up, to see that Neal eyed Cleon with interest. She waited to hear the question behind her friend's look, but Neal saw that she was watching, and smiled at her. "Lady Alanna has been putting me through my paces," he said, buttering a roll. "I swear, if she hears of so much as a sniffle in the village down the road, she has to drag me there to study the healing of sniffles. Would you like to trade with me?"

Kel suddenly realized that if it were possible to be Lady Alanna's squire, she wouldn't do it. She liked where she was. It was a startling thing to know, after thinking her heart would break if she couldn't serve Lady Alanna.

"If you want my place, you can have it," she told Neal, straight-faced. "You'd particularly like the tilting practice we have every day when we aren't in the field."

Neal shuddered. "Tilt with Lord Raoul? Why don't I just lie down in front of an elephant and let him step on me? I bet it feels the same."

"Will you be around later, Kel?" Cleon asked as Kel got ready to go.

She shook her head. "If my lord lets me out of evening lessons, I'll be visiting the Yamani ladies," she replied. He looked disappointed. "I'll see you here tomorrow night, though, if we aren't called out. Try not to spend too many hours writing poems to Yuki's eyebrow," she advised Neal. "Yamani poetry is very different from ours. I doubt she'd appreciate yours." Grinning, she took her tray to the servers. Behind her she heard the squires discuss where they might find books of Yamani poetry.

Conducted into the presence of Princess Shinkokami, Kel greeted her as any Yamani would. She knelt, placed her palms on the floor, and bowed until her forehead touched the silk rug.

"Keladry, no," protested Shinkokami, stepping off the dais where she sat with Yukimi and Lady Haname. "I am an Easterner now—you must greet me in your manner!"

Kel sat up and rested her hands on her knees, gazing at the willowy princess. Shinkokami was lovely enough to break every heart in the mess hall, even those already thumping over Yukimi. She was about five feet seven inches tall, her complexion peach-golden. Unlike Yukimi and Lady Haname she wore no rice powder or lip paint. There was a smile in her eyes even when she was worried, as now. Over a cream-colored inner kimono she wore a golden outer one embroidered with scarlet and gold cranes. Her obi was scarlet, with an ivory figurine of a kimono-clad cat hung below her fan. The short knife carried by all Yamani women was thrust into her obi as well. Her hair, worn in the same very simple style as her ladies', was glossy black and scented lightly with jasmine.

"Cricket?" whispered Kel.

The princess laughed gleefully. "You *do* know me! I told Yuki I did not think you would!"

"You never said that you belonged to the imperial house," Kel told the girl who had taught her Yamani children's games.

"We were in disgrace with my uncle the emperor," Shinkokami explained. "I loved it that you treated me like an ordinary person, so I never told you. And now look! While you learned from me, I learned Eastern ways and speech from you and your family. Who would have dreamed it would bring us here?" A wave of her hand took in the room, hung with tapestries and furnished elegantly in a combination of Yamani and Tortallan styles.

Kel smiled at her. "Just think," she said slyly, "no one here will expect you to be the slave of your mother-in-law."

Yukimi and Shinkokami giggled, their hands covering their mouths. "I was betrothed, you know, before my uncle dissolved that contract and said I was to marry a foreigner," Shinkokami explained. "My mother-in-law-to-be was a terrible old woman. I was so happy to escape her house that I burned incense at every temple I passed on my way to the ship." She turned to the oldest of the three women. "Keladry of Mindelan, I do not believe you know my other attendant, Lady Haname noh Ajikuro."

Shinkokami's request aside, Kel bowed deeply to the lady in the Yamani style. Ajikuro was one of the oldest Yamani noble houses, older even than the emperor's. Her presence was another sign that Shinkokami's uncle wanted the match to work. The lady was in her mid-twenties, clad in a cinnamon-brown kimono over a pale blue one, with a rust-colored obi. She wore a variation on the noble-woman's style, her hair pulled back and tied with a bronze silk bow, the two short, framing locks accenting her pointed chin and serene eyes.

"I am honored to meet the daughter of a redoubtable mother," Lady Haname said. "She told us of some of your exploits. They promise to outshine hers."

Kel bowed deeply. It was the only possible reply. She personally thought it would be a long time before she would do anything as brave as her mother had, protecting imperial relics from pirates.

"So, Keladry, have you forgotten all you know of *naginata*?" Yukimi inquired. "Or do you practice still?"

Kel smiled at her old friend. "From time to time," she replied.

Shinkokami sat on the edge of the dais; Haname knelt on her left, while Yukimi scooted forward on her right. Maids came forward noiselessly with the low tables used by Yamanis, who seldom possessed chairs and conducted all business seated on their floors. Once they were comfortable, the maids served tea and small cakes.

"Would you join us for dawn practice?" Shinkokami wanted to know. "We number five. With one more we can pair off."

Kel bowed. "I would be honored, your highness."

They were telling her where she could find their practice court when the talk was interrupted by a scratching on the door. One of the guards unsheathed his sword and opened the door quickly, meaning to surprise any intruders. Kel realized she would have to find a tactful way to let the Yamanis know that assassination attempts were rare here. She closed her eyes, resigned, as the guard looked up and down the hall and Jump trotted in past him.

Jump had to be introduced, of course, and the guard soothed. Kel watched her scapegrace dog win cakes and scratches from the Yamanis, and thanked him silently. It was hard even for Yamanis to be stiff and guarded when Jump made an effort to be charming.

Rising before dawn was no trial to Kel. She had done it for all her years as a page, to practice weapons and to do strengthening exercises. The staff in this part of the palace knew when she got up: she always found rolls, a dish of smoked fish or beef for the griffin, and hot water outside her door in the morning. Kel shared the rolls with the birds and Jump, dressed, and fed the griffin, then washed off blood and parts of the griffin's meal.

Wearing practice gear, trailed by Jump and the sparrows, Kel searched for the Yamanis. Their practice court was near the royal wing, tucked between the king's stables and an archery yard. She was the last to arrive. The three Yamani women were dressed in their own practice clothes: full breeches bound tight to the leg below the knee, rope sandals, cotton kimonos kilted up, sleeves tied back at the shoulders, and bands around their foreheads to keep their pinned-up hair out of their faces.

Kel had thought the other two present for these mornings would be Yamani maids, but they were Easterners. One wore the Yamani costume. She turned and smiled when Yuki waved Kel over.

"So I have a daughter after all," Ilane of Mindelan said as she came to hug Kel. "I was beginning to think you were an illusion."

"Oh, Mama," Kel said shyly, returning the hug. After years of seeing her mother tower over most people, including Kel's father, it was strange to find that their eyes were now on the same level. The thought that she might outgrow her mother was uncomfortable; the idea that her hair might go white at thirty, as her mother's had, was frightening. She did wish she had her mother's deep, musical voice. "I'm sorry—I've been busy. My lord doesn't exactly sit around."

"So I've heard." Ilane turned to the fifth member of the company and bowed. "Your majesty, I don't believe anyone has introduced my youngest daughter to you: Keladry of Mindelan."

Queen Thayet, called by many "the Peerless," smiled at Kel. She had flawless ivory skin, a ruddy mouth fashioned with a gem cutter's precision, and crow's wing black hair that fought to escape its pins. Her green-hazel eyes were direct; a strong nose made her face human rather than inhumanly beautiful. Like Kel she wore the quilted canvas practice clothes issued to the pages, squires, and Riders. In one small hand she held a glaive. "I hope you'll go easy on me," the queen said. "I've only been training with this thing for a year."

Shinkokami hurriedly assured the queen that she did well for someone who had not started with the weapon as a child. "And you outshoot me all the time," she assured her future mother-in-law.

"That makes me feel a little better," the queen said wryly. "How shall we start?"

Dealing with three Yamanis whose training had not been interrupted as hers had, Kel thought she did rather well that morning. She did have to mind her strength, something she had never considered before. While the other women were fast and tireless, Kel had added months of building her muscles to keep up with males.

At first the queen unnerved her. Thayet finally had to dump Kel on her behind so Kel would stop worrying about the bloodlines of her opponent and conduct a proper defense.

Morning practice became a ritual for all six of them, a quiet time to exercise and prepare for the day. Shinkokami, who had been a lively girl, was shy everywhere in her new home but on the practice court. Kel began to take her walking after the six of them ate breakfast. On those walks she gave Shinkokami tours of the palace. They also discussed the things she sensed made the princess nervous: what Roald was like, the power hierarchies in the east, new gods and religions, even fittings for Eastern-style clothes. Once Shinkokami knew that the brisk dressmaker was Kel's Lalasa, and saw how Lalasa treated Kel, she was more comfortable having clothes pinned and shaped to her form. Lalasa, in turn, liked any female that Kel liked, and took up the shy, reserved Yamani's cause with the palace servants.

The princess was worried about her reception by the country during the coming Grand Progress of the realm. Kel was not. She knew the Tortallans would love her. She even suspected that Prince Roald, when he came home from his knightmaster's castle at Port Legann, would too.

A dry summer and a delay in the winter rains in the south bred problems. First the hill folk near Fief Shaila tried to rebel, laying siege to the local army fort. Third Company rode to free the garrison and hunt those responsible. No sooner had Raoul punished the worst troublemakers and gotten pledges of loyalty from the rest than word came from the village of Sweetspring: forest fires, in the hills between the village and the Drell River. Third Company rode hard to get there and worked harder still to clear wide strips of ground, trapping the fires within them. For two weeks they labored beside hill people, Bazhir, soldiers, and the other inhabitants to save forests and villages. At last the rains came, adding a layer of mud to the soot ground into Kel's skin.

Once the danger was past and the locals back in their homes, Raoul met with his second in command and his squad leaders. He hoped to take Third Company to pass the winter in the south at Kendrach or Pearlmouth.

"I'm sure we'll find plenty to do," he told his

audience in his most charming manner. "Smugglers, flood relief, and so on. And we'll be warmer than in Corus."

"My lord, you know we can't do that," Flyndan told him as Kel served hot cider to the men. "Things are busy at the palace. I'm sure his majesty wants us there."

"Exactly the reason I want to go south," retorted the Knight Commander. "Me dressed in silk and velvet and ermine like a players' bear, while you carouse in the city. *You* don't have matchmaking mothers after you. Me? I'm a hive and they're bees. Kendrach won't turn away a hundred extra swords, not with the Carthakis still fighting over Emperor Kaddar's rule. In Pearlmouth we can help with flooding in the southern Drell, or Tyran smuggling."

"So get married and lose the mothers," Flyn replied without sympathy. "You're the only one who *can* marry and stay in."

"I don't want to," Raoul said flatly.

"Sir, think of the rest of us," Dom said pleadingly. "There's the Midwinter parties, and not all mothers look down their noses at younger sons—"

"At least, not younger sons with money," quipped Lerant, his nose buried in his cider.

"If you're so poor, how'd you finance that pretty dagger, eh?" Dom retorted, pointing at the ivory-hilted blade hanging from Lerant's belt. "If that isn't Raven Armory work, I don't know what is."

"I hear the two Yamani ladies with the princess aren't spoken for," Lerant said, grinning at Dom.

"Thinking you might wangle an introduction, Sergeant Domitan?"

"I hoped my good friend Kel might take pity on me," Dom replied with a wink for her.

Kel's heart turned over in her chest, just as it did whenever he noticed her. It wasn't fair for Dom to be so good-looking, she thought, or worse, so *nice.*

"I still prefer—" Raoul was saying when a sodden messenger walked into the tent. He clutched an oilcloth envelope in his hand. Kel took it, noting the seal: a crossed gavel and sword. Where had she seen that before?

The parchment inside, also sealed, was addressed to her knight-master. She handed it over. Raoul frowned, then broke the seal as Kel ushered the messenger outside.

She made sure he and his mount were cared for, then returned to the meeting tent. The men were leaving.

"Here's Kel," Dom said. He chortled as he clapped Lerant on the back. "Two exotic Yamanis, one for you, and one for me," he told the younger man as they walked away.

"We're going to Corus?" Kel asked Raoul.

He gave her the parchment. "They've found who paid those two rogues to kidnap your maid in April," he told Kel. "We're going back for the trial."

December,
in the 17th year of the reign
of
Jonathan IV and Thayet, his Queen,
456

⇥ eight ⇤

THE PRICE OF A MAID

*T*he trip to Corus was hard. Outside the Royal Forest the rains that had turned the roads into rivers of mud became snow that deepened with every step. Warhorses were sent ahead of the riding horses to break the trail. Kel worried about that, but Peachblossom did his part without sharing his displeasure.

Some weeks before Kel had acquired a big leather pouch for the griffin to travel in during bad weather. Always worried about his health and how much cold and wet he could stand, she had lined the pouch with fleece to keep him warm. Inside the Royal Forest, even this wasn't enough. When she checked him at mid-morning on their second day, the small immortal sat huddled, feathers fluffed out. Gathering her courage, Kel unwound her thick wool scarf, unbuttoned the heavy quilted coat issued by the quartermaster, and opened the top of her fleece-lined jerkin. She took the griffin from its pouch with gloved hands, thought a prayer, and slid him into the front of her jerkin between the fleece and her wool shirt.

"If you savage me, it's back to the pouch for you," she informed her guest, shifting him so his head poked out of her jerkin and coat. The griffin's answer was to tug his head inside the jerkin. Kel rebuttoned her coat and put her scarf on again, leaving a small opening so the griffin could breathe. Either he did not want to return to the pouch or he was so cold he didn't want to do anything at all, even draw Kel's blood. He remained inside her clothes for the rest of the trip.

During the slow ride Kel had time to remember the events of last April. Her old rage at the injustice of it returned. Someone had paid thugs to kidnap Lalasa the night before Kel was to take the great examinations. After holding Lalasa—and Jump, who had refused to leave her—all night, the kidnappers had taken her to the top of Balor's Needle, the tallest structure in the palace. They left her bound, gagged, and blindfolded on the exposed observation platform. Jump was tied up there, too.

If Kel searched for them, she risked being late to the tests. The rules were clear: pages who were late would have to repeat at least one year, perhaps all four, of their page terms, depending on how late they were. The one who'd paid for the kidnapping had bet that Kel would do her duty by Lalasa and Jump and search for them, then give up her dream of a knight's shield rather than repeat her page years. If Kel had left the matter to people who didn't owe Lalasa protection, like the palace Watch, the whole world would learn she had shirked her duty.

As if that weren't bad enough, the kidnappers, or the one who paid them, had waited until Kel walked onto the observation platform, then locked the door to the inside stair of the tower. Their employer knew Kel's terrible fear of heights. Lalasa, Jump, and Kel were forced to descend the outer stair. With Lalasa's help Kel had done it, and lost her fear of heights as well.

The actual kidnappers were caught by the palace dogs before they left the grounds. Now the Watch had found the kidnappers' employer. Kel wanted to see his face. She wanted Lalasa to get justice after being terrorized for no better reason than she worked for the wrong person.

They reached their headquarters in a winter twilight two days after the trial started. Lalasa and her close friend Tian were already waiting for them, seated on a bench in the hall outside Raoul's and Kel's rooms. They took one look at the snow-soaked, weary knight and squire and went into action. They sent orders for hot water, tubs, and food for humans and animals. Then they swept into Raoul's and Kel's rooms. As the dazed pair watched, they lit candles, built fires in every room, put out fresh clothes, and began to strip Raoul and Kel of their wet things. Only when they reached under-clothes did Raoul recover enough to retreat to his own dressing room to await the arrival of his bath.

Kel watched, too exhausted to protest, as she settled the griffin on his platform and set it by her

fire. Technically Lalasa was no longer her maid, and
Tian had never been in her service, but it was so
nice not to have to do anything but what she was
told. At last Kel settled into a tub full of hot water
to soak off the road's grime. Lalasa fed the sparrows
and Jump, and directed the wing's servants at setting
out food in Raoul's dining room.

They couldn't get either woman to share supper,
but Lalasa and Tian agreed to join them in cups of
hot cider before the hearth in Raoul's study.

"How far has the trial come?" Raoul asked the
two young women.

Lalasa smoothed her neat white linen apron
with fingers that trembled. "The men have given
their evidence," she said quietly. "They followed the
man who hired them in case he chose not to pay
them after. I do not properly understand why it took
so long for this man to be captured, but they hold
him now in the waiting room reserved for nobles."

Raoul shook his head. "I bet he was holed up on
his estates and didn't come out before now. The
Crown's having a lot of trouble reducing that set of
noble privileges. On his own lands, a noble is
untouchable."

"Excuse me, my lord," Tian said quietly, "but
why did he leave, then? Surely he did not need to do
so—"

"Unless he wished to earn his knighthood,"
Lalasa interrupted, her voice hard. She looked at
Kel. "He has not been named, but servants talk. Sir
Paxton of Nond has attended each day. So too has
Ebroin of Genlith, who is the Corus steward and

representative of Lord Burchard of Stone Mountain."

When Kel saw who the noble culprit had to be, she almost laughed. Paxton of Nond was the knight-master of Joren of Stone Mountain, Kel's old foe. Of course it would be Joren. He'd pretended he had changed as a squire. She had wondered if that were so. Now she knew.

"His father's steward?" murmured Raoul, as much to himself as to the three young women. "Not his father?"

Tian coughed delicately. "I heard one of the Stone Mountain men-at-arms say the old lord refuses to treat this as if it means anything."

"That sounds like the old stiff-rump," said Raoul. "If arrogance were shoes, he'd never go barefoot." He looked at Kel. "You don't seem surprised."

"I'm *angry*," Kel replied, her voice soft, one fist clenched. The others stared at her, startled. Kel rarely showed temperament of any kind. "Whatever was bad there, it was between me and him. He didn't care about Lalasa or Jump. He didn't care who got hurt, so long as he could fix me. And to put a smile on his face, and tell me how I might get a husband, when he was groping for a plan like this . . . !" She got to her feet, unable to sit any longer. "Lalasa, Tian, thank you. My lord? If you'll excuse me, I need to think a bit."

Raoul nodded. "Kel . . ."

She bowed to him and retreated to her rooms, closing the door firmly behind her.

Joren, she thought, clenching her fists. This time he's gone too far. He'll pay for it. The Crown will see to it he does. Lalasa and Jump will have justice. And when it's over? He can pay some blood to me, when all the legal chants and dances are done.

Forcing herself to sit quietly in Duke Turomot of Wellam's courtroom, Kel wondered if the withered-persimmon look on the Lord Magistrate's face was permanent. Perhaps it was. He had been sour in the spring, when he'd announced that because someone paid ruffians to make Kel late to the big exams, she would be allowed to take them alone. Now that she thought of it, he'd never smiled during the year-end exams, either. So it wasn't just this case that had turned his expression pickle-sour, though it made her insides feel like he looked.

Kel watched Turomot from the bench reserved for the wronged party. She had Lalasa on her right; Jump sat between them on the floor. Lord Raoul was a solid bulwark on Kel's left.

Behind them sat Kel's parents, her brother Inness, Tian, and Lalasa's uncle Gower. Neal, Cleon, and Prince Roald, who had arrived from Port Legann, were there. Lord Wyldon of Cavall came. Kel had expected him: the training master had taken the kidnapping personally.

Across the aisle was Paxton of Nond, Joren's knight-master, a tired, anxious-looking man in his early thirties. On his right was a sleek, dark-haired man in his forties, elegant in gray tunic and hose. Lalasa murmured that he was the Stone Mountain steward, Ebroin of Genlith. With him was an advocate in a white overrobe and a large black skullcap; he was white-haired, mustached, and clever-looking.

"Master Advocate Muirgen of Sigis Hold," Raoul whispered when Kel asked. "He's very good—the best money can buy."

"There's little he can do when everybody knows Joren is guilty," Kel said, her own voice as soft as his.

Raoul frowned and opened his mouth to speak, but was cut off when Duke Turomot struck a bronze disk with a polished granite ball. Everyone rose for the prayer to Mithros, then sat in a rustle of cloth.

Duke Turomot scowled at Kel. "These proceedings are a matter of law, not of noble privilege. Should you have challenges to issue, make them elsewhere. We—"

The Watchmen on guard outside the courtroom doors threw them open. One stepped in to announce, "His royal majesty, King Jonathan the Fourth. Her royal majesty, Queen Thayet."

Everyone rose as the sovereigns walked down the center aisle. Women in skirts sank into curtseys; the men and Kel bowed deeply. Two thronelike chairs, part of every court's furnishings, stood on the magistrate's dais to his right. Normally they were empty, reminders of royal dominion. Today the king and queen went to them and sat. Only when they nodded to Duke Turomot did he resume his own seat, two red rage spots high on his cheekbones. The audience sat when he did.

Kel wasn't sure why their majesties had come, but she could ask Raoul later. He would know.

Duke Turomot's clerk, whose desk was at the foot of the magistrate's dais, stood. To the Watchmen who guarded the common prisoners' chamber off the side of the courtroom he said, "Admit the convicted commoners."

The Watchmen brought out two men in shackles. The clerk read from a sheet of parchment, "Let the record show that the convicted witnesses, Ivath Brand and Urfan Noll, have entered the chamber," he said. "In exchange for their testimony, their fifteen-year sentences to the mines will be reduced to ten."

Kel clenched her hands. Reduced? They should be laboring in mines or sweating and freezing to clear roads, anything, for *more* than fifteen years, not less. They had no right to sit in this warm room with Lalasa! Her mind knew that few people lived more than eight years at hard labor, but her heart wanted them to bear each and every moment of punishment they had earned, with no reductions, even if they weren't alive to serve the entire sentence.

"Proceed, Master Hayward," ordered Duke Turomot.

"Admit the noble prisoner," Clerk Hayward called.

The Watchman on duty at another side door opened it. Out came Joren of Stone Mountain, the same beautiful young man Kel remembered. Although even Kel could see that brown and yellow, his knight-master's colors, were not the best for him, he still looked like an unachievable dream of perfect manhood. He bowed to the monarchs and to Duke Turomot, then went to the bench occupied by Ebroin of Genlith and the advocate. He sat without so much as glancing at Kel or Lalasa.

Every muscle in Kel's body went rigid. He's here to pay for this, she told herself, clutching her self-control. He can't shrug this off. He won't.

"Ivath Brand and Urfan Noll, do you see the man who paid you two gold nobles to kidnap Lalasa Isran?" demanded Clerk Hayward.

Both convicts pointed to Joren. The clank of their chains made Kel look at Joren's wrists and ankles. He had *not* been chained. Arrest didn't seem to have inconvenienced him much. That will change, she thought furiously.

The sleek man rose. "If I may speak, my lord Duke." Turomot nodded. "I am Ebroin of Genlith, steward for his Corus properties to Lord Burchard of Stone Mountain, father of Joren of Stone Mountain. As my lord is in the north and unable to reach the palace at present, I stand in his place. With me is Master Advocate Muirgen of Sigis Hold, licensed to speak in law in Tortall, Tyra, Maren, and Galla. He will serve on Squire Joren's behalf."

"I know Master Advocate Muirgen," said Duke Turomot as that man bowed to the monarchs and to him. "He may speak as required."

Ebroin sat. The Master Advocate spread his hands, jeweled rings accenting his movements. "Your majesties, my Lord Magistrate, the testimony of convicted men in such matters is a jest. They give Squire Joren's name to please the Watch interrogators;

they had to offer a truly big fish to justify any change in their sentence. They—"

"Yatter on, you cake-mouthed money britches," snarled Urfan. "We knows who paid us"—the guard beside him cuffed his ear; he continued despite the blow—"noble or not—" A second, harder cuff shut him up.

The Master Advocate looked at the shackled men as if they were something nasty that clung to his shoe. "Need we include the common element?" he asked. "They have identified Squire Joren, rightly or wrongly."

Duke Turomot nodded. The Watchmen escorted the prisoners out of the room.

"No evidence connects Squire Joren to this tawdry affair," began the Master Advocate.

Duke Turomot raised a leather envelope that dripped with wax seals on ribbons.

"The map of the palace he made for those men," Lalasa whispered to Kel.

"I object to the use of law court mages to determine the truth of Squire Joren's testimony," continued the Master Advocate. "They would not practice inquiry magic if they were fit to make a decent living—"

"Oh, stop this currish babble." Joren's cold, clear voice brought all eyes back to him. "Ebroin and Muirgen have talked at me for days. I'm weary of it." He looked at Duke Turomot. "I paid those idiots to steal the wench and stash her on Balor's Needle. I paid a—"

Muirgen and Ebroin darted to Joren. Kel

glanced at Sir Paxton: the knight sat with his head in his hands.

"Squire, Master Joren, I beg you, not another *word*," Ebroin said hurriedly. "Think of your family, the smirch to your honor. There are ways to handle—"

Joren shook off the steward's restraining hand. "For a man who comes from a great family, you talk like a merchant. My *honor*?" His voice rang throughout the courtroom. "What honor has a nation when a *female* lives among men and pretends to their profession of arms? What honor is there in forcing a good, brave knight like Wyldon of Cavall, a hero of the realm, to accept this creature into training and to allow her to continue?" Kel, humiliated and infuriated, stared at the floor.

"I was not forced, Joren," Lord Wyldon told him. "She earned her right to stay, as much as— more than—you lads. Against odds that might have broken one of you."

"I understand you are honor bound to say so, my lord," Joren said quietly. "The conclusions I draw are my own."

You still don't believe him, thought Kel. Though you know as well as I do that it would just about kill Lord Wyldon to lie. She raised her head to stare at Joren. She didn't want him thinking she couldn't face him.

He spat on the flagstones in front of her and faced Duke Turomot. "I had her coming and going. Either she failed in her duty to her servant—and I'd have made sure the world knew the wonderful

Keladry had shirked her first obligation as a noble—or she'd be so late she'd have to repeat the whole four years. No one would do that."

Except me, Kel thought, staring at that blond head. I would have done it, just to spite you.

"My lord Duke, you and the other examiners made allowance for her, because certain interests in this kingdom mean her to succeed. You allowed her to take the big examinations alone. Of course, she passed." Joren crossed his arms over his chest. "So. I paid those men. I give you leave to sentence me under the law."

Duke Turomot leaned forward. He looks like the griffin about to hiss, Kel thought. "You are fortunate that, by law, a magistrate may not challenge for insult, Joren of Stone Mountain. I submit you knew that much before you found the courage to say such things of me and my examiners. But Mithros waits in judgment, you arrogant puppy. You may twist our law to suit you, but he weighs your every act, and will find you wanting." He sat back, gnarled fingers gripping the granite ball he used as a gavel. "With regard to your actions, the law is specific. According to *The Laws of Tortall*, section five, chapter twelve, paragraph two, in the matter of one noble's interference with the body servant of another noble: the offending noble must pay recompense for the loss of that servant for that period of time, in addition to the time which other servants spend in attempting to help or find the servant thus interfered with; the expense of any care of the servant following the interference; all expenses incurred by the noble with regard to court prosecution; and those costs incurred to bring said noble to court. I therefore fine Stone Mountain one hundred gold crowns, fifty of which are to be paid to Squire Keladry of Mindelan, five to the woman Lalasa Isran, and forty-five of which will be paid to this court for its expenses and those of the Watch."

"One hundred gold crowns!" gasped Ebroin of Genlith. "The wench was gone not even a full day!"

"Silence!" barked Duke Turomot, slamming the granite ball on the brass disk. "You lost your right to speak when your master confessed! The Isran woman earns commissions as a dressmaker to ladies, including, at the time of the interference, her royal majesty. I but include due concern for those delayed commissions."

"Stop whining and get them their filthy money, Ebroin," snapped Joren. "As far as I'm concerned, this country's going to the sewer-mucking merchants." He strode out through the door by which he had entered.

For a moment Kel thought Duke Turomot, rapidly turning purple, would send the Watch to drag him back. King Jonathan cleared his throat. It caught the magistrate's attention; when he glanced at the thrones, the queen shook her head slightly.

Sir Paxton got to his feet. His face was gray. "Your majesties, your grace"—he looked at Kel—"Squire Keladry, I beg pardon for my squire's behavior. I did not know about his crime. Had I known he would act in this fashion, I would have gagged him myself."

Duke Turomot held up a bony hand that still shook with rage. "No noble is responsible for the utterances of other nobles in court, unless there is proof that they are cohorts in the endeavor under study. You are a knight of good repute and standing with the Crown, Paxton of Nond. It is known that you persuaded your squire to face this court. No one believes you had knowledge of Squire Joren's behavior. I would suggest, however, that you use the time remaining of his service to school him in humility."

Sir Paxton bowed and left through the main door.

Turomot looked at Ebroin of Genlith. "Your dispositions, sir?"

Ebroin had been in heated discussion with the Master Advocate. He looked up. "If it please the court, I require three days to raise so great a sum."

"You have until sunset of the first night of Midwinter," barked Duke Turomot. "Each half-day you are late, a third of the sum will be added as penalty, subject to the same division as the original sum."

"A third!" cried Ebroin. He bowed his head as Duke Turomot glared at him. "Very well, my lord Duke."

Kel had boiled since she heard the sentence. Now she stood. "My lord, I would like a question answered, please."

The magistrate looked at her. "Speak, Squire Keladry of Mindelan."

"Did I hear right?" Kel fought to say each word

calmly. "Joren had Lalasa kidnapped, roped, gagged, blindfolded, and dragged here and there in the dark. Then she was left on an open platform where she could have rolled into the opening to the stair and fallen to her death, and all he gets is a *fine*? For the inconvenience?"

"That is the law," said the duke. "A maidservant belongs to her mistress. Squire Joren deprived you of her services—I understand she worked at that time on a gown for her majesty"—he looked at the queen, who inclined her head—"and caused disruption to her work later as a result of disordered nerves. I remind you the woman was also granted five gold crowns in my judgment."

"Lady Kel, please, hush," Lalasa begged, tugging on Kel's arm. "The ones who did it are going to hard labor, that's what matters."

"They wouldn't have touched you if he hadn't paid them," Kel told her. To the magistrate she said, "If he'd kidnapped me he'd have gotten prison or trial by combat." She clenched her hands so tightly that two griffin wounds reopened. "But for her he tosses a few coins in our laps and goes on his way."

"Your tone borders on the insubordinate," Duke Turomot said, his eyes like ice. "My clerk will send you the law pertinent to cases in which nobles interfere with those of common blood under the protection of other nobles. These laws have been in our codes for centuries, squire, worked out by men far wiser than you. If you have no more questions . . . ?"

Lalasa and Raoul tugged Kel back down on the bench. "Choose battleground and enemy when you have a chance to win," Raoul whispered in Kel's ear. "Mithros himself couldn't get old Turomot to admit a law is unfair."

"It's like me giving you my wages," Lalasa added softly. "I told you, most nobles keep nearly all of what their servants earn—it's their right. Maybe you're too full of ideals to do it, but other nobles aren't. My lady, don't make enemies here because of me!"

While they talked, Duke Turomot ended the trial, giving instructions to his clerk and the Master Advocate. Kel sat with her head down, trying to become stone, trying to envision herself as a calm lake. It did no good. She could not let this go without one more try at a protest.

Granite cracked on bronze; she heard the rustle of cloth as everyone got to their feet. King Jonathan stopped to speak quietly to Turomot; the Lord Magistrate nodded. The king gave the queen his arm, and they walked toward the aisle.

Kel stepped around Lalasa.

"Mindelan, don't do this!" hissed Lord Wyldon.

Kel reddened slightly. She didn't want to distress him more than Joren had already. Still, she raised her head and said, "Your majesties, may I speak?"

A big hand rested on her shoulder. Raoul said quietly into her ear, "Not in public, Kel. Ask for a private word."

The monarchs turned. King Jonathan raised his brows. "Squire Keladry?"

Raoul never steered her wrong. "Privately, sire, if possible?" asked Kel, and bowed.

Thayet nodded to her husband. The king looked at Turomot's clerk. The Lord Magistrate had already vanished into his private chambers.

"Sire, my office is empty, if you will excuse the clutter," the clerk offered. He went to one of the doors that led off the chamber and opened it with a low bow.

"May I come, too?" Raoul asked softly.

Kel nodded as the monarchs entered the clerk's chamber. She looked at her maid. "Lalasa?" she asked. "It concerns you."

Lalasa's dark face paled. "My lady, I couldn't. That company's too grand for the likes of me."

And besides, I shouldn't risk the queen taking her custom away if I upset her, Kel realized. She squeezed Lalasa's hand and followed the monarchs, Raoul at her elbow.

⇥ nine ⇤

MIDWINTER LUCK

"Don't confront monarchs in public, Kel," Raoul murmured. "If you make them look bad in front of those who should fear and obey them, they get nasty. Jonathan's a good enough sort as kings go, but that doesn't go far."

Kel nodded. Her heart thudded in her breast. She couldn't let this pass. *It's all of a piece with this king,* she thought. *He doesn't understand what "fair" means.*

The walls in the clerk's office were lined with shelves of books and papers. A double desk took up much of the open space. The king leaned against it, bracing himself with both hands. Queen Thayet sat in a chair, spreading her blue skirts around her. Raoul shut the courtroom door and leaned against it.

Kel bowed to the monarchs, fighting to keep her emotions from her face if not her spirit. Her hands shook. She stood with them locked behind her, so no one but Raoul could see her weakness.

"What may we do for you, Squire Keladry?" inquired the king, smiling. It was an attractive smile. The king himself was attractive, black-haired and -bearded, with sapphire-blue eyes, fair skin, and a good build for a man who spent his time indoors. His velvet tunic and silk hose matched his eyes; his black silk shirt, full in the sleeves and tight at the cuffs, was elegant.

His looks were wasted on Kel. Dom had prettier eyes and a warmer heart. She could not like Jonathan, though she would serve him and his queen. He had made her take a year of probation as a page when no male had to. He relied on charm to get his way. That summer Lalasa told her that Jonathan's oldest daughter, Princess Kalasin, had wanted to be the first female page, until her father talked her out of it. Kel wasn't surprised. She didn't think much of the man, though she had to admit he was a good king. Maybe her father was right, and good kings weren't always good men.

"What just happened? It was wrong, sire," she said firmly. "If Joren had kidnapped me instead of my maid, the legal penalties would have been much worse."

"Because if a member of the old nobility kidnapped one of the new nobility, it would cause a civil war," replied the king. "I like to discourage that kind of thing."

"But by law it's right that I be paid for the inconvenience of my maid being frightened to death? Not even that *she* gets the money, but *I* do? That's not right. It's like saying common folk are slaves. Their rights are measured in coin, not justice." She stopped there, swallowing hard. She'd done her best to keep her voice calm.

For a very long moment the room was silent. Finally the king sighed and crossed his arms. "It's not right," he told Kel, to her profound shock. "Only a fool would say that it was. I am called many things," he admitted with a crooked smile, "but 'fool' isn't one. What do you want?"

Kel swallowed. She was in it this far; it would be silly to blink now. "Change the law, sire."

"Change the law," the king repeated. "Squire, what do you think her majesty and I have done ever since we took the thrones? No, don't answer—I dread to think what you might have the courage to say. We have been *trying* to change laws—not this particular one, but many like it." He smiled bitterly. "The problem is that monarchs who wish to live until their grandchildren are born do not hand down any law they like. We must treat with our nobles, who are equipped to go to war against us; we must compromise with them. We must treat and compromise with merchants, who give loans for pet projects such as dredging Port Legann's harbor. We compromise and treat with farmers, who feed us, and street people, who can burn a city down. There are priests and priestesses, who can tell people the gods have turned their faces from the Crown, so they need not obey us. And the mages—I'll leave it to your imagination what mages will do when angered. Any law Thayet and I propose offends *someone*. We must balance opposing forces. Our successes vary."

Kel blinked. She had never guessed that even the lowliest could exact revenge against their betters, if they didn't mind its cost. "My point is the same, Your Majesty," she repeated. "This particular law is just plain *bad*."

"We could use the story of Lalasa's kidnapping to stir up sentiment for a revision," the king murmured. "My dear? Your opinion?"

"Keladry's right," replied Queen Thayet in her cool, direct manner. "This stinks of slavery. We could get the Mithrans' support—just say we're making it so the same law applies to all. The Goddess's temples will see it as greater protection for female servants."

"I'd hoped you'd want to *spare* us another battle with the nobility," murmured her husband and coruler. "Raoul? Come on, old man, voice an opinion if you dare."

"Now, Jon, you know I have opinions all the time," said Kel's knight-master. "I just don't air them when you've got your ears closed. I'd as soon save my breath."

"And?" the king demanded.

"I'm with Kel," Raoul told him. "The scene we saw in there reeked. That piece of rat dung knew before he came that the worst he would get was a fine. He used that to make the courts *and* the Crown look stupid."

The king winced. "Don't soften your words to spare me," he said drily. "Just speak your mind."

"Stone Mountain can pay fifty times that without a cramp," Raoul said "Old Turomot laid on all the extras he could, and it still didn't faze Joren. I thought that adding Lalasa's dressmaking to raise the fine was inspired, myself."

"You think Turomot would look into changing the law?" Jonathan inquired. "Usually I have to wheedle and grant all kinds of concessions before he'll so much as ask his clerks to look up precedents. He's the stickiest of the conservatives."

"Who just got told by a whelp that he'd given way to royal pressure," Raoul pointed out. "I think right now old Turomot would love to rewrite this law, just in case Squire Joren tries a similar trick one day."

"So there you have it, Keladry," said the king.

Kel blinked, startled to be addressed. She had been dazzled by the speedy discussion. If this was how kingdoms were ruled and people's fates were decided, she wouldn't be happy until she was in Peachblossom's saddle and as far from the palace as she could manage. "Sire?" she asked politely.

"We cannot change the solution in Lalasa's case. We can set the process of change in motion. It's slow—"

"Painfully," remarked the queen.

The king nodded. "But in the end the law will change."

"That's a start," Kel agreed.

"There's a price, my dear," King Jonathan said, capturing her eyes with his own. "In case you were going to challenge Squire Joren, as is your right under ancient custom . . ." He shook his head. "Unacceptable. This chat we've had is about how things must change from the rule of privilege to the rule of law for all. It means *you* must be content to have your quarrels settled by law, not by privilege."

He was right, curse him, thought Kel. If the country were to be governed by one set of laws, there could be exceptions for no one. She would have to accept the law's justice, even when she thought it unfair. Her intent to beat the tar out of Joren had to stay a happy fantasy.

"Very well, your majesty," she said. "If you keep your word to change this particular law, I won't challenge Joren."

The king extended his hands. Kel wasn't sure what he wanted until Raoul nudged her. Then she realized the king wanted her to swear.

She put her hands in his and knelt. "I, Keladry of Mindelan, will forego my privilege to challenge Joren of Stone Mountain, as long as work for a change in that law is made," she said, meeting the king's eyes.

"And I, Jonathan of Conté, do swear on my own behalf and that of Queen Thayet to do all in the Crown's power to have that law changed," replied the king solemnly. "Do you keep faith with me, and I will keep faith with you."

Dismissed from the clerk's office, Kel found Jump whining at the courtroom door. There was a new set of four parallel scratches, fresh and bloody, across the old scars on his heavy muzzle, and a frantic look in his tiny eyes. Kel didn't need to talk to animals like Daine to know there was trouble at home. She followed Jump through the crowded palace at a trot, barely noticing the looks she was given as she passed.

She heard battle before she saw it, sparrow shrieks and the yowls and rasps of an angry young griffin. She burst into her room. The griffin's platform was knocked over, the contents of his dishes scattered on the floor. The griffin himself alternately stood on his hind legs, wings spread, trying to grab sparrows as the birds circled and attacked his head, or hunkered down to protect his eyes. Pinpoints of blood dotted the feathers on his face, showing where his foes had scored a touch. He stood in front of Kel's desk and would not move. Behind him, in the hollow where she put her legs as she worked, Kel heard frantic peeping.

She yanked the coverlet from her bed and threw it over the immortal. The sparrows scattered as it descended. As the griffin thrashed against the heavy folds, Kel knelt to look under the desk. He had trapped one of the male sparrows there. One of the bird's wings trailed on the ground, marked like Jump by a griffin claw.

Kel brought the captive out, cuddling him in her hands. She had named this one Arrow, because the black bib at his throat was shaped like an arrowhead. "Find Daine, somebody," she ordered. Three sparrows zipped out a small window that stood open.

Kel whipped the coverlet off the griffin, knocking him on his back. He struggled to his feet with a hiss, his copper-colored eyes hot.

Kel spanked the griffin as she would a puppy or

kitten, loudly rather than hard. She made sure he saw Arrow so he would connect the sparrow with the punishment—she hoped. Finally she let him escape to the well in the desk where he'd held the sparrow. There he spread his wings in a mantling gesture, cawing at Jump, as if he knew the dog had brought Kel. Holding Arrow against her chest, she poked up the fire, then got a clean cloth. She wadded up the cloth and put the sparrow in it, settling him in her lap.

Suddenly tears spilled from her eyes. It was too much—the griffin, her normal duties, the trial, even her talk with the king. If only someone could help with the griffin! But Daine was the only one who could deal with the grudge held by griffin parents, and she was far busier than Kel.

Arrow peeped with alarm. "It's just monthly glooms," Kel said, wiping her eyes on her sleeve. "Human females get them. I should be as brave as you, defying a griffin."

Daine came and went, leaving behind her a healed sparrow and a griffin with—she and Kel hoped—an aversion to killing small birds. When Raoul knocked on the connecting door, Kel was cleaning up the mess.

"Trouble with the monster?" Raoul asked kindly.

Kel scowled at the griffin, still in his wooden prison with Jump as guard. "All mended, we hope."

Raoul leaned against the door frame, hands stuffed in his pockets. "Do you want help with him? He won't take food, but I could transport him and look after him. I can certainly defend myself from his family."

Kel smiled gratefully at him. It was typical of him to offer. "You're very kind, sir, but we'll muddle along. At least now we can hope he won't be hunting sparrows." Remembering her duty, she asked, "Did you need me for something?" She looked at the dog. "Jump, let him out."

Jump growled at his captive; the griffin hissed. As soon as Jump moved, the griffin stalked out from under the desk, pumped his wings, and hopped onto a chair, up to its back, then onto his platform. There he spread his wings, hissed at Kel, and began to groom himself.

"I was curious about how you felt," Raoul said in answer to Kel's question. "Jon surprised you?"

"He did that," Kel said grudgingly, picking up her comforter and shaking it. Griffin feathers and down stuffing drifted to the floor. As she fumbled with the heavy cover, trying to find the damage, Raoul took one side. He backed up until the comforter was stretched out, then turned it with Kel when she saw no damage on top. The rips were on the underside, five in all. She and Raoul laid the comforter flat on the bed, and Kel got her sewing kit.

"I don't know what I expected, but that wasn't it," she admitted as she prepared needle and thread. "Offering to change the law, or try to, for *me*? Why? Why would the queen agree?"

"Because you were right. It's a bad law. The middle classes are on the rise, Kel. Laws like that one will breed resentment, even bloodshed someday, if they aren't corrected." Raoul helped himself to her thread and needles and began to stitch one rip as Kel worked on another. "And maybe Jon thought this might get you on his side. He never does anything for just one reason." He set tiny stitches and sewed quickly, his big fingers deft. Sparrows lined up on his shoulders and head to watch, fascinated. Jump picked a more comfortable seat on an undamaged part of the comforter.

Looking at her master, Kel thought, Will there ever be a time when he *doesn't* surprise me? "I still don't know what I think," she admitted. "I owe him my duty, anyway."

"Yes, but there's a difference between someone who performs what's required because it's duty, and one who does what's needed because he or she believes in the Crown. You should keep in mind that he probably wants you to be confused about him." Raoul shook his head. "He wasn't this complicated when we were pages. I guess you never know how people will grow up."

"What was it like?" asked Kel. "You, Lady Alanna, the king—it's hard to see you as pages or squires."

Raoul grinned. "Like puppies in a basket," he said. "All paws and tails." He talked as they sewed, telling her stories of his past. Finishing a story about a bully who had beaten the page called Alan, until the day that the disguised Alanna had beaten him in turn, Raoul shook his head. "The only smart thing Ralon ever did was leave after that. He'd never have passed his Ordeal. I'm afraid Squire Joren won't, either."

"Sir?" Kel asked, startled and curious.

Raoul pointed to the longest tear. They had finished the others. "Race you to the middle of that," he offered. As they hurried to thread their needles and start at opposite ends, he continued, "You need a certain amount of, oh, flexibility, to face the Chamber of the Ordeal. You have to know when to bend. If I were training master, I wouldn't have let Joren get this far."

Kel stared at him, mouth open, until she realized he'd already begun to sew and she was falling behind. As she dug her needle into the cloth, she protested, "But if you pass the exams and do the work, and don't do anything really bad, the training master can't stop you from being a squire and then taking the Ordeal."

"Of course he can," Raoul told her, amused. "There are ways to discourage someone who is unfit. And often you're doing them a favor. The Chamber is . . ." He fell silent, shadows in his eyes, though he continued to stitch. "Hard," he said at last. "It's not that it's merciless. To have mercy or lack it, you need humanity. The Chamber hasn't got it. It would be like, oh, hating the griffin because he's a thankless little bit of winged vermin. Yes, you," he told the griffin, who flapped his wings. "Don't let it go to your head. Kel, the griffin can't change what he is, and the Chamber is unchangeable. Squires have broken themselves trying to defeat it." He reached the middle of the tear and tied off his thread with a triumphant smile. "Amazing, the skills a fellow picks up in forty years of bachelordom, don't you think?" he taunted Kel as he got to his feet.

She grinned at him, still finishing her part of the job. "You just did that because you can," she retorted.

"Think about the king," Raoul said. "If you're wary, he won't surprise you too often or too unpleasantly."

She watched him go back to his rooms, then finished her repairs. Done, she inspected his work—it was better than hers.

Was he right about Joren? Raoul saw so much in people, more than anyone she'd ever known, even Neal or her parents. But Lord Wyldon would have seen any great flaws in Joren, surely, and corrected them.

Like Joren's hiring criminals to kidnap someone? asked part of her that had spent too much time conversing with nasty, suspicious Neal. He questioned anything and everything. Worse, he now had some of Kel doing it too, and the rest of her never seemed to have any answers.

Musicians played lilting tunes in the Crystal Room, a gilded jewel box where the largest of the Midwinter First Night parties was held. Garlands of winter flowers and ivy hung on the walls. Heavy logs burned in the two large hearths, releasing piney scents. Candles burned in every window and in the crystal chandelier.

The king and queen sat beside one fire, the queen dramatic in black velvet with a sleeveless overrobe of silver cloth as fine as gauze. Her gown, overrobe, and crown were edged with diamonds and pearls. Kel knew that every stitch was Lalasa's, and glowed with pride in her friend. The king wore a white damask tunic edged with gold trim, white silk hose, and a white silk shirt. Gold lace rose at his collar and cuffs. There were no jewels in his lacy gold crown—they weren't needed. Kel admired the picture they made and kept well away from them. She was still thinking about their conversation three days before.

Kel herself was in Goldenlake colors, her dress outfit: a green velvet tunic so plush she had to stop herself from stroking it, green silk hose, and a pale yellow shirt with full sleeves. Like the queen's clothes, Kel's were made by Lalasa and fit perfectly.

Where her friend had found time to make them Kel didn't know. When she'd taken Lalasa the money from Joren's fine earlier that day, the shop was filled with ladies, their maids, Lalasa, and her helpers. Kel might have argued when Lalasa refused to take more than twenty gold nobles of the fine, but it was so noisy and Lalasa so preoccupied that Kel fled. She returned to her room with the package that contained her Midwinter garb and thirty crowns. Lalasa had been just this stubborn when Kel refused to keep the lion's share of her fees while Lalasa was her maid.

Kel sighed. She'd almost rather be in Lalasa's shop again than walking around this pretty room, carrying a tray of cups filled with mulled cider or grape juice, offering them to those who did not have a drink. Most did. Cleon, Neal, and Quinden of Marti's Hill also carried trays of liquid refreshments: wine, punch, brandy, and, for the Yamanis, rice wine and tea. Four other squires offered food: rolls, tarts, candied fruits, marzipan figures, nuts, and small winter apples, sliced and sprinkled with cinnamon.

They all looked as bored as Kel. Even Prince Roald, the only squire who did not serve, looked bored. When Shinkokami, elegant in a Tortallan-style gown of peach silk, spoke to him, he put a look of interest on his face. Whenever he replied to or addressed his wife-to-be, Shinkokami leaned toward him, offering an attentive ear.

They'll have the politest marriage ever, thought Kel. It was hard to tell if the Yamani was bored, although Kel, watching Shinkokami smooth the bronze silk fan in her lap, suspected that she was. Both princess and prince were more genuinely interested when others came to talk to them. Yukimi, in a sky-blue kimono patterned with gold phoenixes, often returned to her mistress to talk. So did Lady Haname, vivid in a maroon kimono embroidered with white clouds, once she could wriggle out of a cluster of male admirers. She and Yuki were supported by Kel's mother Ilane, Prince Eitaro's wife, and the queen. Roald's visitors included his father, his friends among the squires, and his knight-master, Imrah of Legann. Kel also stopped to chat with Shinkokami. She knew how uncomfortable it was to be among alien people with strange customs.

She worried about the betrothed couple. Shy, both of them, she thought as she collected empty cups from tables and ledges. Something ought to be done.

"You shimmer like a mirage of delight," Cleon murmured as they met in the serving room. They turned in trays of empty cups and plates to take up full ones. "Your teeth call to mind wolfhounds romping in the snow."

Kel smiled up at the redheaded squire. She had never noticed it before, but his eyes were an interesting, clear gray. "Wolfhounds are furry," she pointed out. "I hope my teeth aren't. And teeth aren't cold enough to be snow. How is it you get sillier every time I talk to you?"

"The joy of our nearness cooks my lovestruck heart," he explained with a soulful look.

"Or you've been looking at Scanrans longer than is good for you. Spend time with actual girls," she informed him sternly. "You wouldn't call me things like 'pearl of my heart' then."

"No, it's 'mirage of delight' today. 'Pearl of my heart' was when I was but a mere boy." They stood in the door, looking at the party. "I hate to say it, my dear, but I think our prince is a fathead," Cleon remarked. "There he sits with the most gorgeous creature in shoe leather, excepting your luminous self, of course—"

"Of course," Kel replied, straight-faced.

"—without a word to say. Somebody should tell

him the lady can converse, and sensibly, too." Cleon straightened his shoulders. "If I don't return by dawn, wear my handkerchief beside your heart forever." He disappeared into a clump of guests. Kel lost the chance to say that she didn't have his handkerchief, and if she did, after a while it would begin to smell. *He's right about the prince and princess, though,* she thought, rearranging cups so her tray would balance.

"Did Cleon kiss you for Midwinter luck?" a familiar voice drawled in her ear.

"Did Princess Kalasin ask for a dance at the ball tomorrow night?" she retorted to Neal. "Cleon doesn't mean that stuff. He's just practicing." Changing the subject, she asked, "Is Lady Alanna here?"

Neal shook his head. "Home to Pirate's Swoop," he said. "Happily leaving me to Lord Wyldon's guidance while she embraces the baron and the children."

"You're doomed," Kel teased, and moved on.

She was about to return for a fresh tray when another familiar voice asked, "Squire Keladry, how are you?"

Kel turned and faced Commander Buri. The stocky K'mir looked grand in a crimson silk dress. The shade gave a touch of gold to her skin. Her overrobe was crinkled gold silk with jet beads on the hem. "Commander, you look wonderful," Kel said, trying to remember when she had seen her in anything but mud-splashed working clothes.

"I feel tormented," the woman replied. "And I wish you'd call me Buri. You know Riders don't hold with titles." Her dark eyes flicked around the room. "I haven't seen Raoul about. I suppose he defied their majesties and is hiding in his rooms."

"No, he's here," Kel said. "Not in this room, though, or we'd have seen a big lump behind the hangings."

Buri grinned, white teeth flashing against her dark complexion. "Yes, that's where I'd look. Can't say I blame him. The crowd around Thayet is thinning. I'd best say hello, or she might think I didn't show up per *my* orders." She saluted Kel and wandered off toward the monarchs.

Kel's eyes went to the prince and princess, who now smiled at one another as if their teeth hurt. This is no good, thought Kel. They have to learn how to talk. There must be a way to nudge them along.

She went to a door that opened onto a book room and peered in. Raoul was there, talking with Gareth the Younger, the king's closest advisor and one of his friends. Sir Gareth's wife, Lady Cythera, was tugging on her husband's sleeve. "I hate to interrupt," the lady explained, "but Prince Eitaro wants my husband to meet Lady Eitaro."

Kel moved on to offer drinks to foreign dignitaries. Yuki stopped her briefly. "When things are quieter, would you sit with her highness for a time?" she asked Kel, her usually merry eyes pleading. "She and the prince have nothing to say to one another, and she's sad. When someone mentioned you'd fought a forest campaign this summer, she showed interest. She'd love to hear the details."

Kel's plan came together in the flick of an eye-lash. "Wait a moment, Yuki?" she asked, using her old nickname for the Yamani. She put her tray inside the serving room. "I've been thinking."

"Uh-oh," Yuki murmured wickedly.

Neal and Cleon were talking when Kel approached them. "Come here," she said, leading them to Yuki. The four entered the serving room. "Yuki, have you met my friends?" Kel introduced the young men, who bowed in the proper Yamani manner. "I think we agree, Roald and Shinkokami have to start talking. Now, Shinko—"

"Shinko?" Neal interrupted.

Kel smiled. "It's her nickname—she gave me permission to use it when we were little. Anyway, she wants to hear about that bandit hunt I was on this summer. Lord Raoul is in the book room—he's *really* good at helping people to relax. If you lads—"

"I am a man, I'll have you know," Neal said loftily, putting a hand on his chest. "Five years older—"

Kel elbowed him, ruining his dignity. Yuki covered a giggle with her fan. "Hasn't Lady Alanna taught you not to interrupt?" Kel asked. "Pay attention. Can you two"—she looked from him to Cleon—"get Roald interested? Otherwise he won't come—he'll think Shinko will be bored. And she won't say anything to *him*. She's worried he'll believe she's unmaidenly for wanting to hear about it." Shinko had let a few interesting things slip during morning glaive practices. "If we get them together with Lord Raoul, though, and maybe Commander Buri, they'll be so interesting that Roald and Shinko might relax."

"Why would he think she's unmaidenly?"

protested Cleon. "His own mother hunts bandits."

"Prince Eitaro told my lady that men with unconventional mothers want conventional wives," Yuki said, her round cheeks red with vexation. "I don't think it's true—"

"Me neither," chorused Roald's three friends. They grinned at one another.

"This plan is good," Yuki said, closing her fan with a decisive snap. She tapped Neal's chest with it. "Signal me when you have Prince Roald's interest," she ordered him, and bustled off.

"Bossy little thing," Neal said to no one in particular. "Let's go hook Roald, Cleon."

Kel went to talk with Raoul. He was eager to help, if it didn't mean leaving the book room. Kel suspected he was also glad to have a good excuse if the king asked him where he'd been. She found Buri, who was more than happy to join them.

It was some time before Kel, Neal, and Cleon were finally able to join the book room gathering after the second shift of squires arrived to take their tasks. The prince and princess were caught up, asking sharp questions of the two commanders and of Kel herself. Kel noted Roald's look of wonder and pleasure as Shinko revealed a thorough grasp of strategy, supply problems, and tracking. Pressed by Raoul and Buri to tell what she knew, she described Yamani battles and tactics. From there talk ranged over other battles against immortals, bandit chasing in Tortall and the Yamani Islands, and the latest round of trouble with Scanra.

Others came and left: Lady Haname, Kel's

parents, Sir Gareth and Lady Cythera, the queen. Roald's knight-master, Lord Imrah, stayed for some time. Everyone groaned when Imrah's lady dragged him away at last.

Slowly the group shrank to its original members. Neal and Yuki then left for a mages' party. The prince and princess left together, debating the advantages of crossbows over longbows.

Raoul, Buri, Kel, and Cleon watched them go. "Who would have thought?" murmured Cleon. "She looks like she'd break if you touched her too hard."

Kel got to her feet. "Come to the training yard the queen's ladies use some morning and see how fragile she is." She covered a yawn. "If you'll excuse me, I'm asleep on my feet."

Cleon got up. "Gods, I've yet to finish wrapping gifts."

Buri and Raoul waved to them and continued their conversation.

"So have you survived your first night of squire social duty?" asked Cleon as they wound their way through the last partygoers in the Crystal Room.

"It could've been worse," Kel replied. "I'm just sleepy."

"You see Lord Raoul at parties and balls, and he looks like a piece of wood," Cleon said as they walked down the hall. "But he isn't, is he?"

Kel shook her head. "He's completely different with me and the men." She smiled. "Something he said once—I guess a lot of mothers with daughters to marry off come after him at these things."

Cleon's smile was crooked. "There are a lot of them, and they can be persistent."

They had reached the place where their paths separated. Kel looked up at Cleon. "I wouldn't know," she teased. "I don't have to worry about matchmaking mothers."

Cleon leaned down and pressed his lips gently to hers. "Midwinter luck, Kel," he whispered. He turned crimson, and strode down the hall.

Kel stood there for some time, completely poleaxed.

The next evening Cleon had duty at a different party from Kel. *That's a relief,* she told herself as she offered sweetmeats to the heads of guilds and their wives. *Of course it's a relief, not to see him so soon. I need time to decide what to say to him, or what to do, when I see him. Particularly what I'll* do. *Not that I plan to* do *anything.*

Then they didn't serve together at any other Midwinter parties. Kel only glimpsed him once, at a distance. She told herself that she was *not* unhappy that he hadn't seen her.

She kept busy. She tended the griffin, who was quiet after his encounter with Daine. She practiced weapons with the queen, the Yamanis, and her mother, and rode Peachblossom and Hoshi. She wrapped and sent out her Midwinter gifts the day before the longest night of the year, and opened hers the next morning. Her unknown benefactor had not vanished with Raoul's taking her on—among her gifts was a splendid brass-mounted spyglass, one that Raoul threatened to steal. Raoul himself had given Kel a beautifully made pair of armored gauntlets that were nearly as flexible as cloth gloves, and padded inside for warmth. Kel's gift to him was the best feathers shed by the griffin, each bright orange and perfect. Kel knew she could have sold them, but the look on Raoul's face when he thanked her was more valuable.

Kel had started something with the book room conversation. Others like it continued during the holiday parties. Raoul and Buri presided; Shinkokami and her Yamani ladies and Prince Roald and his friends always came, though plenty of others took part. Warfare wasn't the only topic. The Tortallans were curious about Yamani customs and history; the reverse was true of the Yamanis. They could ask any question about the Eastern Lands and no one would laugh. Kel felt a little smug as she watched Roald and Shinkokami lose their shyness with one another. It was nice to end the old year with a good idea.

During the festivities Kel thought of those squires who faced their Ordeals that year. Each night one of them held vigil; each morning one entered the Chamber at dawn. Did they have visions in the chapel? Kel wondered as she filled glasses and served food. Did they touch that iron door in the night, or were they content to face the Chamber only when the time came to walk into it?

Despite her curiosity she never joined the cluster of family and friends that waited for the squires to leave the Chamber. It didn't seem right, as if it were indecent for her to look on the squires' faces just then.

That year ten of them entered the Chamber, three more than the holiday had nights. Afterward Kel waited three days, to allow for cleaning, before she went into the chapel alone. She didn't think she broke any rules doing this, but she had to be alone in any event.

The chapel smelled of beeswax and cleansing herbs. The sun disk shone from a recent polishing. Only the Chamber door looked the same as it had that summer.

Kel shivered: the room was cold. She blew on her fingers, then pressed her hands flat on the cold iron.

Something bound her from shoulders to feet, locking her arms against her sides and her legs together. The binding was tight, though she saw nothing but the clothes she wore. Another band lay over her mouth, gagging her.

She stood at one end of a long room. Next to her was a line of people who passed without looking her way. One at a time they advanced to a table nearly ten yards from Kel. She could smell them, it was so real: soap, damp wool, fear-sweat. She knew most of them: Lalasa's friend Tian, Bernin from Owlshollow, the girl whose doll she'd found at Haresfield, the girl's mother, Shinkokami, Jump, Peachblossom, Lerant.

Kel twisted frantically, trying to get free, with no luck. She could not move or utter a sound. Fighting to catch her breath, Kel stared at the table. Duke Turomot, the Lord Magistrate, consulted a long sheet of parch-

ment; Ebroin of Genlith, the steward for the lord of Stone Mountain, manipulated a large abacus as the duke spoke. They sat behind the table. Joren of Stone Mountain leaned on it, beautiful in black velvet, his hair pale gold against the dense black. He smiled mockingly at the people in the line.

"Lalasa Isran," Ebroin said clearly, taking up his abacus.

Kel wrenched hard at her bindings. A muscle pulled in her neck, sending a white-hot streak of pain into her skull.

"Dressmaker," Turomot said, drumming his fingers on the table. Ebroin touched a bead on the abacus. "Breeding age, looks well when clean, strong enough for servant's work, rarely ill." For each comment, Ebroin flicked another bead on the abacus. "That is all of worth about her," Turomot said.

Ebroin calculated a sum on the abacus and wrote it on the slate, which he passed to Joren. The young man looked at it.

"Not interested," Joren said. "Cull her."

The centaurs Graystreak and Iriseyes walked out of nowhere to grab Lalasa's arms. They dragged her to one side. There another centaur clubbed her with a spiked mace. Lalasa fell into a pit in the floor.

"Shinkokami, Yamani princess," Turomot said, reading from his parchment. "A good bride price, connections, and an alliance with the Yamani Islands. Embroiders, dances, knows the use of weapons." Ebroin flicked abacus beads and wrote a new total on his slate.

Joren inspected it. "Fifty gold crowns. Not a copper more. It's risky, taking a woman who uses weapons."

Turomot nodded. Graystreak and Iriseyes took Shinko's arms to lead her out.

Bernin stepped up. "Bernin of Owlshollow," Turomot read from his parchment. "Trained shepherd, a guide—"

Joren raised a hand. "I have no need of shepherds or guides," he said. "Cull him."

Kel fought her bonds to stop this, whatever it was, without success. Joren kept Haname and Kel's mother, sending them to some unknown place, then ordered that the Haresfield girl, Yuki, and Jump be culled. They were clubbed down as Kel fought to do something, anything. She was trying to scream to Peachblossom to run when she fell.

She was in the Chapel of the Ordeal, pouring sweat, her throat raw from smothered screams. Her body ached furiously.

Trembling, she staggered to her feet and stared at the Chamber door, fists clenched. You won't beat me this way, she told it silently. You will *never* beat me.

She stalked out, letting the door slam behind her. Only when she reached her room did she allow herself to cry. The sight of those familiar bodies in a bloody heap would haunt her for weeks.

*Spring,
in the 18th year of the reign
of
Jonathan IV and Thayet, his Queen,
457*

ten

THE GREAT PROGRESS
BEGINS

*T*hird Company took to the road just two days after Kel's encounter with the Chamber door, to escort the outgoing Tyran ambassador to his own border. They rode south on a trip Lerant mockingly described as "departing the land of snow and sleet for the land of rain and sleet."

Kel was relieved to be away. She hadn't seen Cleon privately since that astonishing kiss. She couldn't decide if she wanted to see him or never to see him again. She didn't know which would be worse, finding that he'd done it on a dare or that he'd done it because he'd wanted to. Either reason meant a rat's nest of problems.

At the Tyran border they said farewell to the outgoing ambassador and welcomed the new one. Third Company got ten days to recuperate before they escorted the new ambassador and his lady to Corus. Kel, seeing all of the goods in the Pearlmouth marketplaces, did some of her shopping for next Midwinter. The way things went with the Own, she wanted to do such tasks when she could. An emergency might interfere later.

In February after they returned to Corus, Third Company headed down the coast. They were accompanied by Baron George Cooper of Pirate's Swoop, a man people both pitied and looked down on for marrying Alanna the Lioness. Kel watched him intently. She wanted to know why the Lioness had married this man, who wasn't even handsome, for all that he was well muscled for someone in his late forties. The only attractive thing about him was a pair of humorous hazel eyes. Nice eyes hardly seemed to Kel like grounds for marriage.

The baron had heard of pirates who spent the winter near a town called Bay Cove. He led Third Company there over a series of goat trails. It gave them a good vantage point from which to scout the pirates' nest and plan their attack. There was a short, pitched fight, which Third Company won easily. Kel did little more than stand by Raoul, listening to the orders he gave and the reports he got. With pirates in tow, they sought the Port Legann magistrate. That meant another series of trials, another set of executions. More than once she wished there were a different way to handle murderers.

In March they stayed with the Bazhir. Kel, Lerant, Dom, and some of the others raced against the Bazhir, though Kel seldom won. Hoshi was fast and strong, but she was no match for the dainty-boned Bazhir horses, called by their proud owners "children of the wind." Raoul gave her more jousting lessons, something that puzzled Bazhir men and amused Bazhir women. They would gather around Kel afterward to put balm on her bruises and tease her.

They spent April on the banks of the Drell River, which flooded when the winter snows melted. Kel's back was a solid ache as she labored with Raoul and the men to shore up the flood walls.

In early May they returned to the Bazhir and helped the headman of the Sunset Dragon tribe celebrate the birth of twins to his wife. After that Raoul led them back to the palace.

There wasn't a noble in sight. The immense parade of the Great Progress, designed to introduce Tortallans to Shinkokami and to renew the people's ties to the monarchs, had departed. With it rode courtiers, maids, hostlers, clerks, barbers, huntsmen, guards, cooks, errand boys, and anyone else who might prove useful. The palace was not deserted: while the nobles might be gone, hordes of workmen had arrived to fix anything that needed repair, apply fresh coats of paint and whitewash, and pursue other loud, dusty tasks. The kingdom's administrators still worked at their desks. The courts still met; the officials who ran the kingdom's tax collections and postal service labored here. Still, compared to the palace at Midwinter, Kel found the place sadly empty.

"Peace and quiet!" Raoul said as his company rode into their courtyard. "I revel in it!"

"But we *will* be catching up?" prodded Flyndan.

"When we're rested," said Raoul gravely. "I myself feel quite tired."

"And every time you get the bit between your teeth and decide you don't care what the king wants, you two end up butting heads. One day you won't be able to charm your way out of a royal reprimand." Flyn kept his voice low—only Kel heard him, though she pretended she didn't.

"He wouldn't butt heads with me if he didn't keep using us like a garland of pearls to dress up his majesty," Raoul said, keeping his own voice down. "We're a combat unit, not a dance troupe. We leave when we're rested."

Flyndan shook his head and dismounted.

They had two lazy weeks before a firm message arrived from the king. Third Company packed and rode slowly for six days. At last they topped a ridge that overlooked the city of Whitethorn, tucked into a delta formed by the rivers Olorun and Tirragen. There they watched the fat, glittering serpent of the royal progress come into view. The local people had the same idea: they lined the road in their festival best, all wearing some bit of royal blue ribbon. More people flooded onto the road through Whitethorn's open gates, eager to see the realm's notables.

The city was swathed in banners and garlands. Tortallan and Yamani flags waved atop every tower. Grave town fathers in long robes and elegant hats stood on the wall over the main gate. Little girls in white bearing flower garlands stood with them.

The procession came on. With her new spyglass Kel could see the riders behind the heralds. The king and queen rode with Roald and Shinkokami between them. Prince Eitaro scowled on the king's right—Kel knew his arthritis must be bothering him—as his wife serenely guided her mount on the queen's left. Behind Thayet rode her ladies, fourteen young women of good family and education, who could grace a party and ride and shoot well enough to keep up with Queen Thayet in an emergency. Yuki and Lady Haname rode with them. Kel smiled: her Yamani friends had been adopted.

"Don't be greedy," Dom said, elbowing her. "A chivalrous knight shares."

His nearness still did mad things to her emotions, though lately she kept thinking about Cleon, wondering what it would be like to kiss him back. Kel handed over the spyglass. "Try not to steam it up looking for pretty girls," she ordered. The griffin cawed and flapped from his post on the placid Hoshi's saddle horn, as if he echoed Kel.

"You just don't understand a fellow's interest in females," Dom murmured, glued to the spyglass.

"How many fighters are with them?" asked Raoul.

"Four Rider Groups," replied Dom. "The Fourth—the Queen's Rabbits. The . . . First. They don't have a nickname," Dom said when Kel made a questioning noise. "They're just the First. The Fourteenth, Gret's Shadows, and the Seventeenth, Group Askew. There's Commander Buri. Oh, splendid—Captain Glaisdan and First Company. He looks as sour as a pickled beet."

"If he's wearing his old-style armor, probably his face is the same color," Flyndan said. "Why couldn't that fusspot stay at the palace? First Company's all wrong for this."

"If I pretend I like you, squire, can I use the spyglass?" Lerant asked Kel.

"Please don't try," she replied. "You're not that good an actor. Dom, he can look when you're done."

"Some people are cocky ever since they killed a whole centaur," Lerant remarked to the air.

"Some people are annoying," Dom retorted, giving him the spyglass. "So, Kel, about the Yamani ladies . . ."

The royal courier who had twittered at Raoul's elbow all the way from Corus said, "My lord Knight Commander, why do we hesitate? The king was quite firm—"

"So you've said. Often," Raoul growled, black eyes smoldering. He raised his voice. "My dears, there's no help for it. Let us join in the panoply." He urged Amberfire into a careful walk.

Lerant handed the spyglass to Kel and hoisted the Knight Commander's banner, setting his mount forward. Flyndan joined him, his doughy face as gloomy as Raoul's.

"Not too fast," called Raoul. "Let's not scare anyone."

"His majesty said with all deliberate speed!" chirped the courier. He flinched under Lerant's glare.

"That's how we're doing it," Raoul told him. "Deliberately."

Kel hid a smile. Raoul had argued that one company of the Own on progress was sufficient. The king had overruled him and here they were. They merged with the progress, Third Company behind the ranks of nobles as Raoul, attended by Kel, caught up with the monarchs.

The king glanced at Raoul. In a less exalted man his expression might have been called a scowl. Prince Eitaro let Raoul take his place.

"Master Oakbridge has found you hosts to lodge with in the city," Kel heard Jonathan say coldly as they approached the main gates. "Near the governor's palace, so you won't have any excuse for lateness at the social events."

"As my king orders," said Raoul, his voice blandly pleasant. Kel glanced at him. What was he up to? The griffin squawked, and she returned to their game: trying to wrestle a rawhide strip out of his beak. He rarely bit or scratched her while playing.

The king was also suspicious. "It is, eh?"

Raoul indicated the immortal, who growled as he wrestled with the leather. "Did Oakbridge mention our friend?" inquired Raoul. "Where Kel goes, he goes."

"No one's going to want a griffin in his house," the king snapped. "Most folk don't believe it's just people who actually handle the thing who get attacked. She'll have to camp with the rest of the progress."

"I'm to attend balls and banquets without my squire?" demanded Raoul, all innocence. "I can't handle things like requesting water to shave with, or getting my clothes pressed. I need Kel."

"You managed for twenty years," growled the king, blue eyes flashing in anger.

"This is different," Raoul informed him.

Jonathan stared grimly ahead, drumming his fingers on his saddle horn. Finally he ordered, "Tell the Lord Seneschal to give you a place in the camp, then. And I expect you to be on time for social events!"

"Sire," Raoul said, bowing deeply in the saddle. He motioned to the side of the road with his head, and turned Amberfire out of the main parade. Kel followed, her face Yamani-straight.

The Lord Seneschal nearly screamed when he realized he needed to find a place in the camp for the Knight Commander. Drawing up these camps required tact, diplomacy, and quick thinking. Obviously enemies could not pitch their tents side by side, and the most important nobles would not take it well if they camped cheek by jowl with soldiers. For a moment Kel feared the Seneschal was going to have an apoplexy as his face turned a rich plum color. He grabbed a map on a parchment and hurriedly drew a square, putting Raoul's name on it. He squawked a servant's name, then turned to his next problem.

The man he'd summoned did not turn colors or raise his voice. He gave a few commands, then led Raoul and Kel down a grassy lane between tents, explaining the customs and layout of the camp. By the time he'd shown Raoul and Kel the privies and open-air kitchens and escorted them to their assigned space, servants had set up a large tent for Raoul, connected to a smaller one for Kel.

"And they say a stolen griffin's unlucky," Raoul told her smugly as they inspected their new domain.

At Whitethorn castle a servant directed Kel to an

assembly room. She joined other squires to await their usual spate of banquet instructions from the palace master of ceremonies, Upton Oakbridge. He was in hurried conference with a man in Whitethorn colors and a woman who bore the smears and smutches of a cook.

Neal wasn't present. Cleon was, smiling at her in a way that made her feel odd, warm and shivery at the same time. She wasn't sure that she liked it and welcomed the distraction of greeting the others. Her five year-mates were present. So were the newest squires.

"Owen, you've joined our ranks?" Kel teased. Of course he'd passed the big examinations. She didn't have to ask if he'd found a knight-master. His clothes told the tale: he wore the blue shirt and hose and the silver tunic of a squire attached to palace service.

"I've got the title, but not the work," Owen said glumly. He was a plump fourteen-year-old, two inches shorter than Kel, with unruly brown curls and gray eyes. He loved books and had no sense of tact. He also had a wild courage that led him to plunge into battle outnumbered. Gloom was not his natural state.

"What happened?" she asked. "I thought surely you'd be chosen."

"Lord Wyldon says it's like last year," Owen told her. "You had the congress, so everyone took their time picking. Now it's this progress. There are squireless knights everywhere, but they're in no rush. It stinks. And in the meantime I get to answer to *him*." He nodded toward Master Oakbridge, who was sending the Whitethorn man and the cook away.

"Attention!" called Oakbridge. Kel hugged Owen around the shoulders as they faced the master of ceremonies. Oakbridge did his work with dramatics and prophecies that all would go horribly awry. Having dealt with him over Midwinter, Kel wondered why the man hadn't died of a heart attack. Instead he seemed to thrive on disaster and finding people seated in the wrong places. The thought of Owen's having to report to him day and night made her wince in sympathy.

Briskly Oakbridge gave instructions. These banquets were only a little different from page service: squires were assigned to a table where their knight-masters were joined by a dinner companion and other notables. Once the feast was over, guests roamed while squires remained at their posts, refilling glasses, offering sweets, fruits, and cheeses, and providing finger bowls and napkins.

Kel listened, committing what Oakbridge said to memory. When he finished, she found Cleon beside her. He followed Kel to the table where finger bowls and towels were laid out.

"I thought you would never get here," he said as they took up towels and bowls.

"Lord Raoul was just finishing up a few things," she replied, eyes fixed on her bowl. It quivered; she was trembling for some reason, and much too aware of Cleon's warm body at her side.

"Finishing up? Hah," said Merric of Hollyrose

behind them. He was a wiry, lanky boy with very red hair, Kel's year-mate and friend. "Everyone knows the king sent him a message saying catch up *now*."

"Well, is social scheduling what *you* thought you'd do as a knight?" Kel asked as they started for the banquet hall.

"I didn't think," Merric said cheerfully. "I just did what my parents told me, for once."

They split up, going to the tables where their knight-masters sat. Kel looked for Owen, who went to the table where Prince Roald and Princess Shinkokami sat and got a smiling welcome.

Kel was edgy, as she always was when she had new social duties, but tucked it behind her Yamani mask. Raoul had no bland face to hide behind. With the pretty eighteen-year-old daughter of a local baron as his dinner partner, he turned into a block of wood. His companion, made nervous by his rank, age, and silence, chattered. Numair and Daine, seated with them, were too busy talking about books to rescue them.

Kel looked around to see who she could recognize. Buri was as wooden as Raoul. A local guildsman was her partner; he had no trouble talking at the wordless K'mir. The king and queen looked as if they enjoyed talking with the Whitethorn governor and his lady, while the Yamani ladies kept those who shared their tables politely occupied.

At last came Kel's favorite part of a state banquet. Artful creations in jellies, cakes, and sugar called subtleties were served between courses for diners to admire and eat. The first ones were simple, like the spun sugar crowns that represented the four royal personages in attendance. By the end of the feast they were works of art.

Whitethorn's cooks surpassed themselves. Their last subtlety was a silvery winged horse of molded sugar and marzipan. It reared on its hind legs, bat-like wings extended, forelegs pawing the air. Before it stood a foal, wings hanging limply, legs hardly strong enough to support it. But for the size they could be real, thought Kel as she joined the diners in applause. She wished she could make beautiful things like that.

Musicians took the center of the room. Raoul excused himself to his dinner partner and went to greet his friends. As soon as he left, a young man came to lead Raoul's dinner partner into a group of people their own age.

Kel remained at her post, talking with Numair and Daine and waiting on those who came to sit with them. At last Raoul signaled that he was ready to go. Kel turned in her pitcher and tray and ran to fetch Amberfire and Hoshi.

They were halfway back to camp when Raoul broke their comfortable silence. "They're holding a tournament over the next two days. I want you to have a look before we enter you in the competitions—you're about ready. Have you seen one?"

Kel shook her head. "The Yamanis don't have them. They just beat each other half to death in training."

"They sound like sensible people. Do they hold banquets?" Raoul asked wistfully.

"Better," Kel told him. "They have parties where they view the moon in reflecting ponds, or fireflies in lanterns, or patterns of cherry tree blossoms against the sky, and they make up poetry about it."

Raoul shuddered and changed the subject.

The tournament, held just before Kel's sixteenth birthday, was educational. It was also the first time Kel squired for Raoul in the traditional way. Since Raoul was scheduled to joust in the afternoon, she had all morning to inspect, clean, and polish his armor and that of his warhorse, black Drum. The metal pieces were clean—she had scoured them at the palace—but an extra rub of the polishing cloth never hurt. She also checked each of his weapons: an assortment of lances, should one break, his sword, and his mace. He shouldn't need the last two—these were exhibitions, not true combat—but Kel wanted everything ready, just in case. She shook out Drum's saddle blanket and went over his tack, polishing and testing each join and stitch. Lord Wyldon had pounded it into the pages' heads: equipment not in perfect condition was a danger to the one who used it. Kel took his words to heart.

Raoul came to the tent after a light midday meal and changed clothes behind a screen. Wearing breeches, hose, and a loose white shirt, he walked to the center of the room. As he pulled on his quilted gambeson, Kel fit and buckled the leg plates of his armor. Piece by piece they went, Kel snugging the leather straps comfortably, checking the fit of each plate with him before they went on to the next.

"If it were Jerel alone, I'd stick to the padded stuff, not all this clank," Raoul said as he raised his arms for the breastplate. "He knows exhibition rules. But Myles says a couple of charmers from Tusaine are threatening to give me a try. And one of the conservatives has put it about that he'll bash my head in because I, oh, what was that phrase? Encouraged your pretensions, that's it."

"Then I should fight him, sir" Kel tightened a buckle.

"Nonsense. I'll ram some manners into him and tell the king I can't attend the banquet because I pulled a muscle." When Kel didn't reply, Raoul gripped her shoulder and waited until she met his eyes. "Please don't deny me my fun," he said with a smile. "Conservatives haven't found the, er, courage to joust against me in years. Now they'll come out of the woodwork. They think the gods will withdraw their favor from me because I picked you. Haven't you ever noticed that people who win say it's because the gods know they are in the right, but if they lose, it wasn't the gods who declared them wrong? Their opponent cheated, or their equipment was bad."

Kel grinned. She had heard something like that.

"And the money I win from them in penalties will buy armor for you. That's rather fitting, don't you think?"

It *was* fitting, put that way. Kel still shook her head at him. What could she say? He clearly loved to joust; just as clearly he hated the artificiality of the progress. Who was she to deny him some entertainment? When he let go, she picked up a pauldron, or shoulder piece. "Left arm, sir," she told him. Obediently Raoul lifted the requested limb.

Kel watched the jousting from the field itself, where she waited in case Raoul needed her. Cleon, Merric, and Owen kept her company. For the first time in her life she saw knights and squires vie against one another with a variety of weapons.

Competitions like this served more than one purpose. They gave knights who did not live in troubled areas a way to keep their battle skills sharp. Squires got a chance to hone their fighting techniques in a warlike setting. A squire who won combats might earn enough in prize money and penalties against the loser to buy horses and outfit himself and his mount. Monarchs and nobles who spent their time at court could see which of the country's warriors possessed unusual ability and courage: such warriors might be invited to guard the kingdom for the Crown. Nobles settled quarrels at tournaments as an alternative to blood feuds that might last for generations. Noble families showed off marriageable daughters, and the people saw another aspect of the monarchs.

Until nearly ten years ago tournaments, with their padded, guarded weapons and elaborate ceremonies, were seen as interesting but useless exhibitions of old-fashioned skills and a risk to the lives and limbs of those who competed. Then the immortals began to reappear in the human realm. Suddenly tournaments were vital, a way to find those who could best protect the realm. Kel wasn't sure that she liked these contests with their possibilities for injury. At the same time she knew how important this practice was. She gave up trying to decide how she felt and simply prayed that no one got hurt.

Raoul and Jerel of Nenan had their exhibition match. Raoul knocked his friend from the saddle easily. That afternoon he beat one of the two knights from Tusaine, unhorsing him even more swiftly than he had Jerel. A conservative challenged him, Wayland of Darroch. He remained in the saddle after the first charge; Raoul's lance broke. On the second charge Wayland's lance shattered. On the third pass Raoul knocked the conservative from the saddle and collected fifteen gold crowns from him.

"In the old days you could keep the armor and horse of the man you beat," Owen said to Kel. Living in Tortall his whole life, he had seen plenty of tournaments. "Now, though, most people would druther pay in coin."

"It's simpler," Cleon replied absently. It was his second comment of the afternoon, the first being, "Hello."

Raoul went to his tent to drink a pitcher of water and change his clothes, Kel following while Owen and Cleon stayed to watch more contests. Once Raoul left for a bath, Kel hung out his sweat-soaked garments and went to Drum. Lerant was there already. Drum was spotless, testimony to a long grooming. Kel met Lerant's possessive glare with a friendly nod and cleaned the horse's tack. Lerant might think they competed for Raoul's time, but Kel knew better. Her relationship to her knight-master was simply different from, not better than, the standard-bearer's.

The next day she and Raoul did the same tournament routine. She watched him alone as Owen and Cleon entered other competitions. Kel had no interest in risking her own bones to prove her skill. She was content to wait on her knight-master.

She watched the second Tusaine knight tilt against Raoul and lose, wincing in pity every time Raoul's lance smashed into his foe's shield. It looked as painful as she knew it felt. She could have warned Raoul's challengers, but they didn't think to ask her.

Stigand of Fenrigh also lost: he was carried off the field. Once they returned to their tents, Raoul dispatched Kel to check on him.

Duke Baird, chief of the royal healers, was in Stigand's tent. Though the servants refused to talk to Kel, Baird did after he left his patient. "A cracked skull, that's all," Neal's father told Kel. "You'd think it was a thrust to his heart, the way he carried on. He'll be fit to ride in the morning."

"I didn't think anything could open up Stigand's head," Raoul said when Kel brought the news back to him. "It just shows, miracles still happen."

Once Raoul was napping and his armor was clean, Kel went to visit the Yamani ladies. They served her green tea, played with the sparrows and Jump, inquired after the griffin back in Kel's tent, and talked. Finally Shinkokami stood and asked, "Anyone for a game of fan toss?"

"I haven't played in years," Kel demurred, but she followed the Yamanis outside.

Shinko produced a fan, offering it to Kel. The *shukusen* was as heavy as she remembered, cherry-red silk on thin, elegantly pierced steel ribs that were dull at the base, razor sharp on the ends. Kel opened the fan, thought a prayer, and tossed it up, giving it a spin to flip it over. She caught it, the base thunking neatly into her palm.

"See?" asked Yuki. "Your body remembers."

"My body also remembers days in the saddle in the rain," Kel said, straight-faced. "That doesn't mean I like it." The ladies hid their smiles, but their eyes crinkled with amusement. They liked Kel's humor.

The four young women formed a circle on the grass outside Shinko's tent. They started by throwing the fan low. Kel missed the proper flip twice, sending the open fan edge-first into the ground. She retrieved and cleaned it, hiding embarrassment while the ladies hid smiles.

On they played, throwing the fan a little higher each time it completed a circuit of the group. It looked like a giant scarlet butterfly as it turned and spun in the air. The Yamani ladies were as graceful as dancers, Shinkokami in a pink kimono for the afternoon, Yuki in pale blue, Lady Haname in cream with bamboo printed in green. Kel didn't try to be as graceful. She stood well braced, her eyes on that whirling crimson silk. At last she found the rhythm and was catching it one-handed herself.

When they had it ten feet in the air, Shinko gave the Yamani command, "the blossom opens." Now they could throw to anyone in the circle. The fan went from one to another, the players speeding up until it was a crimson blur. Shinko called the word for "sinking sun." They slowed. Now they dipped as they caught the fan, whipped it around both hands, then dipped again before wafting it to the next player. They had a chance to breathe, and the slower pace was a different kind of exercise.

"This is the prettiest thing I've ever seen," Kel heard Neal remark. "May I play?" He stepped among them to catch the fan. There was no time to stop him. The women gasped—and Neal caught the *shukusen* base down. He nearly dropped it, not expecting the weight of steel.

"What *is* this thing?" he demanded, staring at the fan with wide green eyes.

Yuki walked over to him. "There is a saying in the Islands," she told him stiffly. "Beware the women of the warrior class, for all they touch is both decorative and deadly." Taking the fan, she went to a pile of tent poles and picked one up. She carried it back to Neal, unfurled the fan with a snap, and slashed the open edge across the pole. A piece of wood dropped to the ground. She folded the fan with another snap and entered the princess's tent.

Shinkokami and Lady Haname followed her, bowing politely to Neal as they passed, their eyes crinkled with hidden laughter. Neal still had not recovered from the sight of the pretty fan slicing the pole like sausage.

Kel patted his back. "Don't worry," she said. "Yuki cools off pretty quickly."

Neal looked at her. "She's angry?"

"I think you frightened her," Kel replied. "You frightened *me*. Meathead." She cuffed him lightly. "Didn't your mother teach you not to grab things? You could have lost all of your fingers. I doubt your father, good as he is, could put them back on."

"What *was* that?" Neal demanded.

"A *shukusen*—a lady fan," Kel told him. "If a lady thinks she's in danger, but doesn't want to complicate things by openly carrying a weapon, she takes a *shukusen*."

"I want one," the queen said. Kel looked around. They had gathered an audience during their game. It included her majesty, Buri, some local ladies who looked appalled or fascinated, and a stocky female a head shorter than Kel. She wore a dark blue silk tunic over a white linen shirt, full blue silk trousers, and calf-high boots. A sword and dagger hung at her belt: they looked expensive and well used. Coppery hair brushed her shoulders; she regarded Kel with violet eyes.

Kel swallowed. Alanna the Lioness, King's Champion, Baroness of Pirate's Swoop and heir of Barony Olau, gave her the tiniest of nods, then walked into the crowd.

Kel took a breath, remembering Queen Thayet's comments. "I'm sure the princess would be glad to have one made for you, your majesty."

"I'm going to ask right now," the queen said. She entered the princess's tent.

"You could have said the Lioness was here!" Kel whispered to Neal.

"Well, *I'm* here, aren't I? And I didn't exactly have the chance," he pointed out dryly. "We just rode in. Since when do *you* call me Meathead?"

"Since you act like one," retorted Kel. "Let's find something to drink. I'm parched." She dragged him to the food vendors' tents as the crowd broke up.

eleven

CLEON

*T*he progress crawled south, then east. Kel discovered far more was planned than the introduction of the heir's foreign bride-to-be and the production of noble spectacles. At the heart of every camp was a complex of tents where work was done: a new census, a survey of roads for a new, up-to-date map, and a study of local laws and medicines.

The progress also gave the Crown a means to discipline noble houses that had proved trouble-some in the past. Fiefs Tirragen, Malven, Eldorne, and Sinthya all were invited to host the monarchs at extremely expensive banquets. Raoul, Kel, and two squads of Third Company got to carry those invitations to less-than-happy recipients.

On the road to Eldorne to deliver one such message, Kel asked, "Why do these fiefdoms have to pay? I thought the king's careful not to burden the people he visits."

"Except to create an example," Raoul explained. "Gary—Gareth the Younger—calls it 'obedience through poverty.' See, Jon's grandfather, King

Jasson, started it when his wars doubled the realm's size. He let most conquered nobles keep their lands. To make sure they would be good boys and girls, he went on progress and made them pay for everything. When he was done, they couldn't afford handkerchiefs, let alone raise money to rebel. Jonathan is being restrained. He hopes that with just the knowledge of these four draining their treasuries to host us, others who might try the same thing will reconsider." He glanced at Kel. "It isn't just that a girl is a squire or that Joren got a fine for kidnapping a servant. We're all part of a quiet war that's taking place across the Eastern Lands." To Lerant on his other side he said, "If your grandfather Eldorne waxes too outraged, tell him Barnesh in Maren is cancelling *all* of his nobles' royal land grants. They have to petition him to retain their titles and estates, and they get to pay through the nose."

Lerant winced.

They delivered their remaining letters, then rejoined the progress near Fief Eldorne. Once again the train had set a proper camp under the Seneschal's direction: they would be there for several days. Kel could see that preparations for a new tournament were underway. Riding to their part of the camp, she and Raoul wove in and out of a seemingly endless stream of servants, workmen, and vendors, all carrying burdens.

Raoul reined up to let a group pass them in wagons loaded with wood for building grandstands. "Kel, when do you want to start taking part in tournaments?"

The griffin snapped at Kel as she absently preened him with her fingers. *"No,"* she said firmly, smacking him lightly on the beak. "My lord, it seems a waste of time. Let's face it, I haven't beaten you, and I know your work in the saddle better than anyone's. If I'm going to risk breaking my neck, I'd like to do it when I have a chance to win."

Raoul began to chuckle. "Kel, I haven't been unhorsed in, Mithros, a decade." He grinned at her. "I was born with lead in my behind, I know what I can do and what I can't, and every buck who thinks he knows the lance comes to try me sooner or later. Before you start thinking you're no good, get some other opponents."

It occurred to Kel that after her father, Raoul was the nicest man she'd known. He did his best by her, spoke honestly, and never treated her as anything but an equal.

"Maybe so," she replied. "But I'll pick my time." The griffin looked up at her and shrilled. "Hungry again," Kel said wearily. "He eats more than I do, and at least I'm getting bigger."

"So will he," Raoul told her. "Wait till you see an adult up close."

"If it's not trying to kill me, I'll look all I can," Kel replied.

They settled into the life of the progress. Kel practiced her weapons with her knight-master and other squires at stops. In camp she resumed glaive training with the queen, the Yamanis, her mother, and Buri. On tournament days she tended Raoul's armor and weapons. She also made sure Lerant beat her in races to tend Drum after jousting, though she never let the jealous standard-bearer know that she let him win or that she liked the help. It never seemed to occur to him that with a griffin to mind, it was to her advantage to let him cover some of a squire's traditional jobs.

She continued to refuse offers to compete. Raoul did it because he was challenged to fight at every stop and didn't mind showing people that his reputation was well earned. Kel was happy just to assist him and cheer when he rode Drum onto the tilting field.

The weeks of social engagements were blurring together in Kel's mind when the progress reached Fief Sinthya. She had already been here to deliver the monarchs' "request" that its master, a boy of nine, and his mother, who had been spared the old lord's fate when his treason was uncovered, put a lavish meal before their hosts. Kel was so used to the banquet routine that her mind was on other things as she carried the finger bowl and towel to Lord Raoul's table. As she offered them to his female companion, she looked into violet eyes.

Kel dropped the bowl, splattering Lady Alanna's indigo skirts and Lord Raoul's spruce green hose. "I'm sorry," Raoul said wickedly as Kel mopped up the spill. "Should I have warned you?"

Kneeling on the ground, Kel saw Alanna kick Raoul in the shin. "Don't tease," the Champion ordered. "Yes, you should have warned her." To Kel she added, her voice barely audible, "Relax. It's the only way I can say hello without a hundred people saying I put a good-luck spell on you."

Kel mumbled something; she didn't know what. Bowing, she retreated to the service room for a fresh towel and bowl.

"What's this?" demanded Master Oakbridge, pressing cool, dry hands to her cheeks and forehead. "You are warm, and unusually clumsy. Are you ill?" Kel shook her head. For someone who fussed over the problems she presented, being neither a proper young lady or a proper squire, Master Oakbridge could be irritably kind. "If you are ill, tell me. You have no notion of how a summer cold can travel in a group of people like this."

"Thank you, sir, I'm fine." Kel accepted a new bowl and towel from a servant. "I was just surprised by my lord's dinner partner, that's all."

"But surely you've met," Oakbridge said, tugging her tunic until it was straight. Kel shook her head. "Well, she's not demanding, so relax," he ordered her. "At least no one can claim she's magicking you to succeed, not with half the folk here being mages. Go. They'll bring the first course up before you know it. Don't forget you have four people to wait on."

She did, Kel saw as she returned: Harailt of Aili, dean of the royal university and one of Kel's favorite civilians, shared the table; Lady Haname was his companion. "Forgive me, Master Harailt, Lady Haname," Kel said, presenting the bowl to them in turn. "I don't know what came over me."

They assured her that no offense was taken, and

returned to an enthusiastic discussion of Yamani farming.

Kel returned to the service room and took up the first dish, leeks and ginger in almond milk. She served it to all four adults without spilling a drop. "I understand you have the care of a griffin," Alanna remarked, looking out over the room.

"Yes, Lady Knight," Kel replied softly. "Daine is trying to find his family now."

"Doesn't his care cut into your training?" asked the lady, tasting the puree delicately. "They need to be fed quite often, don't they? And they are more like wild creatures than pets." She nodded at Kel's hands, which were a tapestry of scratches and scars.

"He's wild, yes," Kel admitted. "But we get along."

They spoke of innocent things. If anyone overheard, Alanna's questions were those anyone might ask. She was well informed about Kel's weapons skills and training. She even knew about the morning glaive practice and Kel's years in the Islands.

When Kel presented the last finger bowl and the Champion rinsed her hands, she smiled at Kel. "Once you're knighted, perhaps you could teach me to use this glaive," she suggested. "It sounds like a good all-purpose weapon."

Kel walked to the service hall glowing. The lady took it for granted that Kel would win her shield. *She wants* me *to teach her!* Kel thought, elated. She picked up a tray with cups and a pitcher of cordial. *Me, teach the Lioness—who could have dreamed?*

Alanna had gone when Kel returned. Now she

sat with the king, talking to young Lord Sinthya. "Was that so bad?" Raoul asked, pushing back from his chair.

"You could have warned me," Kel said reproachfully.

"I should have," he admitted, looking sheepish. "I'm just used to you taking whatever comes without a blink. It never occurred to me you might need a warning."

Once they were released from banquet service, Kel ate a late supper with her friends among the squires, including Owen, Neal, Merric, and Cleon. Usually some of them walked her back to her tent to watch the griffin's last feeding of the day. They kept a respectful distance as they looked on. None of them wanted to risk a griffin attack just because Kel's charge might scratch or bite him. Instead they fed treats to the sparrows and played with Jump as they talked with Kel.

Another thing all of them did was try to keep Owen's spirits up. "It's terrible," he said that night at Fief Sinthya as he scratched Jump's tattered ears. "I had no idea most knights think having a squire is a pain. I just want to train as a bandit killer, but either the ones who like that have squires, or they say a squire will slow them down. Do you know what Master Oakbridge said?" he demanded, indignant. "He said Myles of Olau wants a secretary. A paper shuffler! And Sir Myles—well, he's a good fellow, even if he's forever saying chivalry is unrealistic and too hard on us, but honestly! I'll never get any field experience with him, unless it's in skulking and sneaking and invisible inks." He looked at his friends, woebegone. "I have to take it. This business of being unattached is worse than shuffling papers. Master Oakbridge makes me run errands and draw seating charts until I think I'll go mad."

"At least Myles won't bite your head off if you venture a comment of your own," Neal said gloomily, tickling the queen sparrow Crown on the chest. "There's a lot to be said for a good-natured knight-master."

"Mine's a decent sort," Cleon remarked without looking at Kel. "Explains things, doesn't expect you to read his mind. I'd best get back. He's in the archery competitions tomorrow, and I think his bowstring's fraying." It was a signal for all of the boys to wander off into the night.

Kel settled the animals and changed into her nightdress, feeling low. And why? Cleon hadn't tried to kiss her or get her alone. He hadn't made excuses to linger after the others left. That was good. It saved her from hurting his feelings. Had he followed up on that kiss, she would have been forced to tell him that she was concentrating on her knighthood alone. That would be awkward, unpleasant, depressing.

I suppose the kiss didn't mean anything to him, Kel told herself, not for the first time. Or he's got a proper girl to admire, someone pretty and small, with big eyes, and hands not all clawed and scarred by an ungrateful immortal she dislikes.

It doesn't matter, she thought as she lay awake

that night. I didn't like his flirting with me anyway.

"Yap all you like, dog." That cold voice stopped Kel as she wound between rows of tents, returning from the ladies' privy. "But a cur dog is all your house whelps. It's only a matter of time before you turn on the hand that feeds you."

"Lord Raoul doesn't think so." That was Lerant of Eldorne's voice. Kel frowned.

"Goldenlake is a dolt without two thoughts in his head," the cutting voice said. "He's shames his blood, consorting with sand scuts"—the scornful name for the Bazhir—"and wenches and sprigs of traitorous trees like *you*."

Kel heard a thud. She moved up closer until she could peer around an open tent flap to see. Three young men stood over the fallen Lerant of Eldorne. Two wore swords and the silver-rimmed tunic badges of knights: one with the flail and sword of Fief Groten, the other with Tirrsmont's spear and fist badge. The third was Joren of Stone Mountain, icily handsome in Paxton's colors.

The man with Groten's badge spoke to the Tirrsmont knight and Joren. It was his voice that Kel had heard. "As I said, our leaders are purblind, dazzled by female flesh and foreign wiles. They shelter traitors," he pointed to Lerant, who wiped blood from his mouth, "and drag those of the noblest blood," he bowed slightly to Joren, "before a magistrate like common highwaymen." To Lerant he said, "Too bad you can't demand satisfaction in the lists, Eldorne, but you're the degenerate son of a degenerate line. Your sire knew you'd be chewed up and spit out by the Chamber of the Ordeal if you got there. *Its* power at least remains uncorrupted."

Lerant tried to stand. The knight from Fief Groten shoved him down.

"We couldn't afford a knight's gear, that's why I didn't become a page," Lerant growled. He spat blood onto Groten's boot. "Why don't we settle this with swords?"

"Because you're neither knight nor squire," Groten told Lerant. "You're just something to wipe on." He smeared his boot across Lerant's tunic.

Kel stepped into the open. "You speak against our knight-master. You must be shown the error of your ways," she said. "And Joren's no highwayman, just a kidnapper." She offered Lerant a hand without taking her eyes from his tormentor. "If it's the lists you want, you shall have them. I am a squire, and I want satisfaction from you." The time-honored phrases of the challenge came from her lips with a sense of strength that grew with each word. Do mages feel like this when they chant spells? wondered Kel.

"I can defend myself!" Lerant snapped, shoving her hand away.

"I'm not concerned about you," Kel said. "For starters, he maligned Lord Raoul. If he weren't a coward, he'd also name those he says are 'dazzled by female flesh'—my flesh? Commander Tourakom's? Or the Champion's, or the queen's, do you suppose? Since he doesn't want to pay for his words, he hides behind his shield. Except now he can't. If he refuses to meet me in the lists, everyone will know what he is."

"I am Sir Ansil of Groten," snapped the knight. He was a grim-faced man in his thirties with eyes like polished stones. "You will have your meeting, *squire*. When you lie in the dirt with my lance through your body, all will see what happens when *men* do the right thing. Tomorrow, at the individual matches. I will enter our names with the tournament clerk."

He stalked away, Joren and the Tirrsmont knight trailing him. Joren looked back once to smirk at Kel.

"Don't growl at me anymore," Kel told Lerant. "That had to be done, and he wasn't going to give you a chance."

"He would if I slapped him," Lerant retorted. "He'd have no choice, then."

"All right—when I'm done, slap him and have your fight," Kel said wearily. A whiff of fish rising from her belt pouch made her grimace. "I have to feed the griffin." She headed for her tent.

Lerant followed her. "He says he'll kill you."

"If he does, then the gods don't want women to be knights. Isn't that how trial by combat works?" Did she have everything for a proper tilt? she wondered, reviewing her list of armor. Raoul had added pieces to it before they left the palace.

"My lord will be angry," Lerant pointed out.

"Why? He said he wanted me to compete in the tournaments. Look." Kel turned to face Lerant. They were of a height, Kel now five foot ten. She met his angry brown eyes. "I have things to do if I'm to fight him, so let me go do them." She walked away.

She was washing her hands after feeding the griffin when Cleon walked into her tent. "Kel, they just put your name up for tomorrow's jousting lists," he said, running his fingers through his red curls. He ignored Jump and the sparrows, who were trying to get his attention. "Against Ansil of Groten. Tell me—" He stopped in mid-sentence, looking her over. "It's true, isn't it? You challenged a full knight—you, a second-year squire."

Kel tried a smile. It didn't feel as confident as she would have liked. "Oh, well, I had to," she replied. "The man's a bully. He insulted my lord."

Her tent had never felt this small before. She liked mathematics, her mind babbled. It was impossible for there to be less room inside a tent with just her and Cleon there than there was when Merric, Neal, and Owen were present as well. Her brain was rattling. In a moment she would start to babble out loud. Instead Kel began to refill the sparrows' seed dishes. She needed to do something with her hands.

"He's asking a winner's purse of ten gold crowns," said Cleon gravely.

"I have that money from Joren. I can pay if I lose." *When* I lose, she thought as she put out the filled dishes. She glanced at Cleon, then looked down. It always surprised her to see him in her family's colors of blue, cream, and gray, wearing the Mindelan gray owl crest.

She knew she ought to find something else to do with her hands, but she looked at Cleon again. He looked good in those colors. Perhaps it wasn't the colors. Perhaps it was the way his shoulders filled out his cream linen shirt, or the way his chest pressed against his blue tunic.

She looked up: his eyes were on her. Warmth flooded Kel's body. Hurriedly she grabbed her breastplate and a polishing cloth. "I have to go over my gear," she mumbled.

Big hands tugged breastplate and cloth from her grip. Cleon put them aside and told Kel softly, "Was I wrong? I thought you liked it when I kissed you but you've avoided being alone with me ever since."

She hung her head. "Midwinter was, it was, nice," she said, cringing inside at her idiotic reply. It was very warm in the tent. "People would talk, if we—if they saw. They might not know it was friendly. They might get the wrong idea."

"Here I am, hoping one person will get the *right* idea," Cleon explained.

Even with her eyes on her shoes, Kel could see his legs; he stood that close. His clothes smelled of orris. The warmth of his body spread to envelop her. "If someone sees . . . ," she whispered.

"Jump, close the flap, there's a good fellow," Cleon said. The dog obeyed immediately.

"That isn't what I meant," Kel protested. Where was Raoul? If he were in his tent next door, he might hear and interrupt. Obviously Jump and the sparrows weren't going to stop whatever was going on, she thought wildly. As chaperons they were useless if they liked the person who was confusing her so. "I meant we shouldn't be, you know, *alone*," she said, dry-mouthed.

"Please look at me, Kel," Cleon asked.

She was ready to refuse, but he'd said "please." It would be churlish not to look up, so she did, meeting his gray eyes with her hazel ones. He was smiling. That was a dirty trick. It was impossible to remind him she was a fellow squire, sexless, when he smiled with so much liking that her insides melted. He lowered his head just a few inches to press his mouth to hers.

Oh, my, thought Kel.

He took his lips away. "That wasn't too bad, was it?"

She was glad to hear his voice crack. She wasn't a complete dolt if this upset him, too.

"Neither of us turned into anything awful," Cleon went on hoarsely, "the tent didn't collapse, even the animals are quiet."

Kel looked around. All eyes—the sparrows', Jump's, the griffin's—were on them. "I . . . ," she began, not sure what to say.

Cleon wrapped big hands around her elbows, leaned in, and touched his mouth to hers once more. Kel gasped, then forgot almost everything else as Cleon drew her snugly against him.

A mocking voice sounded in her mind. It was Joren's, from a talk they'd once had on the palace wall. "You'd make a fine wife for one of those big fellows—Cleon, for instance. You could settle down and raise young giants." Kel stiffened.

Cleon released her instantly. "What's wrong?" he asked. "You have to say if I push too hard. I've just been thinking about this for such a long time—"

"You have?" Kel asked shakily.

"Remember the night you took me to your room to give me a letter for Mindelan, since your brother and I were going that way?" Cleon grinned. "I wanted to kiss you then, but your maid and her friend were there."

"Oh," Kel whispered. I sound stupid, she thought, furious with herself for saying doltish things and for blinking at him like a thunderstruck deer. I had plenty to say to that Groten swine, she thought. Lerant, too.

Cleon kissed her again.

"Kel?" Raoul called. He sounded close. "Are you here?"

They sprang apart like startled rabbits. By the time Raoul entered Kel's tent through the flap that connected it to his own, Cleon sat on the cot, offering seed to Crown, as Kel finger-groomed the griffin.

"It's Cleon of Kennan, isn't it?" Raoul asked Cleon, who got to his feet and nodded. Raoul continued, "Aren't you two hot with the flap closed? Kel, someone put your name on the boards for tilting tomorrow."

"That's right," Kel replied as she went to open her front flap. "I had a philosophical discussion with Ansil of Groten. We couldn't resolve our differences, so we decided to settle it with the lance." Like a page's excuse for having a black eye—"I fell down"—philosophical differences were always to blame for a quarrel settled in a joust.

"Well, come into my tent when you have a moment," Raoul said. "We've some points to discuss. Kennan." He saluted the older squire and went back into his tent.

It was a dismissal, albeit a polite one. Cleon frowned. "You *have* to do this?"

"Yes," Kel replied firmly. "If you'd been there, you'd agree." She met his eyes, willing him to look at her, to see she was also Squire Kel, not just his friend Kel, not just the girl he had kissed.

"Oh, blast," Cleon said ruefully, hooking his hands in his belt. "I've jousted five times already since this progress began." Meeting Kel's eyes, he tried to smile and put the lie to the worry in his face. "Shall I wait for you here afterward? I'll wear a yellow silk tunic and a crown of willow leaves, and carry a bottle of horse liniment to salve your wounds."

The image of him thus dressed and equipped made Kel giggle helplessly. She stopped only when Cleon pulled her into a corner invisible to passersby and kissed her again. Then he strode out of the tent. Kel pressed her fingers to lips that throbbed from this new and different use. Finally she went to see Raoul, Jump and the sparrows following in her wake.

Raoul sat at his camp table with a pitcher of juice and two cups. He motioned to the second chair. Obediently Kel sat.

For a long moment Raoul scratched Jump's ear. At last he said, "I hear this from women of the Queen's Riders, the ones who want to command. Men who join the Riders are able to fight alongside females, or they don't last. But what the women say is that if they take Rider men as lovers, and it's found out, they encounter trouble. Men who dislike their orders offer to work it out in bed. Jealousies spring up, particularly if the woman and the man are in the same Rider group. If the woman is in command and the man isn't, they're both mocked by other men, and the woman gets treated like a trollop."

Kel looked down. "Sir—"

"Nobody makes men surrender private life when they take up arms, Kel," Raoul said, filling their cups. "We only ask that such lives happen off duty. It's more complicated for women. It's not fair, but I think you already know the world isn't."

Kel nodded, sipping grape juice. How many knight-masters would have done this differently, even hurtfully? How many would have said nothing until Kel was so deeply in a mess that she would never get out of it? Only Raoul would treat it as another lesson in the intricacies of command.

"I understand, sir," Kel told him. "I do know there could be problems."

Raoul fiddled with his cup. "As for issues of the body—sex, pregnancy, and so on—perhaps you should discuss those with a woman." He cleared his throat. "If you *want* to discuss them with me, it is my responsibility—"

"No, no!" Kel interrupted, alarmed. She didn't know which of them would be more embarrassed. She didn't want to find out. "I'll ask Mama, truly I will!"

Raoul grinned at her, his cheeks redder than

usual. "Oh, good. I'd probably make a botch of it. I've talked with young men, of course, but even that's been rare. Usually by the time I get them they know where babies come from.

"Now, Ansil of Groten. He's a hesitater. Right when he should set for his impact, he flinches. You can use that."

After that night's service Kel visited her mother. They had talked about lovers and pregnancy, how these things happened, and how important it was to decide if she wanted children when she chose to bed a man. Still, then it had been all theoretical. With Cleon looming in her mind's eye, she wanted her mother's practical advice.

The gods were with her: Ilane of Mindelan was alone in the tent she shared with Kel's father, Piers. She looked up from the book she was reading and smiled at her youngest daughter. "This is lovely," she said as they kissed one another on the cheek. "I haven't had you to myself in ages. How goes all?"

Kel feared that if she didn't blurt the problem out right away, she might lose courage later. The story spilled from her lips in a muddle, one that Ilane needed a few questions to straighten out.

"Well!" she said finally, sitting back in her chair. "You're in a unique position, I'd say."

Kel had thought of several descriptions for her problem, but "unique position" was not one of them. "How so?" she asked.

"Why, most young noblewomen don't have your freedom," replied Ilane. "Our families are so determined to keep their bloodlines pure that they insist their daughters remain virgins before marriage, poor things. You don't see that nonsense in the middle and lower classes. They know a woman's body belongs to herself and the Goddess, and that's the end of it."

Kel was trying to remember if she'd ever heard the matter put in quite this fashion. She hadn't.

Ilane leaned her chin on her hand. "I've often thought the nobility's handling of sex and marriage in their girls is the same as that of horse breeders who try to keep their mares from being mounted by the wrong stallions."

Kel sat bolt upright. "Mama!" Hearing such things in her mother's deep, lovely voice made them even more shocking. She expected this kind of phrasing from her male friends, not her mother.

"You can't say this to noblemen, of course." Ilane got up and went to the small fire that burned in front of the tent. "Tea?"

Kel automatically stood to get the cups. Before she realized she didn't know where they were, her mother had placed a small table between the chairs and was setting out all she would need. Kel sank into her chair. "Why can't this be said to men?"

"The good ones are too romantic to like it, and the bad ones don't care. My papa was the don't-care sort. I overheard him once describing me to a potential suitor. Even though I had small breasts, he said, my hips were big enough that I should foal with ease. It would be easy to find a milk nurse once I dropped a healthy son." Ilane deftly put a tiny scoop of powdered green tea in each of the large, handle-less cups, then added water from the iron Yamani pot. She took up the whisk, beating Kel's tea, then her own, into a green froth. They bowed to one another Yamani-style, then sipped.

Kel sighed with gratitude: she loved freshly made green tea. She enjoyed another sip, then asked, "So what's my unique position?"

"Since you've decided against a noble marriage, you may bed whoever you like," Ilane replied. "You can *choose*, Kel. If you and Cleon want to go to bed, you can."

Goose bumps rolled down Kel's arms. "But I don't want to choose anything like that! I want my shield—I've given up everything for it. And—" She remembered how it had felt, knowing that she cared about Cleon. It had thrilled *and* frightened her. "I don't want to be distracted," she admitted, feeling small with guilt. It seemed selfish, put that way. "I don't think I want to bed anyone, Mama. We were just kissing, that's all."

"Kissing may lead to more serious things, my darling," Ilane said, cupping Kel's cheek in one cool, long-fingered hand. "A girl may be carried away. It's not always love. Lust may feel wonderful enough to be mistaken for love."

"I just want my shield," Kel whispered. "I'll deal with the rest later. The—complications."

"Perhaps you should see a healer," Ilane suggested. "Get a charm to keep you from pregnancy, until you're certain you'd like to be a mother. Then, if you do get carried away, you can surrender to your feelings." Ilane grinned wickedly. "Goddess knows your father and I did."

Kel gulped. She did not want to think of her parents getting carried away. "Well, I certainly don't want babies," she admitted when she could speak again. "But if you think I should get the charm, I will."

Ilane shook her head. "Think about it for yourself. Then decide."

They were finishing their tea when her father strode into the tent. He was a short, stocky man who stood only as tall as his wife's shoulder, a man with Kel's own brown hair and dreamy hazel eyes. Just now there were no dreams in his eyes, but crackling awareness. "Kel!" he snapped. "You're jousting against Ansil of Groten?"

"What?" cried Ilane, sitting bolt upright.

Kel let a little sigh escape. More explanations—just what she needed.

Fall–Midwinter,
in the 18th year of the reign
of
Jonathan IV and Thayet, his Queen,
457

❧ twelve ❦

TOURNAMENT

*T*he night crept by. Kel lay awake, listening to the noises of the progress, until she finally dozed sometime before dawn. She slept late for one of the few times in her life. It wasn't Raoul's preparations for his day that roused her, or the activity of those neighbors whose tents were pitched on the same "street," but the searing pain of sharp claws digging into her head. Kel sat up with a yelp, wide awake, as the griffin clutched her scalp harder still. Jump barked, the birds shrilled, and Raoul shoved through the flap between their tents.

"Kel—Mithros help us," Raoul said.

Kel reached up and closed her hands on feathers and steely muscle. The griffin let go of the hair he gripped so energetically with his forepaws and clamped his beak on her finger. He kicked at her scalp with his hind claws.

"I'll get his breakfast," Raoul said hurriedly, and ducked back into his tent. Kel gritted her teeth and patiently unhooked the griffin from her scalp. The bite on her finger wasn't so bad. The griffin had closed on muscle and bone, not a soft spot. She could endure that better than claws.

Once she had him captive, she got up and carried him over to his platform. The moment she let go, the griffin hissed and launched himself into the air, clumsily chasing sparrows around the tent. Kel swore under her breath. He had learned to fly at last.

By the time Raoul came back with food, Kel had created a leash from a strip of leather. While the griffin ate from his dish, something she had taught him several weeks before, she tied the leash around his leg. As soon as he finished, the griffin turned and bit the leather, severing it.

"Chain?" Raoul asked.

Kel shook her head. "He'll rust it like he did the cage. Let's see how well behaved he is." She felt the top of her head. It was tacky with blood.

Raoul took over, sponging away blood and applying the ointment Kel used on griffin wounds. She winced as it stung in the deep scratches, but didn't try to pull away. The ingredient that made it sting would clean the cuts. There was never any telling what was on his claws, so she scoured all the damage that he did to her with the strongest cleaning ointment she could find.

"He would pick today," Raoul said as he finished and wiped his hands. "Did you sleep at all?"

"Some," Kel said with a shrug.

"Well, get dressed and we'll have breakfast." Seeing she was about to refuse, Raoul shook his head. "You need a big meal now and a small one at noon," he informed her. "What's the point to a joust if you're too weak to last?"

Kel bowed to his experience and obeyed. The morning crawled by. So did the noon break in the tournament proceedings. At last, clad in tilting armor, a visored helm under one arm, Kel waited for the fighters ahead of her to finish their match.

It's a beautiful day for it, she thought as she squinted at the cloudless sky. Autumn was in the mid-September breeze off Lake Naxen, carrying brisk air that made the flags and pennants around the field crack.

A beautiful day to fly into the dirt, she thought ruefully. That wasn't important. Even if she lost, she'd have protested Sir Ansil's poison-spreading. She had to try. It might force him to look twice the next time he bullied a young man, though Lerant must never know that. She had told him she would defend Raoul's name so she wouldn't hurt the irritable standard-bearer's pride.

The field was clear. The chief herald, who instructed the jousters, rode toward Kel. Sir Ansil was at the other end of the field with his friends. Kel had banished hers, including her animals, to the stands. She wanted silence before the fight, time to sink into her Yamani self and prepare.

"You still mean to do this, Squire Keladry?" the herald asked.

"I do, sir," she replied calmly.

"Very well. You have three runs in which to knock your opponent from the saddle. This is considered a victory. If your lance breaks, and lances do, the field monitor will give you a new one. If your horse is lamed, you may either accept a mount provided by the Crown, or concede the victory to your opponent. If neither of you falls from the saddle in three runs, the judges"—he pointed to the box below the king's where they sat—"decide the victor from the strength of blows delivered and accuracy of hits. Do you understand me?" Kel nodded. "Then take your place in your designated lane. Listen for the trumpet to start." He rode off.

Kel rubbed Peachblossom's nose. "Let's scorch him, Peachblossom, what do you say?"

The big gelding stamped, ears pricked and alert. Kel gave her helmet to a field monitor, then mounted. Once she was in the saddle, she accepted her helm and put it on.

She wanted an extra advantage today, more than she'd had in training with Raoul or knights like Jerel. When the trumpet blared, she told Peachblossom, "Charge."

Muscles bunched under her. The gelding flew at his top speed down the dirt lane, hooves thundering in packed dust. For those brief seconds Kel felt like an army of one. She loved no one so much as her horse.

Down came her lance, aimed at Sir Ansil's shield. The long weapon was a feather in her hand. Ansil brought his lance down a breath behind Kel. He doesn't think I'm for true, she thought, her focus narrowing to her target. He doesn't think I'll hit.

She struck his shield dead-on; he struck hers. Her side went mildly numb. Her lance shattered; his didn't. She turned Peachblossom and rode to her start point. This time she checked the lance that was handed to her. She was suspicious of a lance that broke on the first strike.

"You needn't worry, squire," the field monitor assured her. "These is always under our eye. It'd mean a summer mendin' roads if we was bribed to pass a flawed lance."

Kel smiled at him, feeling better. She lowered her visor and urged Peachblossom to their place, her grip on the new lance steady. Ansil gulped water as his friends slapped his legs in congratulation. His destrier did not like their closeness and snapped at them. Like most lone knights, Ansil rode a stallion. Kel thought that was a mistake. Peachblossom was stallion-mean when he wished to be, and he would never take off after the scent of mare.

At last Ansil waved to his friends, rode to his place, and brought his visor down. He nodded to the chief herald, who gave the trumpeter his signal. As the call rang out, Kel told Peachblossom, "Charge." He exploded down the lane.

Kel rose in her stirrups, sure and calm. She had Ansil cold. She knew it from the position of her lance, from the feel of her saddle between her knees, and from the way the air rushed through her visor. Here came Ansil's fraction of hesitation Raoul had mentioned. Kel struck her foe hard. The coromanel on her lance point rammed just under his shield boss. She popped him from the saddle and sent him flying. The stallion reared, screaming, as Ansil smacked the ground in a clatter of plate armor.

Kel brought Peachblossom around and waited a safe distance from the stallion. She prayed she hadn't killed Ansil, though she was fairly sure she hadn't. Field monitors, including a healer, surrounded the fallen knight, removing his shield, helmet, and gauntlets. The healer peeled back an eyelid.

Ansil snarled and cuffed him aside. He sat up very slowly. Joren and the Tirrsmont knight helped him to his feet. He swayed, then waited, eyes on the ground, feet planted wide. Then he looked up. Seeing Kel, he walked toward her. She thought he might collapse when he ducked under the barrier, but he hung onto it until he collected himself.

When he reached Kel, he sneered up at her. "This proves nothing, wench."

Kel said icily, "That doesn't sound like what you're supposed to say, Groten. May I remind you that you just lost?"

"Had we swords—" he began.

"Do you think I don't know how to use a sword?" she wanted to know. "You lost. All those traditions you like tell you what comes now."

Ansil swallowed. "I repent me of the calumny you took from my words with regard to Lord Raoul," he began.

"I took nothing that wasn't there." Something had gripped Kel's tongue to make her most un-Yamani-ly frank. "You called my knight-master a dolt," she continued. "I accept that you wish you'd kept quiet. You called Lerant of Eldorne cur and traitor. You will apologize to him, before witnesses, or we shall return here tomorrow and you can test my skill with a sword. Understand?"

Ansil muttered something, until Kel thumped his shoulder lightly with the butt of her lance. He glared at her. "You won't live until the Ordeal," he snarled. "One of us will spear you through your bitch's heart. I will apologize to Eldorne—need you be a witness?"

"No," she said. "But make sure one of your witnesses tells me he saw and heard you do it, today." She turned Peachblossom, wanting to get away from this man and his poison. At her side of the field, she returned her lance to the monitor with thanks.

He gawped at her. "Is something wrong?" Kel asked, wondering if she had missed anything.

He shook his head and smiled oddly. "This is your first challenge, my lady?"

Kel nodded.

"Your first, and you *won*," the monitor told her. "Well rode, Lady Kel, well rode indeed."

Kel waved him off, embarrassed. Looking at the stands, she saw that Raoul stood with Sir Gareth the Younger. He was holding out a hand. The scowling Gareth counted coins into Raoul's palm.

"So he meant it," Kel murmured to Peachblossom. "He said he was going to win money on me." She hoped he wouldn't bet on her too often. How many times could she fight someone as overconfident and careless as Ansil? Other knights would learn from this. Probably next time she would be the one to fly.

She saw to Peachblossom first. Qasim offered to groom and feed him, but Kel wanted to do that. As she worked she murmured compliments to her wonderful horse. Only when she'd picketed him near enough to Hoshi to gossip but not so close that he could nip, did she return to her tent. There she stripped off her armor and plunged her head into a bucket of cold water. Feeling like herself again, she began to care for her things.

Cleon found her testing her lack of fear of heights in a tree overlooking the lake. "You could have been—gods, Kel, you've seen how jousters get hurt! I thought I could watch, I thought, she's just another squire, but when your lance went . . ." He shook his head.

"He was overconfident," she told him. "And I won, so the gods must have thought I was right. Otherwise they'd have made me lose. You know how trial by combat works."

"You won because you're good," he corrected her. "I find it hard to believe the gods sit forever about the Divine Realms betting on jousts and trials by combat." He looked around to make sure no one was within earshot. "At least come down and let me hold you, make sure you're in one piece," he called softly.

Kel shook her head. "You come up, and no holding. We have to talk about that."

The sparrows cheeped encouragement as he clambered out onto Kel's thick branch. When she repeated what Raoul had said, he nodded. "He's right. We should be careful about . . . anything that might happen. My sister had the same trouble. She's in the Riders," he explained. "I should have thought of that—and of your good name, for that matter."

"Have I got one?" Kel wanted to know.

"You do with your friends, and you'd better with anyone who talks to us," he said bleakly.

His tone made Kel look at him. Someone had said something, she realized. Someone, or many someones. *And my friends got in fights over it, but never told me.*

"I don't deserve my friends," she remarked quietly.

"Sure you do, opal of happiness," Cleon said. "We'd've failed mathematics to a man without you, for one thing."

That made her grin. A rolling grumble made her look at her belly. "I'm hungry," she remarked, surprised.

Cleon dropped to the ground. "Me too. Let's go eat, O queen of squires."

That evening as Kel ate with her friends, a servant gave her a note that bore the Tirrsmont coat of arms. Sir Voelden, who'd been with Ansil and Joren, invited her to joust the following day. This was a match, not a challenge in answer to insult—Kel refused it. That afternoon she had confirmed what she had always thought: jousting was serious business, not a game. As she and her friends left to return to camp, Voelden stopped them in Castle Naxen's inner courtyard. He slapped Kel lightly with a riding glove.

Cleon lunged for the knight with a snarl. Neal grabbed the big redhead. Jump seized Merric of Hollyrose's tunic before Merric could attack, while Owen hung on to Cleon with one hand and Merric with the other. Kel looked at Voelden, feeling cold inside. "I accept," she said quietly. "Ten gold crowns if you lose." As the challenged she could name the penalty.

Kel and Cleon wandered away from Neal, Owen, and Merric once they left Castle Naxen. It did no good. Every time they thought they were alone, others wandered by. They exchanged only two quick, clinging kisses in the shadows, jumping apart both times as people approached.

"It's like having a train of chaperons," Cleon grumbled as he walked Kel to her tent. "Does anyone go to bed here?"

They halted before Raoul's banner. "Bed is where I should be, with a griffin to feed and a challenge tomorrow," Kel pointed out.

Cleon looked around. The lane where Kel's and Raoul's tents stood was filled with nobles returning from the banquet. He sighed. "G'night, moon of my dreams. Send him flying tomorrow."

I hope I can, Kel thought, watching him trudge sadly off. Her nerves, fizzing pleasantly after those kisses, twitched: she faced an unknown knight in the afternoon.

The griffin was wide awake. Lion-like, he paced as Kel lit her lamps and opened a packet of smoked fish. He ate only half of his meal, did not even try to bite Kel, and flew-hopped between his platform and her cot as she cleaned up after him.

Suddenly he began to fly around the narrow confines of the tent, not stopping. The sparrows hid under the cot; Jump barked his objections. At last the griffin dropped onto his platform bed, curled up under spread and trembling wings, and went to sleep. The sparrows came out of hiding to stare at Kel.

"I have no idea," Kel said in response to their unspoken query. "Maybe he thinks he needs practice."

"Whatever that was, it looked really strange," Owen said. He stood in Kel's open tent flap.

Tired as she was, she smiled at him. He'd barely said a word around the others. "Come in," she invited.

Owen shook his head. "You need sleep. I just wanted to ask, could I help you arm up? Myles, he's a good fellow, but . . . It may be the only time I can arm someone for combat."

Though she would rather get ready alone, Kel wasn't coldhearted enough to resist that doleful face. She would feel the same in Owen's shoes. "Would you?" she asked. "I'd like it, if you wouldn't mind."

Owen brightened. "Mind? Not me! Really? You're sure? Wonderful! I'll see you at lunch!" He ran down the lane with a whoop.

Kel shook her head, smiling. She went to tell Raoul, since he'd helped her to arm for Ansil. He agreed to let Owen do it. Kel bade him goodnight, and returned to her quarters for a better night's sleep than she'd had the night before.

The next day Kel sent her friends away again, making them leave her and Peachblossom in the waiting area to watch the jousts that preceded theirs. Owen had done a good job of arming her. Now she settled her gauntlets and took a deep breath. The joust before hers had ended. Monitors cleared the lanes.

The herald in charge came to give Kel her instructions. He had gone and Kel was in the saddle when something ungainly and orange flapped over the stands and glided to the field. The griffin reached the end of Kel's tilting lane as she did, perching clumsily atop the wooden barrier. He panted, beak open, as he glared at Kel.

"Do you feel clever?" Kel demanded. "I thought you couldn't get out of the tent."

The griffin rose on his hind legs, fanned his wings, and voiced a screech that echoed the length and breadth of the tournament field. Kel shivered; the hair stood on the back of her neck. "Stop that," she ordered. "Behave. I mean it. Otherwise I'll chain you next time."

Sir Voelden was ready at the end of his lane. Kel lowered her visor and waited for the trumpet call. "Charge," she whispered to Peachblossom.

Voelden was more sure of himself than Ansil, but he was slower and heavier. Kel adjusted her grip and struck his shield squarely, just as his lance struck hers. They swerved and returned to their original ends of the field.

The griffin shrieked as Kel passed him, his cry ringing in the air. The people in the stands were so quiet that Kel heard alarm calls from distant jays and crows. The griffin had frightened the birds; he'd made Voelden's stallion rear; but Peachblossom's only response was to blow at the immortal as he went by.

In position, Kel waited. The trumpet called.

Peachblossom charged without Kel's saying a word. Rising in the saddle, she aimed at Voelden's shield and shifted to put more force behind her lance, a trick she had learned from Raoul. Voelden's shield ripped free of its straps and went flying. Something hit Kel's ribs like a hammer. She gasped for air. A man shouted, "Foul!" People roared in disapproval. What happened? she wondered, swaying in the saddle.

Peachblossom lunged at Voelden over the barrier. "No!" Kel whispered. She hauled on the reins, trying to breathe. "Peachblossom, curse you, stop it!" she yelled. The command emerged as a breathy squeak. She turned him and headed to their starting point, then checked her breastplate. There was a dimple the size of a fist under her heart. Voelden had tried to run her through.

Kel asked her field monitor for water and a fresh lance. It gave her time to catch her breath. She inhaled, refilling sore lungs, and wondered how to answer Voelden. Deliberately trying to kill an opponent unannounced was dishonorable.

"You can retire from the lists." The monitor passed her a fresh lance.

"Thank you, but no," Kel replied, trying to speak normally. She turned into her lane and waited.

The signal came; Peachblossom charged. Kel rose and braced herself. She angled her shield so Voelden couldn't slide his lance past it, and struck his shield hard. Her lance shattered; so did his. Kel rammed her shield forward and hooked it behind Voelden's. Slamming her body sideways behind the locked shields, she heaved. Voelden popped from his saddle to hit the ground.

The crowd roared and came to its feet.

Kel dismounted and walked over to him, drawing her sword. He hadn't moved. She flipped up his visor with her sword point and pressed the sharp tip to his nose.

"Yield," she advised, her voice even. "Or I carve my initial right there."

He raised gauntleted hands. "I yield."

Kel smiled coldly. "And they say conservatives can't learn."

She walked back to Peachblossom, her ribs making her wince as she ducked under the barrier. Rather than remount, she led Peachblossom back down the field. All around her she heard a chant, and raised her head. Groups of people in the stands were on their feet, crying, "Mindelan! Mindelan! Mindelan!"

Queen Thayet and a group of women that included Kel's mother bore her away despite her protests. Peachblossom would be groomed and watered, Thayet said firmly. Kel was to be quiet and await a healer's inspection. She worried about the griffin until her mother said he now sat on the peak of the queen's tent, having followed them.

Inside, efficient hands unbuckled her breastplate, removed her helmet, and stripped off her mail and gambeson. Her cotton shirt was peeled away to reveal a sweat-soaked breastband and a huge, spreading bruise on her right side. The women hissed in sympathy.

The healer laid gentle fingers on the bruise. Coolness radiated from her touch, easing the ferocious pain. "Nothing's broken," the healer told the queen. "The bones are bruised, but I can handle that." She rested a palm on Kel's bruise. "Don't fight me," she warned.

"My children don't fight healers," remarked Ilane, "or I'll know why."

Kel rolled her eyes. *"Mother,"* she said with disgust, "I haven't done that in *years*."

"Good," Ilane replied, unperturbed. "If you forget, there are plenty of fans here for me to whack you with."

Coolness turned into cold on her side. Painlessness sank into her abused ribs; Kel almost felt them pop in relief. "Ouch," she said as an unexpected sharp pain bit into her side.

"I was wrong; one rib is cracked. Hold still and be quiet," ordered the healer.

Kel stared at the canvas overhead until the healer made the bone whole. At last the woman stepped away. "Sleep, food," she ordered. "Sleep will probably come first."

Already Kel's eyelids were drooping. "The griffin," she murmured.

"I'll mind him." Daine's face appeared in Kel's view. "I need to see why he's so upset."

Kel nodded her understanding, and slept.

Kel returned to her tent late that night after she'd

eaten, still groggy. The sparrows were asleep for the night. Jump, who had found Kel as she ate, curled up under her cot. Only the griffin showed any desire to be awake. Standing on the ground rather than his platform home, he paced back and forth. If Kel hadn't been exhausted, she might have been kept awake by the soft padding of his feet. She had just enough will to remove her boots before she rolled herself up in a blanket and slept the night away.

The camp was nearly quiet when Kel rose. The monarchs had set a rest day with no special events. Once Kel had tended her animals and her gear, she decided a visit to the lake was in order. The griffin needed a bath.

Carrying him, she negotiated the narrow, grassy streets with ease. Everyone moved out of the way rather than risk touching the griffin. He ignored them, trying to groom himself with little success. At the lake Kel sought a large, flat stone she had noted when she and Cleon talked in the tree. There she set up her operation: Jump, drying cloths, a corked bottle with the mildest soap available, and jerky strips for bribes.

She was lowering the griffin into the water for a last rinse when he whirled and raced up her arms, digging into clothes and flesh as he climbed. Kel, half off the rock, yelped and clung desperately as the griffin rose to his hind feet on her back, fanning his wings so hard she felt the breeze. He shrilled, his voice rising and falling in a series of notes that made her skin creep. She scrabbled back from the edge and turned slowly. The griffin dug in, then leaped over Kel to stand on the rock, still voicing that eerie cry. Jump faced the land, growling deep in his throat, his one good ear flat. Kel sat up.

A huge, winged creature, its feathers brindled gold and black, spiraled down from the sky to land beside Kel's rock. A second creature the color of newly minted copper touched the ground ten yards behind the brindled one. Seated, they towered over Kel, the brindled griffin nearly seven feet tall at the shoulder, the coppery one six feet at the shoulder. Kel gulped. She was in very serious trouble with no Third Company or Daine to protect her.

She pulled the young griffin toward her. If these two had sensed him in their territory, they may have come to kill him or drive him off, as mortal predators did with intruders. She did not like their large claws and their cold gazes. Their eyes were intelligent, the brindled griffin's gold, the other's a darker copper than its feathers. If they were the griffin's parents, she was about to die. She only had her belt knife—their claws were longer than it was.

The young griffin screeched and struggled from Kel's hold, leaving long scratches on her arms and chest. He stood on the rock in front of her and rose to his hind legs, wings spread for balance. Kel stayed very still, not sure what was going on.

An eagle hurtled from the sky, landing between Kel's rock and the griffins with an undignified thud. It immediately began to change shape until a small form of Daine's head perched on the eagle's body. "Kel, it's all right!" Daine said without turning away from the griffins. "They're his parents. That's why he was so restless yesterday. They were close enough he could sense them."

Kel looked from one griffin to the other. *"Parents?"* she whispered. She had thought Daine would never find them. Her charge had been with her for over a year.

The youngster trotted over to the brindled adult, twining between its large forelegs like a kitten. Now the copper one hopped ten yards to land beside its mate. It peered under the larger griffin's ribcage to inspect Kel's charge. The young griffin butted his head against the copper griffin's nose. The copper one reached out a forepaw, dragged the little griffin to itself, and began to wash him.

Daine clapped her wings to her human ears. "Please, lady, gently," she said, tears in her eyes. "No need to shout. It hurts." After a moment she took her wings away and looked at Kel. "They gave me their names, but I can't pronounce them. The brindled one is his father. The copper one is his mother." She winced and continued, "They thank you for all you've done. I said you've been searching for them all this time, through me. I also told them you killed the centaur who was going to keep him."

Kel looked at the griffin. Seeing him now with his parents, she realized he was still tiny, still an infant in griffin terms. This had happened before, with wild mortal animals she'd rescued as babies; the time always came when they had to rejoin their kind.

The brindled one—his father—reached over the copper griffin's wings and worked a cloth bag loose of its ties with his beak. He dropped it in front of Kel.

"This is just a token, they say," explained Daine. "They can't really thank you for what you did, but they know humans value their feathers."

The female yanked a trailing feather from her son's tail. The youngster squalled—Kel could have told them he hated to have loose feathers yanked—until his father set a forepaw on his shoulders and pressed him down.

"They say he has learned bad habits," Daine told Kel. "They never allow a young one to make so much noise."

The female laid the orange feather on the bundle. Mother and father traded looks, then nodded to Daine and Kel. Grabbing his son by the scruff of his neck, the male took off first, the young griffin secure and squalling in his beak. The female joined them in the air.

Kel sniffed. She was rid of the little crosspatch, and his mess, and his temper. She ought to be celebrating, not sniveling. "This is ridiculous," she muttered. She found the handkerchief she kept in her boot and blew her nose. "He's with his own kind. I don't even *like* him."

"You did the right thing," Daine said.

Kel nodded. "It's a weight off my mind, or it will be. You get used to anything—" She looked at Daine, still a human head on an eagle's body. "Well, maybe you don't."

Daine chuckled and shaped herself entirely eagle, then took flight. Kel gathered up the bathing things and the griffins' gift. "That's that," she told Jump. "The sparrows will be pleased."

She didn't open the griffins' bag until she reached her tent. It held a fortune in brindled gold and copper griffin feathers. The creatures had said their thanks in an easy way, gathering the results of their last molts. Kel tucked the baby griffin's feathers into the bag with them—she had saved them all, half-thinking his parents might want them—then packed the bag away. For the first time in over a year she could travel light, without platforms, dishes, drying cloths, jerky, and fishing gear. She didn't have to worry about his meals or keeping him away from other human beings.

When she'd rid herself of all the griffin-care baggage, she collapsed onto her cot and put her hands behind her head. "Maybe this won't be so bad," she told Jump and the sparrows.

The progress moved on. At each new tournament location, Kel was offered a match with someone. Once she learned that a refusal meant someone would disrupt time with her friends to slap her with a glove and challenge her, she accepted the matches when proposed. They were safer: padding was worn instead of armor, and lances were padded and tipped with a coromanel to blunt the shock of impact. Matches were supposed to be less a fight than an exhibition of skill. There were fewer injuries and no deaths. Also, unlike a challenge, there was no penalty in equipment or coin paid when she lost. And she did lose from time to time.

Most of Kel's opponents were knights. A handful were squires—Joren was never one of them. Raoul pointed out that those Kel faced were nearly all conservatives. "They want to prove you're not as good as the lads," he explained. "When you show you're equal to most knights, you make those whose brains haven't turned to stone think. They might even remember that once there were female knights throughout the Eastern Lands, in dark times when every sword was needed. It was only a century ago."

She won two out of three matches. She hated to lose, but knew that if she won every time, people would whisper that someone used magic on her behalf. After one loss Kel was massaging her hand—it was numb after three shattered lances in a row—when her opponent rode up. Removing his gauntlet, he offered his hand to shake. Kel removed her own glove and took it, not sure what the man intended.

"I owe you an apology, squire," he said. "I heard things—well, they were untrue. I apologize. I wish you well." He backed his mount to the center of the tilting field and bowed to her, hand over his heart.

The leaves turned color, then fell. It got cold. The progress crossed the Olorun just east of Corus. A tournament was set up outside Fief Blythdin, the festivities brightened by the scarlet-and-gold uniforms of the pages. Lord Wyldon had granted them a holiday of sorts. They got to observe a tournament, and the squires were freed from banquet service as pages did the work.

On the second night of the tournament, Kel

and Cleon stopped so she could read the board that listed the next day's proposed matches. If someone wanted out of the match, he had until midnight to change the listings.

"I'm on again," Kel murmured. It was hard to read the board. She borrowed a torch from the lane and held it up so she could see.

"What a surprise," Cleon joked, tugging a stick out of Jump's mouth.

Kel's mouth popped open when she read her opponent's name. "You'd better see the coffin maker and order me a box," she told Cleon as he threw the stick for Jump to chase.

He straightened, confused, and read the name she pointed to: Wyldon of Cavall.

"Gods protect me, you're going to die a virgin," he whispered. "What say we find a nice private haystack and take care of that?"

Kel elbowed him. She didn't think she was ready to share his bed, though she certainly liked kissing him. She wondered why he joked about making love to her but never tried to do so. Squires tumbled girls of the lower classes all the time; they were infamous for it. Kel feared both possible explanations for his refusal to press her. Either her large, muscular body was ugly to him, which seemed unlikely when they kissed; or he meant to marry her as people of their station married, with the bride a virgin.

"Never mind the haystack, just visit the coffin maker," she told him, and sighed. "I'd best turn in early," she said, resting a hand on his arm. They were in a shadowy pocket with few passersby; they were safe enough for a discreet touch. "I'll need all the rest I can get before he pounds me into the mud."

"He can't still dislike you," Cleon said.

"I don't think he does," Kel replied. "But that won't stop him from pounding me into the mud."

"Maybe you'll win?" Cleon offered. "You're pretty good. You've beaten knights."

Kel just gave him a look, her brows raised.

Cleon hung his head. "I know, I know, but I thought I should mention it. I ought to get credit for the compliment."

Kel smiled at him and put the torch back. "Good night, silly." She walked on down the lane.

He caught her and tugged her into a dark niche by the stands, where he kissed her warmly. Kel matched his warmth with hers: she liked the taste of him. "Good night, sunrise," he whispered, and let her go.

As if the weather gods overheard Kel's mud remarks, rain during the night left a sloppy tilting field in its wake. Peachblossom grumbled, Jump rolled in the stuff, and the sparrows ignored it.

Waiting to take the field, Kel looked down its length at her training master. He and his mount waited alone, hearing the chief herald's instructions. His wife sat in the stands, someone had said; his conservative friends sat with her. Kel knew, though, that Wyldon must like that moment of quiet before he mounted up, just as she did.

Now the herald rode to Kel's side of the field.

She accepted her helmet from a monitor and put it on, then took up her lance and urged Peachblossom to their starting point. Gobbets of mud were thrown up by the herald's trotting mount. Kel grimaced. She hated sloppy ground; it took days to get the grit out of her gear.

"I don't know why I came over," the herald remarked when he was within earshot. "By now you know the rules as well as I. Lord Raoul asked me to tell you that if you get yourself killed, he will never speak to you again."

"So helpful," Kel replied.

The herald saluted her with a raised hand and rode off the field. Kel and Wyldon took their places in the lanes. When the trumpet blew, they charged and came together in a grinding crash; both lances shattered. Kel rode to her end of the field, gasping for air. Lord Wyldon didn't have Raoul's height and weight, but her side was numb from his impact all the same. She waited until she could feel her arm and hand properly, thinking, Lucky for us tournament lances are so easily made. A strong young sapling, a man who's shaped wood all his life, and I'm ready to be pounded again. She accepted a fresh lance and turned Peachblossom for their second run.

The trumpet sounded. On came Wyldon as Kel's focus narrowed to his shield. She barely felt Peachblossom under her, barely noticed Wyldon or his mount, just his shield as she rose, balanced, and hit. Again a splintering crash: Kel's lance went to pieces; a third of Wyldon's snapped off. They returned to their start points for new lances.

I'm doomed, Kel thought. I should have bedded Cleon before I died.

The trumpet blared. Peachblossom flew down the track, an avalanche of a horse. She set herself and realized too late she was wrong; her weight was now in the worst possible spot if she wanted to stay in the saddle. Her lance hit the rim of Wyldon's shield; his struck just under the boss on hers. Kel's bottom rose from the saddle, her boots popped from the stirrups. She went flying.

She set her body for the fall, and landed in a clatter of metal and a splat of mud. She sat up, ears ringing. Removing her helmet improved matters. Her ears didn't stop ringing, but now it wasn't so loud.

Lord Wyldon approached on his horse, helmet tucked under his arm. His clean-shaven face was handsome in a cold way, marked with dark eyes and a scar that went from one eyelid into the cropped hair over his temple. His bald crown gleamed in the sun. "Coming along nicely, Mindelan," he said, his voice as cool and crisp as ever. "I wouldn't have let you joust until your third year, but Lord Raoul was right to let you try. Keep your shield higher by an inch or so. Need a hand up?"

"No, sir, I thank you." Peachblossom had come to urge her to her feet. Kel hauled herself upright by grabbing her saddle.

"Has Joren given you further trouble?"

She was surprised that he'd asked. "No, sir, I don't believe he has."

Lord Wyldon raised dark brows. "You don't

believe so? I taught you to report more precisely, Mindelan."

Kel stood straighter in response to the reprimand in the training master's voice. "He spends time walking about with knights who later challenge me. Of course, his is a very well known family. That might account for it."

"No doubt." For a moment Wyldon looked away, shaking his head. Then he met her eyes again. "Remember what I said about your shield. Hold steady, Keladry." He rode off the field.

"Steady isn't the problem just now," Kel told Peachblossom. "Clean is the problem."

Raoul waited for her at the end of the field. "I haven't seen you do *that* in a while," he remarked cheerfully.

"I thought I was getting better," she grumbled. She hated to lose.

Raoul grinned. "The day you can best Wyldon is the day they put up a statue to you in front of the palace. He's strong, he's fast, he's got powerful horses, and he always knows exactly where to hit," he said. "The last fall I got from any man was from him, ten years ago."

"You've beaten him since?" Kel asked, thinking he might share his secret.

"Mithros, no—I just don't joust with him anymore. I have my pride," Raoul said.

⊰ thirteen ⊱

THE IRON DOOR

*T*hree days before Midwinter's start, the progress returned to the palace. Prince Roald was scheduled to take his Ordeal over the holiday; his parents wanted to be on hand.

Kel visited the Chapel of the Ordeal as soon as she'd unpacked Raoul's gear. No one had entered it to clean for the Midwinter rites yet. A film of dust lay everywhere.

She went directly to the door, determined to do this and get it over with. She had no idea what drove her to keep testing herself against the Chamber, only that she had to do it.

Gingerly she brushed a finger over the cold, dark surface. No dust, she realized. Dust probably doesn't have the nerve to settle here. She wiped her hands on her breeches, bracing herself to put her hands on the iron.

It was a tilting accident, or rather, a joust she had lost, that had crippled her for good. She remembered that loss often as she struggled to learn to walk with a crutch. Her shoulder, broken in the same joust, healed sloppily.

She never got a satisfactory answer as to how a novice healer who specialized in childbirth would be the only one available for a squire who'd taken lances in a shoulder and a hip. Now Kel lived with a shoulder that was so much lumpy meat, and a leg that was too weak to take her weight.

She was limping down a village street with a basket on her back when she heard shouting. Men, armed and mounted on horses, galloped down the street, coming straight at her. One leaned down, longsword in hand. "We don't need no cripples, dearie!" he cried as she fought to shed the basket. Her bad leg collapsed; she toppled as the man's sword bit deep into her good shoulder. She lay on her side in the dust, blood pooling under her, unable to move or close her eyes.

Armed men killed two small children, then grabbed their mother and a teenaged girl and slung them over their saddles. A local man came out waving a rusted old broadaxe. He was shot through the throat by a raider bowman. The temple was on fire: she heard the screams of those trapped inside. No matter how hard she struggled, she couldn't get up. She couldn't put a stop to it. She was helpless and dying in some dusty street.

When the door freed her, she raced outside the chapel. She reached a small, snow-covered garden just in time, and threw up till she had nothing more in her belly.

Lies, she told herself grimly. All lies, to make me lose my nerve. And I won't. I won't ever lose my nerve.

Kel scrubbed her face with snow, ate a handful to clean her mouth, and shoved more over her mess.

Then slowly, holding her shoulder and limping, she walked to her rooms.

Cleon's was the first name drawn of the squires who faced the Ordeal. He would take the ritual bath at sunset on the first night of Midwinter, with two knights there to instruct him in the laws of chivalry. Next would come his solitary vigil in the chapel throughout the night with only his thoughts for company. At dawn he would enter the Chamber. Though he didn't mention Cleon, Raoul gave Kel the first day of the holiday to herself.

That morning she put on a pale pink shift, pink wool stockings, and a fine wool gown in a delicate brown Lalasa called "fawn." Over her clothes she wore a hooded wine-colored coat with the look of a kimono. Lalasa had assured her it was the newest fashion. Kel chose dress boots to walk in. Ladies wore wooden pattens outdoors in winter, to lift their feet clear of the slush, but whenever Kel put them on, she turned an ankle. Boots were safer.

Seeing herself in the mirror, Kel thought she'd made herself into the girl she would have been had she not tried for her shield. The feeling was odd, more good than bad. Maybe I'm the same whatever I wear, she thought. It's just easier to fight in breeches.

She saw Cleon before he saw her. He stood at the foot of King Jasson's statue, where the Palace Way met Gold Street. He missed her as he scanned the crowds coming down from the palace. Kel slid back her hood and smiled when he finally looked at her.

"A dress?" he asked, grinning. Kel opened her coat. "You look *beautiful*," he said, taking her hand.

"It's not me, silly, it's the gown," Kel told him. "Lalasa can make anyone look good."

Cleon pulled her into a nook in the base of the statue and kissed her warmly. "It *is* you, silly." He kissed her again, then held her tight. "I love tall women. Pearl of squires, have I mentioned how lovely it is not to have to bend in two to kiss you?"

"Only a hundred times," she replied.

They let go of each other reluctantly. Cleon looked to see if anyone they knew was about. Finding no one, he signaled "all safe." Kel walked out to join him, covering her hair again.

They had lunch at a quiet eating house, where they could hold hands as they talked. Then they visited Raven Armory to covet the displayed weapons. "One of those swords would cost Mother a year's income," Cleon said. "But I can dream. Maybe I'll do something heroic, and the king will reward me. He does that, with knights who serve the Crown."

"I know," Kel replied. "Conal, Inness, and Anders all got purses for things they did." As Inness's squire Cleon knew her older brothers.

On they walked through the crowds. If Cleon was nervous about his Ordeal, he said nothing. His grip on her fingers got tighter, the stops in alleys and corners for kisses more frequent, as the afternoon wore on. When a shopkeeper placed lit torches on either side of his door, they knew their day was over. They found one last doorway. Wrapping their arms around each other, they kissed long and hard. Kel felt Cleon's heart beating against his ribs. She clung to him with all her strength as he clung back.

A street boy saw them and chanted obscene rhymes until they separated. Cleon shook his fist at the boy, then drew Kel's hood up.

"Who's instructing you in the bath?" she asked, straightening his stubborn red curls with fingers that shook. "Inness, and . . . ?"

"It's a very great honor," Cleon told her, cupping her cheek in one large hand. "Lord Raoul."

Kel shook her head. "He didn't say a word."

"You know those big fellows—sneaky." He kissed her softly one more time. "Midwinter luck, Kel," he told her with a smile.

She kissed him. "Midwinter luck, Cleon."

"Y'goan t'start again?" The street boy was unimpressed by their farewell. Cleon sighed, flipped a coin to the boy for luck, and began the long walk back to the palace.

She lingered briefly to savor the warmth that filled her veins when he kissed her. Then, whistling, she took the street to the Temple District to say Midwinter prayers.

Even the monarchs were tired of entertaining. They chose not to hold large parties this year, though Kel would have liked to have something to do. She settled down to read the night away, but with Jump and the birds asleep, the silence was too big, the time between the Watchmen's calls too long. When Raoul came in after his part in Cleon's vigil was done, he and Kel played chess. Kel nearly had him boxed in when someone knocked.

It was Prince Roald, Princess Shinkokami,

Inness of Mindelan, Buri, Neal, Yuki, Jerel of Nenan, and Owen. All had cakes, fruit, jugs of cider, and other things to eat and drink. Raoul and Kel welcomed them with relief.

They talked, played games, and traded songs, Tortallan for Yamani and K'miri. The night was well along by the time everyone left. Kel slept without dreaming.

Despite her late bedtime she woke before dawn, as usual. Together with the sparrows and Jump, Kel went to the Chapel of the Ordeal. Cleon was inside the Chamber by the time they arrived. They waited.

Kel bit down a feeling of panic at the sight of the iron door, suddenly afraid it would send her a vision. It can't reach to the back of the room, surely, she told herself as the sparrows huddled in her lap. She covered them with her hands and tried to ignore the Chamber door. Instead her mind presented her with a roll call of those who had failed their Ordeal. Kel squelched that fear, too. Counting the failures since the time her oldest brother became a page, she had less than a handful. Cleon would be fine.

A clank: Kel flinched. Was the door opening? It was. Inness hurried forward to grab Cleon as he tottered into the chapel. Kel bit her lip: Cleon was pale, sweating, and shaky. Inness asked him something—Cleon nodded, and searched the room with his eyes. When he saw Kel, he smiled wearily. He was all right, or as all right as anyone who had survived the Ordeal can be. "It's a hammer," her brother Anders had described it. Cleon looked pounded.

Kel smiled back. As others crowded around him, she stayed where she was. Her knees had gone all quivery. Too little sleep, she told herself, though she knew it was relief.

For the second night of Midwinter, Raoul decided he liked parties the size of the one they'd had the night before. At his request palace servants filled a table with food and drink. Invitations went to people throughout the palace, including Third Company. Most of the men stopped in to say hello. Flyn, Lerant, Qasim, and the squad leaders, including Dom, stayed. When Dom saw Kel, he smiled at her. Her stomach did flip-flops. The old worry stirred: was she hopelessly fickle? She liked Cleon, but she still melted like butter when Dom looked her way.

Cleon was knighted at sunset. Kel thought she would burst with pride in him. That pride filled her again when he walked into Raoul's chambers. Most of her feelings about Dom evaporated.

Everyone who had been there the night before returned, including Buri. She and Raoul talked frequently, leaning against the wall side by side. Kel had to smile, looking at them: Buri stood only as high as Raoul's shoulder. They made a comical pair.

When Cleon slipped into her dark room, Kel waited a moment, then announced a trip to get more fruit. She left Raoul's, then eased through her front door into her chambers. The connecting door was ajar: she saw Cleon by the light from the party. He caught her up in a warm, fierce hug, then kissed her as if he thought he might lose her. They were fumbling at one another's clothes, to what end a sane Kel couldn't guess, when Jump nudged the connecting door wider. The sudden increase in sound brought them to their senses. They kissed again, then separated, Cleon to return to the party, Kel to get fruit.

They went home at a respectable hour. Kel slept past dawn, exhausted by late nights and relief. A hand shook her rudely awake. It was Raoul's. The expression in his eyes told her the news was odd.

"Sir?" Kel asked, sitting up.

"It's that Vinson of Genlith." Lalasa stood beside Raoul, grim-faced, hands clenched under her embroidered apron. Her friend Tian stood just behind her. "His Ordeal was this morning."

"He left the Chamber and requested an audience, with Turomot present," Raoul told Kel. "Get dressed. When they want something after they come out, it's usually not good." He left her, closing his door.

"How did you know?" Kel asked Lalasa and Tian as she washed her face.

"We have rooms for the holiday in the royal wing," Lalasa said. "We are finishing dresses for the princesses and her majesty."

Kel looked into her former maid's eyes. "You wanted to be here in case something happened." Vinson had attacked Lalasa once, trying to kiss her, frightening her half to death. If Peg the sparrow hadn't fetched Kel, he might have done worse.

Lalasa nodded. "Oh, no," she said, dark eyes sharp, as Kel buttoned a shirt. "You've gone and added more muscle—that shirt doesn't set right."

"Worry about my clothes later," Kel said.

Lalasa held up a pair of breeches. "Look at these pockets. My lady, you are so hard on your clothes!"

"I've been hard them for years," retorted Kel, putting the breeches on. "It's not like I'll change now."

Lalasa fed the birds as Kel finished dressing. Once the animals were tended, the three young women and Jump left. As they passed through the halls they were joined by more sleepy-looking people, nobles and servants alike.

Soon after Kel, Tian, and Lalasa took places between Raoul and Kel's parents, the door behind the dais in the Great Throne Room opened for the king and queen, Prince Roald, and Princess Kalasin. At another time Kel would have been curious about the princess, who had spent the last four years with the countess at King's Reach, but not today. Instead Kel looked for Vinson's cronies. There was Joren with his knight-master, Paxton. Garvey of Runnerspring stood nearby with Jerel. Vinson's family—his parents, uncle, and grandfather—and his knight-master, Nualt of Rosemark, stood near the throne. All looked like proud folk trying to hide fear.

With the monarchs seated, the Lord Magistrate, Turomot of Wellam, took a place one step down from the thrones and nodded to the guards at the doors. A herald announced, "Vinson of Genlith, squire and—" He fell silent, astonished. Vinson ran past him to drop to his knees before the dais.

Vinson's eyes were red and swollen—had he been weeping? He trembled visibly, and he still wore his vigil clothes, though surely he'd had time to change. There were marks over his shoulders, as if someone had grabbed him so hard that he'd bled through the cloth. Shadow bruises played over his face and hands, signs of a beating, or beatings. He flinched or twitched as each new one appeared, as if they caused him pain.

"I have a confession." His voice cracked, as if he'd broken it with screams. "I must—confess. I confess." He shuddered. "Two years ago, there—there was trouble in the Lower City. Two—two slum wenches, no better than—No!" he cried, raising an arm as if he shielded himself from a blow. "No! I meant, two girls of the Lower City were attacked, beaten. A third was—must I say it?—a third was beaten and raped. I did it. Sir Nualt had no knowledge. None. He'd have denounced me if he'd known. I didn't—the women made me angry. They're teases, leading a man—" He screamed then and dropped to the floor, sobbing. One of his hands swelled, turned purple, shrank. A cut opened on his scalp, bled, then faded.

The king reached a hand toward Vinson and twisted his fingers. The blue fire of his magic settled over the weeping squire. It blazed fiercely white, then vanished. "He tells the truth," King Jonathan said grimly.

"Tell the Chamber I confessed," Vinson begged, raising his face. "Tell it I did what it wanted me to. Make it let me go! Make it stop hurting me!"

The queen's face was hard. "The Chamber is commanded by no one, Vinson of Genlith. It will release you as it chooses."

Duke Turomot came forward, the brass-shod foot of his tall walking stick rapping sharply on the stone floor. "Guards!" he called. "Arrest this man on the charges of assault and rape. Take him to the provost. I want a confession in full." He looked to Vinson's family. "Send your advocate," he ordered. "You may visit him once his confession is witnessed."

The men bowed, the lady curtsied—to him or to the monarchs, it was hard to say. Then they scurried after the guards who carried Vinson away.

Kel turned to Lalasa. The older girl's eyes burned with a fierce light; there was a triumphant smile on her lips.

She doesn't realize it, Kel thought, feeling sick. She hasn't seen that if we'd reported his attack on her, he might not have hurt those girls. She begged me not to—but I knew it wasn't right. And I kept my mouth shut anyway.

The royal family walked out. The audience was over.

Kel fled out a side exit and down less-used halls, making for her rooms. She didn't want to talk to anyone. Guilt made her stomach roil; pity for the women Vinson had hurt burned her eyes. Yamani discipline helped defeat tears, as it had done in all the time Kel had been at the palace. It did nothing to lessen her guilt.

Blind with emotion, Kel turned into the hall that ended at her quarters. She didn't realize someone waited in a niche until an arm shot out and grabbed her shoulder. She reacted instantly, ramming her captor into the wall. Her free hand shoved his head up and back; her fingers touched his eyes.

Joren of Stone Mountain waited. "Are you happy?" he snapped. "You got one of us somehow, you progressives. You can't even fight your own battles—"

Kel jerked back. "You'll be a wonderful father someday," she replied. "You're good at bedtime tales."

"Once I'm a knight, you'd best keep an eye behind you, bitch." His voice was a viper's hiss, dripping venom. "I'll be in your shadow, until one day you won't cast one ever again."

Kel refused to dignify that with an answer or even a reaction, gazing at him with level eyes until he cursed her and walked off. No doubt she *would* have to keep an eye on him once he was knighted, Kel thought, but it wasn't precisely a new idea for her since his trial.

She went into her room, shutting the door firmly. A maid sweeping the floor jumped and began to babble apologies. Kel shook her head and entered Raoul's rooms. Two maids were there, talking as they cleaned.

Kel tried other refuges. No matter where she went, knots of people discussed the scandal. At last she returned to her room, dressed warmly, grabbed a Yamani bow and quiver, and went out. Servants' paths and the main road to the stables were cleared, but the practice yards that served the pages and squires were two feet deep in snow. Kel stamped her way through to the archery yard and chose a target. She cleared a space for herself, tamping down snow furiously, then stuffed her gloves into her quilted coat pockets. She strung the long Yamani bow with a grunt of effort and chose an arrow. Bitterly she began to shoot, concentrating on the half-remembered weapon, which she hadn't used for six years, and the target. Her arms and shoulders began to ache. This bow was drawn differently, the arrow held to the string in a thumb-and-forefinger pinch, not guided between her index and middle fingers. She had to pull the string farther back than with an Eastern bow, past her ear. It was hard work.

She improved. Arrow after arrow came closer to the center, as if she marched them in from the outer edges deliberately. Once she had emptied the quiver, she stalked down to the target, yanked the arrows free, and returned to start again. She didn't realize anyone was near until Buri said, "When one of my Riders said there was a crazy woman out here with a stripey bow, I thought he was pulling a fool's gambit on his old commander. I thought only our Yamani lilies shot those things."

"I used to," Kel replied.

"I don't see how they can ride without the horses tripping over the bow." Buri knocked snow off of the topmost rail of the fence and hoisted herself up. "When will you try our recurves? You won't want a longbow after that."

"Once we're on progress, maybe," Kel said. "I just wanted to get out."

"What's wrong?" asked the K'mir. "You walked out of that throne room as if you'd seen your death."

"Not exactly," Kel said. "I don't think I can say."

"Sure you can," Buri replied. "Leave out names if you like, though anyone who knows you can see it had to do with Lalasa. He attacked her, didn't he?"

Kel had not meant to say a word, but a basketful spilled out. "She didn't want me to report it. I should have." She tried to sight on the target, but she was so angry she couldn't steady the arrow. "She said it was her word against his. She said *he'd* say she led him on, then struggled when she saw me so I wouldn't blame her for dallying. I could have reported it at the Goddess's temple, too, but I didn't. And he went after three more girls."

Buri sighed. Hopping down from the fence, she trudged over. "Let me try," she said. Kel gave her the bow and arrow. Her eyes watered in the cold; she wiped them with icy fingers. If she'd felt like being amused, the sight of Buri, who was not much taller than the bow, would have made Kel smile.

Buri held the arrow to the string properly. When she shot, she hit the center of the target. She unstrung the bow, coiled the string, and fetched the arrows from the target. "I've tried it, on progress," she said as she put away the arrows. "I still prefer my bow. Come on, let's get something warm to drink."

She led Kel to the Rider mess, sat her at a table, then went to the servers' window. Kel had never come here; she looked around. Midwinter decorations were everywhere: holly and ivy, candles, branches of pine. Clusters of Riders sat at the other tables. There were only twenty or so, most still half asleep.

Buri returned with a tray. She set it down and poured hot cider into two cups. "To your health. Drink, you look frozen."

Kel scalded her tongue on the first sip, and blew on the stuff before she took a second. It set a fire warming her belly. She wasn't sure she deserved warmth.

"Were you not listening when they told you that a noble who kidnapped a maid only owed a fine?" Buri asked, dark eyes sharp on Kel's face. "The mistress of chambermaids used to call the palace cleaning women 'sluts.' Thayet made her stop, but it's coppers to a Midwinter bun that she still does, and that any maid who tells her majesty will lose her place." Buri put a Midwinter bun in front of Kel and began to eat one herself, piece by piece. "You're an idealist, Kel. I've noticed that about you. See, I try to beat idealism out of Rider trainees. It just ruins their ability to give a fair report. So long as there are nobles and commoners, the wealthy and the poor, those with power will be heard, and those without ignored. That's the world."

"I don't accept that," Kel said grimly, shredding her bun without eating it.

"I didn't say you should," the Buri replied.

Kel looked at her, startled.

"Three nights a week your Lalasa closes her shop early," Buri told her after a sip from her cup. "She teaches city girls—commoners—holds, blows, and kicks that will help them to escape an attacker. She learned all that somewhere. And it does girls more good than your courting frostbite to shoot a bow you don't even like. There's now a demand for arms teachers for young noble*women*. Seven female Riders this year asked me for references to get them such posts. And may I remind you that a particular law is being revised right now because you had the nerve to tell King Jonathan it should be changed?"

"I still should have reported Vinson at the Temple of the Goddess," Kel said stubbornly.

"Very well, you should have done," Buri agreed, her face sober. "Next time, you will. And while it won't heal his victims, here's something for you to drink besides self-pity. No court in the land could put him through what he did to those girls. The Chamber did. I've seen the marks of beatings. The Chamber is making him feel every blow, kick, and punch he doled out. And I bet that will continue for a while." She sighed and picked up a second bun. "The world is imperfect, Kel. But you do more than your share to set things right. Next time, report it. Even if nothing is done because the one reported is too powerful, a record will be made. When he does it again, the record will show he won't stop."

Kel smiled ruefully. "I'm sorry. I wasn't trying to wallow in guilt."

"You take chivalry too seriously," Buri informed her. "Just like Raoul. It's sweet, in an impractical way."

Kel shook her head. They would have to agree to disagree about that. Still, she felt better now, though she would never, ever forget.

⇥ fourteen ⇤

FRIENDS

That evening Raoul hosted another gathering in his quarters. Next came the longest night of the year, the night the crown prince kept his vigil. Kel and her friends stayed up late talking, then rose early to go to the chapel. The king and queen were already there, holding hands. When Roald emerged from the Chamber, white and dazed, the packed room echoed with cheers.

Kel returned to her quarters to find Midwinter gifts on her desk, delivered by servants. Most were small, tokens that her friends thought would amuse or please her, like the gifts she had given them. Cleon had given her a griffin brooch. Raoul had given Kel a warhammer, a weapon with a flat head for striking blows on one side, and a curved, spiked head, used to pierce armor and yank it off, on the other. It was a beautiful weapon, well crafted, with a plain wire hilt like those on her sword and dagger.

There was nothing from her unknown benefactor. Kel sighed and felt sheepish. "I'm greedy," she told Jump and the birds as she fed them. "Really, what else could I need? Besides finding out who it was."

After she tidied her rooms and dressed, she went to the stable with Midwinter treats for Peachblossom and Hoshi. On the gate to Hoshi's stall was a new saddle and tack that matched the gelding's. Kel laughed. Her benefactor hadn't forgotten her after all.

She returned to her quarters after a run with Jump, then settled for a lazy morning. She finished reading a book of battles that Raoul had lent her and returned it to his study. He was there, doing paperwork.

"You're not supposed to work during holidays," Kel scolded as she put the book on its shelf.

"I can't fob it off on Glaisdan because this beslubbering progress doesn't leave either of us time to do it, so I'm stuck," he replied. "If you liked that, try Emry of Haryse." He indicated the book with his quill. "It's not fair that he could write and general, but what in life is fair?"

Kel grinned. "*You're* in a splendid mood," she remarked. Getting the book, she saw that Raoul's second-best tunic, wine-colored velvet with gold borders, was laid out. "Is there a party tonight?" she asked, puzzled. She'd received no instructions to report for service.

"I wish," he replied gloomily. "I've received an imperial command." He lifted a sheet of parchment. "My great-aunt Sebila of Disart, my sire's aunt, matriarch of our clan, orders me to present myself at her house tonight. She and the other local relatives will be there to greet me."

Kel didn't understand. "But, sir—Midwinter, and . . . family. They go together."

"Which is why I dare not refuse, or I'll hear from my father as quickly as letters can travel. Have you any female dragons in your family?"

Put that way, Kel saw his point. Her grandmother on her mother's side ruled her clan with an iron fist.

"They'll want to know why I'm not married," Raoul said, long-faced. "They'll have lists of eligible women—not the best of the crop, of course, because I've let things go much too long and will have to be happy with those no one else wanted. And Greataunt Sebila will explain all this at full bellow, with the women present, because her hearing is not what it was. Gods help you if you suggest she talk to a healer about it. Nothing wrong with *her* ears—we young people never learned to listen, that's our problem."

"Why not bring someone?" asked Kel sensibly. "They can't try to match you up if you bring an eligible female. Not me, though. Not even for you, sir, would I face at your great-aunt's what I get at Grandmama's."

That startled a bark of laughter out of him. Then his face turned gloomy again. "If I bring a lady of our rank, Kel, she might think I mean something by it. I don't want to hurt someone that way. I may be 'a feckless gawp of an overage boy,' Aunt told me once, but I don't play fast and loose with people."

Kel leafed through her book without seeing it. "Why not Buri?" she suggested at last. "She won't get any romantic notions, you'll have someone to talk to, and maybe your relatives will leave you alone, at least about marriage."

Raoul thought about this, rubbing his chin. "Why would she put herself through something like that if she didn't have to?"

"Aren't you friends?" Kel wanted to know. "I'd help my friends in a situation like that."

"She'll never agree," Raoul said, one hand inching toward a sheet of parchment.

Kel smiled and put the book down. "Not if you don't ask her. I'll take the message."

Reading his note, Buri grinned. "Poor lad! A big man-creature like him, needing protection! Oh, I can't turn my back on him. Tell him I'll do it. A sacrifice for friendship—what's more appropriate at Midwinter?"

Kel returned late after an evening spent with the Yamanis. There were no candles burning in Raoul's quarters: was he still at his great-aunt's? Yawning, she lit a candle in his study so he would have it to see by, then entered her rooms and lit a branch of candles for herself. She would read until he came in. She wanted to hear how the evening had gone.

With the best intentions she nodded off over her book. The sound of her front door smashing open woke her.

"Bitch!" a man screamed. Jump attacked the intruder. Sparrows followed like feathered brown darts, gouging the newcomer's face. Kel threw herself out of bed to yank her glaive from the wall.

"Trollop, you killed my boy!" shouted the man who fought Jump and the birds. Kel pulled a shutter open, admitting cold air and early morning light—it was shortly after dawn. Jump gripped one of the man's wrists in his jaws, drawing blood. The birds continued to strike his face and eyes as he flailed at them with his free hand.

Kel didn't know this well-dressed, white-haired stranger. Neither did she know the woman and man who ran in to grab him, the woman clinging to his waist, the man with one hand on the stranger's tunic as he tried to knock Jump away.

The door to Raoul's chambers sprang open. Raoul was in his loincloth, holding his unsheathed sword. Buri, clad only in a blanket, stood at his elbow, a dagger in her free hand. "Birds, move," ordered Raoul. The sparrows darted off. Raoul grabbed the snarling man one-handed and smashed him against the wall, shaking off his human companions. "Jump, let go," ordered Raoul. Jump obeyed.

The woman, her face red and tearstained, wrung her hands as she and the other man babbled to Raoul. Kel tried to hear what they said, without success. Raoul's captive continued to swear at her. He craned around Raoul to stare at Kel with blue eyes that bulged in their sockets.

Kel came forward, glaive ready in case the other two attacked her. When the captive shut up long enough to breathe, she said quietly, "I don't even know you."

He answered with curses. Raoul changed his

grip to press a broad forearm across the man's throat, cutting off air and voice. "My lord of Stone Mountain, you forget yourself," he said icily. His captive wheezed. "If you try to carry out your threats, I will break your jaw."

"He is distraught," the woman said, her voice breaking. "My lord, please, Burchard is out of his mind with grief."

"My nephew is dead," the other stranger cried. "The Chamber of the Ordeal opened on his corpse."

"Joren? Dead?" whispered Kel, horrified.

Joren's uncle and mother glanced at her and away, as if they could not bear to see her. "It is the shock," Joren's mother whispered, fresh tears on her face. "Don't hold my husband responsible."

Raoul eased the pressure on Burchard of Stone Mountain's throat. The man was not white haired but pale blond, as Joren was. "He was to be the greatest of us," Burchard whispered. "My lord Wyldon said, after that first year, he was the most promising lad he'd seen." His eyes were adder-poisonous as he looked at Kel. "Jumped-up merchant slut," he whispered. "He was never the same after you arrived. Never. You witched him, cursed him—" His voice was cut off as Raoul reapplied pressure.

"I am tired of you," Raoul said, his voice deadly soft. "Nothing affects the Chamber of the Ordeal, you stupid bigot. Ask Numair Salmalín—"

"A progressive!" snapped Joren's uncle.

"Ask him under oath, then," rapped out Buri, hoisting her blanket around her shoulders. "Numair is the most powerful mage in the realm, politics or none. He knows what everyone knows—no one has ever been able to affect the Chamber."

"I am sorry for your loss," Raoul told Joren's mother, "but Kel didn't kill your son. I won't ask to settle this insult to my squire's honor, and thus to mine, by combat. In that I respect your grief." He released Burchard.

The man fell to the floor. "Two lives destroyed in that Chamber this year," he whispered, staring at Kel through a sparrow-made mask of blood. "How did you do it?"

"I didn't!" Kel protested, shocked.

"Hush, Kel," Raoul ordered. To Burchard he said, "One more chunk of spew and you answer me by the sword, understand?"

Burchard said nothing, only rubbed his throat. Raoul looked at Joren's mother and uncle.

"We understand," Joren's mother told Raoul. She tried to pull her husband to his feet.

"We understand our realm has strayed so far from tradition that the gods' gifts fail," Joren's uncle snapped. "The Chamber is breaking down. What more proof do we need that we have lost divine favor? What have you people left untouched? You school the whelps of farmers, let women make war, intermarry with foreigners—"

"*I make allowance for your grief.*" Kel had never heard that tone in Raoul's voice. White-hot rage seem to smoke off his skin. "Go. Bury your boy." Raoul hauled the lord of Stone Mountain up one-handed and thrust him at his wife and brother. "While you do, ask yourselves where he learned to be so rigid that he shattered under the Ordeal. Get out."

They left. Kel shut the door, trembling.

Raoul rubbed his face with both hands. "Gods," he whispered, "I need a drink."

"Shall I get you one?" Kel asked, unsure.

"Not the kind I meant, if you don't mind," he replied. "Juice, water—no liquor." He smiled crookedly. "It turns me into someone I don't like."

"I'll find something," Kel promised, looking for her clothes.

"Kel." Raoul grasped her shoulder. "That was bile, pure and simple. You had nothing to do with Joren's fate—you do understand that?"

Kel thought about it. "Yes, sir," she said at last.

"Raoul, maybe you're not entirely right," said Buri, leaning on the door to his rooms. "You heard Lord Fart-face. Joren was a golden boy before our Kel arrived. Maybe the Chamber just found the selves that Vinson and Joren revealed around Kel."

"I thought only Alanna was lucky enough to be the tool of the gods," Raoul commented.

"Don't the gods say when they choose you?" Kel asked. "I've never heard from them."

"Oh, maybe I'm just giddy," Buri said with a shrug. "Who goes tonight?"

"Garvey of Runnerspring," Kel replied. "One of Joren's cronies."

"He'll have an audience tomorrow," said the K'mir, walking into Raoul's study. "And I am going back to bed." She glanced at Raoul. "Well?"

He grinned, then looked at Kel. "Don't let them poison you," he told her. "Your coming was a fine thing, for the realm, for all those girls who come to watch you tilt, even for an old bachelor like me." He went into his rooms and pulled the door shut after him.

Quite a few people visited the Chapel the next morning as Garvey of Runnerspring entered the Chamber. Kel did not, though she heard about it from Owen. The watchers had a long, quiet wait. When Garvey emerged, weak and shaken but otherwise fine, a sigh of relief went up.

The next morning Zahir ibn Alhaz, another of Joren's friends, entered the Chamber. He too walked out alive, sane, and confessionless.

Prince Roald's year was larger than the previous one: eleven squires awaited the Ordeal. The court remained at the palace as every squire entered the Chamber. There were no more upsets, and the departure of the progress was announced the day of the last Ordeal. Kel was packing Raoul's things when someone knocked at his door. She opened it to find the king and several of his chief councillors: Sir Gareth of Naxen, Alanna the Lioness, Sir Myles of Olau, and Lord Imrah of Port Legann, Prince Roald's former knight-master. Raoul stood at his desk, frowning. "Sire, to what—"

The king said flatly, "Wyldon of Cavall has resigned. He won't reconsider." He looked at Kel. "I don't want your friends to hear this before the official announcement," he ordered. Kel nodded and brought chairs for everyone.

"*Resigned?*" demanded Raoul. "In Mithros's

name, why? He's done a cursed fine job!"

The king looked meaningfully at Kel. She read his expression: he did not want her there. She fetched cups, brought a pitcher of cider in from the window ledge, and poured drinks for everyone, then left.

The king had forbidden her only to talk to her friends, she thought as she headed for the pages' wing. The training master's door was open; Wyldon was inside, packing things in a crate. He looked up when she knocked.

Only then did she think that Wyldon might not approve of her coming when she wasn't supposed to know of his resignation. She was about to make a lame excuse and go when his mouth jerked sideways.

"I suppose they're with Raoul, trying to name a new training master," he remarked. "What brings you here?"

"My lord said it, and I agree—you're a wonderful training master," she replied, worried for him. "You can't go."

"I can, and I will," replied Wyldon. "I must." He sighed, rubbing the arm that had been raked by a savage winged horse called a hurrok. It always bothered him when snow was about to fall. "Come in and close the door," he ordered. "Did you hear why?"

"No, sir," Kel replied, doing as he bid. It felt odd to sit in his presence. She perched on the edge of the chair, a compromise between standing and being comfortable. "I gave them something to drink and left."

He wrapped a stone hawk figure in cloth and stowed it in his crate. "Two failures in one year—it's never happened. I think my training, my approach, is flawed. Maybe I've done this for too long—fifteen years, after all. It's time for someone new."

"But sir, you can't blame yourself," Kel protested. "Joren and Vinson . . ." She stopped, suddenly unsure. She had often thought that Wyldon ignored the bullying of first-year pages, encouraging boys to fight and to use their strength without thinking.

"You see?" Wyldon asked, sardonic. "You aren't sure that I didn't help to create Vinson and Joren either. I told lads to be aggressive, to concentrate on the goal. Mindelan, it may be that the best thing said of my tenure is that you were my student. Should that be the case, I *am* the wrong man for this post. I did all I could to get rid of you. Your probation was wrong. You know that, I know it. I was harder on you than any lad. Thank Mithros I remembered my honor and let you stay when you met the conditions—but it was a near thing. Next time I might not heed the voice of honor."

Kel watched him pack for a while, unable to think of a reply. He had confirmed what she had wondered about for years. Still, she didn't think he should go. "Sir, I learned so much from you," she said at last. "You're the kind of knight I want to be."

He regarded her with the strangest expression in his eyes. "I am not," he said. "But that you believe it is the greatest compliment I will ever receive. Go back to your master, Kel. If they can't decide, tell them I said Padraig haMinch. He's old blood, conservative, and a Minchi."

Knowing she was dismissed, Kel stood. Before

she could leave, she had to ask: "Sir, what will you do?"

Wyldon massaged his bad arm. "Go home. Idle about until my wife threatens to leave me. I've asked for a post on the northern border come spring. Scanra is on the move. I'd like to do what I can." He waved an impatient hand. "Go, Mindelan. If you're going to snivel, do it outside my office."

Kel nodded, unable to trust her voice, bowed, then went. She didn't snivel, but she did blow her nose.

Something occurred to her; she ran back to his open door. "Sir?" she asked.

Wyldon looked up from a book. "Weren't you leaving?"

"Sir, if you'll only consider," she began nervously. She wasn't at all sure that her idea was good, but her instinct was to pursue it.

"Consider . . . ?" he prodded.

Kel blurted, "Owen of Jesslaw."

"Owen?" he asked. "That hellion?" He folded his arms, looking thoughtful. "All right," he said finally. "Tell Myles I would like a word when he's free."

When she reached her room, she stopped to listen at the door. Should she tell them Lord Wyldon's suggestion?

"It's settled, then. Padraig haMinch." That was the king's voice. Kel heard chairs scrape. "Gary, take over with the pages—you've been complaining how your paperwork is backed up. I'll see if there's a scry-mage at haMinch. I'd like to give Lord Padraig word as soon as possible."

As they emerged from Raoul's chambers, Kel

stopped Sir Myles to relay Lord Wyldon's other request.

That night Kel was packing when her door burst open. She was reaching for her sword when she saw that the newcomer was not Burchard again, but Owen. His eyes bulged and his curls looked as if he'd been yanking on them. He ignored Jump and the sparrows, who greeted him with enthusiasm.

"Kel!" he cried. "Kel, I'm a squire!"

She tried not to giggle and succeeded, barely. "You've been a squire for months."

"Not like *you're* a squire, not like Neal. Kel, my brain's going to pop! I'm not in service to Sir Myles anymore. Lord Wyldon resigned, and he's going home a while, and come spring he's going to fight Scanrans. With me! He's going to work me like a horse, he says, but Kel, I'll be a squire to a fighting knight! Isn't it the jolliest? And he'll teach me to breed dogs!"

He launched himself across the room and hugged her wildly, then stepped back, looking sheepish. "Um, sorry. I didn't mean to, uh, treat you like a girl or anything."

Kel sank down on her bed, head in hands. She lost the battle to appear serious and laughed until she couldn't catch her breath.

Kel missed the departure of the progress. Raoul took Third Company out ahead to scout the road. Buri rode along with her own Group Askew and two more Rider Groups, the Sixth, called Thayet's

Dogs, and the Fifteenth, Stickers. Both Riders and Third Company were detailed to watch the front, sides, and rear of the train, as Glaisdan and First Company stayed close to the monarchs and looked noble. They were welcome to it, as far as Kel was concerned. She preferred scout detail. For one thing, no court gossips were out here, teasing her to say whether Raoul slept alone these days.

The progress stopped in Irontown for a week, then continued south, leaving the forest to enter drier country, Tortall's grain lands. Crawling on, they reached the borders of the desert. The snows of the north turned to rain. The nights were cold, the days bearable. When they came to the desert itself, the king ordered the units in advance of and at the rear of the progress to rejoin it.

"As if we wouldn't know to come back," grumbled Dom. He and Kel rode together one morning, guarding the supply train.

Kel grinned at him. "But we wouldn't have, unless ordered to. You know we wouldn't."

Dom grinned back, making Kel's pulse speed up. "Well, yes, but still, he shouldn't treat us like unruly children."

Kel, who knew the pranks the Own and the Riders played when left alone, raised her eyebrows. Dom chuckled. "You look just like my lord when he does that," he informed her. To Cleon, who rode up, he said, "Doesn't she look like Lord Raoul when she raises her eyebrows?"

Cleon scowled. "She looks like herself," he retorted.

Dom looked at Kel; his mouth curled in a wry smile. He shivered. "Does it seem cold to you all of a sudden? I believe I'll find a blanket." He rode off with a wink at Kel.

"That wasn't nice," she commented as Cleon fell in beside her.

"He was flirting with you," growled the newly made knight. Kel had worried he would be assigned away from the progress now that he had his shield, but for the moment, at least, Cleon was allowed to stay. "I know what flirting is, and he was doing it."

"Dom flirts with everyone. It runs in the family— you know how Neal gets."

"Both of them can flirt with someone else," Cleon snapped. Suddenly he looked ashamed of himself. "Oh, rats, Kel, don't mind me. I'm grumpy. Lately all we do is wave at each other as we pass."

"I know," she said. "At least we *see* each other. We couldn't even do that in the forest."

Quietly he said, "I don't know what I'll do if they separate us. There's too much of me to go into a decline, but . . ."

Kel met his eyes wordlessly. Sooner or later Cleon would be sent away in service to the Crown, probably to deal with the growing pressures from Scanra.

"Hullo," he said, shading his eyes to look east. "What's this?"

Kel smiled as a multitude of horsemen in the white robes of the Bazhir crested the hills. On they came, their tack and the colors in the cords that fastened their burnooses telling their tribe. She counted six tribes among the riders who came over the eastern hills; falling back to look between wagons, she counted three more tribes coming from the west.

"It's the Bazhir," she told Cleon. "They're greeting the king. Cheer up—they'll feed us." She grinned. "I can't dislike people who welcome guests like the Bazhir do!"

For a week the tribes enveloped the progress, treating their guests lavishly. On the eighth day the train reached a fortress city, a granite monument that sheltered eleven springs and wells inside its walls. "Persopolis," Raoul told Kel. "The only city the Bazhir ever constructed." He shook his head with a sigh. "I don't like it."

"That's because you're a tent boy," Captain Flyndan, riding beside them, commented in his dour way. "Me, I like the real beds in Persopolis just fine."

They were joined at supper that night by Lady Alanna and her husband, Baron George Cooper, who had just arrived with Neal in tow. They were still relating news from the western coast when a man at the table asked, "Did you hear about Lord Wyldon's resignation?"

Alanna's face hardened; she drummed her fingers beside her plate. The baron covered her hand with his and smiled at the questioner. "The world knows, surely. It's good for the lads to change teachers—gives them a broad training base. Don't you agree, squire?" he asked Kel. She, Neal, and Merric were not servants at these Bazhir-hosted gatherings, but guests, seated with their knight-masters. The Bazhir took care of serving.

Kel looked at Raoul. "It's very educational, my lord Baron," she told George Cooper gravely.

Alanna grinned at her own squire, seated beside Kel. "So, Neal, do you feel educated?"

"Incredibly," Neal replied in his wry drawl. "Why, words simply fail me about how educated I'm getting."

Everyone laughed. The possibility of a famed Lioness explosion over Lord Wyldon faded. The talk turned to the news from Scanra and Carthak. The new Scanran warlord troubled the knights. Everyone was praying that the northern clans, notoriously difficult when it came to working together, would arrange his downfall. "Preferably during the winter," Baron George said, "so they'll be accusing and killing each other come spring."

Kel woke at her usual hour the next morning. First she had glaive practice, then sword practice with her fellow squires. She had to clean Raoul's weapons and her own afterward, then go riding with her friends.

"Jump, Crown, Freckle," she said quietly. "Time to get up." Chances were that she wouldn't wake Raoul in the next room, but with no door to close between them, she didn't want to chance it. He and Buri had been out late. "Jump." Kel nudged her dog, who slept draped over her feet. He grunted and flopped over, freeing her. She turned to the sparrows, who slept between her and the wall. They were already awake and looking at her.

All but one. Crown lay on Kel's pillow on her side, eyes closed, tiny feet curled up tight. Kel touched the bird with a gentle fingertip. Crown didn't move. When Kel picked her up, she found the sparrow was cold.

She took the small body to Daine. With the griffin restored to his family, the Wildmage was now a permanent member of the progress, and easier to find.

"I'm sorry," Daine said, tears in her eyes. "But Kel, understand, she was eight or so. For a sparrow, that's *old*. Some that are pets last longer, but the wild ones have six or seven years, that's all." She put a hand over the small body. "Do you want me to take care of her?"

Kel shook her head and bore Crown away. She rode to a public garden in the city, attended by Jump, the other sparrows, and Peachblossom, and buried Crown under an olive tree. Olives symbolized healing and peace. Crown had earned both.

Kel stayed away from people for the rest of the day. She didn't weep after she buried her fierce sparrow, but she wanted to be quiet with her animals. And she wanted to remember Crown's bravery in the safety of silence.

Around sunset Cleon found her. He held her, then took her to supper. Kel hadn't eaten all day. Neal joined them; so did Yuki, Roald, Shinkokami, and Merric. The group was leaving the feasting hall when a man approached Kel and slapped her with his glove: Sir Hildrec of Meron. Kel throttled the urge to pick the man up and throw him at a tree.

"I'm sick of this," she snapped. "Call me what you like, say I'm without honor, I don't care. I'm not getting on any more horses to whack you people with a stick."

She walked away.

Two mornings later she found Freckle's body on her pillow. She had not expected him to outlive his mate for long. In a way Kel was grateful that he'd died in Persopolis so she could place him beside Crown. This time Cleon went with her. Once she had scooped earth over the sparrows, Kel blew her nose. "It's the only bad thing about animals," she told Cleon. "Most don't live as long as we do."

"I know, sweet," Cleon said, kissing first one of her eyelids, then the other. "But think how bleak life would be without them."

*In the 19th and 20th years of the reign
of
Jonathan IV and Thayet, his Queen,
Spring 458–Spring 459*

⊰ fifteen ⊱

TILT-SILLY

The progress left Persopolis, turning east into the hill country, then south. The succession of events and meetings with people from Tusaine and Tyra blurred together, along with the names of those who held large and small fiefdoms along the way. Fed up, Kel still refused all challenges and matches, no matter how many insults her would-be foes paid her. Instead she practiced her weapons with her own circle.

Kel did enjoy some new things they encountered, like dishes of rice studded with raisins, almonds, and peas, or balls of chickpea batter fried and served with a creamy sauce. But it seemed to her that grape leaves stuffed with ground lamb, and hot mud baths for the skin, were jokes the locals played on gullible northerners. The markets of Pearlmouth, just across the border from Tyra, were interesting, particularly those that showed the work of Carthaki smiths. Kel wanted one of those blades. She loved the rippled tempering that made art out of steel, art that helped it hold on to its edge longer. Someday, she told herself, if she did so great a service that the Crown gave her a purse of gold, she would buy such a blade for herself.

They were camped outside Port Legann when Kel, bored, decided to use some of her bounty of griffin feathers. Raoul found her working behind their tents so the wind would blow away the smell of the glue she used.

"This is good," he said with approval, inspecting a finished arrow. "If you give up this mad knighthood thing, you'll do well as a fletcher."

Kel grinned at his joke. "Some of these are for you, sir," she pointed out.

"I accept them happily. In the meantime, do you remember Bay Cove?"

Kel had to think. It seemed as though she'd been there ages past, but in truth it had been less than a year. "Smugglers," she said at last.

"They might be glad we captured them. The place was struck with an earthquake last night—their mage reached the king through his crystal. The town's about to slide into the ocean." He glanced at the sun's position. "Grab supper as you pack. We have a serious ride to make."

Group Askew and Thayet's Dogs joined them. Raoul only took six squads that night; the other four would come at a slower pace with wagons of supplies. They would have a bad time of it, Kel realized as they rode on roads turned to mud by winter rains. It was a wet, cold, windy trek north along the coast, but their thanks came from Bay Cove's people, driven into the open in winter. The town, perched on a rocky slope to the sea, was a shambles. The few buildings that stood looked like collapses waiting to happen.

The locals needed all they had brought in their saddlebags and more. The Riders and Raoul's men scoured the countryside for miles to find households that could take refugees or donate supplies, a hard choice with at least a month of winter to go. Men of the Own, whose big horses didn't tire as quickly as Rider ponies in icy mud, found the bogged-down wagons, filled their packs, and brought emergency supplies to the town. Once the wagons finally came in, they bore away whole families to any town or castle that could take them.

Eight days after their arrival Kel and Raoul joined a crew that pulled down buildings too unstable to leave standing. Peachblossom and Raoul's warhorse, Drum, were hitched to heavy ropes; these in turn were tied to support beams inside a two-story house.

"The glory of knighthood is lovely, isn't it?" Raoul asked as they urged the indignant Peachblossom and the calm Drum to pull. "The brilliance and fury of battle, the sound of trumpets in the air, the flowers, and the pretty girls—or pretty boys, in your case—climbing all over us."

Kel, every bit as muddy and weary as her knight-master, grinned. "I've said it before, and I'll say it again, my lord. You are a bad man."

The progress moved inland while they continued to labor in Bay Cove. Kel missed Cleon desperately, but duty meant helping those in need as winter faded and spring arrived. If the town were to survive the next winter, its people needed help. Kel was better at some kinds than others. For one thing, she had no talent for carpentry.

"This is silly," Dom told her one night, inspecting blood blisters under three of Kel's nails. "My lord, this is silly," he told Raoul, who came to see why one of his sergeants held his squire's hand. "She hits the nail half the time and herself the other half. Let Kel hunt. She's a fine shot, and she won't kill herself with a hammer."

"I'm fine," Kel said, pulling her hand away. She was almost immune to Dom by now. When her attraction to him surfaced, she made herself think of Cleon. "And I'm learning carpentry."

"Peachblossom is a better plough horse than you are a carpenter," Raoul said with cheerful brutality. "We've been selfish, having fun while others suffer on progress. Besides, we're out of work." He beckoned to Emmit of Fenrigh, one of their healers. "Tend those fingers, will you?" he asked Emmit. "She'll need them if she jousts again. I'll tell the lads to pack. We'll relax in Corus a week, and catch up with their majesties by the River Tellerun."

Kel's Yamani calm evaporated. She'd see Cleon soon! She jumped up, hugged her knight-master fiercely, and ran to her tent to pack. Emmit had to follow her to work a healing on her fingers.

Corus was a delight, particularly the palace baths, but it was better still to ride north after the progress.

Kel fidgeted every inch of the way. What if Cleon had found someone new, someone small and lovely? What if he'd found someone with dimples? Dimpled girls were her worst daymare: men were supposed to be unable to defend themselves against them. She had decided years before that she was no prize on the romance market. Being away from Cleon for so long, she forgot the things about herself that made him like her.

After hard riding they caught up with the rear of the train late one spring afternoon. The progress had already stopped for the day. Its camp sprawled over the lands on either side of the road. Raoul went on alone to learn where they were supposed to go. As he returned, he looked at the western sky. It was growing dark. Kel's heart sank.

"Well?" Buri asked when he reached them. "I was right, wasn't I? Barely room to swing a stunted cat, let alone camp, until we get to Arenaver."

Raoul nodded, with a rueful look at Kel. She hadn't mentioned Cleon, but she wasn't surprised that Raoul knew she'd like to see him. Raising his hand, the knight signed for the double column of Riders and Third Company to turn. "That pond a mile back had plenty of room," he told Flyndan. "And we have enough no-bugs potion with us."

Flyn turned and galloped down the columns, telling them where they were bound.

"Sorry, Kel," Raoul said quietly.

"No, sir, you're right," Kel replied cheerfully. "Better to stop now, while there's room."

Once she had pitched her tent and cared for her

animals, Kel sat on her cot, dejected. It was silly to fall into gloom when she would see Cleon tomorrow, the day after at the most. They couldn't have gone on today, not when ground fit to camp on would be so jammed over the next ten miles that they'd have to sleep standing up.

Kel was about to leave for supper when the flap blew open. She was yanked into a hug against a body as hard as a tree. Strong arms clutched her tightly as Cleon whispered, "My sunrise!" His lips met Kel's and they clung to each other. When he drew his mouth away, he brought it back instantly, as if he couldn't bear to stop. Kel felt the same. He was wonderfully solid in her arms, and she wanted to keep him there.

At last she got a chance to breathe. Calmly she asked, "You missed me, then?"

That got her another round of very warm kisses. They had each other's tunics off and were fumbling with shirt lacings when Raoul called outside, "Kel? Suppertime."

"Festering tree stumps," Cleon whispered.

"That's mild," protested Kel.

"I don't *feel* mild," Cleon told her, and kissed her so sweetly that she half-hoped she might faint.

"Whose horse is that?" asked Buri. She sounded close enough to make the pair jump apart. Hurriedly they untangled their discarded tunics and put them on.

"We're all right," Kel called to Raoul and Buri, then grimaced for that slip of the tongue.

"*We?*" asked Raoul. He opened the tent flap.

By then Kel sat cross-legged on the ground, roughhousing with Jump. Cleon stood peering into the mirror attached to a tent pole, straightening his red curls. He bowed courteously to Raoul and Buri as they looked in.

"Hullo," he said cheerfully. "Have you enough food for a hungry knight who's been riding sweeps all day?"

Later Kel would wonder about those discarded tunics and half-opened shirts. Did they almost make love? Ought she to look into a mage-charm against pregnancy? She didn't want a child she couldn't look after, not after seeing how well her own parents had done the job. Any child Kel had, in the very distant future, would be born into a family, not dragged hither and yon by a knight-mother. In the meantime she was nearly seventeen and not planning to marry. Why shouldn't they go to bed?

Quietly she found a midwife-healer traveling with the progress and purchased the charm against pregnancy. It hung around her neck on a fine gold chain, tucked under her clothes. If she and Cleon got carried away without interruptions, she would be prepared.

As they rode north, the progress dictated their time alone. This meant that she and Cleon returned to kisses and an occasional embrace. Kel wore the charm anyway, as a declaration that she could decide some things for herself.

Northern roads were narrower than southern ones. Rocky hills and dense forests made them so, forcing the progress to slow down until the pace that had annoyed Kel the year before now seemed lightning-like. She had not jousted since Persopolis, but these days, frustrated with dawdling and having so little time alone with Cleon, pounding an opponent in the lists began to look attractive.

Blue Harbor was the last big port on the northern coast. Since it was also the largest colony for merfolk in Tortall, the monarchs would stay longer than usual. There would be more celebrations and more serving duties. Reading the schedule, Kel could bear it no longer. She put her name on the boards for matches.

"Frustrated?" Neal asked as she wrote.

"You'll be too, with all the banquets they mean to stage," she retorted.

Neal shrugged. "I won't be here. Lady Alanna, seeing the floating pavilion built for these affairs, tells me we are riding ahead." His smugness made Kel long to beat him with a loaf of bread, as she had when they were pages. "Simply viewing the gentle slap of wavelets on anything makes her seasick."

"You're joking," Kel said. How could the Lioness, the King's Champion, be prey to something that inglorious?

"Ask Lord Raoul. He had a sea voyage with her, when she brought the Dominion Jewel home."

Kel asked Raoul that night when she returned his cleaned armor to his tent. "Gods," he said with a laugh. He was shaving. "Green the whole trip, I swear."

"Well, she's riding ahead, since she gets seasick," Kel said glumly. "She and Neal are going tomorrow."

Raoul wiped lather away from his ear. "His majesty tells me I have no excuses. He believes I took advantage of our efforts in Bay Cove to stay away. He won't admit I'm right and all this mummery is not the best use of Third Company. Instead he's decided that, like a dog, I have to be retrained to remember who is king and who is not."

"He wouldn't take the Own away, would he?" Kel asked, horrified. The king could be unfair, but surely not *that* unfair.

"Worse." Raoul patted his face with a cloth. "He said if I take more time away from his bootheels for my own pleasure, he'll seat me with the greediest matchmaking mother in each district."

Kel winced. Surely there ought to be laws against that kind of punishment. She had to compliment the king on underhandedness, though. He'd picked the penalty Raoul dreaded more than fines or the loss of noble privileges.

That night after supper, Kel took a long walk with Cleon, Neal, and Esmond of Nicoline. Owen joined them: he had arrived with Lord Wyldon the day before, stopping for a few days before they headed to Northwatch Fortress and the Scanran border. The squires wandered in the city, then headed back to camp. On the way Kel asked to stop at the challenge boards. She wanted to see who she would face the next day.

Neal, Esmond, and Owen left them at the tournament grounds. Neal had to pack, he said. Esmond had a letter to write. Owen, after his arms were tugged by the other two, decided he had stockings to mend. Cleon smiled at Kel as their friends left, trailing weak excuses.

"Apart from Raoul and Buri, we must be the worst-kept secret in this traveling gossip show," he remarked as they read the lists of matches. "Have you—Mithros, guide us. We're back to this. Do you really want to die a virgin? I keep telling you, we can fix that."

Kel looked at Lord Wyldon's name and shook her head. Then she rounded on Cleon. Stabbing him in the chest with a forefinger, she demanded, "What if I took you up on it? What if I said, All right, I *don't* want to die a virgin?" She mock-glared up into his eyes, noting with glee that he looked panicked. "*You* are just trifling with my maiden's heart. I've heard about fellows like you, who talk so beautifully and run when they might have to keep their promises!" She turned and folded her arms over her chest. Charm or no, accusations or not, she was as timid as he, but she needed to know, did he want her? When he kissed her or looked at her with liking and pride, she went all warm inside. Did he feel the same?

After a moment he muttered, "I—I need to talk Mother around."

Her blood went cold. She was justly punished for teasing him. There was only one reason he would feel he couldn't bed her until he talked his mother around. That scared her far more than sex.

He'd told her about his mother, his father's early

Once more, and then I can lie down, she told herself grimly, turning to face Lord Wyldon.

The trumpet called. Peachblossom hurtled down the lane. Kel shifted, then sank a little, looking for the best way to hit that oncoming shield. She leaned in and braced herself for the impact.

When it came, it slammed so hard Kel's vision went gray. Peachblossom danced to keep her in the saddle until she could settle back. Her ears roared; her vision slowly cleared. She nearly dropped her lance, but clung to it grimly as Peachblossom carried her back to her side of the field.

When the monitor tugged the lance, Kel needed a moment to see that he wanted to take it. "Judges gave the victory to my lord Wyldon," he told her.

"Oh, good," Kel said weakly, body pounding, muscle and bone telling her in no uncertain terms how they felt about this treatment. She didn't see the monitor flag another man to help him get her shield off, or she might have scolded when Peachblossom tried to bite him. Instead she swayed in the saddle, grateful it was there, knowing she really ought to dismount. It seemed like such an effort.

"Mindelan." Once that voice had driven through solid terror to make her pay heed. She turned toward it now, and saw a broad hand held out to her. She took it. "Very well done. Very well indeed. You listened to my advice about your shield—but then, I expected no less. I only wish—"

Kel grinned foolishly, her ears still ringing. They made a nice counterpoint to Lord Wyldon's voice, she thought. "I know, my lord," she managed to say. "You wish I were a boy. But being a girl is more fun. More fun-er? Is that right?"

"Go lie down, Mindelan," Wyldon advised. "You're tilt-silly."

"Yessir," she said, automatically obeying the command. Somehow she climbed out of the tilting saddle and slithered to the ground. The two monitors caught her.

"Mithros watch over you, Keladry," Wyldon said. Kel waved her thanks. To Peachblossom Kel's training master said, "Let the monitors unsaddle you and groom you. None of this temperamental nonsense."

Peachblossom regarded him for a moment, then snorted. Flicking his tail, he followed Kel and her escort, with Jump bringing up the rear.

Voices woke her. "Is she going to sleep *forever*?"

"I can't believe she stayed in the saddle. Papa says Lord Wyldon unseats everybody."

"When he hit her that third time? *I* thought his lance would go straight through her. But he didn't unseat her. He shook her hand!"

"We should go, if she's asleep. It's just, we won't know anything, if we don't ask."

Girls. There were three girls near her, talking in hushed voices. Girls, and they wanted to talk to her. She was hungry enough to eat a cow, horns and all, but duty came first.

Kel opened her eyes. The three curious faces that filled her vision jerked back.

"It's . . . all right," Kel mumbled. "I was waking up." She licked her lips—she was stone dry. Looking around, she saw she was in her own tent. Jump rose on his hind legs, planted his forepaws on the side of her cot, and dropped an apple onto the sheet that covered her. Four sparrows landed beside his offering, each with a grape in its claws.

"Is there water about, and a cup?" inquired the oldest of the three girls. Jump towed her to the small table where the water pitcher sat. The girl filled the cup and brought it to Kel. The water was warm, but it cleaned the stickiness from Kel's tongue. She started to eat the apple, while the sparrows continued to ferry single grapes to her from a bowl next to the pitcher.

"My thanks," Kel said to the girl and to her animals. It was nearly sunset, judging by the light that flowed through the open tent flap. It was enough that Kel could see her guests were very well dressed. They watched her with eyes as bright as stars, lighting three very different faces. The oldest looked to be about twelve, the other two ten or so.

"You broke his lance!" The most energetic of the three was blond; she beamed at Kel. "It was *beautiful*."

"Beautiful is Yvenne's word for the week," the oldest girl told Kel.

"Mama says, if me and Fianola still really want to, in a year, she'll let us try." The speaker, the other youngster, looked to be a sister to the oldest. Both had similar brown eyes, olive skin, and brown hair so curly it fought the pins that confined it.

"Fianola will do it even though she's too old."

The oldest girl looked down, as if two extra years were something shameful. "Fianola and *I*," she corrected her younger sibling.

Here was something Kel could fix. "My best friend, Nealan of Queenscove, was fifteen when he started," she said gravely. "He's squire to Alanna the Lioness now."

The three faces looked equally awed. Kel knew how they felt.

"We hoped," Fianola said shyly, "if—you don't mind . . ."

"Have you advice for us?" asked the blond Yvenne. "Things we can practice, like archery, and horseback riding, except we know about those."

"Do we have to be as big as you?" asked the younger brunette. "I don't think I'm going to be very tall."

Kel sat up. Someone had laid a clean shirt and breeches on a nearby stool. She reached for them wearily. Fianola took up the shirt, shook it out, and held it for Kel.

Well, it's not like they've never seen female ribs and legs before, thought Kel. She started to rise. Her whole body protested the effort. The two young girls each grabbed an arm and hauled her up. Kel thanked them, and pulled her shirt over her head. "I'm just lucky that I'm big," she told them. "Alanna the Lioness is a head shorter than me, and she manages. It will help if you run," she told them, slowly tying the lacings of her shirt. "Up and down stairs, on broken ground. Run for a long time. That builds up your wind and your stamina and your legs. Climb. Hunt. Really work on archery and riding. Lift heavy things. I worked hard—I still do. Don't let anyone say it's easy." She accepted her breeches from Fianola and drew them on, one tree-stump leg at a time.

Sitting on her chair, she looked each of them in the eyes for a long moment. She wasn't sure about the blonde, for all her energy and eagerness. She could be one who jumped from wonderful idea to wonderful idea. One of Kel's brothers, presently a student in the royal university, was like that. But the sisters felt different. The older girl seemed as if she wouldn't go after things lightly. If she did choose to be a page, it would be because she'd found out all she could and chose to do it anyway. The younger one—Kel saw a fire in her small, dark face. The younger one needed it. She would manage.

"More importantly," she said, speaking carefully and firmly so they would remember, "be ready to put up with things—insults, practical jokes, dirty tricks. Nobody will make it easy. You'll be called names and accused of doing things you'd expect from the worst slattern who works the upstairs rooms at inns." Though girls of their age and station weren't supposed to know of such things, Kel's experience was that they nearly always did. "None of that is important, so long as you win through to your goal." She met each pair of eyes in turn, making sure they had heard her, then nodded a dismissal. "Shoo, please," she told them with a smile. "I need to go eat."

They tumbled toward the door. Fianola was the first to stop, turn, and curtsy. The two younger girls did the same. Then all three raced down the grassy lane.

"Good luck, and Goddess bless," Kel whispered. "I hope I see at least one of you again someday."

sixteen

THE NORTH

*T*hey left Blue Harbor at last. On rolled the progress up the coast. They pitched camp for a week on the western edge of Fief Mindelan, a sign of royal favor to the house that had negotiated the Yamani treaty. Kel saw her nieces and nephews for the first time in six years. They were shy with this large stranger, who looked nothing like their memory of her. Seeing her oldest brother, Anders, who managed the fief, was also a shock: they were the same height. At first Anders goggled. Then he laughed, shook his head, and gave Kel a hug.

"Don't worry," he assured Kel as the children kept their distance. "In a little while they'll besiege you. Would you mind talking to Lachran about page training? He goes in the fall. He'd never say as much to his father, but I think he's nervous."

Kel nodded. That was the least she could do for her oldest nephew. Anders had given her useful advice before she had left for Corus.

As luck had it, her seventeenth birthday came while she was at Mindelan. There was a party just for family and friends; the monarchs went hunting with other local nobles. It's nice to have a meal without having to wait on everyone, Kel thought. Nicer still was the sight of Cleon with her nieces and nephews. They knew him—Mindelan was Inness's home as well as Anders's—and shamelessly pestered Cleon for games and treats.

Once he looked up from a knot of children to see Kel watching. His eyes filled with longing, so much that Kel had to go. He was thinking of the children they could have. Kel shivered. She didn't want to consider that at all. Her shield awaited her, if the Chamber of the Ordeal didn't grind her to cat meat. An heiress, and his duty to the tenants on his lands, awaited him.

Two days later the progress was about to heave itself onto the road when urgent messages came from Fiefs Seabeth and Seajen. Scanran wolf-ships had been sighted off the coast, though they had yet to attack. That same afternoon a messenger from Northwatch galloped through Mindelan's gates. Scanrans had crossed the border in three places. General Vanget haMinch, in charge of the border defenses, needed troops and supplies immediately. He also wanted the progress to head inland and south, out of danger. He could not promise their safety if they followed their scheduled route north.

When Kel heard the news, she knew what was coming. To put it off—and to hear it in private— she went down to the River Domin. Someone had rolled a log nearly to the water's edge. Kel sat on it, looking across the shallow band of water. Seven years ago she had tried to kill a spidren with a handful of rocks here.

Steps in the undergrowth made her look around. Cleon sat next to her. For a long while they simply shared the quiet chuckle of the water and the calls of birds. Finally Cleon said, "Half of us are off to Northwatch. We leave tonight at moonrise. The ones to defend the coast are going now. They're taking three of the Rider Groups—not Buri's Seventeenth, though."

"My lord?" Kel asked.

Cleon shook his head. "The king's decided that First Company of the King's Own has been at court too long and needs to remember why they wear the pretty mail. Glaisdan and his men are on their way to the coast. My lord Raoul and Third Company stay with the progress."

"Maybe I'll sleep here tonight," Kel said with a shudder. "He'll be angrier than a stung boar."

Cleon smiled. "The queen sent him to his room."

Kel gaped at him. "She *what*?"

"Oh, not in front of anyone," Cleon assured Kel hastily. "They were in that tower of yours. I wouldn't have heard if I hadn't been using the, er, necessary that's on the floor right below. The queen said if Raoul was going to squall like an infant cheated of a sweet he could go to his room until he grew up."

Kel hid her face in her hands, not sure if she would laugh or cry. "Definitely I stay out here tonight." Then she thought to ask, "Did he go?"

Cleon nodded. "Sooner or later he'll realize the

monarchs will want to see things for themselves, and that he'll have to keep them safe with one hundred men. Maybe he's figured it out by now, that it's why Commander Buri didn't squeak about *her* staying with the progress." He sighed. "I wish I were sleeping out here with you tonight."

Kel didn't care if anyone saw. She wrapped her arms around him and buried her face against his chest. "How long?" she whispered.

He stroked her hair. "All summer, at least."

She had nothing to say that wasn't pointless. Instead she turned her face up for his kiss.

The much smaller progress was east of Mindelan when Cleon's prediction came true. The king and queen let most of the train, led by Roald and Shinkokami, follow the Godsroad east. The monarchs, with the mages Numair and Daine and the realm's chief healer, Baird of Queenscove, remained behind. Raoul, Kel, and Third Company were their guards, along with Buri and the Seventeenth Rider Group. Dressed plainly, moving quietly, their party visited fiefs and towns below the Scanran border. They noted what was needed, then Numair magically transmitted their requests to mages in Corus. Further news of Scanran activity came as Daine sent out hawks and eagles to spy for her and flew as an eagle herself. From their reports she drew maps and sent them to General Vanget through bird messengers. Unlike the monarchs, she had not been requested to leave the district.

They had been riding through mountain terrain

for two weeks when General Vanget caught them. Kel stood guard at the tent as the fiery Minchi expressed overburdened feelings to his king and queen, with Buri and Raoul in attendance. The king's explanation of what he'd been doing did little to appease the general. He demanded that they not add to his worries and get their royal behinds back to the progress.

"You can't expect me to do nothing while my people are in danger!" snapped the king.

"But I expect you to do what you must away from the danger zone!" barked the general. "I can't chase after clan war parties *and* guard you. And if you think the realm won't go to pieces if you're killed, sire, then you don't know your people."

"Roald is of an age—" King Jonathan began.

To Kel's astonishment, Vanget interrupted his king. "Roald does not command the Dominion Jewel and thus its power over each pond and leaf of this kingdom. People think if you fall, the land falls." There was a long silence before he said wearily, "So if you will *please* go away?"

"We'll go," Kel heard the queen say firmly.

By the time Vanget left the tent, Kel had schooled her face to blankness. For the first time she felt sorry for the king. His people were in danger, and he could only ask others to protect them.

"Why doesn't he use the Jewel to protect the north?" she asked Raoul that night. Like all pages she had studied the magical artifact and its power to hold a kingdom together if a strong-willed ruler held it.

He shook his head. "Anyone ever mention the famine of 438 to you?"

"No, sir," Kel replied, putting her weapons-cleaning gear aside.

"You know Roger of Conté tried to magic an earthquake to destroy most of Tortall and quite a chunk of our neighbors, right?" Kel nodded. Raoul stirred up their campfire before he said, "It didn't happen because Jon called on the Jewel to hold the land together. The problem was, the strength it drew to stop the quake had to come from somewhere. We had a famine throughout the realm the next year. All the year's seed, with that magical potential for life, was dead. He and Thayet beggared Tortall for three years to buy food, to keep the kingdom from starving. All magic has a price. Pay now or later, with your own substance or someone else's, but you will pay."

"Enough. We lived and you're depressing me," Buri said, nudging his foot with hers. "Tell her about the giantess who fell in love with you that year."

"Aw, Buri!" he protested.

"Giantess?" Kel asked, wide-eyed. "Come on, tell!"

They rejoined the progress at Fief Hannalof and traveled east to the sprawling lands held by members of the Minchi clan, north of Fief Dunlath on the Gallan border. After a week of celebrations the progress took a meandering route south and west. There were tournaments: Kel entered as many contests as she could. It was the only way she could even briefly stop worrying about Cleon, in battle as a knight for the first time. There were fewer knights to joust against. Everyone who could be spared was sent north. To fill empty hours, Shinko talked Kel into doing exhibitions of glaive combat and Yamani archery with her ladies. Kel mentioned that she would have thought that with the border in trouble, people would frown on expensive, showy affairs like the progress.

"Not so," Shinko told her. "If the rest of this were canceled, people would think the realm is in real danger. They would panic."

Kel shook her head. "I'll stick to jousting," she told her friend. "It's nice and simple, just like me."

They came to Corus as the last leaves fell from the trees. The Grand Progress was over at last.

Feeling obsessed, Kel went to the Chapel of the Ordeal as soon as she left her gear in her room. Midwinter would not come for nearly two months. She saw dust on the benches, though altar and sun disk had been cleaned recently.

They must come every month, Kel thought, walking down the aisle, whether this place needs dusting or not. A giggle that tasted nervous bubbled up in her throat. She swallowed it, ignoring her brain as it clamored to know why she kept doing this to herself. She wiped her hands on her breeches and laid her palms against the iron door.

For a moment she had the oddest fancy that something in the metal breathed, *You again.*

"Yes, of course it's me," she whispered. "I'm proving to myself that I'm not afraid of you."

But you are, that strange not-voice replied.

"I like lying to myself. It's fun. Would you just please do it?"

It did.

Cleon stood halfway across a grassy meadow, longsword in hand. A blond man with tags of fur braided into his beard rode down on him, one hand gripping a big-bladed axe. Kel tried to scream, only to find she couldn't. Cleon ducked, letting the rider pass him by.

The blond man yanked his steed to a halt and dismounted, gripping the haft of his axe with confidence. Roaring, he charged Cleon.

Cleon blocked the swings of the axe, then tried to cut in under the other man's guard. The blond man—Scanran, from his clothes—was fast, dancing out of reach, then lunging back in with that murderous axe. They circled, looking for an opening. The only sounds Kel heard were their panting and the swish of meadow grass. She tried to move, tried to get to Cleon, but she was helpless, frozen in place.

Cleon darted to the side, slashed at the foe, and stumbled, falling to the ground. Kel heard him curse. He struggled to get to his feet. The Scanran was on him with a triumphant yell. He raised the axe and brought it down.

The Scanran was gone. Kel was free. She ran through the grass, sobbing, hunting for Cleon. She nearly fell over him. He was so white that his summer freckles stood out on his skin. A huge slash from his left shoulder to the ribs on his right side bled sluggishly. Somehow he was still alive.

Kel had no belt knife, no edged weapon at all. She took his and hastily cut strips from her tunic. She wadded the rest of it into a long pad and laid it over that dreadful wound, then worked to tie it down, to hold the pad secure until a healer could be found. Within minutes the pad was soaked. She screamed for a healer and hauled Cleon's dead weight up. She fumbled, supporting his head on her shoulder to keep pressure on the wound with her hands.

No healer came. Cleon never opened his eyes. She didn't know how long she'd been holding him before she realized that the bleeding had stopped. So had his breath. He was gone.

This time she drew away from the iron door slowly. She had to prove that she was as strong as the Chamber of the Ordeal. There had to be some gesture she could make, to prove it would not break her.

It took Kel time to call moisture into her paper-dry mouth. When she had it, she spat on the ground in front of the Chamber. Then she turned and walked out.

The weeks before Midwinter were quiet. The court had gotten all the parties and banquets it could stand, and everyone worried about the situation in the north. Kel looked in vain for Cleon, Neal, and Owen. By Midwinter she had to face it: they had stayed. It was going to be a long winter. She couldn't even hope for letters. Little came south once the snows began to fall.

The only excitement to Midwinter was the

squires' Ordeals, and the fear that the Chamber would break more young men. Each day Kel went to the Chapel of the Ordeal, watching the iron door with her hands fisted in her lap. Though she had no close friends among the fourth-year squires, she liked Balduin and Yancen. They and all the other fourth-years emerged from the Chamber to be made knights, with no deaths or failures. Kel shook their hands and wished them well. She and they knew that, come spring, they would be sent to the border.

The holiday over, Third Company looked for work. They went out into the Royal Forest, visiting every village. They hunted game and helped to repair snow and ice damage. Seeing people's relief when they appeared in isolated villages lit a fire inside Kel. She remembered that she wanted to be a knight not to play at killing someone for an audience's entertainment, but to help people.

One February morning Raoul decided that Kel could learn a great deal by working on Third Company's supplies. She was given sheafs of lists. To make sure the company had all that was on them and that what they had was in good condition, Kel inspected leather and tack, sacks of flour and grain, barrels of dried apples and beans. One afternoon she reviewed the shoes of every horse belonging to the Own and gave orders for those that should be replaced. Another day she went to suppliers of medicinal and edible herbs to restock after the demands of the progress. She did her best to be careful with their money, with mixed results.

"I swear," she told Raoul one night, "the moment these merchants see you're working for the Crown, they add a gold noble to every price listed."

Raoul's face twitched with amusement. "I have faith in you, Kel," he replied solemnly.

It took her two weeks to see what he was up to. Enlightenment struck as she finished bargaining for canvas with a royal supplier. Once the sale was made, Kel marched back to her knight-master's rooms. He was reviewing maps on what was supposed to be his dining table, explaining them to Jump and the fascinated sparrows. Raoul looked up, saw Kel, and raised his brows.

"We're going north in the spring, aren't we?" she asked, holding out the sheaf of notes and orders. "And for a long stay at that."

"Not too long. You have to be here next Midwinter, remember." Raoul twisted from side to side, his spine crackling. "Well, Flyn owes me a gold crown. He said it would take you a month. He keeps underestimating you." Raoul shook his head. "He doesn't have your intuition."

Kel sat, her heart drumming. Border duty, with the Scanrans so bold, was as close to full-out war as she might come as a squire or knight. "You're bringing Second Company back here?"

Raoul nodded. "They've been out three years. That's a year longer than I wanted, but there was that poxy progress. Second Company needs to recruit. They're down twenty-three men." He rolled up a map of the lands around Anak's Eyrie. "I'll tell you right now, Kel, border duty will be work."

"Needed work," she pointed out.

"Badly needed," he agreed. "The warlord has another three clans under his banner. It's rare that Scanrans unite, but they do manage every twenty or thirty years. I guess they forgot what happened the last time."

"This is worse than last time." Myles of Olau stood in Raoul's open door with the king and Flyndan. "Is yours a private party, or may anyone come?"

Kel brewed tea as the visitors settled into chairs. Once she had served it, Myles said, "We have news from the north. It's not good. Join us, please, Keladry."

The king and Flyndan frowned at the plump, shaggy knight who had been Kel's teacher in history and law. Myles showed a completely bland expression to both. Kel glanced at Raoul, who nodded. She drew up a chair.

"Every night I thank the gods for Daine," Myles said, adding honey to his tea. "Since she came to us we have sources of information year-round—we're not blind in winter." He sipped from his cup and made a sound of approval. "Maggur Rathhausak has been a busy boy. He now has nine clans under his banner. The remaining clans on their Great Council brawl over trade monopolies and blood feuds, while this southern wolf munches them up one by one."

"I don't understand," said Flyndan. "I thought it was impossible to get three Scanrans to—" He glanced at Kel and changed the word he was about to use. "—eat together, let alone fight. How did he unite nine clans sworn to drink each other's blood?"

"Warlord Maggur is clever," Myles replied. "He keeps hostages."

"What?" chorused Raoul and Flyndan.

"He spirits those dearest to the clan chiefs to his stronghold, where he keeps them safe. From assassins, he says." Myles shook his head. "If we could free them, we might unravel his army. And if wishes were pies, I'd weigh more than I do."

"Why don't your people try to free them?" asked Flyndan.

Myles's eyebrows flew toward his bald crown. "Do you know how long it takes to place an agent in a clan house?" he inquired. "Much too long to risk those I have on heroics. I need every scrap of news they smuggle out. When you go north—"

"Me?" asked Raoul, all innocence.

"I may not get perfect information from a gaggle of clans who live only among their own blood kin and slaves, but I certainly get it here," Myles said drily. "Or did you think if Kel did the work I wouldn't notice you're stockpiling for a prolonged jaunt?"

"It's an exercise in logistics and supply," Kel said, her face as innocent as Raoul's. "He makes me study such things."

Myles began to chuckle. "Very good, my dear," he said. "Very good. If you ever want work as an agent, I hope you'll come to me."

The king shifted in his chair. "He warned me a

week ago what was in the wind," he told Raoul. "You could have told me yourself, instead of letting me hear it from my intelligence chief."

Raoul fidgeted. When he spoke, his cheeks were redder than usual. "I thought you were so intent on having me dance attendance on you to reaffirm your kingliness that next you'd bid me open an etiquette academy," he growled.

Kel felt breathless. This was the man who'd told *her* not to beard a monarch in public! Even this small group counted as public, or so it seemed to her.

King Jonathan glared at Raoul. "You acted like a sullen, spoiled child who's told he has to do chores."

"I didn't take this post to spend nights bowing and fussing!" snapped Raoul, his cheeks redder yet. "I took it to do something *real*. If you want a dancing master, get Glaisdan and the First down here!"

The king flinched. Lord Raoul looked at him, then at Sir Myles. Very quietly Myles said, "Glaisdan of Haryse is dead."

Kel froze; so did Raoul and Flyndan. Finally Raoul asked, "What happened?" in a much softer voice.

"He heard of a late autumn raid on Carmine Tower. He thought two squads would be enough to capture the raiders. One man made it back." Myles rubbed his eyes. "He said Glaisdan misinterpreted trail signs and took them into the middle of a three-clan war party."

Kel and Flyndan made the sign against evil on their chests.

Raoul glanced down. His big hands clenched

and unclenched. Then he looked at his king. "I told you he wasn't fit for a field command."

King Jonathan slumped. "You were right. I let my temper get the better of me, and now twenty men are dead. I'm sorry, Raoul. I think you know how sorry I am."

Raoul nodded. "I do know."

Kel struggled with pity. It was such a costly mistake.

The king got to his feet. "You'll go north with the first thaw, along with five Rider Groups. Try not to get killed." He looked at Kel, Flyndan, and Raoul. "*I* need all of you."

"*I* need every prisoner you can take," Myles told Raoul once the king had gone. "We don't know enough. My spies are with the clans, not the armies. We're getting wild reports of strange machines—metal beasts and walking stones. None of ours who are still alive have seen them. I need something definite." He passed a document dripping ribbons and seals to Flyndan. "Another thousand crowns have been deposited in your treasury for supplies." To Kel he said, "Thank you for the tea—and good luck."

When the door closed behind Myles, Raoul rested his face in his hands. "That fathead Glaisdan," he said, his voice muffled. "He kept telling me that one Tortallan horseman was the equal of ten northern savages."

"Maybe they are," said Flyndan dourly. "It's the eleventh savage that gets you."

They were traveling again, but the difference made

Kel edgy and eager. The men called war "going to see the kraken." Krakens were sea-monsters so rare and powerful that none of the few who'd survived an encounter with one forgot the experience, just as nobody forgot his first encounter with war.

"We learn more of ourselves, seeing the kraken, than we can learn in ten years at home," Qasim said over that first campfire on the Great Road North.

"Speak for your own home," Lerant quipped. "My aunt Deliah *was* a kraken." The men chuckled.

"Only two arms," Dom insisted, mouth full. That raised a laugh.

"But you've all done battle," Kel said as the mood turned quiet again.

"So have you," Dom pointed out. "Maresgift's bandits—"

"Housekeeping," Kel replied.

"That time in the hills," Dom said.

"What time in the hills?" someone demanded.

"Or when the spidrens attacked our hunting party from the rear," added Qasim. "If that wasn't the kraken, what was it?"

Kel smiled crookedly. "That was one of my friends losing his head because spidrens killed his father," she explained.

"And the hill bandits?" Dom repeated.

"An unpleasant surprise," Kel said.

"Well, by the time you walk into the Chamber of the Ordeal, you'll have seen the kraken by anybody's terms," Lerant told her. "And then you'll know."

Then I'll know, thought Kel, rubbing Jump's

chest. I'll know if I can keep my head in war.

After a day at Northwatch with General Vanget, Raoul and Flyndan led Third Company to the meadow that was to be their northern home. It was between the fiefdoms of Trebond and Carmine Tower, meant to serve as a plug for this hole in the border defenses.

Their first task was to build a permanent camp. Out of the supplies they had brought in wagons came shovels, cutting tools, and nails. Men cut down trees and turned the trunks into pointed logs, fitting them into ten-foot-wide sections. Others dug a broad ditch in the shape of a square, building up one side with the dirt they'd moved. In that side they dug a trench. The ground was sloppy and loose: early April was half-winter this far north.

At last they raised the stockade walls in the trench atop the large ditch and filled in the gaps. A crew planted sharpened logs in the outer edge of the ditch, to stop horses if not humans. When they were able to withdraw behind their wall and close the gate, everyone heaved a sigh of relief. No one liked sleeping in the open when the enemy might be close.

Work did not stop with the wall and ditch enclosures. Healers directed the placement of latrines inside the fort and helped build sheds for them. Carpenters set up the wooden skeletons of an infirmary, a mess hall and kitchen, and a corral. Raoul and Flyndan helped with every job, getting as dirty as everyone else.

Kel was put to limb-lopping and trench-digging, while the sparrows offered commentary and Jump hunted rabbits. "Don't take any does," Kel told him while the men joked. "They've got babies or they'll have them soon. Only take males." The men stopped laughing when they found that all of Jump's kills were male.

"Why don't they mention hammering and digging and sawing, when they talk about war?" Kel asked Dom over breakfast one morning. "They never talk about mud in your teeth."

He laughed. "If they did, who would be crazy enough to fight?" he asked. "Pretty girls would look oddly at a fellow if he talked about mud in his teeth, instead of the enemies he killed so *they* might sleep safe."

Once their camp was set, local guides took the squads on patrol, familiarizing them with the country they were to defend. There was a lot of it. Most, Kel discovered, was uphill. When the terrain got too bad for horses, they left their mounts to graze under guard and covered the ground on foot.

The patrol area assigned by General Vanget included three villages, part of a river, two roads, silver mines, and a logging camp. One of the villages, Riversedge, was almost big enough to be called a town. Raoul decided that each squad would spend a week there, to add to the local defenders while enjoying soft duty that included baths, shops, and female companionship.

Kel wasn't sure that she would ever get to Riversedge, since Raoul didn't go. With the fort built, she rode along for one of every three patrols. She would have liked to go more often, but Flyndan insisted that as the owner of a spyglass she take duty shifts atop a tall tree on a bluff, serving as lookout.

"I'll override him, if you like," Raoul had offered her quietly.

Kel shook her head and climbed with grim determination. Her walk down Balor's Needle had broken her fear of heights, but she would never like them. At least her time in the tree was limited by the watch schedule. Several hours after dawn she gladly handed her post and spyglass to someone else.

Soon she discovered what most of Third Company knew: war was boring. They were ready for the Scanrans in April. The Scanrans were not ready for them. There were no reports of enemy activity until May—even then the action took place on the coast. Third Company planted small gardens inside the stockade and a large one outside. Lerant found an orphaned squirrel and raised it as May wore into June. Kel entered a chess tournament and found herself in pitched battle with Osbern for third place as Qasim and Raoul duelled for first. They practiced weapons and horseback riding. Men hunted with dogs and hawks, and fished, in squad strength. Kel celebrated her eighteenth birthday.

One foggy June day the squads commanded by Aiden and Volorin found the enemy. By the time Raoul brought up five more squads in response to their horn calls, the Scanrans had fled. Five of Third Company were wounded. One was dead.

Kel was ashamed that she had longed for battle.

She'd forgotten that people might die when she chafed at the top of a tree.

Osbern's squad found a Scanran band robbing travelers five days later. This time the enemy left two men dead and three wounded. The wounded were sent to Northwatch to be questioned, nursed to health, and shipped to Sir Myles for more questioning.

Two days later Gildes of Veldine was the first rider in Osbern's squad as they followed a game trail on patrol. He didn't see the danger until his horse walked onto it, breaking through the leafy cover of a wolf pit. Down fell horse and rider onto sharpened stakes.

"Stupid!" growled Osbern, his sergeant, wiping away tears at the funeral pyre. "I told him, keep your eyes ahead—Scanrans love traps."

Raoul and Kel were on patrol with a squad when the sparrows, flying as scouts, came in shrieking. Behind them was a Scanran war party, fifteen men armed with swords or double-bladed axes. They plainly thought they outnumbered the Tortallans, but they reckoned without the horses. Peachblossom, trained as a warhorse, trampled a man who tried to pull Kel from the saddle. The man who followed him carried a sword: Kel parried his cut at Peachblossom and ran him through.

Raoul was pressed by two men, one on either side, who kept trying to pull him down as they dodged Drum's hooves. Kel clubbed one with the butt of her glaive; she remembered Myles's plea for prisoners. Her hardest battle was to keep

Peachblossom from killing her captive. By the time she got her mount under control, the fight was over, the Scanrans gone.

"Is that the kraken?" Kel asked, wiping sweat from her forehead. "It felt like bandits to me."

Raoul, dismounting to inspect the fallen, sighed. "Me too." He riffled through one man's clothes, grimacing as he shook lice off his hand. "These aren't much better than bandits."

"A diversion?" asked the squad's sergeant.

Raoul glanced down the road. This patrol area included the silver mines. "Leave 'em," he ordered. "Mount up!"

They hit the Scanrans besieging the mines from the rear. Caught between the Own and the miners, most surrendered. Kel joined the party that rode to Northwatch with the prisoners. It was anxious duty that left her with a headache. Even with the sparrows and Jump to warn them, she feared the enemy might come to take their people back.

Thus it went throughout the summer: multiple small attacks like biting flies as Scanrans hit and ran. Kel fought twice in June, five times in July. A bout of overconfidence—she had thought she was immune to arrows and forgot to wear a helm—resulted in a painful head graze.

"Could be worse," Osbern told her cheerfully as he escorted her to the healers. "I know a fellow . . ." He regaled her with absurd wound stories, taking her mind off the pain of her wound. Mental pain was another matter.

"I was *stupid*," she told Raoul when she saw him next.

"Good. You know it. Now you won't make that mistake again," he said with a grin. "You'll get to make others. Try to remember that armor works much better when it's on."

The hit-and-run battles had one good result. No one, not even Flyn, questioned her ability to fight anymore.

Summer,
in the 20th year of the reign
of
Jonathan IV and Thayet, his Queen,
459

seventeen

THE KRAKEN

*T*he worst thing about her observation post, with its sweeping view of the forested lands between their camp and the river, was that in mid-August it was *hot.* The tree was a pine: beads of sap that were hard in April were glue. Every time she found a new position, blobs of resin clung to her.

Kel fanned herself with her broad-brimmed hat, wiped her face on her sleeve, replaced the hat, and put the glass to her eye. Slowly she scanned the horizon, then the middle ground, then nearby terrain. She froze. There, northwest. Movement.

She took the glass from her eye, wiped her forehead, and searched the area again. Movement for certain, on a road abandoned twenty years before. It was overgrown but still offered easier marching than untouched forest.

Sun glinted off metal. This was no raiding party. It was a small army, headed for Northwatch. Kel put her things away and slowly, carefully, began her descent of the tree.

Raoul and Flyndan heard her out. "Flyn, send a

messenger to Northwatch," said Raoul when Kel had finished her report. "Vanget will put his army in the field against this lot. It's stragglers and side parties we have to worry about. One squad to the logging camp, one to the mines. Get those people out of there, I don't care what excuses they give to stay. Send Osbern to the mines as well. Tell him to break heads if they don't heed sense. That's three squads. Three to defend this camp. Who's in Riversedge this week?"

"Volorin's squad," replied Flyn and Kel together.

"Flash them a warning with the mirrors. Flyn, you're in command here. I want Dom's squad, Balim's squad, and whoever's left with me."

"Sir?" asked Flyndan. "Where will you—"

"They've been making two-pronged attacks all summer," Raoul reminded him. "And that merchant caravan is due at Riversedge today."

Flyndan swore. Riversedge was normally a raider's plum. A big merchant caravan like the one expected made it juicier still. The town could hold for a time with their own fighters and Volorin's squad, but how long depended on the enemy's numbers and weapons.

Kel saddled Drum and Peachblossom—with so little time they took only one horse each. Once they were ready, she donned her armor. She didn't worry about Raoul. Lerant was probably there already, thinking he'd stolen a march on her as he assisted Raoul with his full suit of plate metal armor.

Dressed, she gathered her weapons. After a

moment's hesitation she took the quiver that held her griffin-fletched arrows instead of her everyday one. Today she might need all the help she could get.

She returned to the command tent to find Lerant securing Raoul's greaves to his shins. Raoul winked at Kel as she collected his weapons. By the time she had fetched their mounts, he was armored. He slung a long-handled, double-bladed axe on his back. His lance he kept in his hand. There had been reports that giants fought for Scanra. They might be with the force Kel had seen, invisible among the trees.

Lerant already wore his own mail and weapons. He ran to get his horse, saddled by one of his friends, as Kel and Raoul mounted up. Kel held the banner as they waited for him and for the rest of the men to assemble.

Raoul urged Drum to the gate as the squads formed a double column. Kel followed, Jump in his carrier behind her, the sparrows clutching perches on her gear, Peachblossom, and Raoul's saddlebags. When Lerant rode into his place, Kel gave him their flag.

"Try to stay in one piece, my lord," Flyn, at the gate, told Raoul. "The king'll have my head if you get killed." The gates swung open. Raoul raised a gauntleted hand and chopped down twice, briskly, the signal for the horses to trot. The column followed him onto the road.

The gates closed. The locking bar thumped as it was thrust into place. The camp was on its own.

Halfway to Riversedge Raoul called a halt and sent Lerant up a tree with his spyglass. Lerant came down fast in a half-fall that Kel envied, though she would never try it. She could live with heights; she couldn't defy them.

"They're at Northwatch, my lord," he said, flipping sweaty hair from his eyes. "There's fires burning that way. And it looks like a second party's headed for Riversedge. They're about three miles off and there's two giants with 'em. Maybe sixty or so men, and a covered wagon."

Raoul swore. "Time was they never had enough warriors to hit two places at once. Mithros curse this Maggur maggot." He signaled for a trotting pace. "A wagon for a *raiding* party?" Kel heard him mutter.

At Riversedge the gates were shut, the walls lined with armed men. Sergeant Volorin and the town's headman came out through a small door in the main gate. "The caravan?" Raoul asked.

"No sign of 'em," the sergeant replied.

"Scouts saw 'em camped by Trebond Gorge last night," added the headman. "Loaded heavy, moving slow. They might be as far as Forgotten Well by now."

Raoul ran his fingers through his hair. Kel tried to guess what he was thinking. Forgotten Well was five miles away. Riversedge was fortified. It had a steep-sided ditch lined with stones at the base of its wooden wall. Like so many isolated towns, its back was to the river. Nearly all of the men were archers. They should be able to hold the enemy off.

"Which, Kel?" he asked quietly. "Town or merchants?"

"Merchants, sir," she said promptly. "They're

just about naked out there. This is a bad time to think the enemy won't try a three-pronged attack."

"Or that after going for one tough nut in Northwatch, they'd also want a second tough nut in Riversedge," Dom commented. "Smarter to go for the easier fight and merchant loot."

Raoul turned to Volorin and the headman. "I'll see to those merchants. You'll manage fine without us, for now."

"Good hunting, my lord," said the headman.

"Mithros ward you," added Volorin before he followed the headman inside the walls.

Raoul looked at the five squads behind him and signaled for a trot. Kel's skin prickled. She listened hard, trying to hear what lay under the jingle of tack and thump of hooves. Was that movement deep in the woods to her right? She sent the sparrows after it: they could now read hand signs. They'd picked up "go there" and "scout" within days of their arrival in the north. Now five went and returned quietly, which meant they'd found nothing.

Kel sent other sparrows farther ahead. The company had ridden a mile when the birds came back in a straight line, peeping their alarm call.

"Pox-rotted, money-blinded, mud-wallowing, donkey-whipping merchants," snapped Raoul. After three summers with the sparrows he knew their signals. He gave the sign for "gallop."

They heard battle sounds: the clash of metal, the whistle of arrows, the screams of men and animals. Sergeants ordered men off the sides of the road to sweep the woods for the enemy. Kel sent two sparrows to watch the road in back of their column to make sure no one fell on them from behind. She hoisted her glaive, checking that her grip was firm as they galloped around a bend in the road.

The caravan was backed against tumbled boulders at the foot of the hill where the village of Forgotten Well had been. Three wagons were turned on their sides to give archers cover. The merchants were behind the wagons, fighting the enemy with coolness and precision: they were used to attacks on lonely roads.

Facing them were about thirty Scanrans, mounted and afoot. Kel saw no giants. From the bodies, abandoned goods, and spent arrows littering the road between them and the merchants, the Scanrans had already tried an assault, and been driven back.

Raoul's force slammed the Scanran left like a hammer, breaking up their columns. Drum and Peachblossom reared, flailing at anyone foolish enough to approach. Jump leaped at a man about to attack Kel, thudding into his chest. The Scanran yelped and fell. Kel chopped an enemy down with her glaive and closed with Drum, not wanting to get separated from Raoul. She saw only a sea of arms, legs, and weapons ahead, rising up and down as Peachblossom wielded his murderous hooves.

Suddenly the enemy turned and ran for the shelter of the trees. Raoul's high-raised hand kept his squads from chasing them, though the archers continued to shoot until the last Scanran was out of range.

Raoul turned Drum and signaled the order to

fall back on the rocks, where the caravan waited. "They came out of nowhere," said a man whose arm was being splinted. "Our wounded, our animals . . . Are we to lose everything?"

"No," Raoul told him. "This was only half of the war party reported in this area, and two we didn't see were giants. We'll stand here until it's safe to move. Vanget haMinch has five companies of infantry and two of light cavalry at Northwatch— he'll be along as soon as he can." He didn't say that Northwatch was besieged.

He's afraid they'll spook if they know, Kel realized.

Raoul looked at the stones, pulling a handkerchief from under the poleyn that covered his right knee to wipe his face. They had been over this place several times that summer. Kel knew he was visualizing it as a map, seeing a series of natural walls to fall back on. Behind these boulders that girdled the hill rose a small stone bluff. Trees grew at irregular intervals on its sides. The ruins of Forgotten Well's stockade and buildings crowned the top.

He looked at the merchants. "Let's get you up there"—he pointed to the overgrown dip that was the original road—"behind the walls, what there are of them."

"My wagons," said an old man, clutching a bundle.

"Buy new ones. Get moving," he snapped. "Put your wounded on blankets and carry them up. The animals can go if they'll follow. If not, leave them. Who's in charge?"

"My—my husband's dead," said a small, fragile-looking brunette with huge brown eyes. "I suppose—"

"If he was in charge, let's make it you, unless someone argues. Get going," Raoul ordered. "Don't flutter, mistress, just do it."

The brunette turned away from Raoul. Kel watched her, thinking she would crumble or delay. Instead the woman squared her shoulders against the no-nonsense gray cotton of her dress. Her chin went up. She began to call out names, her voice firm as she went on. A slender man carrying a longbow and quiver came to stand beside her. Those who hesitated at her orders behaved after that.

"Kel, will your sparrows tell us when the enemy gets within a hundred yards of the tree line?" Raoul asked, nodding to the woods just twenty yards away. All but four birds flew off without Kel saying a word.

"Nice to have sentries," Raoul commented, scratching a rough map in the dirt. "Squad leaders, to me."

They gathered around.

Raoul marked his points on his map. "As we face the enemy, I want the squads out along the base of the hill, behind these boulders. Drag dead animals and the wagons to cover the bare spots between them. We hold them here," he told the squad leaders grimly. "Detail two men to walk your horses up to the merchants. Lerant, picket Drum behind those rocks—I may need him in a hurry. Kel will take Lerant's mount and Peachblossom up."

Kel raised a hand. "Peachblossom will go on his own."

Raoul looked at her. "As long as you're sure. He'd probably cripple anyone else who took his rein.

Now. Keep your weapons and your water bottles. It's going to get hot. Places. Balim's squad has the far left flank. Woodcutters left a huge pile of dead trees and trash on that side, like a natural wall between you and the river."

He named squad after squad, showing positions at the base of the hill. Dom's squad would take the far right flank, the other end of the crescent anchored by Balim's squad. "I'll be here, by this road, and I'll roam afoot—unless those giants show. I need to go up there"—he jerked a thumb at the bluff—"get them to send up a smoke signal for Northwatch. If you even *smell* a giant, horn call. Lerant, you're message runner. Kel, you're with Dom's squad." He straightened and looked at them all. "Move. It won't take them long to find their friends. When they do, we'll reap a field of hurt."

Kel sent Peachblossom to the top of the bluff: he hadn't wanted to go, but finally obeyed. The four sparrows not on scout duty stayed with Kel. They were led by the new chief female Kel had named Nari, the Yamani word for thunder. On her way to her post she checked the hill just in time to see Peachblossom walk through what had once been a gate. Above the ruins of the stockade wall a pillar of smoke began to rise. It would be visible for miles. If the general saw it, he would come with troops, if he could.

Dom's position was sheltered by trees on the hill and in front. They wouldn't bake in the sun, as the men to their left would. On the other hand, more trees made it easier for the enemy to get close. At

Kel's request Nari and the other three sparrows went to scout.

Dom signaled her to take the rock next to his. She slid down behind it and whispered, "Jump, sit. If anyone gets close enough, you know what to do."

Jump wagged his tail in agreement and took his post. Like the company's wolfhounds, he had done his share of fighting that summer.

Kel set her glaive to one side and rested her quiver on the boulder. Quickly she strung her longbow and laid it down. She checked the weapons on her belt—sword, dagger, warhammer behind her right hip—and took a mouthful of water.

Jump whuffed; Kel's four sparrows fled the wood, shrieking. In the distance Kel heard an alarm call from more sparrows in an otherwise silent wood. The Scanrans were advancing. Dom signaled the man on his right; Kel signaled the last man in the squad on her left. She then drew a griffin-fletched arrow from her quiver and set it to the bowstring. Carefully she looked around the side of the boulder.

There they were, still ill-defined lumps of movement behind the screening brush at the edge of the trees thirty yards ahead. Two taller moving shapes looked to be horsemen—nobles, then, or officers. Among the Own there were two opinions: kill the soldiers because they fight and officers are useless, or kill the officers because they think and the soldiers will break up and panic without them. Kel and Dom belonged to the second camp. As the Scanrans exploded from cover, shrieking war cries, both Kel and Dom waited until the two horsemen emerged. As one they stood behind their covering rocks and loosed. Dom hit his man in the thigh. Someone else's shot caught that Scanran in the shoulder; he reeled in the saddle and fell.

Kel shot her officer squarely in the throat. He too dropped. Kel ducked as arrows rattled on the stones around her, and fitted another arrow to her string. Up she went, taking a perilous moment to choose her target: a blond man the size of a bear, frothing at the mouth as Scanrans did when they claimed war demons had possessed them.

This is for you, thought Kel, and loosed. Her arrow punched into the frothing man's eye. He dropped like a stone, war demon or no. Kel took cover to choose two arrows this time, holding one in her mouth she set the other to her string. Once more she chose a target and shot; the man she hit keeled over as she put her second arrow to the string. About to draw, she stopped. The enemy was racing back into the tree-cover. Dom signaled everyone to stop and save arrows. The squad on Kel's left did the same.

"Nice shooting, Kel," Dom said with approval, taking a swallow of water.

"It's these feathers the griffins gave me," she told him, showing him one. "I think if I shot straight in the air I'd still hit a target."

"Modest, modest, modest," he teased, shaking his head. "Do you think it's a requirement for lady knights or something? Lady Alanna isn't modest— at least, not about the things she does well."

Nari and her trio zipped past, crying the alarm. Dom and Kel readied to face the enemy's next rush.

The Scanrans were more careful this time. Arrows preceded them, raining behind the squads' rock wall. A man yelped on Kel's left; another screamed on Dom's far right. Dom cursed. Now Scanran foot soldiers came on in a single ragged line, instead of each man charging as he pleased. They had shields, round ones they tried to keep overlapped with their neighbors' as they advanced. Dom's men shot at their thighs or at those who didn't keep their heads down. Kel trusted to the griffin fletching and shot at eyes and throats when they became visible. Five shots later, the Scanrans retreated again.

Dom sagged against his rock. "Mithros, I *hate* it when the enemy learns new things!"

Kel, sipping water, asked, "What things?" She took a handkerchief from her pouch and blotted her face.

"Formation to create a shield wall. Advancing in order," replied Dom. "Curse this Maggur what's-his-name. He's trained with a real army, or he's studied them. Did you see that ugly one back on the edge of the trees, the one with the peaked fur hat?"

"Mage?" asked the man on Dom's far side.

Dom nodded. "My arrows all swerved when I shot at him. I can hear him singing back there—he's cooking up something nasty. Probably something to hide them on the next advance." He sucked a tooth in thought. "Kel, I've got an idea. Nobody can lie around griffins, right? Maybe some of that carries over to their feathers. Maybe you could see through illusions if you tied some on your forehead, over your eyes."

Kel shook her head. "This had better not be a

joke to make me look silly. If you say Sakuyo laughs, you will be in deep trouble."

"Saku—what?"

"A Yamani god. On his feast day people play tricks on one another, and if someone gets angry, the other one says Sakuyo laughs." She always carried spare griffin feathers in her belt pouch, just in case. She took two out and used a pair of handkerchiefs as a band to hold them over her eyes. Holding two arrows, she slid up until she could look over her sheltering rock. The old man in the pointed fur cap stood just in front of the trees. He sang as he hopped around a tiny fire that cast off threads of glittering smoke. Around him the enemy was massing, preparing to attack.

"What do you see?" asked Dom. "I can't see a thing."

"You can't see the enemy?" Kel whispered.

"Everything turns to kind of a smoky blot about ten feet in front of us," he replied. "Now we know what the mage is up to."

Kel exhaled. Dom was right. With those feathers against her skin, she saw what the others could not.

"When in doubt," the mage Numair Salmalín had taught the pages, "shoot the wizard."

Kel straightened, drew her bowstring back to her ear, and loosed. The old man pointed to her arrow and screeched. It slowed in midair, then sped again, knocking off his fur cap. Kel laid the second arrow to the string the moment she loosed the first, in case he magicked her first shot. That arrow struck the old man squarely in the chest. He grabbed the end of the shaft, greatly surprised, and fell into his fire, smothering it.

Instantly the Own shot a deadly rain of arrows that flew at the Scanran lines. The northerners retreated, howling, until they were out of sight and out of range.

"Who took care of the mage?" Raoul asked.

Kel jumped a foot. She didn't even know he was behind her. He laid a hand on her arm. "Steady on," he said, then asked Dom, "Well?"

Dom pointed at Kel as she peeled the band from her forehead, showing Raoul the griffin feathers.

"May I borrow that?" Raoul asked.

"Of course," Kel told him. She tied it to his forehead.

"I'll bring it back. Good work, you two. Try to save arrows." Raoul hurried back down the line of men, walking half-bent so he didn't give the enemy a target.

Word came to Dom: the man who had screamed during the second volley of arrows was one of his corporals, Derom. He was dead.

"Stay here," Dom told Kel. "I've got to shift the line so we don't have a gap." He ran behind the rocks as Kel sent her sparrows to keep watch in the woods.

Here they came with the alarm. Arrows flew in their wake, a dark wave that crested the sheltering rocks. Dom, returning to his post, went down face-first. An arrow was buried in the thick muscle between his neck and shoulder. He grimaced and got to one knee; the man on his far side crawled over to help him up.

The rain of arrows stopped. "Nari, get my lord," Kel told the sparrow, watching the trees for Scanrans. Nari soon returned, Raoul behind her.

"Dom's hit," Kel said, without taking her eyes from her view. The Scanran archers were putting up a fresh rain of arrows to keep everyone pinned down. There was something about the way they fell that bothered her. I'm sorry, Dom, thought Kel, straining her eyes to see the enemy's movements. I'll go all shaky over you when this is over.

Arrows fell, some of them like rain. They're shooting *down*, Kel realized. But from where? She fit an arrow to her bow and slowly looked around her rock shield, waiting for movement in the wall of greenery. There. They had climbed the trees. An arrow shattered on the rock just beside her.

She hand-signaled the archers' new positions to the man on her left and to the man who'd helped Dom, then swung her longbow up and loosed. There was a scream, then a crash of broken tree limbs. The archer plummeted to the ground. A second Tortallan arrow dropped another archer; a third fell halfway to the ground, where he was trapped by a tangle of branches.

"Nice shot," Raoul said in her ear, approving. "Take command of Dom's squad."

Kel stared at him. "What about Symric?" she asked, naming Dom's other corporal.

"A good man, but no commander. Dom knows it was a mistake to promote him. Worse, Symric knows. You've got the squad, Kel." Raoul gripped her arm, making sure he had her undivided attention.

"There's a least one giant on our left. I think the foot soldiers will try to rush the center of our line while the giant rushes our left flank. Kel, you've got our right. If they get around you here, we're cooked, do you understand?"

Kel nodded.

Raoul squeezed her shoulder through her mail. "Mithros guide you," he said.

"And you, sir," she replied. This might be the last time they ever spoke. Giants were clumsy, but they were big, and Raoul was just one man.

No, she told herself firmly. The men of the Own won't sit back and let him do it alone. She watched for a second as he went back to his work, then prepared to do hers.

Kel turned. Men from the caravan had crept up while she and Raoul talked. They shifted Dom onto a blanket, and carried him to the scant safety uphill. Kel moved to Dom's position and signaled the squad to gather. The sparrow Nari had gone to scout; Jump had his nose in the air. They would sound the alarm if the enemy moved in.

The men clustered around her, keeping an eye on the open ground in front. Symric, the remaining corporal, watched her with haunted eyes. "Fulcher's got Derom's old place by the river," he whispered. "He'll sing out if he sees anything."

Kel nodded. "Lord Raoul's put me in command," she told them firmly. She thought she heard a sigh of relief from Symric, but she wasn't sure.

"You aren't even—" someone hissed. Kel looked at him: Wolset, a man who talked bigger than he was.

"Shurrup," growled Symric. "Better Kel than me."

She told them Raoul's orders and sent them back to their places, with instructions to spread the line out now that they were short two men. Symric she kept with her. Maybe Raoul thought she could command these men, but she wanted one of them near to advise her, just in case.

Once the men were moving, she turned back to the view and picked up her bow, listening for movement in the trees ahead. Something was not right. She strained her ears and heard the noises of men crashing through the woods, but their sounds were fading.

"They're moving off," Wolset hissed. In shifting to fill the gaps Wolset had placed himself on the corporal's right.

"Shurrup," ordered Symric.

"I'm telling you, they're *leaving*," argued Wolset. "We can reinforce the center of the line instead of dawdling here—"

Kel had to do something. He'd call for a vote next, while the Scanrans prepared their next move. She had to risk getting shot.

Kel got up and walked over to him. Grabbing his mail and the shirt under it, she twisted hard and yanked until his face was near hers. "Listen, yatter-mouth," she whispered, locking her eyes on his, "shut up, do as you're told. Or you'll have worse than Scanrans to fret over." She tightened her grip as he struggled. *"Do you understand?"*

Wolset nodded, his face beet red. Kel dropped

him. "Next time remember I'm bigger than you," she told him.

The men were sneaking wide-eyed glances at them. When Kel glared, they turned their eyes front.

Jump whined. Kel stared at him—had she ever heard him whine before?—and listened to the sounds in front. The noise of movement faded, as if the Scanrans worked their way to the center and to Kel's left, away from her position. Why? She heard a roar and the clang of battle, but in the distance. She settled down to wait, puzzled, but sure of herself. It didn't matter if the whole Scanran army attacked on the left. Raoul's orders were clear.

Sparrows exploded from the trees opposite and sped across the open ground, screaming. They tumbled to the dirt behind Kel, so clearly terrified that it frightened her. Jump paced and whined, then stood on his hind legs to watch the trees.

"Maybe we should . . . ?" Symric hissed across Wolset, jerking his head to the left. "At least send a man for word?"

Kel checked that her sword and dagger were loose in their sheaths, shifted her warhammer to the back of her belt, where she could reach it easily, and made sure her glaive lay under her hand. Then she shook her head. "Something's out there. These birds aren't scared of much. Neither's Jump."

"It's probably a cat," someone muttered.

Kel ignored that. She and these animals had done too much together for her to discount them now. The mutterer would learn his mistake soon enough.

There—a sound, the crack of breaking twigs, a series of thumps like running feet in the brush. Branches flailed. Kel snatched up the bow and put an arrow to the string, drawing it. She loosed just as the black thing burst from the trees ahead, but the arrow glanced off its head.

Kel gaped. She had *never* seen anything like this. The long, black, curved shape that served as a head swiveled back and forth on the dull metal body without exposing a neck. The eyes were set deep in the metal, if those dark pits were eyes. The limbs seemed formed of large metal-coated bones— giants' bones?—and fine metal chains and rods that acted like muscles. Pulleys served as joints. There were three joints in each limb between the splays of knife-tipped digits on its feet and hands and the limb's connection to the body. That gave the thing two extra elbows and two extra knees. Its slender tail coiled and whipped, snakelike; it was tipped with a ball of spikes. The whole construction was nearly seven feet tall.

The thing stood erect at the center of the meadow, curved head questing. Could it smell? Kel wondered. A visor that might be lips clacked open, revealing a mouth full of sharp metal teeth as long as Kel's fingers.

The clack woke her from stupefaction. She seized a fresh arrow and put it to her bowstring.

The thing dropped to its fours and leaped, landing on her rock. She dropped her bow to seize her glaive. As the thing pounced, Kel drove the glaive's iron-shod butt into the monster's black metal torso with all her strength. The blow dented the thing and smacked it back into her boulder. The monster swiped viciously at Kel—she jumped back, to go sprawling as a branch rolled under her boot.

Jump leaped to seize a jointed metal arm. Kel shrieked, "No!" The dog bit and let go with a yelp, scrambling out of the monster's reach. The four sparrows darted in and around the thing's head. It jerked, trying to follow their flight, razored hands clacking as it tried to grab the birds.

Symric lunged in, sword raised. The thing took his weapon and beheaded the corporal with its blade-fingers.

"Ropes!" Kel shouted, scrambling to her feet, still clutching her glaive. She smashed its butt into one empty eye-pit. "Tie this thing up! Ropes, chains, now!"

The thing regarded her, cocking its head. Kel thought the men had run. She didn't blame them. How could anyone fight this creature? They didn't even know what it was.

The monster slashed at her. Kel dodged the knives and slammed the glaive against its head over and over—the noise seemed to confuse it, which was better than nothing. It flailed its arms. Kel had to keep moving; if she stayed in one position too long, it would have her.

She heard scrambling in leaves: Wolset, his face white with terror, climbed the rocks, a clear target if enemy archers waited in the woods. From the top of the large rock at the monster's back, he tossed a loop of rope over the thing. His rope caught under its head, in the neck groove. Wolset slid down the far side of the rock. His weight drew the rope taut, pulling the monster flat against the stone.

Another rope lasso settled over and caught one of the monster's arms. A man from the squad wrapped the free end around his hands and pulled as he backed up, yanking the arm out straight.

The monster slashed at the rope with its free hand. Kel grabbed that hand close to its wrist-pulley and hung on. The monster was horribly strong. Over and over it smashed her against the rock as if she weighed no more than a rag doll, trying to shake her loose. Balancing on one leg, it lashed at her with the other, trying to cut her with its knife-clawed toes. Gasping for air, Kel raised her legs out of the way. Her belly muscles burned with the effort.

A white shape raced past Kel. Jump carried a hank of rope that unrolled as he ran. At the other end one of the men anchored the rope to a heavy tree. Jump leaped over the slashing leg, trailing his rope. Nimbly he ran under the leg and jumped over it again, wrapping the rope around it twice. He galloped back to the man, who grabbed and yanked the rope, drawing the leg straight out to the side, then secured the rope to the anchoring tree. The monster's leg was safely trapped, temporarily, at least.

Another coil of rope, one end trailing, settled across the arm that Kel gripped. Hanging on with one hand, she wound it around the metal-and-bone limb. She tossed the rest back to the man who had thrown it. He gripped it and pulled as Kel jumped clear of the arm. She lurched and nearly fell, her back a thudding, grinding source of pain.

Two other men were on the ground, trying to trap the monster's remaining limb. Letting its full weight hang on Wolset's rope, it had freed the leg on which it stood. Now it hacked with it, cutting a long slash in one man's scalp as he tried to thread a rope through metal bones and rods. He shook blood from his eyes and finished the job, giving the free end to his companion. They separated and ran to tie each end of rope to opposite trees. The thing was secured, for the moment. It struggled like a fly on a spiderweb.

Gasping, Kel reviewed the situation. The thing wasn't beaten, only halted. As it struggled, even the thickest of the trees that anchored its ropes shook. It was slowly pulling Wolset back up from the far side of its rock. If he were shot or if his body crested the boulder, the thing's head would be free. It would be able to put its entire strength into its battle with their ropes. Kel was reasonably sure it would free itself. They had to kill it now.

Someone had to get close to it.

She yanked the warhammer from her belt and grabbed a fist-sized rock. "Mithros, don't let me die," she pleaded, and ran to the trapped monster. Turning her warhammer so the long spike faced out, she dug it into the cables and bone of the monster's torso and pulled herself up like a mountain climber.

The men yelled for her to stop. "We can hold it!" one insisted. Kel knew they were wrong.

To the monster that had just tried to bite her she said, "You don't scare me."

The thing turned its head toward her, its mouth

on the same level as her face. "Mama?" it asked in a child's voice. The visor opened; razor-teeth snapped. Kel jammed the stone between them. She'd picked the right size: the monster couldn't close its mouth. Kel heard metal grind as it kept trying to shut those visor-lips.

She took a deep breath. Grabbing the cables of one arm with her free hand, she dug a toe into a metal crevice and worked her warhammer free. She raised her weapon and smashed the hammer's spiked head onto the monster's metal crown. It dented— the spike was made to pierce armor. Kel raised the hammer and smashed it down in the same place. The monster thrashed, fighting its bonds.

One more blow ought to do it, she thought.

Kel wedged one foot in the slot between the monster's outstretched arm and the boulder. Bracing her knee on its shoulder, she extracted the other leg and pulled it up onto the thing's opposite shoulder. She balanced shakily, freeing both hands. Third time for luck, she told herself, and drove the warhammer down into the thing's head with all that remained of her strength.

The spike caught. Yanking it free, she lost her balance. Down she fell, twisting an ankle and landing flat on her very sore back. She yelped and struggled to her feet.

White steam, or something like it, hissed from the hole in the thing's skull. It formed a pale, wavering shape that cried, "Mama?" in the same voice as the monster. The wind blew the shape apart. The creature collapsed against its ropes.

Kel pressed a hand against her aching side. "You, and you." She chose men who had not been forced to wrestle the thing. They looked fresher than those who had. "Get more ropes on this creature. Wrap it up like a spidren's supper. I don't want it waking to cut our throats." She looked up at Wolset, who had dragged himself to the top of the boulder. "You're promoted to corporal," she croaked. "For understanding that the head had to be trapped. What have we forgotten?"

He blinked at her, then looked at the men. "Weapons, positions, eyes front," he ordered as he slid to the ground. "We don't want the enemy following this thing to us!" He faced Kel as the men scrambled back to their places. "That was right, wasn't it?"

Kel nodded.

"Then, sir—lady, may I ask something?"

"Ask," Kel said, and coughed.

He pointed to the thing as Kel's chosen men cocooned it in rope. "Is that enough kraken for you?"

It was dark when men in army uniforms reached them with torches. Lerant came too. "We can stand down," he told Kel. "General Vanget rolled up our friends, including the other giant. My lord already did for one. Dom's going to be fine."

They all sighed their relief. Kel hadn't thought the wound deadly, but it was always good to know.

Lerant goggled at their prize. "What in the name of Torsen Hammersmith is that?"

"Good question," croaked Kel, whose voice was

raw. She must have been shouting, though she hardly remembered it. "So happy you asked. Give us another, if you like."

Lerant shook his head. "You get more like my lord every day. I suppose you'll want combat pay for the dog and birdies next."

"They earned it," Wolset told him. The other exhausted men nodded.

Lerant went away, still shaking his head. The squad discovered that the army reliefs had brought soup and bread as well as torches. The soldiers had to be reminded to hand over the food as they stared at the Own's prize.

Kel and her men ate as if they hadn't done so in weeks, feeding Jump and the sparrows as well as themselves. Kel knew she ought to tell the birds to go to sleep, but it hurt too much to talk. She sipped her soup cautiously, letting the warm liquid soothe her throat.

Footsteps made her look up. It was Raoul. His head was bandaged; another bandage on one arm showed a red stain. Kel waved to him weakly.

"My lord bagged himself another giant, we hear," said Wolset with admiration.

"Those big fellows are all alike," Raoul said with a weary smile. "Smash 'em on the toe and they turn into kittens." He approached the monster, now wrapped in rope, and inspected it thoroughly. Then he turned to Sergeant Balim, who had come with him. "Send for General Vanget. He should see this, but tell him I also want Numair Salmalín up here, now. I don't care where he is or what it takes, I want

Numair here yesterday." As Balim hurried off, Raoul turned to look at the thing once more. "Tell me, someone," he ordered.

Kel looked at Wolset and nodded. He squared his shoulders and tried to stand.

"Oh, stop dancing, stay sat, and tell," Raoul said impatiently. Wolset obeyed. The others added details as they saw fit. When the report was done, Raoul hunkered down beside the thing and pulled coils of rope aside for a better look. Kel gripped her warhammer; she saw the men reach for their weapons. The monster remained a dead pile of metal and bone, no more alive than the rocks on which they sat.

Finally Raoul looked at Kel. "So here's one of those machines that Myles spoke of." Worry filled his eyes. "What are they cooking, up there in the north?" he asked very quietly. "How many of these things are they going to send us?"

Kel shook her head. She had wondered the same thing.

Winter,
in the 20th year of the reign
of
Jonathan IV and Thayet, his Queen,
459

⇥ eighteen ⇤

ORDEAL

*T*he Scanrans were not beaten, or even mildly inconvenienced. Kel was in groups that fought them once more before the end of August and once in early September; other squads added four more clashes to the total. Around mid-September encounters with the northerners dropped. There was a nip in the air. Unless the Scanrans chose to stay, this was the time of year to pack their loot and sail or march home.

One morning near the end of September Kel was working on Third Company's account books when Raoul entered the new command hut rubbing his hands. "Frost last night," he commented, pouring a cup of tea. "The leaves will . . ."

Kel looked up when he didn't finish his sentence. "Sir? Leaves?"

Raoul went to the table that served as his desk and checked his almanac. "Kel, it's the end of September."

"Yes, sir." She wasn't sure why this was important, though his tone said it was.

"How long to finish what you're doing?" he asked.

"I'm nearly done," she said. "Just one more page."

"Good. You need to pack." Reading her puzzled look correctly, he told her, "We have to go to Corus—unless you've changed your mind about that shield and want to join us. I won't say no if you do."

The words left her breathless. December. Midwinter. The Chamber of the Ordeal. "Oops," she said.

"We'll leave in the morning," he said. He strode out of the hut. A moment later he stuck his head back inside. "I don't want to get rid of you, mind. I could certainly use you. It's just that the realm needs you more as a knight." He vanished again.

Kel heard him call loudly for Flyndan and Lerant.

The next morning Lerant came to the stable as Kel saddled Hoshi. He clapped the girl on the shoulder. "Good riddance," he said. "Don't mess up your Ordeal. If you do and you come back here for a place, I'll have to hurt you."

Kel grinned. She and Lerant understood each other quite well these days. "Now that I've shown you how, look after my lord when he gets back," she retorted, and swung herself into the saddle. Lerant got out of Peachblossom's way as Kel tugged on the gelding's lead rein.

Third Company turned out to see her and Raoul off. They said little, but scratched Jump's good ear, or fed the birds, or slapped Kel on the back. They patted Hoshi, though not Peachblossom. To Kel's surprise, even Flyndan wished her luck. Her Yamani training kept her from crying as they rode through the gate, but it was a closely fought battle. If she leaked a tear or two, Raoul pretended not to notice.

Kel enjoyed the ride south. She and Raoul set their own pace, not having to rush to a crisis or dawdle in a dusty train of nobles. They had chosen a perfect time to go: the realm was dressed in fall gold and the air was heady.

One day in mid-October they halted on top of a bluff. Corus sprawled on both sides of the Olorun below. Opposite, on the southern heights, was the palace.

Kel sighed. Raoul looked at her. In reply to his silent question she said, "I was wishing we didn't have to stop."

He nodded. "I thought the same. But you know, Buri might object."

Kel shivered. "As much as I like you, my lord, I'd sooner deal with the objections of a cobra. It's safer."

Chuckling, Raoul led the way back to the road. It was time to go home.

To Raoul's disappointment, Buri was in the south with her Seventeenth Rider Group. Kel expected the K'mir's absence would mean uneven numbers in the morning glaive practices, but instead she found no lack of partners. Several young noblewomen had joined the group. Being part of the circle around Shinkokami, Kel was also called in on plans for that spring's royal wedding: after allowing the realm to recover from the Grand Progress, Roald and Shinkokami would marry at last. Kel thought asking her for wedding ideas was like asking a cat how to raise horses, but she did her best.

She did not visit the Chapel of the Ordeal. She would spend the night there soon enough.

Raoul continued her lessons as winter set in. Using their tactical experience of the Scanran raids in their district, he helped her put them together with the reports from all the other districts on the northern border. From that knowledge they worked out the Scanran warlord's overall strategy for the summer—Raoul called it the eagle's-eye view, instead of the vole's. Kel liked this as much as she did chess.

The King's Own was recruiting: Captain Linden of Second Company had assembled candidates for Raoul's approval. If they were accepted, they would begin training with Second Company among the Bazhir. Kel sat in on Raoul's interviews, taking notes and giving her impressions of each candidate at his request. He called it part of her continuing education in command. She still thought he was optimistic.

Neal and Merric returned in early November, the Ordeal clearly on their minds, though they talked of everything but that during meals and time off. Kel worried about them: Neal and Merric were the most imaginative of all those in her year. She understood their nerves, of course. No one could forget Vinson or Joren, and her own experiences of the iron door gave her dreams that woke her gasping in the night.

Buri and the Seventeenth returned. So did other knights and squires, most from the north. Cleon did not come, but wrote instead. General Vanget had ordered him to drill local boys in the defense of themselves and their villages. The best time for such lessons was in the winter, when the crops were in. Kel wrote back that she knew orders were orders, though she had to throw out three efforts before she had a letter she could send. The others had splotches on them.

Six knight-masters prepared their part of the Ordeal ritual. The timetable was that followed by knights and squires for centuries: a bath, instruction in the code of chivalry by two knights, a night-long vigil in the chapel until the first ray of sun touched the wall, then entry into the Chamber. One instructor would be the squire's knight-master, who also found the second knight for the ritual. The other could be a family member, but it was more proper if he were someone less closely connected. Lady Alanna had bespoken the king for Neal's instruction that summer. The lady, Neal told Kel in his wry drawl, left very little to chance.

Kel was afraid to ask Raoul if he'd approached anyone for her. She didn't want to hear that he'd been refused. What if she were the first in memory to be instructed by one knight? It was bad enough that her own ritual differed slightly from the others'. As Lady Alanna had done, with knights who knew she was female, Kel would bathe alone, and be instructed in the code after she dressed.

She knew she was silly to worry about bad luck following any changes in the steps of the rite. Clean was clean, no matter who did or did not see her wash. Many knights owed Raoul favors and would help him, if not The Girl. When she caught herself worrying about things she couldn't fix, she found work to keep her busy. Raoul would say if there were a problem.

One December morning he returned from a meeting to find Kel in his study, sorting his notes about the Own's applicants. "Well," he said, digging his hands into his pockets, "we have a second knight. I don't know what you'll think. I took him up on the offer. I thought he had a point."

Kel stared at him. "He who?"

Raoul grimaced, a sheepish look in his eyes. "Turomot of Wellam."

She knew that name, though she hadn't thought of its owner as a candidate. Turomot of Wellam, when did she . . . "The magistrate?" she cried, her voice squeaking.

Raoul nodded.

"The Lord Magistrate?" she persisted.

Raoul nodded again.

"The conservative?"

Raoul nodded a third time. "Kel, it was his idea."

"He hates me," Kel said, her knees wobbling. "And he isn't a knight. Is he?"

"Actually, yes," Raoul told her. "He hasn't lifted a sword in fifty years, of course. And he doesn't hate you. At least, I don't think he does. What he hates, what he told me, is that people meddled with his procedures to validate pages. He's going to make sure no one tries that with you again. Look, if he's there, no one will dare say anyone gave you any help."

"The vigil?" Kel looked at Raoul with pleading eyes.

"He's, um, going to sit up with you. That's been done before, so you don't have to worry about a jinx."

Kel's head ached. "He's too old to be up all night. That place isn't even heated."

"Gods above, don't tell *him* that! He already told me he wasn't in his grave yet and he'd thank me to stop hinting he was decrepit!"

The day before the holiday, the knight-masters of the squires to take the Ordeal met for their own ceremony with the new training master and the king and queen. They drank a toast to the new year, wrote the squires' names on bits of paper, and shook them up in a plain clay bowl. The order in which the queen drew names was the order in which the squires faced the Chamber. When Kel heard the results, she thought that the Yamani trickster god Sakuyo had danced in that bowl.

Neal was first. She was last.

As candidates for the Ordeal, they were excused from Midwinter service. Kel wondered if someone had miscalculated—it couldn't help them to have more time to imagine the worst—but that was the way it was done. She also knew Neal. If he wasn't distracted, he would make himself sick with worry.

She enlisted Yuki to help her. Neal and Yuki always had something to talk, or argue, about. That Midwinter day the three of them went to the city for an early supper and a visit to the winter fair. They played games, watched jugglers and fire-eaters, and listened to a storyteller relate the birth of Mithros. By the time they climbed the hill to the palace, they had to rush; the sun had set.

The girls left Neal in the squires' wing and walked on through the palace in silence. Kel was about to bid her friend a good evening when she realized that Yuki's silence might not be due to weariness. The Yamani's mouth was drawn tight and her eyes were haunted.

"You're afraid for him," Kel remarked as they crossed the main hall.

Yuki automatically reached for her fan, popped it open, and hid her face behind it. It was the Yamani way to say the fan holder was embarrassed.

"I'm not a Yamani anymore. I'm allowed to be rude. Foreigners don't know any better," Kel pointed out. She pushed the trembling fan aside. "Yukimi noh Daiomoru, it is going to be a long night. You're worried for him. So am I. We'd best sit it out together, don't you think?"

Yuki furled her fan and traced the pattern on one slender steel rib. "I was there, when they carried the beautiful Joren out. Not—as a sightseer. But there were shadows in him, for all his beauty. I wanted to see if this Ordeal purged them." She tucked her fan in her obi. "He looked as if he'd lost all hope of sunrise. Neal . . . If something happens . . ."

"I wondered," Kel admitted. "But you flirt with so many men that I wasn't sure."

"Neither was I," Yuki said with a shaky smile. "Not until today."

"Time for glaive practice," Kel said, glad to have someone to look after. "Then a bath, a massage, some archery in one of the indoor courts. If you don't sleep after all that, I will admit defeat."

Yuki did sleep, in one of her armchairs. Kel stayed awake through the long night, deep in meditation. She woke Yuki before dawn and helped her change into fresh clothes. The sun was half over the horizon by the time they reached the Chapel of the Ordeal.

They weren't alone. The chapel was crowded. Even though last year's squires had taken their Ordeals without problems, everyone remembered Joren and Vinson.

It felt like forever before the iron door to the Chamber creaked open. Yuki grabbed Kel's arm.

Neal stumbled out. His hair and the undyed cotton garments he wore were dark with sweat. His face was gray, his green eyes hectic and red-rimmed, as if he'd wept.

Lady Alanna wrapped a blanket around him and led her former squire toward the door. They were passing Kel and Yuki when Neal halted and turned toward them. There was a question in his eyes for Yuki. The Yamani girl looked down, then drew her folded *shukusen* from her obi and offered it to him, dull end first. Neal took the fan with trembling fingers, then let Alanna guide him out of the chapel.

That night, when the king knighted him, Neal wore Yuki's delicate, deadly *shukusen* in his belt.

Kel was there each morning as her year-mates emerged from the Chamber. Esmond of Nicoline was second. Seaver of Tasride was third, followed by Quinden of Marti's Hill. They looked as if they'd been ground up and spat out, just as Neal had. Each was whole in mind and body; by the time they were knighted at sunset, their terror was hidden, replaced by awe that this moment had come at last.

Then it was Merric's turn. Kel, Neal, and Seaver spent the afternoon with him. They rode, sledded, and practiced quarterstaves, anything to keep him moving and unthinking. It didn't work. He got paler as the sun began to set; he couldn't eat supper. Finally they went to his room to wait until the Watch called the hour when he had to prepare for the bath. As Kel, Seaver, and Neal rose to go, Merric asked, "Kel? A word?"

She waited until Neal closed the door after him. "What is it?"

He swallowed. "Are you scared?" he asked, blue eyes huge in his bone-white face.

Kel reviewed the answers she could give, then said, "Witless."

Merric nodded. Taking a deep breath, he lifted his chin. "I can do this."

She smiled. "I know you can."

He clasped her hand warmly, then shooed her from his room. She kept her own kind of vigil again with Neal and Seaver. They spent the long watch in her room, dozing in chairs as they waited.

Dawn. They went to the Chapel, arriving just as Merric left the Chamber. He looked exhausted, but oddly reassured. He grinned at his friends when he saw them. "Too scared to scream," he told them, before his knight-master towed him off for a bath, food, and rest.

In the morning Kel had breakfast with her parents and visited Lalasa, just in case. Then she took Peachblossom, Jump, and the birds, and went for a long ride in the Royal Forest, where she heard nothing but the calls of birds and the plop of snow falling from the trees. She drew that quiet into her. What would come would come, whether she fretted herself to pieces or not. She would rather enjoy the weather, which wasn't too cold, and the quiet. As much as she loved her friends, sometimes it was good to hear no one at all.

She returned to her room late in the day and sat down to write to Cleon. More than anything, she wished he were here. That was her main regret, that he wasn't here. If something were to happen tonight, she wouldn't have seen him, talked with him, or kissed him good-bye.

She lost track of how long she sat looking at blank parchment, unable to think of something graceful to say. The ink was dry on her quill when she finally tried to write. Frowning, she trimmed the pen and waited this time until she came to a decision, then dipped her quill. She wrote, "Dear Cleon—I love you and I will miss you. Kel." After all, if she survived, he would never read one of their two forbidden words, "love," in her note. If she didn't, it wouldn't matter.

"I could do better," she told Jump, "but I can't seem to manage it right now."

She didn't want to eat with people who'd talk to her. Instead she went to the kitchens and cajoled a maid into giving her a plate of food. She ate in a little-used pantry and returned the plate with thanks, then went to visit Peachblossom and Hoshi. Her last stop was her room. She gathered up the clothes she was to wear during her vigil, then went to the sparrows to give each one a caress.

She kissed Jump on the head. "Be good and be careful, all of you," she said, her voice shaking. She gripped her fear with an iron hand before it made her weak. Thinking back on the things she had seen when she touched the Chamber door, she knew that it could resurrect all that terrified her and make it real. This time would be the last, one way or another. "Goddess bless," she told her animals, and closed her door behind her. Inside her room, baffled by her strange behavior, upset at being locked in, Jump began to bark.

The room where the bath was held was attached to the Chapel, but at least it was heated. Raoul and Turomot met her there. No one's added sugar to Duke Turomot's lemon, Kel thought as she bowed and thanked the Lord Magistrate for honoring her.

The men waited in the hall while she scrubbed every inch of herself from crown to soles. Once she had put on the undyed cotton breeches and shirt, the rough material chafing her damp skin, she admitted Raoul and Turomot.

"Keladry of Mindelan, are you prepared to be instructed?" asked the duke. He would not sit this night out shoeless in thin cotton. Over his clothes he wore a heavy velvet robe with a fur collar and lining; on his head was a velvet cap with flaps that covered his ears. He even wore gloves.

"I am," Kel replied firmly.

Ritual dictated each man's words.

"If you survive the Ordeal of Knighthood, you will be a Knight of the Realm," said Raoul gravely. "You will be sworn to protect those weaker than you, to obey your overlord, to live in a way that honors your kingdom and your gods."

Turomot cleared his throat, then said, "To wear the shield of a knight is an important thing. You may not ignore a cry for help. It means that rich and poor, young and old, male and female may look to you for rescue, and you cannot deny them."

Back and forth they continued the instruction, reminding her of her duty to uphold the law and her own honor, to keep her word, to heed the rules of chivalry. Kel let all of it fall into her heart like stones into a still pool, sending ripples through her spirit as they fell. Those words were the reason she had come this far, the whole reason she needed to be a knight. She wanted them to be as much a part of her as blood and bone.

At last Raoul opened the door to the chapel. Cold air swept over Kel's skin. "Remember," he said gravely, "you must make no sound between now and the time you leave the Chamber of the Ordeal." Leaning down, he kissed her forehead as her father might, then gave her a hug. She hugged back, praying that it wouldn't be the last time she would see this man.

Turomot cleared his throat meaningfully. Taking a breath, Kel walked into that cold room. A single lamp burning in front of the gold sun disk behind the altar was the only light in the room. Kel followed it to the bench positioned in front of the Chamber of the Ordeal and sat.

Her feet were cold. Her skin and hair were cold. She could see wisps of steam from her skin and breath. If she thought about physical comfort, it would be a long and bitter night. That would not do.

She had been told to think about the code of chivalry, what it could mean to her and the realm. She was to think about her life, and choose where she wanted to go. No one had said she could not do that as she meditated.

Behind her she could hear Lord Turomot settling himself in the chair that had been set at the back of the chapel for him. She wished he hadn't done this. Of course he'd done it before—he was a knight, after all—but he was far too old to spend hours in an unheated room in the dead of winter. Still, his resolve to do his duty, to make sure that no one interfered with her vigil as Joren had interfered with her big examinations, awed her. If she could do as well at eighteen as he did tonight at almost eighty, she could take pride in herself.

Kel settled on the bench and placed her hands face-up in her lap, pressing thumbs to forefingers to show wholeness and emptiness, as the emperor's armsmistress had taught her. Yamani warriors meditated with broken limbs, in sleet and snow, even as their wounds got stitched up. I can do this, she thought. She let her thoughts and fears stream away from the still pond that was her image of herself as she wanted to be.

That pond showed her a man, stubborn, harsh, old, who spent the night in discomfort. He did not do it for the squire who kept vigil there, but for the sake of duty, and for the web of custom and law that was the realm.

The realm. In her time as a squire she had seen more of it than most people knew existed, from the damp and mossy streets of Pearlmouth to Northwatch Fortress. She had hunted pirates in the west, built up dams against floods in the east. Mountains, green valleys, desert—she had ridden or walked in them all, measuring them with blisters and grit. Was this what was meant by "the realm"? Or was it other things: a little girl with a muddy doll, Burchard of Stone Mountain livid with grief and rage, a king who admitted a law was wrong, Lalasa in her bustling shop with pins in her mouth. If they were the realm, then so were griffins, sparrows, dogs ugly and beautiful, Stormwings, foul- and sweet-tempered horses, spidrens.

If she owed duty to the realm, then it was not

the dry, withered thing it sounded in people's mouths. Duty was what was owed, good parts and bad, to keep the realm growing, to keep it as fair as life could be kept. Duty was an old man, snug in his fur-lined robe, snoring lightly somewhere behind her.

A hand touched her shoulder, calling her into the present.

Kel looked at the priest. The lamp had guttered out. In the back of the Chapel, Duke Turomot cleared his throat.

The door to the Chamber of the Ordeal was open.

She tried to stand and almost pitched onto her face. Her legs were stiff after a long, motionless night. The priest caught her and held her until she could walk. With a nod of thanks Kel entered the Chamber. It was a small, boxlike room, its ceiling, walls, and floor all plain gray stone flags. The door clanged shut, leaving her in total darkness. Terror surged through Kel: anything could come at her now, and she would never see it.

Clenching her fists until they hurt, she stuffed her fear into the smallest out-of-the-way corner she could find. Of course she was afraid; she was always afraid. She just didn't have to admit it.

Within herself she thought she heard a voice say, *Now we shall see.*

She stood on a grassy plain. The only sound was the endless whistle of the wind as it blew, shaping tall grasses into shiny, rippling waves. She looked for the sun to fix her position and found solid, high, pale clouds. Later the sun would come out, or night would fall. She could guess her position then.

Kel turned in a circle. There: a tree, a pine, a lone tower on the plain. The sky arched down to the ground in almost every direction, without mountains or any other trees to break the horizon. Kel listened, searching for the sound of animals or running water. All she heard was the constant sigh of the wind.

If she was to survive for long, she would need water. That made her choice of action clear. The tree would be her goal. If she found no water by the time she reached it, she could use it as a watch post to find water. Kel stretched her muscles, then started to walk.

She thought she trudged onward for a long time, but it was impossible to tell. The light never changed, the wind never stopped, and she didn't get tired. She did get very bored. About to hum a song for company, she stopped just in time. If this was part of her Ordeal, she had to keep silent.

Finally she reached the tree. It was a fir, like her northern watch post. Gripping a low branch, Kel hoisted herself up and began to climb. Bark and pieces of broken limbs bit into her sore feet. Patches of sap stuck to her hands. She climbed despite them, determined to see where she was. Up and up she went. She refused to think of how high she must be, far higher than she'd been in that border fir. *I climbed down the outer stair of Balor's Needle,* she told herself grimly. *At least here, if I fall, the branches will slow me down till I can grab on.*

The wind picked up, tugging her clothes. Worse, it pressed the tree until the fir began to sway. Reaching for the next branch, Kel missed. Her foot slipped. One-handed she clung to the overhead branch as the wind dragged at her.

Is this the best you can do? she thought at the Chamber as she got both feet on a branch again. Balor's Needle was scarier—

She closed her eyes. Even in her own mind she couldn't hold her tongue. How clever was it to anger the thing in the Chamber while she was in its power?

Below she heard wood break. It was followed by the sound of heavy, leafy branches falling in an avalanche. When Kel opened her eyes, knowing she would not like what she saw, she found that the ground was now visible. It was hundreds of feet below, a distance far greater than that from the observation platform to the base of Balor's Needle. Kel's head swam. She trembled as she clutched the tree, and sweat poured from her body.

She closed her eyelids—they fought their way open, though she wanted them shut. The pine swayed. A gust made the trunk whip away from the clinging Kel: she hung on, somehow, wrapping legs and arms around it. The trunk shook as the wind grabbed her clothes.

Now her stomach rolled as she rode the trunk to and fro on arcs that grew gradually wider. The tree started to whip. She knew what was coming as clearly as if the Chamber shouted it in her ear. She could hang on as her grasp on the trunk weakened, or she could die when it snapped.

Her chief regret was that they would think her death here meant that girls were not supposed to be knights. That Lady Alanna was a fluke or a miracle. Fianola, her sister, and Yvenne would have to find other dreams. It was no longer a matter of Kel's surviving the Ordeal: the Chamber meant to kill her. What she could refuse it was the banquet of fear she would feed it if she clung to the very last. Perhaps it was her fate to die in such a fall—that would be why heights had always scared her.

Kel let go of the lashing tree trunk, and dropped.

She landed on sand with a thump. She was twelve again, in a familiar-looking valley in the hill country, with sand on the ground, reddish-brown stone cliffs in front of her. Faleron, Neal, Prosper of Tameran, Merric, Owen, and Seaver clustered around her. They carried hunting weapons and looked panic-stricken.

Bandits rode around them on rugged horses, cutting the pages off from any escape. There were more than twenty raiders; hard, desperate men without so much as a patchless shirt between them. Their weapons were the only good things they had—good enough to carve up pages silly enough to stumble into their camp, at least.

"Kel, help us!" cried Faleron. "What do we do?"

It hadn't been that way six years before. Faleron, the senior page, had been in command. He hadn't asked for help from anyone; he had frozen. So had Neal, the oldest. They lived that day because Kel had kept her head.

She wasn't keeping it now. She couldn't breathe; she couldn't think. The archers among the bandits fitted arrows to strings. The pages had to do something, but what? If they broke left, they ran back into the bandit camp. The men blocked them in front and on the right. The cliff was at their backs. She couldn't decide. If the page archers shot, what would happen if they missed? What if they ran out of arrows?

But if those like Kel, bearing spears, attacked, wouldn't the bandits shoot them?

An arrow sprouted in one of Faleron's eyes. He collapsed, trying to pull it out as he died. Kel looked at the man who had shot him, her mouth trembling. They would have to kill all of the pages, she realized. No word of a bandit camp must get back to Lord Wyldon, who would summon the army. . . .

"Kel, help us!" Merric yelled. He loosed an arrow, grazing a bandit, and fumbled getting another to its string. Two arrows buried themselves in his chest.

Owen screamed defiance and ran at a horseman, his spear raised.

The man grinned, showing blackened teeth, and chopped Owen's spear in two. She had to do something, Kel thought, sweating, queasy. She had done it before, why not now? Did her group have mages with them? She thought they did, but she wasn't sure.

The horseman beheaded Owen.

The Chamber made her watch all of them die as she tried to think, as she tried to jerk free of her paralysis. She could have saved them, she knew. She did save them once. Was this how normal people felt when forced to battle? Frozen and witless?

As an axe-wielding bandit walked toward her, Kel thought at the Chamber furiously, *I thought you would be grand and terrible! I thought you would make us grow up, make us accept knighthood's duties and sacrifices. This is just mean—you're a nightmare device, bringing bad dreams to people who want to help others!*

She thumped to her knees on flagstones. Once again she was in a gray stone box with an iron door on one side. Her body steamed in the chilly room.

You'll do, a cold, whispering voice said somewhere between the inside of her ears and her mind. *You'll do quite nicely.*

On the inside of the door frame, in the keystone, a face was carved. Its eyes glinted yellow as they surveyed Kel. The face was as lined and lipless as the mummies curiosity-seekers had found in a very old Yamani tomb. Kel wondered if she were seeing ghosts.

Or was it an attempt to trick her into speaking?

It was no trick. The stone lips did not move. The voice still sounded within her head, not without, but she knew somehow that voice and stone face were both the Chamber's. *This is no part of your test. This is something you must remember.*

One end of the Chamber went to shadows. In their depths grew an image. First she saw a little nothing of a man. He was short, scrawny, with mouse-brown, unruly hair clumsily cut, bewildered eyes that blinked constantly, and a thin, selfish mouth. He wore a dark, musty robe covered with stains and scorch marks. He could not stay still: he dug absently at a pimple on his face, chewed a fingernail, and picked hairs from his robe.

Blackness moved out of the shadows. Kel stepped back, forgetting this was an image, not reality. Like so many alien beetles, the dreadful machine of the battle at Forgotten Well, multiplied by eleven, walked from the dark to form a half-circle at the back of the little man. They all turned their smoothly curved heads toward him with eerie attention.

Kel blinked. She had not seen that something lay on the ground between the little man and the machines. It was actually a pile of something, she thought, trying to get a better look. She took two steps forward. Several somethings. Her eyes saw the gleam of dark, fresh liquid on a doll's face. And there—who would make a doll with a black eye? All had bruised faces. . . .

Later she would understand why she had refused to believe what she saw. It was too vile. A twelfth black killing device forced her to see things as they really were. It stepped out of the shadows. It tossed a dead child onto the pile. They were all battered, dead children.

There is your task, the whispering voice told her shocked brain. You will know when it has found you.

Tell me where, she demanded silently, fiercely. Tell me where this is!

The Chamber door swung open. She could see Raoul, her parents, Jump, and the sparrows. They waited for her.

It will find you, the Chamber told her. When it does, fix it.

A force urged Kel forward. She walked out of the Chamber of the Ordeal.

The king struck each of Kel's shoulders with the flat of his sword, hard enough to bruise, then gently tapped her crown. "You are dubbed Lady Knight, Keladry of Mindelan," he announced solemnly as his court watched. "Remember your vows and service to this Crown. Remember your promise of chivalry."

I'll remember, she thought as her family and friends applauded. Particularly will I remember it when I find that little man.

Ilane of Mindelan wept openly, smiling at her youngest daughter as she wiped her eyes.

"Mama, you'll lose face if you cry," Kel pointed out, returning Ilane's hug.

"I don't care," her mother said. "I am so proud of you, Lady Knight!"

Kel bent slightly to return her father's hug. The sight of tears on his cheeks left her speechless. She blotted them with her sleeve, making him laugh. Then there was Raoul to hug, and Neal, and her other friends.

She was beginning to think wistfully about food when Raoul tapped her shoulder. "Take a look," he told her, pointing to the dais.

The king had stepped aside, leaving three women to stand there: the queen, Buri, and in the center, holding a cloth-covered shield, Princess Shinkokami. As Kel watched, they removed the shield's cover.

There was the Mindelan device: a gray owl, wings outstretched, on a blue field rimmed with cream. There were two differences between this shield and those of her brothers. On Kel's, the owl hovered over a pair of crossed glaives, cream embroidered in gold, matches for a Yamani glaive. The other difference was the shield's border: it was formed by two thin rings, the outer blue, the inner cream. A distaff border, the heralds had named it, the coat of arms of a lady knight. They had studied them as pages, but distaff borders had not been used in over one hundred years. Not even Lady Alanna had ever claimed one.

Kel stepped forward in a daze. Buri and Shinko helped slide the shield on her arm. It fit perfectly—Kel looked around to see Lalasa, teary-eyed, beaming at her. Of course the shield fit, if Lalasa had anything to say about it.

"Wear it in health and victory," Queen Thayet said. "Now, show the nice people."

Kel turned, and showed them.

Her family and friends offered to wait in the courtyard while she put her new shield away: Raoul had arranged for a dinner at the city's best eating-house as a celebration. Since horses had to be saddled and brought, Kel decided to tidy up again once she had placed her new shield on the bed for the animals to admire. Nari had already left some droppings on the Mindelan owl.

"I hope that's a comment on owls and not my family," Kel told her as she combed her hair and cleaned her teeth. When she looked at the bed next, Jump stood on the shield, using his nose to rub a wet cloth over the besmirched owl.

Kel, laughing, almost missed the very quiet knock on the door that connected her rooms to Raoul's. Puzzled, since he was with the others, Kel opened the door.

Lady Alanna stood there, a sheathed longsword

in one hand. "I asked Raoul if I could see you privately," she explained to the baffled Kel. "May I come in?"

"My—my lady, of course," Kel stammered. "Please. I would brew tea—"

"Please don't," Alanna said with a smile. "I know you have people waiting." Once inside, she knelt and gave Jump a moment's attention—from the way the dog carried on, Kel thought, they must have made friends on progress.

At last the King's Champion straightened with a groan, her free hand going to her lower back. "Nobody ever says that, even with healers, your body still adds up your breaks and bruises, then gives you the bill in your mid-thirties," she said wryly. She sat in Kel's chair and offered the sword to her. "You've grown since the last sword I gave you, and I got a better idea of your fighting style on progress."

Kel took the blade in hands that shook. How casually this woman answered a question that had bothered her for eight years! "It was you?" she whispered. "The bruise balm, the exercise balls, the dagger, the—?"

Alanna nodded. "It nearly killed me, that I couldn't help you. Not with magic, like those mammering conservatives claimed, but with things like what works best on heavy opponents, and how to build up shoulder muscle. So I did what I could."

Thinking of all those gifts over the years, truly expensive things chosen with so much thought about what she would need, Kel shook her head.

"Neal mentioned there were times when you thought I didn't care," the lady said, violet eyes serious. "I wanted to tell you, it was the opposite. And you went so far beyond what I hoped, for the next girl page, and squire, and knight. All those tournaments, and those girls in the stands, right down by the field, watching you hungrily—"

"Oh, my lady, no!" protested Kel, shocked.

"Yes," the King's Champion said firmly. "I had the magic, don't you see, and the hand of the Goddess on me. Everyone could and did say I was a freak, one of those once-a-century people. No one else needs to strive for what I did, because they couldn't reach it." Alanna smiled crookedly. "But you, bless you, you are real. Those girls watched you, and talked about your style in the saddle, and the things you did. They swore they'd take up archery, or riding, or Shang combat, because you had shown them it was all right. I was so proud." She cleared her throat. Kel realized that the Champion was beet red. "You know, those things look better out of the sheath," she remarked, pointing to the sword Kel held.

"Oh!" She had forgotten it was in her hand. Looking at it, she admired the style of the plain black leather sheath and neat, wire-wrapped hilt: they matched the sword and the dagger Alanna had given her. She looked under the cross-guard. There it was: the stylized enamel raven that was the sign of Raven Armory.

The blade, when she worked up the nerve to draw it, did not match the sword and dagger. It showed the blue wave tempering of the finest Yamani steel. She held a fortune in metal in her hands.

"My lady, you can't—I can't—" she stammered, trembling. Her hands ached from the tree she had climbed for so long during her Ordeal, and the blade teetered in her grip. Forgetting herself, Kel grabbed the metal and sliced the thick muscle at the base of her thumb. She flinched and dug for a handkerchief to wipe the blade.

"Now you have to keep it," Alanna said, presenting her own handkerchief. "You've bled on it; it's yours. You know sword lore as well as I do."

Kel had to smile: she did know. She ducked her head and finished wiping that lovely blade. It was heavier and longer than her present sword, better suited to her hand and height.

"I do wish you'd been a runt like me." Alanna was straight-faced, her eyes mischievous. "That would have made it perfect."

Kel sighed and told the lady solemnly, "I would have been smaller if I could, Lioness." Alanna laughed. She laid a small, hard hand over Kel's as Kel gripped the hilt of her wonderful new sword. "Gods all bless, Lady Knight," she said quietly.

Jump chose that moment to flop on the woman's feet in a play for attention. Kel was grateful to him—her feelings, and she suspected Alanna's, were just too intense to bear. With Jump to act the clown, they were able to catch their wind.

Alanna scratched his belly and told him he was a rogue, then turned to go.

"Lady Alanna," Kel said, "would you like to come to supper with us? Someone has to keep Neal from making speeches."

Alanna cackled. "Well, I'm definitely the woman to do that," she admitted. "I thank you, and I accept."

After she left to get a coat, Kel remained for a moment, looking at her sword. The blue tempering shone in the light from her candles, pulling her eye to that elegant blade.

"I dub thee Griffin," she whispered, running her fingertips along its length. "We have work to do."

CAST OF CHARACTERS

Aiden	sergeant/squad leader, Third Company of the King's Own
Alanna of Pirate's Swoop and Olau	the King's Champion, also called "the Lioness," born Alanna of Trebond
Ansil of Groten	conservative knight
Arrow	one of Kel's sparrow flock
Baird of Queenscove	duke, chief of Tortall's healers, Neal's father
Balduin of Disart	acquaintance of Kel's
Balim	sergeant/squad leader, Third Company of the King's Own
Burchard of Stone Mountain	Joren's father, conservative
Buriram Tourakom	called Buri, commander of the Queen's Riders
Cleon of Kennan	squire to Inness of Mindelan, Kel's friend
Crown	female sparrow who leads Kel's flock
Cythera of Naxen	wife of Sir Gareth the Younger

Derom	corporal in Dom's squad, Third Company of the King's Own
Domitan of Masbolle	called Dom; sergeant/squad leader, Third Company of the King's Own; Neal's cousin
Ebroin of Genlith	steward for Stone Mountain holdings in Corus
Eitaro noh Nakuji	prince, head of Yamani delegation to Tortall
Emmet of Fenrigh	in Aiden's squad, Third Company of the King's Own
Fianola	twelve-year-old noble girl, wants to be a page
Flyndan Whiteford	called Flyn; captain, Third Company of the King's Own; second-in-command to Lord Raoul
Freckle	male sparrow with white-spotted head in Kel's flock
Fulcher	in Dom's squad, Third Company of the King's Own
Gareth of Naxen	called "the Younger," one of King Jonathan's most trusted counselors, married to Cythera
Garvey of Runnerspring	squire to Jerel of Nenan, Joren's crony

Gavan	Haresfield youth
George of Pirate's Swoop	baron, born George Cooper, a commoner, married to Alanna
Gildes of Veldine	in Dom's squad, Third Company of the King's Own
Glaisdan of Haryse	captain, First Company of the King's Own
Graystreak	centaur herd leader
Haname noh Ajikuro	Yamani lady-in-waiting
Harailt of Aili	mage, head of the royal university in Corus
Hildrec of Meron	heir to fief Meron
Hoshi	brown mare with white socks, star on forehead, placid, Kel's riding horse
Ilane of Mindelan	baroness, Kel's mother
Imrah of Legann	lord, knight-master to Prince Roald
Inness of Mindelan	Kel's second-oldest brother, knight-master to Cleon of Kennan
Iriseyes	female centaur
Ivath Brand	convicted criminal
Jasson of Conté	called "the Old King," King Jonathan's deceased grandfather
Jealousani	rebel centaur

Jerel of Nenan	knight-master to Garvey of Runnerspring
Jonathan of Conté	King of Tortall, co-ruler with his queen, Thayet
Joren of Stone Mountain	squire, old foe of Kel's
Jump	bull terrier, Kel's friend
Kaddar Iliniat	emperor of Carthak
Kalasin of Conté	oldest princess of Tortall
Keladry of Mindelan	known as Kel, youngest daughter of Piers and Ilane of Mindelan, first girl to openly serve as page and squire in over a century
Lachran of Mindelan	Kel's brother Anders's oldest son
Lalasa Isran	Kel's former maid, now a dressmaker
Lerant of Eldorne	standard-bearer, Third Company of the King's Own
Macorm	Haresfield renegade
Maggur Rathhausak	newest Scanran warlord
Maresgift	rebel centaur
Merric of Hollyrose	squire, Kel's friend
Muirgen of Sigis Hold	master advocate (attorney)
Myles of Olau	baron, head of royal intelligence service

Nealan of Queenscove	called Neal, squire, Kel's friend and page sponsor, son of Baird of Queenscove, Dom's cousin
Noack	servingman, Third Company of the King's Own
Nualt of Rosemark	knight-master to Vinson of Genlith
Numair Salmalín	mage, born Arram Draper, Daine's lover
Onua Chamtong	horsemistress to the Queen's Riders
Osbern	sergeant/squad leader, Third Company of the King's Own
Owen of Jesslaw	page, then squire, Kel's friend
Padraig haMinch	senior member of powerful haMinch clan
Paxton of Nond	knight-master to Joren of Stone Mountain
Peachblossom	cross-grained strawberry-roan gelding destrier
Peg	one-footed female sparrow in Kel's flock
Piers of Mindelan	baron, Kel's father
Prosper of Tameran	squire, Kel's friend

Qasim ibn Zirhud	Bazhir corporal, Third Company of the King's Own
Raoul of Goldenlake and Malorie's Peak	lord, Knight Commander of the King's Own, Tortallan hero, known as "the Giant Killer"
Roald of Conté	prince, squire to Imrah of Legann, heir to the Tortallan throne
Salma Aynnar	head of servants in the pages' and squires' wings
Seaver of Tasride	squire, Kel's friend
Sebila of Disart	Raoul's great-aunt
Shinkokami	Yamani princess, betrothed to Roald, called Shinko by her friends
Stigand of Fenrigh	conservative knight
Symric	corporal in Dom's squad, Third Company of the King's Own
Thayet of Conté	Queen of Tortall, co-ruler with her husband, King Jonathan
Tianine Plowman	called Tian, maid, Lalasa's friend
Turomot of Wellam	duke, Lord Magistrate, chief examiner of pages

GLOSSARY

Balor's Needle: a tower, the highest part of the royal palace in Corus, used mostly by astronomers and mages.

basilisk: an immortal that resembles a seven-to-eight-foot-tall lizard, with slit-pupiled eyes that face forward and silver talons. It walks upright on its hind feet. Its hobby is travel; it loves gossip and learns languages easily. It possesses some magical skills, including a kind of screech that turns people to stone. Its colors are various shades of gray and white.

Bazhir: the collective name for the nomadic tribes of Tortall's Great Southern Desert.

Bonnett River: runs through the Royal Forest near Owlshollow.

Carthak: the slaveholding empire that includes all of the Southern Lands, ancient and powerful, a storehouse of learning, sophistication, and culture. Its university was at one time without a rival for teaching. Its people reflect the many lands that have been consumed by the empire, their colors ranging from white to brown to black. Its former emperor Ozorne Tasikhe was forced to abdicate when he was turned into a Stormwing. (He was later killed.) He was succeeded by his nephew Kaddar Iliniat, who is still getting his farflung lands under control.

centaur: an immortal shaped like a human from the waist up, with the body of a horse from the waist down. Like humans, centaurs can be good, bad, or a mixture of both. For a male to keep females in his herd, he must constantly provide them with presents: if he does not, they will turn on him. Among the gods worshiped by centaurs are the Mares with Bloody Teeth, goddesses of vengeance. Centaurs consider horses to be slaves.

charcoal burners: people who make charcoal by cutting logs and building them into large, layered stacks that are set on fire and made to burn slowly, without consuming the wood.

Code of Ten: the set of laws that form the basis of government for most of the Eastern Lands.

Copper Isles: a slaveholding island nation to the south and west of Tortall. The Isles' lowlands are hot, wet jungles, their highlands cold and rocky. Traditionally their ties are to Carthak rather than Tortall, and their pirates often raid along the Tortallan coast. There is a strain of insanity in their ruling line. The Isles hold an old grudge against Tortall, since one of their princesses was killed there the day that Jonathan was crowned.

coromanel: a flat, crown-shaped piece fitted over the tip of a lance. It spreads the power of a lance's impact in several directions, to make the force less severe.

Corus: the capital city of Tortall, located on the northern and southern banks of the River Olorun. Corus is the home of the new royal university as well as the royal palace.

Domin River: runs through fief Mindelan.

dragon: a large, winged, lizard-like immortal capable of crossing from the Divine Realms to the mortal ones and back. Dragons are intelligent, possess their own magic, and are rarely seen by humans. The infant dragon Skysong, known as Kitten, lives in the mortal world with her foster mother, Daine Sarrasri.

Eastern Lands: name used to refer to those lands north of the Inland Sea and east of the Emerald Ocean: Scanra, Tortall, Tyra, Tusaine, Galla, Maren, Sarain.

Galla: the country to the north and east of Tortall, famous for its mountains and forests, with an ancient royal line. Daine was born there.

Gift, the: human, academic magic, the use of which must be taught.

glaive: a pole arm including a four- or five-foot staff capped with a long metal blade.

Great Mother Goddess: the chief goddess in the

Tortallan pantheon, protector of women; her symbol is the moon.

griffin: a feathered immortal with a cat-like body, wings, and a beak. The males grow to a height of six and a half to seven feet at the shoulder; females are slightly bigger. No one can tell lies in a griffin's vicinity (a range of about a hundred feet). Their young have bright orange feathers to make them more visible. If adult griffin parents sense that a human has handled their infant griffin, they will try to kill that human.

halberd: a pole arm, a six-foot staff capped by an ax head or a pike (long spear) head.

headman: leader of a tribe, mayor of a small town.

Human Era (H.E.): the calendar in use in the Eastern and Southern Lands and in the Copper Isles is dated the Human Era to commemorate the years since the one in which the immortals were originally sealed into the Divine Realms, over four hundred and fifty years previous to the years covered by *Protector of the Small*.

hurrok: an immortal shaped like a horse with leathery bat wings, claws, and fangs.

Immortals War: a short, vicious war fought in 452 H.E., the thirteenth year of Jonathan and Thayet's reign, named for the number of immortal creatures that fought, but also waged by Carthakis (rebels against the new Emperor Kaddar), Copper Islanders, and Scanran raiders. These forces were defeated by the residents of the Eastern Lands, particularly Tortall, but recovery is slow.

kimono: Yamani robe dress that wraps around the body and is secured in front by a stiff sash called an obi. The sleeves are long and rectangular and can serve as pockets. Usually Yamanis wear at least two or three kimonos, the bottom one of very light cloth.

King's Council: the monarch's private council, made up of those advisers he trusts the most.

King's Own: a cavalry/police group answering to the king, whose members serve as royal bodyguards and as protective troops throughout the realm. Their Knight Commander is Lord Sir Raoul of Goldenlake and Malorie's Peak. The ranks are filled by younger sons of noble houses, Bazhir, and the sons of wealthy merchants. The Own is made of three companies of one hundred fighters each, in addition to the servingmen, who care for supplies and remounts. First Company, a show company, traditionally provides palace bodyguards and security for the monarchs. Under Lord Raoul, Second and Third Company were added and dedicated to active service away from the palace, helping to guard the realm.

K'mir, K'miri: the K'mir are the matriarchal,

nomadic tribes of the mountains in Sarain. They herd ponies and are ferocious warriors and riders. The Saren lowlanders despise the K'mir and are continuously at war with them. There is a small, growing K'miri population in Tortall, where Queen Thayet is half K'mir and a number of the Queen's Riders are also of K'miri descent.

logistics: military study that involves the purchase, maintenance, and transport of supplies, equipment, and people.

mage: wizard.

Maren: a large, powerful country east of Tusaine and Tyra, the grain basket of the Eastern Lands, with plenty of farms and trade.

merlon: one of the solid stone pieces between the crenels (notches) of a crenelated wall.

Midwinter Festival: a seven-day holiday centering around the longest night of the year and the sun's rebirth afterward. It is the beginning of the new year. Gifts are exchanged and feasts held.

Mithros: the chief god in the Tortallan pantheon, god of war and the law; his symbol is the sun.

naginata: the Yamani term for the glaive used by Kel.

obi: a wide, stiff sash or band that secures a kimono

around the waist. Yamanis wear ornaments on obis and tuck items such as fans into them.

ogre: an immortal with aqua-colored skin, shaped like a human, from ten to twelve feet in height.

Olorun River: its main sources are Lake Naxen and Lake Tirragen in the eastern part of Tortall; it flows through the capital, Corus, and into the Emerald Ocean at Port Caynn.

pauldron: a piece of armor that protects the shoulder.

pole arm: any weapon consisting of a long wooden staff or pole capped by a sharp blade of some kind, including spears, glaives, and pikes.

poleyn: a curved piece of armor that protects the knee.

Queen's ladies: term used to refer to fifteen or so young, active women of noble birth who can ride and use a bow as well as dance and converse with all manner of people. Queen Thayet takes them to small, isolated fiefs or to meetings when there is a possibility of danger. They handle emergencies that may arise.

Queen's Riders: a cavalry/police group charged with protecting Tortallans who live in hard-to-reach parts of the country. They enforce the law and teach local residents to defend themselves. The basic unit is a Rider Group, with eight to nine members. Rank in a Group is simply that of commander and second-in-command; the head of the Riders is the Commander. They accept both women and men in their ranks, unlike the army, the navy, and the King's Own. Their headquarters lies between the palace and the Royal Forest. Buriram Tourakom is now the Commander; Queen Thayet was the Commander but has since passed the title to Buri.

quintain: a dummy with a shield mounted on a post. One outstretched "arm" is weighted with a sandbag, while the other is covered by the shield. The object in tilting at a quintain is to strike the shield precisely, causing the dummy to pivot 180 degrees. The jouster can then ride by safely. Striking the dummy anywhere but the target circle on the shield causes the dummy to swing 360 degrees, so the sandbag wallops the passing rider.

remount: a rider's second horse, to ride when the primary horse gets tired. In the case of knights and the King's Own, remounts are often warhorses, heavier mounts trained to fight.

rowel: a star-shaped piece on a spur, which cuts into a horse to get it to pick up its speed.

Sakuyo: Yamani trickster god, who loves jokes.

Scanra: the country to the north of Tortall, wild, rocky, and cold, with very little land that can be farmed. Scanrans are masters of the sea and are feared anywhere there is a coastline. They also frequently raid over land. Their government is a loose one, consisting of a figurehead king and a Great Council (formerly the Council of Ten, expanded in the disruptions following the Immortals War) made up of the heads of the clans. Recently some clans have been uniting to follow a new warlord, Maggur Rathhausak.

Shang: an order of warriors, mostly commoners, whose principal school is in northern Maren. They specialize in hand-to-hand combat.

shukusen: Yamani "lady fan," silk on steel ribs that are often engraved or pierced with a design. The outer ends of the ribs are very sharp, acting as a thrusting weapon when the fan is closed and as a slashing weapon when it is opened. Traditionally carried by Yamani ladies when they don't wish to be seen with a weapon.

Southern Lands: another name for the Carthaki Empire, which has conquered all of the independent nations that once were part of the continent south of the Inland Sea.

spidren: an immortal whose body is that of a furred spider four to five feet in height; its head is that of a human with sharp, silvery teeth. Spidrens can use weapons. They also use their webs as weapons and ropes. Spidren web is gray-green in color and it glows after dark. Their blood is black and burns like acid. Their favorite food is human blood.

squad: ten soldiers commanded by a sergeant and two corporals.

standard-bearer: young man or boy who carries the company flag.

stockade: wall made of whole logs, the upper ends cut into rough points.

Stormwing: an immortal with a human head and chest and bird legs and wings, with steel feathers and claws. Stormwings have sharp teeth, but use them only to add to the terror of their presence by tearing apart bodies. They live on human fear and have their own magic; their special province is the desecration of battlefield dead.

strategy: planning for a battle or war from a distance, working out the movements of armies and setting goals for them.

string: a group or train of horses on a lead rein.

tactics: planning for a battle at short range, as it happens.

tauros: a seven-foot-tall immortal, male only, that has a bull-like head with large teeth and eyes that point forward (the mark of a predator). It is reddish brown, human-like from the neck down, with a bull's splayed hooves and tail. It preys on women and girls.

Temple District: the religious quarter of Corus, between the city proper and the royal palace, where the city's largest temples are located.

Tortall: the chief kingdom in which the Alanna, Daine, and Keladry books take place, between the Inland Sea and Scanra.

Tusaine: a small country tucked between Tortall and Maren. Tortall went to war with Tusaine in the years Alanna the Lioness was a squire and Jonathan was crown prince; Tusaine lost.

Tyra: a merchant republic on the Inland Sea between Tortall and Maren. Tyra is mostly swamp, and its people rely on trade and banking for an income. Numair Salmalín was born there.

warhorse: a large horse or greathorse, trained for combat—the mount of an armored knight.

Wave Walker: sea goddess, the goddess of sailors, storms, and shipwrecks.

wildmage: a mage who deals in wild magic, the kind of magic that is part of nature. Daine Sarrasri is often called the Wildmage for her ability to communicate with animals, heal them, and shapeshift.

wild magic: the magic that is part of the natural world. Unlike the human Gift, it cannot be drained or done away with; it is always present.

Yama: chief goddess of the Yamani pantheon, goddess of fire, who created the Yamanis and their islands.

Yamani Islands: island nation to the north and west of Tortall and the west of Scanra, ruled by an ancient line of emperors, whose claim to their throne comes from the goddess Yama. The country is beautiful and mountainous. Its vulnerability to pirate raids means that most Yamanis, including the women, get some training in combat arts. Keladry of Mindelan lived there for six years while her father was the Tortallan ambassador.

ACKNOWLEDGMENTS

My most heartfelt thanks for this goes to my wonderful editrix, Mallory Loehr, who gave me another hundred pages in which to tell the story—my brain might have melted down without them, because I could think of nothing to cut. Thus, indirect thanks are due to British author J. K. Rowling (nope, don't know her personally), whose wild success with the Harry Potter books has convinced American publishers that perhaps their authors could manage to sell longer books too.

My gratitude goes to Alicia Craig-Lich, manager of the National Audubon Society Important Bird Area in Indiana and Senior Manager of Nature Education, Wild Birds Unlimited, Inc., for her quick assistance with information on sparrow biology. She and the other folks at Wild Birds Unlimited online (www.wbu.com) are a tremendous resource for those who want to know more about birds.

Thanks also to my continual support team: my parents, forever answering crazed garden information questions without once suggesting that I need my head examined; my agent, Craig Tenney, who has a delicate touch for what works and what doesn't; Raquel Starace, for horse breeds, riding, and monster creation advice; Richard McCaffery Robinson, for his many instructive thoughts on the nature of royal progresses; and my very own Spouse-Creature, Tim Liebe, who had his hands full with me this time, and offered many sage thoughts on the nature of romance, ordeals, and training relationships.

To Iris Mori and her family, *arigato goziemashita* for Japanese names and weapons feedback—errors here are strictly mine.

Finally, I express a debt to Crown, Freckle, Peg, and the house sparrows of Riverside Park in New York City, who have taught me that big hearts and large courage can be found in the smallest of creatures; to Pidge the dove, who taught me that whoever said doves are birds of peace had never been anywhere near one; and to Shortstop the crow, who taught me in a short time the pains and joys of caring for a wild bird.

*Turn the page
for a preview of Tamora Pierce's
fourth* Protector of the Small *book*

LADY KNIGHT

*Now in hardcover from
Random House,
paperback coming in 2003*

STORM WARNINGS

*K*eladry of Mindelan lay with the comfortable black blanket of sleep wrapped around her. Then, against the blackness, light moved and strengthened to show twelve large, vaguely rat- or insectlike metal creatures, devices built for murder. The killing devices were magical machines made of iron-coated giants' bones, chains, pulleys, dagger-fingers and toes, and a long, whiplike tail. The seven-foot-tall devices stood motionless in a half circle as the light revealed what lay at their feet: a pile of dead children.

With the devices and the bodies visible, the light spread to find the man who seemed to be the master of the creations. To Keladry of Mindelan, known as Kel, he was the Nothing Man. He was almost two feet shorter than the killing devices, long-nosed and narrow-mouthed, with small, rapidly blinking eyes and dull brown hair. His dark robe was marked with stains and burns; his hair was unkempt. He always gnawed a fingernail, or scratched a pimple, or shifted from foot to foot.

Once that image—devices, bodies, man—was complete, Kel woke. She stared at the shadowed ceiling and cursed the Chamber of the Ordeal. The Chamber had shown Kel this vision, or variations of it, after her formal Ordeal of knighthood. As far as Kel knew, no one else had been given any visions of people to be found once a squire was knighted. As everyone she knew understood it, the Ordeal was straightforward enough. The Chamber forced would-be knights to live through their fears. If they did this without making a sound, they were released, to be proclaimed knights, and that was the end of the matter.

Kel was different. Three or four times a week, the Chamber sent her this dream. It was a reminder of the task it had set her. After her Ordeal, before the Chamber set her free, it had shown her the killing devices, the Nothing Man, and the dead children. It had demanded that Kel stop it all.

Kel guessed that the Nothing Man would be in Scanra, to the north, since the killing devices had appeared during Scanran raids on Tortall last summer. Trapped in the capital by a hard winter, with travel to the border nearly impossible, Kel had lived with growing tension. She had to ride north as soon as the mountain passes opened if she was to sneak into Scanra and begin her search for the Nothing Man. Every moment she remained in Tortall invited the growing risk that the king would issue orders to most knights, including Kel, to defend the northern border. The moment Kel got those orders, she would be trapped. She had vowed to defend the realm and obey its monarchs, which would mean fighting soldiers, not hunting for a mage whose location was unknown.

"Maybe I'll get lucky. Maybe I'll ride out one day and find there's a line of killing devices from the palace right up to the Nothing Man's door," she grumbled, easing herself out from under her covers. Kel never threw off her blankets. With a number of sparrows and her dog sharing her bed, she might smother a friend if she hurried. Even taking care, she heard muffled cheeps of protest. "Sorry," she told her companions, and set her feet on the cold flagstones of her floor.

She made her way across her dark room and opened the shutters on one of her windows. Before her lay a courtyard and a stable where the men of the King's Own kept their horses. The torches that lit the courtyard were nearly out. The pearly radiance that came to the eastern sky in the hour before dawn fell over snow, stable, and the edges of the palace wall beyond.

The scant light showed a big girl of eighteen, broad-shouldered and solid-waisted, with straight mouse-brown hair cut short below her earlobes and across her forehead. She had a dreamer's hazel eyes, set beneath long, curling lashes, odd in contrast to the many fine scars on her hands and the muscles that flexed and bunched under her nightshirt. Her nose was still unbroken and delicate after eight years of palace combat training, her lips full and quicker to smile than frown. Determination filled every inch of her strong body.

Motion in the shadows at the base of the courtyard

wall caught her eye. Kel gasped as a winged creature waddled out into the open courtyard, as ungainly on its feet as a vulture. The flickering torchlight caught and sparked along the edges of metal feathers on wings and legs. Steel legs, flexible and limber, ended in steel-clawed feet. Between the metal wings and above the metal legs and feet was human flesh, naked, hairless, grimy, and in this case, male.

The Stormwing looked at Kel and grinned, baring sharp steel teeth. His face was lumpy and unattractive, marked by a large nose, small eyes, and a thin upper lip with a full lower one. He had the taunting smile of someone born impudent. "Startle you, did I?" he inquired.

Kel thanked the gods that the cold protected her sensitive nose, banishing most of the Stormwing's foul stench. Stormwings loved battlefields, where they tore corpses to pieces, urinated on them, smeared them with dung, then rolled in the mess. The result was a nauseating odor that made even the strongest stomach rebel. Her teachers had explained that the purpose of Stormwings was to make people think twice before they chose to fight, knowing what might happen to the dead when Stormwings arrived. So far they hadn't done much good as far as Kel could see: people still fought battles and killed each other, Stormwings or no. Tortall's Stormwing population was thriving. But this was the first time she'd seen one on palace grounds.

Kel glared at him. "Get out of here, you nasty thing! Shoo!"

"Is that any way to greet a future companion?" demanded the Stormwing, raising thin brown brows. "You people are getting ready to stage an entertainment for our benefit up north. You'll be seeing a lot of us this year."

"Not if I can help it," Kel retorted. Grimly she walked across her dark room, stubbing her toe on the trunk at the foot of her bed. She cursed and limped over to the racks where she kept her weapons. When she found her bow and a quiver of arrows, she strung the bow and hopped back to her window. She placed the quiver on her window seat and put an arrow on the string. Outside, the court-yard was empty. The Stormwing's footprints in the snow ended right under Kel's window.

Scowling, Kel looked up and around. There he was, perched on the peak of the stable roof, a steel-dressed portent of war. Kel raised her bow. She wouldn't actually kill the creature, just make him go away.

He looked down at her, cackled, and took to the air, spiraling out of Kel's range. He flipped his tail at her three times in a mockery of a wave, then sailed away over the palace wall.

"I *hate* those things," grumbled Kel as she removed the bowstring. The thought of anyone's dead body providing Stormwings with entertainment gave her the shudders. And she knew chances were good that *she* might become a Stormwing toy very soon.

There was no point in going back to sleep now. Instead, Kel cleaned up, dressed, and took down her